To Amy / the best
agent in the world!
♡ Candice
Thank you
for every-

FINDING
FAMOUS
thing!

A Mashad Family Novel

FINDING FAMOUS

A Mashad Family Novel

CANDICE JALILI

HYPERION

Los Angeles   New York

First Edition, July 2024

1 3 5 7 9 10 8 6 4 2

FAC-004510-24158

Printed in the United States of America

This book is set in Stempel Garamond LT Pro/Linotype

Stock image credit: emojis 1073375483/Shutterstock

Designed by Zareen Johnson

Library of Congress Cataloging-in-Publication Data

Names: Jalili, Candice, author.
Title: Finding famous : a Mashad family novel / Candice Jalili.
Description: First edition. • Los Angeles : Disney-Hyperion, 2024. •
    Audience: Ages 12-18 • Audience: Grades 7-12 • Summary: "An Iranian
    American girl discovers she is part of the most powerful family in
    reality TV history"—Provided by publisher.
Identifiers: LCCN 2023034795 • ISBN 9781368094733 (hardcover) •
ISBN 9781368094986 (ebook)
Subjects: CYAC: Reality television programs—Fiction. • Iranian
    Americans—Fiction. • Families—Fiction. • LCGFT: Novels.
Classification: LCC PZ7.1.J3846 Fi 2024 • DDC [Fic]—dc23
LC record available at https://lccn.loc.gov/2023034795

Reinforced binding

Visit www.HyperionTeens.com

For the two best parents in the world.

Dad, thank you for encouraging me to read whatever I want and be whoever I want.

Mom, at its core, this book is a celebration of strong women. And who's stronger than you?

I love you both so much.

MEET THE MASHADS:

This month's *Savvy* cover stars fill
out our famous *Savvy* Celeb Quizzes.

Name: Melody Farrah Mashad

Nickname: Mel

One item you never leave your house without: I swear I'm not even trying to push product—it's my Melody Mashad organic lip balm. I literally keep a tin in each of my handbags.

Words you live by: "You can catch more bees with honey than vinegar."

Biggest pet peeve: I honestly don't get annoyed that easily, but if I had to pick, it would maybe be flakiness??

Favorite sister: I love them both equally!

Last person you FaceTimed with: My fiancé, Axle. He's on a spiritual retreat in Sri Lanka right now, and he let me virtually join for a guided meditation. I miss him so much </3

Best thing your dad taught you: How to connect with people on a deeper level.

Advice you would give your younger self: "You're good enough."

HUGS AND KISSES,
Melody Mashad <3

Name: Meesha Mahsa Mashad

Nickname: Meesh

One item you never leave your house without: My mom is going to kill me for not saying something from my new collection, but the honest answer is probably just my phone.

Words you live by: "Protect your energy."

Biggest pet peeve: Fake people.

Favorite sister: Today it's Melody. Mona is really on one right now.

Last person you FaceTimed with: My girlfriend, Bunny. She's on tour in Asia, and last night she FaceTimed me while she was onstage at this massive stadium in Tokyo. I'm pretty sure, like, 50,000 Japanese Bunny Lee fans saw me in bed with a greasy bun and a face mask on, LOL.

Best thing your dad taught you: How to stick up for myself.

Advice you would give your younger self: "You'll get through this."

xo *Meesha Mashad*

Name: Mona Niloufar Mashad

Nickname: I've been trying to make Mo happen, but my family refuses to comply.

One item you never leave your house without: Pepper spray.

Words you live by: F*ck the haters.

Biggest pet peeve: Liars. Ugh, nothing worse.

Favorite sister: They're both kind of annoying me today, if I'm being totally honest.

Last person you FaceTimed with: My mom, five minutes ago. She can't be here today and she keeps calling us to check in on how the interview is going. The woman needs to get a life.

Best thing your dad taught you: How to have a great time.

Advice you would give your younger self: "Dump him." (Yes, I'm referring to the *him* you're thinking of.)

xoxo Mona Mashad

Chapter 1

"Hey Siri," I panic-whisper into my phone as I stand locked in Oliver Blair's mom's bathroom. "Can Vibe Tea kill you?"

"Sorry, I didn't catch that," she responds, totally unfazed by the sheer panic in my voice.

"Can. Vibe. Tea. Kill. You," I try again, this time carefully enunciating each word.

"I didn't get that. Could you try again?"

"Caaaaaan. Viiiiiiibee. Teeeeeeeea. Kiiiiillll. Youuuuuuuuuuu," I try one last time, now dragging out each word as long as possible.

"I didn't get that. Could you try again?"

My mouth is bone dry. Oh gosh. Maybe it's too late. Maybe this is it. Maybe the Vibe Tea is *currently* killing me. I can practically feel my cells shutting down one by one. Oh gosh. Oh gosh. Oh GOSH. What will Matt do? Midway through picturing my sweet stepfather tearfully delivering the eulogy at the funeral of yet another woman he loves, I hear a bang on the door.

"JOSIE, OPEN UP."

Shoot. It's Louise.

"Hey, Lou," I say as I breezily open the door, trying my hardest not to sound like someone on the brink of death. "Sup?"

She rolls her giant green eyes, exactly the color of seafoam, and pushes past me, shutting the door behind us. "I heard you asking Siri if you're dying."

"Oh."

Great. So *she* can hear me, but Siri can't.

"Josie, you had *one* Vibe Tea. And I was proud of you for drinking it! I mean, not like I care whether or not you drink, but it was nice to see you take a walk on the wild side for a split second."

I stare at my much-cooler best friend, who looks like a high-fashion Hell's Angel in her cropped black cami and black leather pants. Lou's always been into fashion, but this was her first go at actually sewing her own clothes.

"Lou, I can't believe how good this outfit came out," I say, both meaning it and trying to change the subject. "Honestly. I know I'm no fashion critic, but it looks incredible."

"Thank you," she says, giving herself a proud once-over in the mirror before turning back toward me. "But back to the point. You lived on the edge a bit! I'm proud of you."

I can't tell her the truth, which is that I didn't even know the stupid Vibe Tea was alcoholic. I mean, to be fair, the package literally says TEA. And the soccer girls were using it as a chaser! But halfway through the admittedly delicious bottle of what I thought was iced tea, I looked at the label, and there it was: 3.7 PERCENT ALCOHOL. A lifetime of safely avoiding the stuff down the tubes. Just like that.

"If you were freaking out so much," Louise continues, "why wouldn't you just tell me? You've ignored, like, all eight of my texts since you've been locked in here."

"I would have obviously answered your texts, but I never got them, see?" I show her my phone for proof. "The service in this bathroom isn't great. I can't even get Siri to answer my question."

"Let me answer it for you: No. You're not going to die because you had ONE Vibe Tea. Besides, Vibe Tea is Melody Mashad's brand, and she's, like, super into everything being all organic and natural."

"You know arsenic is technically organic and natural," I say, my heart racing even more as I make the connection. "And same with asbestos! Remember when our third-grade gym teacher got asbestos poisoning from his apartment and was in the hospital for *months*?"

"Yes, I remember," Lou says. "But Melody Mashad can't afford to be as negligent as the Burbank slumlord who managed Mr. Nealy's building. She's a *Mashad*."

"What does that have to do with anything?"

"I just mean she's part of the most powerful family in the world. Mary Mashad, the most powerful woman in the world, is her *mother*. Their family is collectively worth almost a *trillion* dollars. They have wayyyy too much at stake to just be mass-producing dicey beverages that are killing teens."

"But what if it's not killing *teens*? What if it's just killing this *singular* teen?" I feel my palms getting increasingly sweaty. I can't die. Not like this. Matt just really wouldn't be able to take it. I can't do this to him. And Lou! She acts all tough now, but she would *crumble* without me.

"Josie, you have to stop letting your anxiety hijack your brain like this," Lou says, giving me a light shake. "Just because you have a *feeling* alcohol is going to kill you doesn't mean it's actually going to."

"How do you *know* that, Louise? Like, for a fact?"

"Think about how many things you've had *feelings* would kill you that never did—roller coasters, gluten, the scent of marijuana, glitter, sleepovers, those disposable flip-flops they give you at the nail salon, standing front row at concerts, public speaking, literally any form of confrontation . . . Should I keep going?"

"No. You've made your point."

Louise always does this. She speaks with such conviction that for a millisecond I convince myself she has the medical savvy of a leading neurologist at Harvard . . .

. . . but then the millisecond passes, and I remember she's a senior in high school failing physiology. Before I can question her, though, she continues. "If anything, this was good for you. Another piece of evidence that, despite what you cuh-*learly* believe, taking a risk won't kill you."

"We'll see about that," I retort, once again certain I'll be dead by sunrise. "Listen, Lou. It was so nice of Grant to invite me to tag along tonight. But I think I should just go home. Spend my last hours with Matt before he must lose me forever."

"You can't go home!" Lou protests. "You turn eighteen in an hour. Just stay and celebrate."

"You know I'm not a big birthday person," I tell Lou. "Thank you for trying to make this one special. Really. But I think this death scare is just further proof that birthdays are no longer for me."

My mom and I used to love birthdays so much that the rest of the year almost felt like a 364-day-long planning period for whichever one was coming up next. Then she died. And, no matter how many years go by, birthdays still feel like a giant annual reminder that she's not here to celebrate them with me.

"*What* death scare?" Lou asks, dramatically placing a hand on her hip as she gives me one of her patented eye rolls. "Josie, I know how much you miss your mom, especially today. But the last thing Sharzad would have wanted is for you to spend your eighteenth birthday cooped up in the apartment worrying yourself to death because you had three sips of one Vibe Tea."

Lou's right. I can practically hear my mom saying, "Josie Joonam, chillax," her faint Farsi accent making it come out more as *cheelax*. I don't know where she got the term *chillax* from. My best guess is some old sitcom rerun she was falling asleep to. All I know is she heard it once and never looked back. Every time I was freaking out about anything, she would laugh and repeat the same phrase: "Josie Joonam, chillax."

"Also." Lou interrupts my trip down memory lane with a smirk and one eyebrow raised. "Did I mention Isaac Taylor just got here five minutes ago?"

This changes everything.

"OMG. You're kidding me." My heart starts pounding—TBD if it's the Vibe Tea killing me or the sheer thrill of being alive at this very moment. "Isaac freaking Taylor?! Newly single and HERE?!"

Lou smiles so big I worry her cheeks might burst. "I'm not kidding! He's here!"

"Lou," I say. "This is huge."

"I know," she solemnly agrees. "You know I haven't always been his number one fan, considering the guy has not *once* said hi to you outside of class. . . ."

"Um, you're forgetting that day in fourth grade," I quickly remind her. Ugh, Lou *always* forgets the day in fourth grade.

"I'm forgetting about it because it didn't mean anything, Josie." She rolls her eyes. "The jerk asked you out on a dare! How are we still talking about this?!"

"He is *not* a jerk!" I exclaim. "If you just saw us together in math class, you'd understand. And what we have in math class wouldn't even exist if it weren't for that day in fourth grade. It's all connected! Our bond is as magical as it is because we have a *history*."

"Really?" she retorts. "You think a foundation for some magical bond with this guy—the one where you allegedly have inside jokes and heart-to-hearts about your families—is built on the fact that you dated for one day eight years ago?"

"Kind of," I admit. "I mean, technically speaking, we're exes. It changes the whole dynamic."

"Okay, fine," she says. "You're right. He's your ex. Now can we move on to tonight?"

The reason why it's such a majorly gigantic deal that Isaac's here *tonight*, of all nights, is—well, (1) because I'm here and I've never been to a party before, (2) because I've spent the past four years waiting for the perfect opportunity to show him that I'm more than just his dorky math partner, (3) because it's almost my birthday and he might be the only person on Earth who has the power to make me enjoy my birthday again, and (4) because he's finally broken up with the most evil girl in our grade, Genevieve Lang.

Up until eighth grade, Genevieve, Lou, and I used to be a trio. The three of us were inseparable. But something changed the summer going into eighth grade. Genevieve's flat chest developed into a C-cup, she got her unibrow waxed at Benefit, and her mom took her to Beverly Hills to get a new wardrobe and her mousy brown hair dyed platinum blond. Somewhere between the new boobs and the new hair, she decided that she also needed new friends. Friends who more closely fit her new aesthetic. Well, to be fair, she decided *I* was really the only one who did not fit with her new aesthetic. Lou, with her perfectly symmetrical face and consistently trendy outfits, was just collateral damage.

It started with a slow fade. Genevieve wouldn't respond to our texts or show up to hang out with us all summer. When she didn't come to my mom's funeral the week before school started, I pretty much knew it was over. But Genevieve didn't just need *us* to know we were no longer friends; she needed the whole school to know. When I came to sit next to her in math class the first day of school, she made a big show of making fun of the new Asics she *knew* my doctor told my mom I had to wear for my tendonitis and moved two seats over. From then on out, Genevieve has made it her mission in life to make my adolescence a waking nightmare. She spent all of eighth grade calling me Chewbacca because I was the last girl in our grade to start shaving my legs. Even to this day, if she's able to make out the *faintest* trace of a mustache growing above my lip, Genevieve is all, "Ooh, look, everyone! It's Chewy!"

It's like her soul entered some sort of demonic Brita that filtered out any ounce of good she had in her. The girl has become pure, unadulterated evil.

But because she's a master manipulator with boobs and blond hair, boys like Genevieve. Even sweet, sensitive, soulful boys like Isaac. And for the past two years Genevieve and Isaac have been in an on-again-off-again relationship so dramatic they could have their own reality TV show. But the word is they're off again—for good, this time.

And now my sweet, sensitive ex/soulmate/math partner is here at this party. And SINGLE.

Lou shuffles through the Staud moon bag her sister got her for Christmas and pulls out a tube of dark red lip gloss. "This stuff is the best," she raves as she carefully applies the bloodlike goo onto her perfectly full lips. "Want some?"

I glance over at the mirror above Oliver Blair's mom's bathroom sink and take a quick look at my own makeup-free face, complete with chapped lips, a gigantic pimple, and dark circles under both eyes. "I'm good," I tell Lou.

"God, I wish I could have your confidence sometimes," she says, sighing.

Listen, I know I'm no Genevieve Lang. But I'm okay with that. Besides, who really wants to be with a boy who only likes them because of the way they look?! Genevieve and her minions have made it *abundantly* clear both IRL and on their finstas that I have a mustache and that my Supercuts haircut makes me look like a young, more Middle Eastern Hillary Clinton. And Lou has offered multiple times to tweeze the little jet-black hairs off my nipples, so I'm pretty sure those aren't classically hot, either. But, to be honest, I don't really care. I feel my best without any frills. Au naturel. That's how my mom always was, and I loved that about her. Besides, as far as finding *love* goes, I want someone who loves me for me. The way Matt loved my mom.

Hopefully Isaac's finally ready for that kind of love. I mean, he tried out the whole hot-girl-with-a-bad-personality thing, and it didn't work out for him. Maybe he's finally ready to be with a woman of *substance*. (Like me.)

Lou finishes applying her lip gloss after what feels like fifty years and moves onto her hair. She pulls her long, perfectly waved chestnut locks into a bun, then reconsiders and lets them spill back down over her shoulders. "Do you like my hair more up or down?"

"Down. You spent *forever* waving it before we left, why let that go to waste?"

"You're right," she agrees, before looking me up and down. "Isaac Taylor is the luckiest boy in the world to get to talk to you tonight."

I smile because I know Lou actually means it. It's wild what having one friend who loves you for you does for your confidence. It's like she's my living human proof that I'm not actually the freak everyone else at school seems to have decided I am.

I take a deep breath and grab Lou's hand, and we head back

into the party. Okay, "party" is a loose term. Oliver Blair's mom is a dental hygienist and is away at some sort of dental conference, so he invited the twenty most popular kids (the soccer girls and basketball boys) in my grade who do everything together to hang out in his garage. Plus me and Lou. The only reason we're even here is because Lou has been hooking up with Grant Miller, class president, captain of the basketball team, and certified hunk-and-a-half. This is *his* friend group.

Despite his questionable choice in friends, Grant's a pretty nice guy. I like him way more than the other guys Lou hooks up with, who typically treat me like an annoying fly they're trying to swat out of the picture. Lou told me he even specifically told her to bring me along tonight to celebrate my birthday. It's the only reason I came in the first place. I may not love my birthday anymore, but I do appreciate a nice gesture.

Looking across the room, though, I honestly can't believe *these* are the events the popular kids have been raving about every Monday since our freshman year. Some rap song Lou told me is by Drake is playing quietly over the speakers so as not to wake up Oliver Blair's neighbors, and people are chatting in little groups dispersed throughout the garage. In the center of the musty-smelling room is a flimsy-looking foldout table lined with red Solo cups on either end for beer pong. Playing beer pong, of course, is Genevieve. She's being extra loud tonight and majorly flirting with Oliver Blair, who I think is her teammate. (Either that, or she's playing against him. I don't really know how beer pong works.)

The girls who aren't playing beer pong—mostly Genevieve's

crew—are seated on an old dusty-green pullout couch facing the table. They've spent pretty much the entire night seated there, taking selfies of themselves chugging vodka out of plastic water bottles and chasing it with Vibe Teas.

I tried hanging with them earlier while Lou was busy flirting with Grant, but they didn't exactly seem interested in acknowledging my existence.

"Hey, Alicia," I'd tried to say as I took a seat on the couch next to my Environmental Action Club cochair.

She gave me a curt "Hey" back, then returned to gossiping with her friends with her back turned toward me for about forty-five minutes until I finally decided to treat myself to a Vibe Tea. Then . . . well, I already explained how the story went from there.

I look slightly to the left of Alicia's crew, and, finally, I see him. Six feet and two inches of pure sexy. "Oh my gosh," I whisper to Lou as we make our way past a clump of popular girls taking selfies. "Grant is talking to Isaac!"

Lou squeezes my hand and whispers back, "This is *perfect*."

We make our way over to the two boys. "Hey, babe," Lou murmurs in the singsongy voice she only ever uses to talk to boys.

"Sup, sexy?" Grant excitedly engulfs her in a bear hug, and I worry he might legitimately squeeze Lou to death. Before I know it, they're aggressively making out.

I know I'm a virgin and don't know anything about this stuff, but I just don't get how these two logistically work. Lou is so tiny, and Grant is, like, a seven-foot-tall beef castle. He's bending down practically two feet right now just to stick his tongue down Lou's throat! Seems like a lot of work, if you ask me.

But, hey, they both seem to be enjoying it. Who am I to judge? Maybe Grant sees the squatting as bonus basketball practice.

I shift my attention over to the Greek god of an eighteen-year-old standing in front of me. Tonight, Isaac's dressed in gray shorts made of some sweatpant material, a bright yellow USC T-shirt, and Vans. His dreamy hazel eyes are covered with a pair of black Oakley sunglasses like the ones my dad Matt wears riding his bike, which makes me worry a bit about his corneal health. (But, like, come on. Even his *eyes* are sensitive. Swoon!!)

I want to make conversation, but instead I wind up staring at him silently for what feels like ten years but is probably realistically ten seconds. My heart is beating so fast I worry it might jump out of my chest and onto this grimy alcohol-covered party floor. Part of me just wants to run back to the bathroom where it's safe, but I remind myself I'm likely dying tomorrow. This could be my last chance to make a move on the greatest man who's ever lived.

Just pretend you're in math class, Josie. It's just the two of you, hanging out, talking calc. Maybe he'll remember your birthday!

"H-hi, Isaac," I finally muster.

He stares at me blankly, seemingly not registering what I said.

"Uh, Isaac?" I ask, gently tapping his perfectly chiseled chest with my index finger. "You okay?"

He straightens up at my touch, frantically running his hand through the middle part of his shaggy brown hair. Was he asleep? Is that why he was wearing the sunglasses? To hide the fact that he's sleeping upright at a party? Ugh, we're so meant to be. We would both rather sleep than be at this party.

He lifts the sunglasses up onto his forehead, revealing his excessively bloodshot eyes. He seems surprised to see me standing in front of him.

"Sssup," he finally says, his words a little more slurry than they typically are in math class. He puts his sunglasses back on and takes a long drag on his joint.

"Uh, nothing," I say, trying to suppress my fear of the smell of marijuana killing me by reminding myself that the Vibe Tea pretty much already sealed my fate earlier tonight. "How about you?"

He takes another million-year-long drag of his joint and finally responds, "Nothing, man. *Nothing.*"

Okay, so that conversation was a bust. But that was on me. *Nothing, how about you?* I gave the guy nothing to work with!

"Cool," I say, desperate to keep things flowing forward. "So, uh, how's your mom doing?"

He takes a sip of his Vibe Tea. Then another. Then another. And just stands there, staring at me blankly, occasionally wobbling left to right. It's funny. He's a pretty big guy. And years of P.E. being my worst subject have proven that I'm no athlete.

But I sort of feel like I could topple him over right now with just one flick of my index finger.

Five more seconds go by. Yes, I know, because I counted.

Maybe I need to be louder. That's gotta be it. He's just not *hearing* me.

"COOL," I try again, this time louder. "SO, HOW'S YOUR MOM DOING?"

Shoot. Maybe that was too loud. Thankfully Genevieve has headed off into the house with Oliver Blair, but Alicia and her whole crew are staring from the couch. Even Lou and Grant take a pause from their tonsil-hockey session to see what I'm yelling about.

"You got this," Lou mouths to me, her lips still somehow perfectly glossed, before she goes back to sucking off Grant's face.

Isaac smiles. He has the world's CUTEST smile. In *The Great Gatsby*, Nick described Gatsby's smile as a smile that "understood you just as far as you wanted to be understood, believed in you as you would like to believe in yourself." Well, Isaac has that *exact* smile.

I wait expectantly as he takes another long sip of his Vibe Tea. I'm honestly curious. I know they have their issues, based on what he's told me in class, but I like his mom, Carol. She's a nice lady, always makes the best brownies for the bake sale, and gave me a totally unnecessary ten-dollar tip that one time I babysat his little sister Avery last year.

He sets the Vibe Tea down and turns his attention back over to me. He stares blankly for seven excruciating seconds before taking another long drag on his joint. Now, completely out of nowhere, he bursts into giggles. Not laughs. Giggles. He's giggling like his little sister Avery did when we watched a particularly funny episode of *Peppa Pig* together.

"Sssorry," he finally says. "Do I know you?"

The whole room stops. Alicia and her friends stop whispering to each other and stare, mesmerized by the real-life piece of gossip unfolding before their very eyes. Lou pushes Grant off her and rushes over to me.

"Oh! Yeah," I say, grabbing Lou's hand for support as I try to blink away the burning-hot tears desperately trying to escape. "It's me. Josie. Your math partner." More giggles. "Josie Lawrence. I babysat your little sister one day last year," I try again. He gives me a shrug and keeps giggling, so I continue. "We carpooled together in third grade?"

Even more giggles.

"Josie," Lou whispers in my ear. "Just let it go. He's a jerk."

But I can't. This is *Isaac*. The love of my life! He knows who I am.

"We have three separate inside jokes about parabolas?"

"Oh God, Josie." I can hear the panic in Lou's voice rising. "Don't."

But I have to. "We dated for a day in fourth grade?"

"I'm sorry," he slurs between giggles, wiping away the tears that have now streamed down his face. "I just have no idea who you are. But, like, you clearly know me. This is so trippy, dude."

Alicia and her friends erupt into laughter, and I turn to see they've all been filming the whole exchange on their phones. "Just *wait* till Genevieve sees this, she's gonna die," I hear one of them say.

The room starts feeling like it's closing in around me, and I'm not sure if the sensation is a result of the Vibe Tea working to kill me from within or the sheer humiliation of being alive during this very moment. Lou wraps me in a hug that may be even stronger than Grant's and shifts her attention to Isaac. "You know what you are? You're a weasel," she says in an almost yell. "A disgusting, tiny, pathetic weasel—"

"Lou, stop," I quietly interrupt, my face growing as hot as a furnace. "Isaac probably didn't mean it. He's had too many Vibe Teas. He's wearing sunglasses inside, the guy's practically blind!"

Even as the words escape my mouth, I know there's no use. Lou has no off button when she's mad. All I can do is hold my breath, wait, and hope she doesn't make Isaac cry.

"NO," she responds to me, now fully yelling. "I'm not done." Her attention is back on Isaac. "You would be so *lucky* to know someone as perfect as Josie. And you know what? She's lucky she doesn't have to waste another ounce of her energy thinking about a *painfully* insecure loser like you."

Then she turns all her attention to me. "Come on, Josie," she says. "Let's go."

"Sorry," I mumble to no one in particular as I grab her hand and follow her out of the house.

Lou tries to pep me up when we first get in the Uber to my apartment, but eventually she stops. She knows there's nothing to say.

He was just drunk, he didn't mean it. He was just drunk, he didn't mean it. He was just drunk, he didn't mean it. I repeat the words in my head over and over again until they start to feel true. I mean, I *know* Isaac knows who I am. His best friend Grant is the one who invited me tonight! And, like, yes, Grant is hooking up with my best friend. But part of that invite had to be Isaac related, right? Like, I'm sure Isaac has told him about our math class bond. And maybe Grant thought inviting me, the secret love of Isaac's life, to the party tonight could cheer his buddy up after his breakup. And then Isaac was so excited that I was coming that he got too drunk and was unable to recognize my existence. Yes. That's the only logical conclusion.

"Hey," Lou says, breaking the silence ten minutes into our drive. "It's midnight."

"Oh," I say. "Got it."

I try to force a smile but my lips are quivering too much to curve into the right proportions. I wish I hadn't had that Vibe Tea. I wish my mom were here. And, even if it was an accident, I wish Isaac had remembered me. As sucky as all my birthdays have been since my mom died, this might have to take the cake for the worst yet.

"Happy birthday, Jos," Lou says, scooching closer to me in the back seat to give me a hug. "I love you."

"Thanks, Lou," I say, resting my head on her shoulder. "Love you, too."

We ride a few more minutes in silence until an unpleasant thought creeps into the back of my mind. I try pushing it away, but it persists. Finally, the question just blurts out of me. "Lou, did Grant really tell you to invite me tonight?"

"Yeah! Of course!" Her response is almost too quick. "Well," she adds, sensing my disbelief. "I mean, he didn't say the words 'invite Josie' exactly, but it was totally implied. Like, he told me I could bring a friend and obviously you're my only friend, so that was a given."

"Yeah," I mutter as I try to blink away the second wave of scorching-hot tears. "Totally."

Chapter 2

Hi Josie Boob Man you're asleep just one room over from me but it's midnight and you're officially on Evan. Happy birthday ___. I love you so much and can't wait to see you in the morning.

I stare at the lazy iPhone transcription of the voicemail my mom left me now exactly seven years ago, hoping it might distract me from the horrors of last night. It's become sort of a birthday ritual. As soon as I wake up, I read the transcript and try to imagine it's her little birthday message to me. Actually listening to the voicemail is too sad. But reading the transcript I can handle. Something about my phone assuming my mother would have been calling me *Boob Man* instead of the Farsi term of endearment *Joonam* and wanting to chat about me being on top of a guy named Evan gives the sentimental message just the right dash of humor to make it palatable.

Besides, I listened to that voicemail so many times after she first passed away that I know what she actually said, and how she actually said it, by heart. If I focus really hard, I can hear

Matt softly snoring in the background as she whispers: *Hi, Josie Joonam, you're asleep just one room over from me, but it's midnight and you're officially eleven! Happy birthday, azizam. I love you so much and can't wait to see you in the morning.* I like knowing that version exists in my head. It's proof I still remember her voice.

"Josie?" Matt calls from outside my door. "My birthday girl up?"

Oh gosh. I was so busy dwelling on . . . well, everything that I forgot about Matt. He probably wants to take me out to Delaney's for a birthday breakfast. It's our tradition. Neither of us liked celebrating our birthdays after Mom died, so we decided our only celebration would be a breakfast at Delaney's. Delaney's is the only place we could think of that has no association with her. The only place in all of Van Nuys that wasn't touched by her magic. A place where we could go browse a menu without instantly thinking of what she would have ordered if she were with us.

"Jos." He knocks again. "You in there?"

Oh no. He sounds tense. What if he knows about last night? About the Vibe Teas? He can't know about this. First, my mom died. Then he had to give up his beloved comedy club. Now he's working double shifts at the California Pizza Kitchen to keep us in this tiny one-bedroom just so that we don't have to move out of my school district.

The man already has enough on his plate. He gets about one waking hour at home when he's not working, and my job is to make sure that hour is as stress free as possible.

I try shaking Louise awake to see if there's any way her mom might have already told Matt we went to Oli's, but it's no use. I've had enough sleepovers with her over the past decade and a half to know not even a tsunami could wake her up before eleven on a Sunday morning.

I take some deep breaths. *Chillax, Josie.*

"Sorry, Matt," I finally respond. "Coming out in a sec!"

When I open the door, I find my stepdad nervously pacing up and down the brown shag carpet in our tiny hallway. Well, *pacing* is a loose term. He's more stiffly marching, then pausing to crack his back every few seconds.

"Matt," I say as I walk toward him. "I've already told you a million times. Please just let me take the pullout couch and you take the bed."

"And I've told *you* a million times." He smiles. "The pullout couch is better for my back. Trust me."

"Okay." I sigh, knowing from experience this fight isn't a winnable one. "But I'm telling you. Whenever you want the room, it's yours. You need a good night's sleep more than I do! I'm not the one spending sixteen hours a day on my feet."

"That's because you're the brains of the family, Jos," he says, giving me a pat on the back. "My Stanford girl. We need you resting that noggin of yours."

A pang of guilt strikes me like a punch in the face. Here he is literally breaking his back to make sure I get a good night's sleep, and I'm out secretly partying it up drinking gross Vibe Teas with the popular kids.

"So, um, what's up?" I ask. "We going to Delaney's?"

"I'm sorry, Jos," he says, nervously biting his lower lip. "I know it's our tradition, but Melissa's sister just had a baby, so

I told her I would pick up her shift at the restaurant this morning. You don't mind, do you?"

"Oh," I say, my heart sinking a little more than I care to admit. "No, not at all. I get it."

I try my best to slap on a forced smile. The last thing he needs is me making him feel guilty about missing a dumb little birthday breakfast.

"I knew you would understand," he says with a relieved smile. "But don't worry. I didn't *completely* throw our birthday traditions aside." He gestures for me to come meet him at the kitchen table, where he has re-created my exact order from Delaney's: a Mexican scramble with a side of chorizo. A dish I never once saw Mom order or speak of. Wonderfully unfamiliar.

"What time did you have to wake up to make all of this?" I ask, my eyes welling up. "It's perfect."

"Wait!" he exclaims before I take a seat at the table. "There's one final touch."

He comes out with a candle and carefully secures it into my mound of eggs. "Make a wish."

I close my eyes and wish for the first thing that comes to mind: *I wish that Isaac completely forgets last night ever happened.* Then I blow it out.

"Yum, this is so good," I lie, taking a bite out of the rubbery scramble. "Like, better than Delaney's!!!"

Matt laughs. "You know I'm not a chef, but I tried."

"No, seriously!" I insist, forcing the widest smile I can muster as I shove another spoonful down. "It's so good." If Lou was awake, she would tell me to just tell him I don't love the stupid scramble. But what's the point? He went to all this effort.

"Good. I'm glad you like it." Matt finally relents, before his face tenses up again. "But listen, Jos . . . I really have to talk to you about something before I go to work."

"Oh no," I say. "You seem stressed. Is this about last night?"

"What?" he asks. "What was last night?"

"Oh, um, nothing." Relief washes over me like a warm bath as I scarf down another bite of the subpar scramble. "No big deal. I was just out a little later than usual. Wanted to make sure you weren't worried."

"No. If anything, I'm happy to hear you were getting out of here on a Saturday night," he says, getting up to grab something from the counter. "I . . . I just have to talk to you about what's in here."

He sits back down across from me, tentatively placing a large manila envelope between us. I still don't know what's going on, but my heart starts to beat faster.

I wait for him to say something, but instead he wordlessly starts tapping his fingers to the tune of Tom Petty's "I Won't Back Down." *Oh, this must be really bad.* The last time I saw him tapping his fingers this feverishly to the '80s hit, he'd found out he was losing the club.

"So, okay, here we go," Matt begins. Then, muttering under his breath: *"So here we go? Are you kidding me, Matt? What, are you about to kick off a dance routine?"*

I try my best to maneuver my face into a calm, unbothered-by-his-weird-muttering position, hoping my unfazed vibe will relax him enough to just tell me what's going on.

"Okay, before I get into it, let me just start by saying you *know* that you are my whole world," Matt says, his eyes welling up. "And I know that we don't do the whole 'dad' thing, but when I signed those adoption papers the day I married your mom, I never looked back. You are my kid. My only kid."

"Of course," I say, my eyes now also moistening. "And you are my only dad."

"Well, that's the thing," he says, his attention now back on the envelope. "This envelope has a letter in it . . . from your biological father."

I instinctively shove the envelope back toward him. It's the same one that's been sitting between us since he placed it there, but now even just looking at it feels like a betrayal to my mom.

"You mean the guy who completely abandoned Mom when she was pregnant with his baby?" I ask. "Matt, I want nothing to do with him or his stupid letter. *You* are the only dad I need."

"And you will *always* be the only daughter I'll ever need. Whatever that letter says doesn't change what we have," he says, pausing for a beat before adding, "but your mom wanted you to have this."

"What?" I ask, my voice shaking. "But she hated him."

"I know, sweetie," Matt says, reaching his hand across the table to clasp my trembling one.

"How long have you had it?"

I stare at the envelope like it's a bomb, wondering where it's been hiding for all these years, waiting to blow up my life.

"She told me about it a year before she died," Matt says.

"You were going into seventh grade. She placed it in that safe we had in our bedroom closet and told me she wanted to give it to you on your eighteenth birthday, said she was trusting me to get it to you if God forbid anything happened to her. Of course, I never thought anything would actually happen. But . . . well, here we are."

"Here we are," I repeat, unable to think of anything cleverer.

I keep staring at the envelope, remembering our move into this apartment. I imagine it bouncing around in a box under our family photos, like a fiery piece of coal scorching the entire foundation our family was built upon.

"I still don't get it," I say, my eyes watering as I more seriously consider opening the mysterious envelope. "She hated him. All she would ever say about him was how he abandoned us both. Why would she want me to have this?"

"I don't know, Jos," Matt admits. "I didn't ask any questions when she mentioned it, and now she's gone and it's too late. I haven't even seen what's in there. It felt like an invasion of your privacy to peek. All I knew up until now was that there was a letter from your birth father and she wanted to get it to you on your eighteenth birthday. Then this morning, I got a call."

"What? From my birth father?"

I feel my fingernails digging into the flesh of my palms. *Now* he calls? The guy leaves me abandoned for years, and now suddenly he's pestering me with letters and calls? The nerve.

"Not quite. It was his wife. She wanted to make sure you got the letter."

"His wife?" I ask, my brain trying desperately to piece this increasingly difficult puzzle together. "My birth father's *wife* called you? Why wouldn't he call you himself?"

Matt pauses, gazing everywhere around the room except for where I'm sitting.

"Oh, Jos," he says, nervously running his hand through his hair. "I just . . . I wish your mom were here. She knew how to handle these things. Here I am, blowing this conversation like an idiot."

My heart sinks. I can't make this about me. Matt needs me to be strong.

I take a deep breath and try to channel my mom's brave energy, the word *CHILLAX* blaring at me in neon lights in my mind's eye.

"It's okay, Matt," I say. "You're not an idiot. It's fine. Just tell me."

"Okay, um, well. Jos, I know you are not a huge pop culture person," he begins. "But you do know the Mashads . . . right?"

"Like, the reality TV people?"

"Yes," he confirms with a nod. "Them."

"Yeah, of course I know them," I say. "I have to pass, like, a million billboards with their faces on them just to get from here to school every morning."

"Yep. They're big," he says slowly and carefully, like he's practiced this. "And, again, I want you to know I really didn't know what I'm about to tell you. You know, until this morning."

"I know," I say, my voice coming out a little too perky. "I believe you."

Chillax. Chillax. Chillax. Don't make this about you. Stay calm for Matt.

"So, what is it?" I ask, doing my best to exude nonchalance. "Matt, just tell me."

"Josie, your biological father was Ali Mashad," he says, his voice barely audible. "You're one of them."

Chapter 3

"Josie, hurry up!" Lou yells from our living room. "It's starting!"

It's Christmas break of seventh grade, and I know I don't really have to do any homework. But Mrs. Zhang said if we read and did a book report on *Of Mice and Men* over break, we could earn twenty extra credit points. How am I supposed to pass up a deal like that?!

I finish the last sentence of my book report and head out to the living room, plopping myself down on the couch between Lou and Genevieve.

"What is this again?" I ask, my eyes staring at what appears to be a funeral unfolding on our TV screen.

"It's Ali Mashad's funeral!" Genevieve reminds me, quickly grabbing the Kleenex from Lou's lap to wipe her own tears. "According to Twitter, there are already 155 million viewers tuned in."

"I just can't believe he's gone." Lou solemnly nods, soaking another bunch of Kleenex. "I feel like my own dad just died."

"I don't think I would be as sad if my own dad died," Genevieve says, a snot bubble making its way out of her nostrils. "Ali Mashad was my dream dad."

I look at my two best friends and try my best not to laugh.

"You guys are seriously this sad over some random guy's death?"

"He's not some random guy," Genevieve insists. "He's Ali Mashad!"

A sniffly Lou nods in agreement. "This is projected to be the most-watched event in American television history since the moon landing!"

"Whoa," I say, watching as a stoic Iranian lady makes her way up to the podium by his burial plot. "Who's that?"

"Josie, *how* do you live on planet Earth without knowing who Mary Mashad is?" Genevieve asks. "She's, like, America's hot mom."

"Girls, I brought some snacks," my mom says, as she makes her way in from the kitchen, setting a plate of kookoo sabzi on the coffee table in front of us.

"Oooh, you made the ones with the raisiny things in them," I say, excitedly grabbing a square from the plate. "My favorite."

"Those raisiny things are called zereshk," she says, giving me a kiss on the forehead. "And yes. We had some extra bites left over at the café this afternoon, so I brought them home for you girls."

"Thanks, Sharzad," Lou says. "But I don't think I have much of an appetite."

"Speak for yourself," Genevieve says, stuffing her face with two squares at once. "I think I'm going to have to eat this pain away."

My mom glances at the TV, the camera zoomed in on Mary Mashad's flawless face, then back at my two teary-eyed best friends.

"Are you girls this upset over the Mashads?" she asks with a sigh. "That family is ridiculous. An embarrassment to the entire Persian American community."

"But Ali Mashad died," Genevieve replies, bursting into a sob.

Louise joins in, now loudly wailing. "He was, like, the best dad America has ever seen, and now he's dead! The least we can do is watch his funeral."

"They are mourning as if he was their real-life dad," I say with a laugh, expecting her to join in. "Isn't that nuts???"

But she doesn't speak. Instead, my mom sinks down onto the couch beside Genevieve, her eyes tightening as she watches Mary begin to stoically deliver her eulogy.

"Um, Mom?" I ask. "You good?"

"Oh, yes. Sorry, azizam. I guess I got a bit distracted. I get how they suck people in with this junk," my mom says lightly before turning her attention to Genevieve and Lou. "You girls really shouldn't waste your precious little tears on this stranger. It's probably all made up anyway."

"It's not!" Genevieve insists. "This is his real funeral."

"She's right," Lou agrees. "They're streaming it live."

"Even worse," my mom says, shaking her head in disbelief. "Capitalizing on a *funeral* for profit. It's deplorable. Is anything sacred to these people? We really shouldn't even be giving them our attention."

But her eyes are still glued to the TV.

"Mom, you don't have to stay and watch," I say. "I know you hate this stuff. I mean, I'm not a fan, either. I'm just here for moral support."

"And we appreciate it," Lou says, soaking my shoulder with tears as she rests her head on it.

"I don't *hate* them, Josie Joonam," my mom says, still hanging on Mary Mashad's every last word. "I more . . . fundamentally disagree with everything they stand for."

I've never seen her like this before. It's like she's here but she's also somewhere else entirely.

"Um, okay," I say. "So, you don't hate them. Just have no respect for them and instinctively roll your eyes any time you see their billboards on the way to school?"

She lets out a small laugh and reaches over Genevieve to give me a playful smack on the top of my head. "Pedar sookhteh. You know me so well."

Then her attention turns back to the TV, and although she quickly tries to blink them away, I see the small pool of tears forming as Mary Mashad describes the husband she just lost.

"Mom . . . are you crying?" I ask. "Over a *Mashad*?"

"Azizam, it's death," she says, giving a teary Lou and Genevieve a tight squeeze. "It's always sad."

✦ ✦ ✦

"I just can't believe she even *knew* him," I tell Lou for what must be the thousandth time since she woke up. "Let alone slept with him."

"I know," Lou agrees. "She hated that family more than anything."

"This must be why she hated them as much as she did, though," I say, memories from my past suddenly clicking into place like a set of Legos. "It was personal. He's the jerk who left her. Who left *us*. Ugh, this makes it so much worse. She had to see him everywhere, just being the 'perfect' husband and father, knowing that he totally abandoned us. Can you imagine what that must have been like for her?"

My heart sinks, wishing I could go back in time and rip up every stupid magazine with his face on the cover before she even had a chance to roll her eyes at it.

"I honestly can't imagine," Lou says, visibly shuddering. "The woman lived through a literal nightmare."

"Do you think she knew he was married?" I ask, the thought just now crossing my mind. "I mean, he had been with Mary Mashad since college, right?"

I'm not sure how I know this, but I do. Whether or not you actively pay attention to them, the Mashads seem to be an inescapable fact of life. Basic information about their family is as seamlessly etched into my mind as the color of the sky or the date of Lou's birthday.

"I'm sure there was some sort of explanation," Lou reassures me, seemingly sensing how badly I need this to be the case. "Maybe he didn't wear a ring and she just assumed he was single. My aunt Jackie—the single one who lives in Chicago—says that happens all the time."

"Yeah," I say. "Or maybe they privately went on a break for a bit before they became famous."

Too much has been turned upside down in the past twenty-four hours. I just need this one thing to be true.

"I mean, it's not totally impossible," Lou admits. "People take breaks from their marriages all the time."

"Right!" I say, feeling vindicated. "I'm sure that's what happened. They were on a break way before he was famous or anything. A brief break, and he somehow met my mom. And she was there for him, and they briefly fell in love, and she got pregnant with me, and then he went back to his wife and his fancy life and decided to completely forget about us."

"Well, he didn't *completely* forget about you," Lou says. "He wrote you that letter."

I scoff. "The letter?! Louise. Please. The guy lived less than an hour away, and instead of coming to see me in person even just once, he wrote me a stupid letter that I wouldn't get until I was an adult and he was dead. I was an afterthought, at best."

"I don't know, maybe he was scared," Lou says with a shrug. "Your mom hated him. And you were obviously going to be loyal to her. Maybe he was afraid of being rejected by you."

"Well, then he was a coward," I say firmly.

"He was a coward, says the girl who spent all night horrified that she had a few sips of a Vibe Tea," Lou fires back. "Maybe a little cowardice runs in the family."

"I'm a coward in a tangible way," I say. "Like in an 'I avoid doing things that might kill me' sort of way. Not in an 'I abandon my responsibilities and moral obligations as a human being' kind of way."

"Fair." Lou nods. "I'll give you that. . . . But this is just so weird. Ali was, like, America's favorite dad. He, at the very least, *seemed* like a great guy."

"Well, Bill Cosby also had America convinced he was a great guy," I remind her. "People aren't always how they seem."

"So you're really not gonna read the letter?" Lou asks, willfully ignoring my Cosby parallel. "You're not even a little bit curious?"

"I don't care at all what he has to say," I tell Lou. "His actions already told me everything I need to know about him. But it's just . . . it's the fact that my mom wanted to give it to me. It's weird. I feel like I shouldn't open it, out of loyalty to her. But then, she was the one who wanted me to open it. It sort of feels like one last birthday gift from her? A really, really weird birthday gift."

I try to visualize my mom handing me the letter, hoping maybe it will conjure up some sort of idea of what she would have said to me in this moment, but I come up blank. We sit there quietly for a few minutes, giving all this new information a minute to marinate.

"Okay," Lou finally says. "I am really trying my hardest to be your calm rock here, but can you please give me, like, five seconds to fully freak out about this?"

"Fine," I concede.

"My best friend is a freaking MASHAD," Lou squeals. "Oh, I wish we could tell Isaac and rub it in his stupid little twerp face. And Genevieve! Remember she bragged for an entire year that she went on one date with an intern on the set of *Making Mashad*? And you literally *are* a Mashad!"

"Louise, we CAN'T TELL," I remind her. "Seriously, this has to stay a secret."

It really does. Shortly after delivering the news, Matt gave me the NDAs Mary's team required that we sign that basically give her the right to sue the three of us for millions if we blab about any of this.

"I'm not going to tell," she says with an overly dramatic eye roll. "*Relax*. I just think this is absolutely iconic information. Honestly, it makes sense. Before we found out about all of this, Ali was always my favorite. Probably because he reminded me of you. Because *you* are a Mashad. Holy crap. This is just too much. Do you think you might get to go on the show?"

I stare at her for a second, wondering if maybe someone slipped some meth into her beers last night. Has she met me?! How could she possibly be talking about this as if it's even a remotely real possibility?

"Lou, are you kidding?" I ask. "In what world am I going to go be on national television? That's absurd. And I'm sure Mary would agree the minute she sees me. I am not fame worthy. People I've gone to school with for fifteen years barely even know I exist!"

"I think America would love you," Lou says. "I mean, they loved Ali. And he clearly had some major character flaws behind closed doors. You're like a better version of him. You have all of his quirkiness without the skeletons in the closet."

"Even on the off chance that they *did* invite me on the show, we both know I'm not the reality TV kind of gal," I say. "I want to be pre-med at Stanford. Not really trying to peddle diet teas on Instagram for a living."

"Okay, fine," Lou concedes. "Just at least open the letter. For your mom."

I stare at it, my hands instinctively tapping the same rendition of Tom Petty's "I Won't Back Down" Matt was drumming on our kitchen table earlier this morning.

"I'm scared," I admit. "What if there's something in there I don't want to know?"

"How about I read it first?" Lou suggests. "Then, if it's not upsetting, I'll give it to you to read?"

I consider this for a moment. If anyone knows exactly what would upset me, it's Lou. This might be my best option. All reward, no risk.

"Fine," I say. "BUT you cannot tell me a single thing about what it says if you think it's going to make me too sad. Deal?"

"Deal," she confirms, snatching the envelope from my side of the table.

As soon as she pulls the paper out of the envelope, I can tell it was penned by a Fancy Man. I've spent enough hours of my life at Paper Source to know fancy paper when I see it. And I can tell just sheerly based on the cardstock-ish thickness to that sheet and the initials *AM* embossed in navy at the top that this man spared no expense. Not even on his paper. Plus, the front side of the beautiful sheet of fancy paper is littered with what is the unmistakably aggressive all-caps handwriting of a powerful man with a way-too-expensive pen.

I sit there waiting in excruciating silence for Louise to finish reading. If she weren't so intent on going into fashion, I would say she should become a professional poker player. The girl has an absolutely killer poker face. It is totally and completely blank. I can't tell if he just told me that he has another secret child who he murdered in a dumpster fire or that he loves me and giving me up was the biggest regret of his entire life. Honestly, I'm not sure which version I prefer. On the one hand, I guess it would be nice to know that my birth father actually cared about me. On the other, if the letter is cruel and awful, it only means my mom and I were right. He really was a horrible monster, and I really was better off spending my life not knowing him . . . but then if he really was a horrible monster, does that make me half horrible monster, too? *Ugh*. I need Lou to get through this letter already.

The suspense is only magnified by the fact that she's the slowest reader of all time. Man, I really wish she hadn't refused to take that speed-reading course with me in seventh grade. Or maybe she's dyslexic? I make a mental note to ask her to get tested when we're done with this important moment.

"Okay," she says, finally putting the letter down. "I think you should read it."

"You're sure?" I ask.

"Yes," she replies confidently. "I'm sure. It's really nice and gives some backstory on, you know, *you*."

Nice, I think to myself, surprised by how relieved I am to hear her say the word. I guess that's what I was hoping for.

Lou gently scoots next to me and holds my hand as I prepare to read whatever's on the piece of fancy paper.

DEAR JOSIE,

IF YOU'RE GETTING THIS, IT MEANS THAT I WAS NEVER ABLE TO SAY "I'M SORRY" WHILE I WAS ALIVE. I HAVE BEEN A COWARD—SO DEEPLY AFRAID OF RUINING MY EXISTING FAMILY THAT I DELUDED MYSELF INTO THINKING YOU WEREN'T MY FAMILY, TOO.

THE LEAST I CAN DO NOW IS TELL YOU A BIT ABOUT WHERE YOU CAME FROM. WHILE I'M SURE YOUR MOTHER HAS FILLED YOU IN ON HER SIDE OF THE STORY, WHAT I CAN TELL YOU FROM MY VANTAGE POINT IS THAT I TRULY LOVED HER, AND, IN TURN, WE BOTH TRULY LOVED YOU. I CAN ONLY IMAGINE WHAT A DYNAMITE WOMAN YOU HAVE BECOME WITH HER TO GUIDE YOU THROUGH LIFE.

THINGS DID NOT ULTIMATELY WORK OUT BETWEEN YOUR MOTHER AND ME. IT WAS COMPLICATED, AS I'M SURE YOU CAN IMAGINE. BUT PLEASE KNOW THAT YOU WERE THE FRUIT OF WHAT REALLY WAS A GENUINE LOVE.

WHILE I WAS NOT ABLE TO BE THERE IN THE WAY I WOULD HAVE LIKED, I HOPE YOU KNOW I DID LOVE YOU IN MY OWN WAY. I LET YOU GO BECAUSE I HAD TO SAVE MY MARRIAGE. BUT A DAY DIDN'T GO BY WHEN I DIDN'T THINK ABOUT YOU. WHAT YOU LOOK LIKE. WHAT YOU SOUND LIKE. WHAT YOUR INTERESTS ARE. WHAT INSPIRES YOU. WHAT ANGERS YOU. I'VE SPENT YOUR WHOLE LIFE WONDERING FROM AFAR.

I HAVE SET UP A TRUST IN YOUR NAME. IT KICKS IN WHEN YOU TURN 18. I KNOW THAT MONEY CANNOT COMPARE TO A FATHER'S PRESENCE IN YOUR LIFE. I WISH I COULD HAVE GIVEN YOU THAT. BUT I HOPE THIS HELPS.

NOW, HERE'S WHERE I HAVE THE AUDACITY TO REQUEST SOMETHING OF YOU: PLEASE MEET YOUR SISTERS. SPEND TIME WITH THEM. I KNOW THIS MAY BE HOPING FOR TOO MUCH—BUT

MAYBE YOU'LL FIND A SENSE OF FAMILY WITH THEM. I MAY NEVER HAVE THE PLEASURE OF GETTING TO KNOW YOU, BUT I HOPE YOUR SISTERS MIGHT.

I AM VERY SICK AND WILL LIKELY BE GONE WHEN YOU READ THIS, SO PLEASE. BE IN TOUCH WITH MARY. SHE CAN PUT YOU IN TOUCH WITH THE FAMILY AND GIVE YOU MORE DETAILS ON THE TRUST.

WITH ALL THE LOVE IN THE WORLD,

ALI MASHAD (DAD)

I set the letter down, a little taken aback by the power a virtual stranger managed to have over my emotions. Maybe the letter is just the icing on the cake after last night's events and this morning's revelation, but my eyeballs have somehow transformed into the Niagara freaking Falls.

"It was nice, though, right?" Lou asks nervously as she embraces me in a tight hug. "He clearly loved you. Also, you might be rich?!"

"I don't want his money," I say through sniffles. "I just . . . I don't know. I guess I wasn't expecting it to affect me like this."

"Oh." Lou laughs. "You didn't expect a letter from your deceased estranged biological father to make you a wee bit emotional?"

I laugh. "Okay, fair point," I say. "But you're right. It was nice. I mean, I still think he's a coward. But at least *he* also thought he was a coward?"

"Yeah," Lou agrees. "I guess you two were aligned on that."

We sit in silence for a bit, my mind flooding with questions I'll likely never have answers to. Did my mom ever read this letter? How did she get it? Was she talking to him? How long did she have it before she mentioned it to Matt? What would she say to me right now if she were here? What about him? What would he say? Would he have ever written to me if he wasn't literally on his deathbed? Would I have ever met him if he were alive?

"I know I have Matt, but does this technically make me an orphan?" I finally ask Lou.

"No!" Lou exclaims. "Well, yes. Technically. Yes. But you have Matt. So, no."

The realization lands on my heart like a ton of bricks. Somehow, the fact that he's gone only works to highlight the fact that she's gone, too. One more link to her, gone.

"It's not like I would have even wanted to meet him if he were alive," I tell Lou. "But I sort of always imagined my birth father was out there existing somewhere. It's just kind of bizarre to think the two people who put me in this world are no longer in it."

"Yeah," Lou says, wrapping an arm around me. "It is weird. But hey. You have Matt. And you have me. Until the very, very, very end."

"I know," I say, a small smile finding its way onto my face.

"And you *do* technically have three sisters," Lou quietly adds. "Do you think you're going to call Mary? Not to be on the show or for the money, but just to meet your sisters. Like he wanted."

I glance over to where Mary Mashad's number is casually scribbled on a yellow sticky note clinging to the fridge, like she's just the plumber or someone else who hasn't won twenty-three People's Choice Awards. The truth is, sometimes

I do fantasize about what it would have been like to have a big family. But in that fantasy, I'm not the estranged love child who pops out of nowhere. I'm wanted.

"Honestly? I think I just want to put all of this behind me," I say, feeling surprisingly confident in my decision. "I got my closure. I know who my birth dad is. Now I just want to be done."

"Okay!" Lou says, ripping Mary's number off the fridge and throwing it in the trash. "Then we're done."

Chapter 4

"REMEMBER HE HUMILIATED YOU," Lou yells down the hall as I turn away from her and Grant and head over to Mrs. Lopez's classroom a few doors down. "HAVE A BACKBONE!"

For the past four years, math with Isaac has been the highlight of my day. It's like our own little slice of heaven. And honestly? I could really use a little heavenly energy right now. As much as I have tried to forget about yesterday's revelation, I'm quickly learning that it's impossible to be a functioning member of modern society without being reminded of the Mashads every hour or so. First, I had to take the bus down the Ali Mashad Memorial Highway to get to school this morning. As if the name of the highway weren't enough, it also happened to be lined with *six* billboards promoting the new season of *Making Mashad*. Then I got changed for first period P.E. in a locker room filled with girls throwing on their Meesha Mashad–brand sports bras and lathering their skin with Melody Mashad–brand body lotion. It's a lot.

So, yeah. Today of all days, I was *really* hoping our heavenly oasis could be protected, despite the horror that was Saturday night. And, honestly, I think I had a fair shot. According to my research, 50 percent of alcohol drinkers experience black-outs at some point in their lifetime. Who's to say Isaac wasn't blacked out for that entire brutal exchange? Not that I *want* him to experience a blackout. Trust me, I am well aware of the cognitive damage those cause. But maybe, just this once, it would have been okay.

But, of course, Genevieve *had* to make sure my humiliation went viral, posting the video Alicia took on TikTok with the caption isaac dsnt know rand0 😭😭 . I never told a soul when you peed your pants at that sleepover in third grade, Genevieve, and now I'm a rando?! Her evil simply knows no bounds.

When Genevieve first posted the video, I was still cling-ing to the hope that everyone *but* Isaac would see it. (At this point, Lou said I had "totally and completely lost any grip on reality.") But nope. Despite thinking the birthday gods might throw me a bone and just let this one little wish come true, I was told by Lou that Isaac commented on Genevieve's video: *haha so faded.* So he's most definitely seen it. And, as of yes-terday, Genevieve and Isaac are officially back together.

So now my little slice of heaven has officially been destroyed. My palms are so sweaty as I approach Mrs. Lopez's that I can barely get a grip on the round brass doorknob. How do I handle this? What if he *still* doesn't recognize me? Do I say hi or do I wait for him to say hi? If I say hi, what tone do I go with? Like, a chipper "Hi!"? Or more like a chill "Hi"?

How do I normally greet him in class? Have I ever said hi to him before? Were we ever even friends?! Did I make this all up in my head? Oh my gosh, what if something's wrong with my brain?

My phone lights up with a text from Lou:

HELL HATH NO FURY LIKE A WOMAN SCORNED!!!!!
SCORN THAT MOFO!!!!!!!!

I turn around to see her standing at the other end of the hall, mouthing, "LIGHT HIM UP." The thing is, we both know I won't "light him up." That's more Lou's department, whereas I'm just hoping that Isaac gives me some sort of confirmation that our beautiful in-class friendship was not just a wild fever dream I made up in my head, and that we can move on as if Saturday night never happened. Even though we are now both very much aware of the fact that it *did* happen.

I finally make my way into the classroom three minutes before the bell rings to find Isaac already sitting in his seat next to mine, scrolling past a picture of a bikini-clad Mona Mashad on his IG feed.

Ugh. The billboards and merch were one thing. But this?! The love of my life casually liking a picture of my bikini-clad half sister blowing a kiss from what appears to be a mega yacht? In the middle of our math class oasis?

"Josie! Hey," he says, shoving his phone in his pocket as I take my seat next to his.

Okay, so he does know me. Things are looking up!

"Hey, Isaac," I say, shocked by how easily the words flow

out of my mouth as I try to wipe the image of my estranged half sister from my brain.

"Listen," he starts, nervously twisting the silver ring he has on his index finger. "I really do owe you an apology."

"Don't worry about it," I say, thankful Lou's not around to hear me. "Seriously. It's fine."

"No," he retorts. "It's really not. I just . . . I had a lot on my mind on Saturday before Oliver's. It would've been my dad's fortieth birthday. I've told you about how weird I get around his birthday. And I know it wasn't the most *responsible* decision, but I decided to get wasted to deal. Of course I know who you are! You're my math bud!"

How could I have forgotten his dad's birthday?! I knew there would be a logical explanation here somewhere.

"Really, Isaac." I try to reassure him. "It's okay. I get it."

"And about Genevieve," he continues. "I'll make sure she takes the TikTok down. She was probably just jealous I was talking to another girl. She can be possessive like that."

"Oh," I say, simultaneously flattered he thinks Genevieve would see me as a threat and disturbed he named her within the sacred confines of math class. "Yeah. I mean, it's no big deal. I'm sure she was just . . . messing around."

"That's what I love about you," he says, patting my shoulder with one of his giant hands. "You're so chill."

Um, I'm sorry. Did he just basically say he loves me?!

"Thanks" is pretty much all I can get out without literally falling out of my seat and onto the linoleum classroom floor.

"Wait," he says, his eyes growing wide. "It was my dad's birthday. . . . Didn't you mention your birthday is around his?"

"Uh, yeah," I say, my heart doing backflips at the fact that he remembered. "It just passed."

I mean, the best-case scenario I was prepared for was him fully ignoring what happened. An apology and a full birthday acknowledgment??? This might be even better than my birthday wish.

"Oh no," Isaac says, smashing his head down onto his desk. "Don't tell me it was Saturday. . . ."

"No, it was Sunday," I say, hoping the technicality gives him some solace.

"Shit, Josie, I'm a jerk," he says. "Did you have a good birthday otherwise?"

"Yeah," I lie. "It was great."

He flashes me one of his perfect smiles. "Okay, phew. Then I won't worry too much. So, in other news, how about Louise and Grant?" he asks, referring to the fact that Grant asked Lou to be official last night. "Now my boy and your bestie are dating. Pretty tight, right?"

"Yeah." I nod. "This is Lou's first *official* relationship. I'm pumped for her. Plus, she's been into Grant forever. And, I mean, he seems super nice." Grant *did* send me a text Sunday morning saying he "definitely" invited me to Oliver's. I know he's lying because I saw Lou sending him the exact text to copy and paste and send me when she thought I was sleeping Saturday night. But still. I appreciate the effort.

"Grant is my dude. He's the man," Isaac says, before nervously adding, "So, uh, did you manage to get through part two of the assignment this weekend? I was just so stressed with my family stuff, and then Genevieve and I had some stuff to work out. . . . I didn't manage to finish that last set of problems."

"Oh! Yeah," I say, pulling out my binder. "Wanna just copy mine?"

"You're the best, Josie," he says, pulling out his own binder. "Seriously. What would I do without you?"

Just as my heart is about to melt into pure liquid, Mrs. Lopez enters the classroom. "Isaac, stop doing last night's homework. Josie, you're wanted in the principal's office."

Chapter 5

"Give me one minute," a woman is saying when I enter Mr. Schwartz's tiny office, her back toward me. "I'm just wrapping up an important email."

She's seated in Mr. Schwartz's swivel chair, which has been turned around so that it's facing the DREAM BIG poster he has hanging above his desk. Who the heck is this lady?

Before I can wonder any further, she swivels the chair around, Bond villain style, to face me. Oh my gosh. Oh my gosh. No.

"Okay, all set," she says, shoving the phone into what I know from Lou's many aspirational fashion Pinterest boards is a large Birkin bag before she shifts her gaze up at me. "Hi, Josie Joon."

I close my eyes and open them again to make sure I'm seeing correctly. No. This cannot be happening. Am I hallucinating? "You're not . . ." I begin to ask, failing before I try again. "You can't actually be . . ."

"Mary Mashad? I am and I can," she replies matter-of-factly, before continuing, with a laugh. "You know, that was not my plan—the whole swiveling in the chair thing. But it worked out, didn't it? Really upped the drama there for a moment."

I know she's speaking, but I'm too distracted by her sheer presence to make sense of anything she's said since *Hi, Josie Joon*. I'm convinced no human being has ever looked more colossally out of place in any setting, ever. Her Pilates-toned, designer-suit-clad butt is just casually resting on the disgusting pleather chair I'm sure Mr. Schwartz has farted on dozens of times, as she takes a long sip out of her black Prada water bottle. Staring at her is like staring at the sun. I mean, like, she literally *gleams* like the sun. She's shinier than anyone I've ever seen in real life.

I stare at her, dumbfounded, as she gazes nonchalantly back at me, like hanging out in my principal's office is just something she and I do from time to time.

I want to say something—literally *anything*—but I am just standing here frozen, like it's 2016 and I'm recording a mannequin challenge.

"My mom used to call me that. *Josie Joon*" is all I can muster as I finally take the seat across from Mary's. "She was Persian, too." I resist the urge to choke up as I realize this might be the first time anyone has called me that since she died. The last thing I need to do is cry in front of my newfound A-list billionaire stalker.

"Yes, well, that's common in our culture," Mary says, completely unaffected by my emotional revelation. "You know, Joon is a term of endearment. It means—"

"Dear. I know," I say, cutting her off. "I speak Farsi." Shoot, was that rude? Wait, why do I even care if I'm being rude? She's the one literally *stalking* me.

"Oh!" Mary exclaims. "That's wonderful. You know, Ali tried *everything* to get our girls to speak Farsi. Meesha is actually not bad. But Mona and Melody are useless."

"Well, to be fair, I'm not sure how good I would be now," I admit. "I haven't spoken it since my mom passed away."

"I heard about your mother's passing," Mary says. "A car crash, correct?" She says this like it's just any other piece of information, a semi-interesting headline she skimmed over in the paper this morning. I can't decide if the total and complete lack of pity is offensive or refreshing.

"Yeah," I confirm. "She was rushing to pick me up from math camp."

"My parents died when I was young, too," Mary says casually, like we're bonding over having the same color socks. "In the revolution back in Iran. Luckily, I was in France for a summer program. But they killed everyone I had back home—my mom, my dad, my siblings, my grandparents. Everyone."

I already knew this about Mary. According to Wikipedia, her family was connected to the Shah, which is kind of weird because so was my mom's. But she and my grandma, my Maman Farrah, came here before the revolution, so they never faced any danger. I wonder what would have happened if they had stayed. Would my mom's story have been as tragic as Mary's? Honestly, considering their endings, did my mom's story wind up *more* tragic than Mary's?

Mary doesn't need to continue her story, because I know it. It doesn't matter that I'm not a devout Mashad fan. Their family's story is American folklore at this point. Mary met Ali at UCLA—when Matt and I went for my tour of the campus there, the guide stopped by a bench on the main quad to show us "where Ali Mashad famously asked Mary Mashad out for the first time." And the rest is history. The two created the richest, most famous family in the world.

The Wikipedia version of the story sounds so Hollywood and glamorous. But when I look at her, as outrageously well dressed and poised and nonchalant as she is, it's impossible to ignore the fact that she's a real human being. A living, breathing human being sitting across from me.

"I'm so sorry," I tell Mary. "That must have been horrible to go through."

"It was," she confirms. "They took our money, too. I went from having everything a girl could ask for to being stuck in a foreign country with no money, no parents, and no home to return to. But you know what? It made me resilient. And you don't get to where I have without some resilience."

"Right." I nod, unsure of how to react. "Resilience is super important."

Mary stares at me, squinting like she's trying to figure me out but not quite getting there. Maybe she's trying to understand how someone like me could possibly share DNA with her A-list daughters. *Trust me*, I want to say, *I am just as lost as you are.*

"So, *Josie Lawrence*," she says, relaxing her gaze. "That is one hell of an American name for a girl with two Iranian parents."

"Well, when I was born, my mom gave me her last name.

So my name was actually Josie Asadi until I was five. Then she married Matt and he adopted me, so we both changed our last name to Lawrence," I say, before adding, "but my middle name is Iranian. It's Farrah."

"Ah," Mary says. "Melody has the same middle name."

"Really?" I ask, suddenly nervous Mary might think my mom copied her. "My mom named me after my grandma. Her name was Farrah."

"Farrahs are a dime a dozen in Iran. It's like naming a kid Lauren in America," Mary points out before moving on. "And Josie? Where did that come from?"

"Well, my mom moved to America at ten, and after spending all of middle school and high school being called *Shart*zad, she swore she would give her own kid an American first name," I tell her. "*Josie and the Pussycats* was her favorite movie, so she went with Josie."

"I would have *loved* to have given my girls American first names," Mary says. "Especially for the sake of the show. You know, *now* people are very into diversity. But when we first started the show fifteen years ago, nobody even knew what being Iranian meant. American names would have given us a huge leg up when it came to being accepted early on."

I know I've only known her for about twelve minutes, but it's virtually impossible to imagine this woman doing anything other than exactly what she wants to do.

I have to ask. "So why didn't you just give them American first names?"

"Ali," she says with a sigh. "He was so insistent on Iranian names. He even hated that I shortened my name, Marjan, to

Mary. So I agreed the girls could have Iranian names as long as he would let *me* pick the names. God, he was awful with names. I tried to give him a shot when Melody was born, and you know what he picked? Mahboubeh. *Mahboubeh.* Can you imagine me trying to get a branding deal in the 2000s for *Mahboubeh* Mashad?"

"Uh, no?" It comes out more like a question, because let's be real here: What else does she expect me—a teen girl who has never in her life booked a brand deal—to say?

"It's *boiling* out today, isn't it?" she asks out of nowhere, loosening the buttons on her blazer as she casually rests her legs on top of the stacks of paper scattered across Mr. Schwartz's desk. "I wore this blazer thinking it was going to be cooler. Or that your school would have air-conditioning."

She won't stop talking. I stare at her, confused. What is *happening*? Did the most famous woman in the world hijack my principal's office to just . . . hang out with me? She wishes she'd worn something different, she says. Maybe some athleisure. Have I tried her daughter Meesha's line? In addition to making the panties and the bras I noticed everyone wearing after P.E. today, Meesha apparently makes the *best* athleisure. She'll send me some samples!

Finally, I can't take it anymore. Who does she think she is? Strolling into my principal's office, pulling me out of class, and wasting twenty minutes of my day for *chitchat*?

"Um, I'm sorry, Mrs. Mashad—" I begin, way more nervously than I was hoping to sound.

"You can call me Mary Joon," she interrupts with an unbothered smile.

"Mary Joon," I echo back, like the invertebrate I am. "Not to be rude, but, uh, well . . . would you mind please telling me why you're here?"

"Ah, yes," she says. "The point! Well, Josie Joonam—I'm sure you know this, but when you add the *am* to *Joon*, it becomes possessive, like you're *my* dear Josie."

"Right," I say, dying for her to just get to it already. "I do know what Joonam means."

"You know what my husband said to me right before he died?"

There's a long, awkward pause before I realize her question was not rhetorical. "Oh, uh. No, I don't."

"Guess," she dares me.

Is she kidding me? How in the world am I supposed to know? I never knew the guy.

"Uh, 'I love you'?" I venture.

"That's what you'd think, right?" she replies, seemingly satisfied with my answer. "That's what I always say in interviews. That he told me he loved me. But that's a lie. The last time he told me he loved me was twelve hours before he died. I had called him from his favorite restaurant, Craig's. You know, the steak house?"

I don't, but I nod anyway.

"He was feeling good that night, better than he had in a while," she says. "So much so that we thought something might have changed. Maybe he was going to make it after all. So I went to pick up Craig's. To celebrate. When I called and asked what he wanted, he said a medium-rare rib eye with a side of jalapeño creamed corn, and I said 'You got it,

Ali Joonam,' and he said 'I love you, Marjan.' Remember I told you that's my real name? Marjan. I changed it before we started the show. You know, to be a little more commercially viable. Americans can never pronounce Marjan. They always think it's *margin.* Or *Mar-JAN*. But Ali never called me Mary—"

Oh gosh. She is not going to stop speaking unless I say something.

"I'm sorry, Mary Joon," I interrupt, my eyes glancing up at the analog clock above Mr. Schwartz's desk. "I don't mean to cut you off, but it's just . . . I have a math quiz tomorrow, and if I don't make it back to class in the next ten minutes, I'm going to miss all of Mrs. Lopez's review." My heart sinks as I realize I'll probably have to wait another full twenty-four hours to have quality time with Isaac again. And for what? Listening to this kooky lady tell me stories about the guy who abandoned me?

"Interrupting me in the middle of a story? You really *must* be a Mashad." Mary cracks a smile. "Fine, I'll land the plane. You can watch the Craig's call on the show, anyway. Season fourteen, episode nineteen. There it is. The last time my husband told me he loved me."

"Wow," I say, my eyes still glued to the clock. "I'll be sure to give that a watch. But, um . . . I really have got to get going."

"The last words he said to me were spoken in private," she continues, totally unbothered by my antsy energy. "We knew he was on his way out. So the doctor gave us a minute in private, and I sent everyone else out. No cameras. No crew. No security. The kids had just left. And we were sitting there. Just me and him at his deathbed. And he says to me, 'Find Josie. Please. When she's eighteen, there's a letter. Make sure she reads it, and make sure she spends time with her sisters.'"

I can tell Mary wants this to move me. But the truth is, it doesn't. I just . . . I still don't get it. Yes, he was dying. But he wasn't *dead*. He could have picked up the phone. He could have invited my mom and me over. He could have . . . I stop myself before I descend into a complete spiral. The bottom line is I can pretty much think of a million things he could have done that would have been better than leaving it to his widow to relay this message to me years after his death.

I haven't said a word, and Mary doesn't seem to mind. "I didn't even know your name. That was the first time he said it out loud to me," she continues. "But, of course, when he said the line about your sisters, I knew. I knew he was talking about *you*. And it stung, but I loved him so much that it was okay. I knew I would do it. I would have done anything for that man. So here I am. Asking you to spend time with your sisters. Better yet, come on the show. Film a season with us. That's it. Just one season. Be a *real* part of our family. Please. For my husband. For your father."

My father. I really wish people would stop calling him that. He's not my father. He's a guy who assisted my mom in the biological process of creating me. *Matt* is my father.

"That was really . . . it was really so moving," I say, sensing that's what she might want to hear. "But I'm just . . . Well, look at me. I'm not reality TV material. I'm just a hairy nerd from Van Nuys. And I already have a family. I have a dad I love, and

I'm not sure I'm ready to meet the children my birth father chose over me."

"I understand," Mary responds calmly. "But I disagree. Josie, no matter how hard you try to deny it, you have that Mashad blood coursing through your veins. It's part of who you *are*. It's written in your genetic code."

Oh gosh. This woman isn't going to get off my back, is she?

"Fine." I relent. "How about I just get lunch with them? He just wanted me to meet them, right? Why don't we get lunch? No cameras. Just a quick lunch to make Ali happy, and then I can go back to my life."

"That won't do," she retorts sharply. "He didn't want you girls getting one awkward lunch. He wanted you to get to *know* each other. He wanted you to be one of us. And the only way to do that is through the show."

"Listen, I wish you and your family nothing but the best," I say. "Really, I do. Honestly, I didn't know much about you guys before all of . . . this. But my best friend, Lou, is a huge fan and filled me in. Really, I have nothing but respect for the empire you've been able to build. . . ."

"Great!" Mary exclaims. "Then it's settled. You'll be on the show."

"Um, well, no," I say, reaching for my backpack on the floor next to me. "I'm sorry. I just . . . I don't think reality TV is for me."

I look up at the clock. If I hustle, I can still squeeze in some Isaac time.

"Okay," Mary says, letting out a big sigh as she pulls a stack of paperwork out of her bag. "I didn't want it to come to this, but he left you quite a bit of money. And, in the fine print here, you will see that the money is contingent on you participating in the show for at least one season. It was important to him, Josie Joonam. He really wanted you to get to know your sisters in a real way, and, if you don't care about his wish, I would at least hope you'd have the good sense to do it for the money."

I can't help but laugh. What kind of sellout does she take me for?

"I'm sorry," I say, finally gathering myself. "It's just . . . I don't care about his money. I don't want it. I'm a pretty low-maintenance girl. I don't drink out of designer water bottles and wear fancy shoes. The only thing I really need money for is Stanford, and my mom already left that behind for me."

"Yes, right," she says, unamused. "Your *mother*."

"Wait," I say, the thought just crossing my mind. "Did you . . . know her?"

"The woman who almost destroyed my marriage?" Mary asks. "Yes, I was familiar."

"But you guys were on a break, right?" I ask, suddenly hopeful. "Like you and Ali weren't together when he and my mom—"

"Had an affair?" she interrupts. "No, we were not on a break."

"Oh, so then you had one of those open marriages?" I ask, convinced this must be it. "I heard those are really common in progressive Hollywood circles. And I'm all for it! If monogamy is not for you, who are we as a society to enforce it upon you?"

"Ali thought ripped jeans were too progressive," Mary fires back. "I'm not sure what circles you're referring to, but swinging was not for us. Your mother had an affair with him. Plain and simple. That's what happened."

"Well, as far as you know," I insist. "I'm sure it was a misunderstanding. Like on *Friends*!"

"Come again?" Mary asks, her face blank.

"You know, *Friends*," I repeat. "Like, the show. Maybe it was that sort of miscommunication. Ross thought they were on a break, but Rachel thought they were still together. Maybe that's what was happening with you and Ali. And my poor mom got dragged in the middle."

"Josie Joonam, I can tell you loved your mother," Mary says. "But I can assure you she was *not* the victim here. Ali and I were together. It was an indisputable fact, and it was not one that seemed to sway her decision-making."

We sit in silence, her words just lingering in the air between us. Who does this woman think she is? Coming into *my* school telling me what kind of person *my* mother was?! I know my mom. I saw her working as hard as she could to raise me on her own because this Ali guy left her. There *is* a victim here, and there's no doubt in my mind that it was her. I open my mouth to say all of this, then shut it. There's no point. I'm not changing Mary's mind, and she's not changing mine.

"Anyway." Mary cuts through the silence. "What's the good in rehashing the transgressions of the dead? Let's discuss this money you say your mother left you."

"No offense, but I don't really see what there is to discuss," I say, my voice soft but surprisingly firm. "My mom's biggest dream was for me to go to Stanford. By the time the car accident happened, she had already saved up everything I need to go there."

"Right," Mary says, pausing for a beat. "Now, I'm sure you already know this, but could you remind me how much Stanford tuition costs for four years, Josie Joonam?"

"Um, sure. It's about two hundred thousand dollars."

"$214,116, to be exact," she corrects. "And, of course, that's just tuition. Once you factor in fees and living expenses, you're looking at around 298,280 dollars."

"Well, whatever it is, it's fine," I say, itching for this conversation to be over. "I have enough. I've asked Matt multiple times. There's more than enough in my fund."

"Ah, I see. You don't know. Josie Joonam, I hate to meddle," she says, though her tone suggests otherwise. "But I did some digging. And were you aware that this magical college fund of yours only has 84,237 dollars in it?"

I gulp hard. It's like she just slapped an eerie new filter over the past five years of my life. All those extra shifts. Selling the club. Selling the house. I know we've had money troubles. I guess I just believed the tuition money was exempt from those troubles.

"You're a smart girl," Mary continues. "I think we both know your adoptive father who works at California Pizza Kitchen isn't quite going to be able to afford the extra two hundred *thousand* dollars it's going to take to put you through college."

But it's Matt. I get how this looks on paper. But Mary doesn't *know* Matt the way I do.

"He told me—"

"Whatever he told you is bullshit," she cuts in. "Excuse my language. But it is. Your adoptive father has taken out three loans to cover the remainder of your tuition. The sweet man is going into debt to make your college dreams come true. Now it's up to you, Josie Joonam. Are you going to step up and do the right thing, or are you going to let him drown?"

Chapter 6

Signing up to be on the longest-running reality show in television history alongside my estranged family after hearing my mom may or may not have really broken a home and my only living parent has been lying to me for years? Yeah, that calls for a school-night sleepover.

It's been five hours since my terrifying meeting with Mary, and I'm frantically pacing around my room as Lou lies sprawled across my full-size bed in her feather-trimmed silk pajamas.

"You're right," Lou says. "It must have been a Ross and Rachel situation. Mary is just too firmly in Rachel Land to see it."

"Right?!" I ask, thrilled that Lou's bought into the theory. "It's the only explanation. My mom would have never—"

"No, never," Lou finishes the thought for me. "Sharzad was a girls' girl."

"Yeah." I nod a little too aggressively. "A total girls' girl."

"Even if she *did* sleep with him while he was married, I'm sure there was some sort of explanation."

Lou's right. There was an explanation. There had to be one.

"Wait," Lou says, shooting upright. "Remember what happened when I gave Mark Whittmore a hand job sophomore year?"

"And he was still with Alyssa Steinem . . . ?" I ask, quickly realizing where she's going with this. "But he *told* you they were broken up!"

"Yes!" Lou exclaims. "Alyssa still doesn't believe it. But he really did lie to me! I would have never hooked up with him if I knew they were together. What if Sharzad was in the same position? Maybe Ali lied and *said* they were getting divorced. So Mary knew she and Ali were still together. And Ali knew they were together. Your mom was the only one in the dark."

Oh, the guy who completely ditched his lover and child was also a liar? Now *this* adds up.

"Lou, you are a genius!" I exclaim. "How did we not think of this earlier? She was lied to! Obviously."

"Obviously," Lou confirms. "And Mary was lied to *about* the lie, which is why she's defending the fact that they were still together so intensely. It's the most logical explanation."

We sit there for a few silent moments, satisfied with this new theory, until Lou finally changes the subject. "I still can't believe you're going to be on my favorite TV show. And not just as, like, a 'friend of.' You are *part of the freaking family*. Josie, I know you don't see it this way, but this is, like, a fairy tale."

"Lou, you have to *swear* not to tell anyone," I repeat for what must be the thousandth time. "Mary is super serious about us keeping this a total and complete secret until the show airs. She's convinced 'the numbers will be shot' if people find out about me beforehand. Then I don't get the money, and we're stuck back at square one."

"Oh my *God*, Josie," Lou says, also for what must be the thousandth time. "What do you want, a vial of my blood? I pinkie promised, I swore on my mom, and I even signed that terrifying contract. I've kept secrets for much less. Don't worry, I'm not telling."

"I know, I know. Sorry. This is all just . . ."

"Absolutely, completely, totally insane?"

"Yeah."

"Are we even sure she's telling the truth about your tuition money?!" Lou asks. "I mean, how does she even know all this?"

"I guess she had a P.I. look into it? She had all these files with her. She showed me everything. Matt's taken out three massive loans that he'll probably have to spend his whole life paying off."

"But why would he lie to you about all this?" she presses on. "People take out student loans all the time. You could have even taken them out under your name instead of his. I mean, my mom has *no* issue making me do that."

"You know how Matt is," I remind her. "He hates admitting everything's not fine, no matter how blatantly unfine everything is. Even when we moved in here after he lost the club, he swore we were just downsizing because he loved the 'sense of community' we'd get living in an apartment building."

"Yep," Lou says. "I remember that. Kind of like when he swore that he *wanted* to sell the club for a quarter of what it's worth, because 'comedy isn't about the money.'"

"Exactly," I say. "He's been promising me my college fund is safe ever since the accident. All I have to do is get in. And now he's going into debt to prove everything's still fine. It's classic him."

"Yeah. It is pretty on brand. So . . . did you tell him everything?"

"Louise. Have you gotten nothing from observing our family dynamics all these years? We show each other love by *shielding* each other from the truth."

"I think going on national television is going to be a bit hard to hide from him."

"I agree, which is why I didn't lie to him about that part," I say. "I just told him I've agreed to go on the show to get to know my sisters better."

"And he was fine with that?"

"Yeah," I say, recalling Matt's surprisingly nonchalant reaction. "I mean, he was rushing back to work for the night shift, so we didn't really talk about it extensively. But, if anything, he was excited for me to 'do something fun for a change.'"

"Did he ask about anything to do with money?"

"No," I say. "I mean, he's not an idiot. I'm sure he assumes I'll be making some money just for being on the show. But as far as he knows, I still think I'm set in terms of my college tuition."

"So what's your game plan here?"

"Easy. I do a season of the show, get my money, then surprise Matt by telling him I've decided to spend the money on my tuition. Once that's covered, I'll buy back our old house and his club. The rest I'll probably just donate to charity."

"Are you sure it wouldn't be easier to just tell him you know? Maybe it would take a load off his shoulders."

"Are you kidding? What would I even say? 'Hi, Matt! Mary Mashad surprised me at school today and told me that the private investigator she hired to look into your finances found out you're actually going into hundreds of thousands of dollars of debt to fund my education. But don't worry! She's offering me three million dollars—'"

"Wait, wait, wait, wait, WAIT." Lou jumps off the bed. "She's offering you *three MILLION dollars*? YOU DIDN'T SAY IT WAS THREE MILLION DOLLARS. Josie, you're, like, rich!"

My face grows red, which happens all the time, but this might be the first time it's ever happened in front of Lou. The girl was with me when I pooped my pants at Rite Aid our sophomore year. She's seen it all. But something about this revelation feels even more mortifying than sharting in the middle of the shampoo aisle.

"That's just the fee for the show," I sheepishly add. "If I complete a full season, my trust is unlocked, and it's . . . thirty-seven million dollars." It's my first time saying the number out loud. It's so large that it almost feels fake.

"You're joking," Lou says, her eyes wide. "You know that's exactly what the girls got from him. Your sisters. I've googled it a zillion times. They each have a thirty-seven-million-dollar trust fund. And they each get paid three million dollars a season for the show. You're getting paid like a real Mashad. Josie. This is *wild*."

"Yeah, Mary told me I'm getting paid exactly what they get paid," I say. "The document she showed me for the trust is covered with lines about everything being 'fair' and 'equal.' But it's not like I'm even going to do much with the money. I told you already."

"Oh my God, Josie," says Lou, who at this point is pacing more frantically than I am. "Once you buy it back, do you know how many people will go to Matt's club if you just get *one* of your sisters to post about it?! Mona posted a selfie eating a burger from the In-N-Out in Westwood yesterday, and they literally sold out of burgers within the hour."

I honestly had not considered that. But something about the possibility of me becoming tight with these mega celebrities feels even more fake than the money.

"Yeah, I guess that would be cool," I admit. "But these girls aren't even really my *sisters*. They're strangers I just so happen to share DNA with. People I've gone to school with for years don't even like me enough to acknowledge my existence at a party. I have a feeling the most famous women on Earth aren't exactly going to welcome me, the love child of their dead dad, with open arms."

"Ugh, I really wish you just watched the show with me," Lou says with a sigh. "They're honestly really nice. All about family. I think they'll *love* you."

"I hope so," I say, taking a seat on the edge of the bed as a pit starts taking shape in my gut. "Hey, Lou?"

"What's up?" she asks.

"My mom always said I knew her better than anybody. Do you think there was just a whole other side to her that I was blind to?"

"No," Lou quickly retorts. "Absolutely not. Are you kidding? I mean, did you know every detail of her history? Probably not, considering it would frankly have been weird and not age appropriate for her to have told her tween daughter about all of her sexcapades. But Josie. You *knew* her. The two of you were the closest mother-daughter duo I've ever known."

"But I just don't get it," I say. "The mom I know would have never fallen for a guy like him."

Lou rolls her eyes. "Josie, you know nothing about him! I totally see why she would have fallen for him. What he did to you and your mom was undeniably shitty. But there's a very real reason why his funeral is still the most viewed event in American television history. People really loved him."

"Yeah. I guess that's true."

It's just so hard to imagine. How was my mom ever in the same room as this man, let alone his lover?? My brain flashes to all the times she almost instinctively flipped the channel the minute he and his perfect-looking family popped on the screen.

"Do you think she would want me to do this?" I ask Lou, nervous about what the answer might be. "To go on the show? With the family he chose over us?"

Lou considers my question for a while. "She must have," she

finally says. "Why else would she have wanted you to get that letter on your eighteenth birthday? There's no way she didn't know what was inside it."

"Yeah, but what if she just wanted me to know the option was on the table? Like, for the sake of transparency? But really she didn't want me to do it?"

"I don't know, Jos," Lou admits. "This situation is obviously complicated. But what I *do* know is your mom would have done anything for the people she loved. And I think if she were in your shoes, she would have made the same choice. Even if it scared the shit out of her."

"Promise?"

"Promise."

I smile at Lou, my separation anxiety beginning to settle in. This is a new feeling because, well, I've never had to separate from Lou before. We've been inseparable since the day we met in preschool. How in the world am I supposed to get through the most terrifying thing I've ever done without her by my side?

Chapter 7

"You sure about this, Jos?" Matt asks as his old Hyundai finally pulls up to the end of Mary's acres-long driveway. "If you want out, we can turn around right now."

The truth is, all I want to do in this moment is Krazy Glue myself onto the scratchy fabric of the passenger seat and never leave this car. But Matt can't know that. He needs to believe I want this.

"I'm sure," I say, willing my voice to shake as little as possible. "I think it will be nice. You know, getting to know my sisters and stuff." *Get it together, Josie. Your voice is coming out wobblier than the Ruth Bader Ginsburg bobblehead Mrs. Lopez keeps on her desk.*

"I think so, too," Matt says with a reassuring smile. "And remember, they may be rich and famous, but you're Josie freaking Lawrence. *They're* the lucky ones to be getting to meet *you*."

I shoot him the best smile I can muster while holding back

this growing mountain of nerves. *This* is why I'm doing this. Because if there's something I can do to even kind of repay him for the love he's given me, even if that something petrifies me, there's just no question. I have to do it.

"Thanks, Matt," I say, trying to steady my racing heart as I get a look at the time. "What time do you have to be back at work?" I was honestly shocked when Matt said he could give me a ride here from school today. His workday typically starts right when my school day ends.

"I took the afternoon off," he says. "Melissa said she would cover for me after I helped her out last weekend."

"You didn't have to do that," I say, but I'm grateful he did. Even though keeping this secret from him is adding a million levels of stress to an already stressful situation, Matt's presence has always made me feel safe. When my mom first brought him to our house when I was four, I remember immediately feeling like everything was going to be okay. Things have changed a *lot* since then, but his presence still has that effect on me.

"So, based on what that last security guard told us, I think you have one more security clearance you're going to have to pass before entering the house," Matt says before giving me a light nudge. "I have no idea how long that one will take, but you might want to head out there if you're going to make it to your meeting on time."

"*Another* security clearance?" I groan. "How is that even possible?!"

Before we could even enter Beverly Palms, the invite-only

gated neighborhood Ali Mashad developed within Beverly Hills exclusively for the *most* rich and the *most* famous, the guards at the gate had to scan both Matt's and my IDs and call Mary to confirm she knew us. Then we got to Mary's ginormous compound, which makes Fort Knox look like a public park. Before we were let into her driveway, the six beefy security guards at the gate gave us a series of forms to fill out—not only did I have to sign another NDA, I also had to give them my social security number, my blood type, and my thumbprint to have on file. Then I had to check my phone in for a full "history search," which they're still conducting to make sure they don't find any "suspicious plotting or activity." What more does this woman want from me?

"I'll get out in a minute," I tell Matt as I take another look out the car window at Mary's palatial estate, no longer capable of hiding my nerves. "This sort of feels like the summer Lou and I went to Camp Walla Moo. Remember how nervous I was before drop-off?"

"How could I forget?" Matt asks with a laugh. "You threw up all over the back seat."

"Yeah, this feels like that multiplied by a thousand," I say, my heart racing so fast that I think it could qualify for the Indy 500. "I mean, don't get me wrong. I *really* want to do this. It's just . . . you know I'm not great with new experiences."

"But remember the end of Camp Walla Moo?" Matt asks. "You loved it!"

"Right," I lie. "Good point. I forgot about that."

He doesn't know I hated Camp Walla Moo. They separated

me from Lou, and the girls in my cabin dipped my hand in water while I was asleep, so I peed my sleeping bag and spent the rest of the summer being referred to as "Pee Girl." I just told Matt I loved it because I didn't want him to feel bad for encouraging me to go.

"Hey," Matt says. "How about you check out that study guide Lou made you one more time?"

"It was on my phone that they're still looking through," I say. "But I'm not sure it was helping that much anyway."

Lou's extensive study guide included details on each of the Mashads—Mary, the matriarch; Mona, the wild child coming off of a breakup; Meesha, the retired supermodel who's dating mega pop star Bunny Lee; and Melody, the oldest, who's engaged to sweatpants designer/grocery store heir Axle. I thought getting to know them as people might help calm my nerves a bit, but I'm realizing it's no use. I can't humanize these people, because not one thing about them feels even remotely human.

I take a look outside my tinted window. Mary lives here—in a gigantic mansion with multiple infinity pools and tennis courts, a horse stable, a full security team, and fourteen different exotic sports cars parked in each driveway. How could I possibly relate to them on any level?

Every single cell in my body wants to take Matt up on his offer to turn the car around. But then I remember the money and how this is the first shift he's taken off since starting the job at CPK two years ago. I'm not doing this for me. I'm doing this for *us*. He's faced plenty of discomfort to help me; now it's my turn.

I close my eyes and take a deep breath in, my mom's *cheelax* ringing in my head like a mantra.

Just as I start to feel my heart rate finally sinking, I hear a knock on my window.

"Josie!" the peppy voice on the other side of the tinted window exclaims. "Is that you? I saw you pull up on the security camera! I'm *so* excited to meet you. Another sister? Pinch me! Why don't you get out here and give me a hug?!"

Chapter 8

I was dreading opening the car door even before Melody knocked on it. But as soon as I sheepishly set one Asics-clad foot out of Matt's car and on Mary's smooth concrete driveway, Melody practically pounced.

Then, when she was done squeezing me with her perfectly toned arms, she—get this—*complimented* my outfit. To be clear, Melody looks like a bohemian goddess in her long, flowy white dress, and is rocking on her slender ring finger what is without a doubt the largest diamond I have ever seen. Meanwhile, I'm dressed in purple Asics I found on sale at Big 5, a pair of old basketball shorts with a hole in the butt that Genevieve relentlessly mocked me all day for wearing, and a giant T-shirt I found at Goodwill that says ROLLIN' WITH THE HOMIES over a drawing of two hamsters rolling in a hamster wheel together. It's not exactly the sort of outfit you'd see sprawled across the pages of *Vogue*, which Melody has been on the cover of six times (seven, if you count *Vogue Italia*). But my tiny, barely five-foot-tall half sister swears my look is "a vibe" and "off trend in the best way." She even asked where I got my shorts and, when I told her I bought them at Target years ago, she took a picture of them, sent it to her assistant, and told him to hunt them down for her. Coming from anyone else, the over-the-top friendliness might come off as fake. But something about Melody's kindness feels almost palpably genuine.

Once we passed my third round of security at the front door, she gave me a full tour of her mom's absolutely bonkers twenty-thousand-square-foot home, which ended with the giant conference room we're seated in now.

The meeting has not technically started yet, but Scott Sanderson, the Yay! Network CEO, is giving me a little introduction until everyone gets here.

"We're like family," he's telling me. "That's how I knew these people were destined for television. I just knew America would love them as much as I did. And let me tell you, your birth father was near impossible to convince. It took years of me begging, pleading, showing him business models." Oh right, Scott also happens to have been my biological dad's best friend from college.

"And then I stepped in," Mary adds, having joined us a few minutes ago. "When Ali and I hit our little . . . rough patch, I thought going into business together—as a *family*—could be the thing to save us. Not many people go into reality TV to save a marriage, but it worked for us."

I gulp hard as Mary breezily references Ali's romance with my mom as some sort of blip in her marriage. Now, looking around this wild estate Mary calls a home, it's more difficult than ever to imagine how my mom even crossed paths with these people.

"Their marriage isn't the only thing *Making Mashad* saved," Scott notes. "This show saved Yay! Network. It revolutionized reality TV as we know it. It revolutionized the concept of *fame* as we know it. You know, before she quit to do this, Mary was a shark of an agent at CAA. She has tons of connections and phenomenal business savvy. Lots of families have that initial appeal, but they don't have the staying power. With her at the helm, I knew they'd make it. And, well, I think we can all agree my instinct was right."

Before Mary can chime in, Meesha Mashad walks in through the sleek white conference room door. One look at her and I instantly get why she has been Lou's style icon since we were kids. According to Lou's study guide, she has walked the runways of every major brand at Fashion Weeks across the globe. And it shows. She's currently wearing a loose-fitting pair of jeans with a simple, slightly cropped white tank and still looks like the best-dressed person I've ever seen. But it's more than just the way she dresses. Even without looking up from her phone or saying a single word, the way she carries herself exudes a bone-chilling level of icy coolness.

Meesha slinks into her seat and homes her honey-brown eyes in on me. Somehow her gaze does two completely contradictory things at once. It feels both deeply intense, like I'm the only thing in the world that matters to her at this very moment, and also like she could not care less if someone were to pick me up and toss me in the trash right at this very moment.

"So, you're our new little sister?" she asks, her eyes still fixed on me like we're in some sort of staring contest I didn't sign up for.

"Um, yeah," I say. "I'm Josie."

"Nice," she says, flashing me a quick smile. "I'm Meesha."

Her phone vibrates, and immediately her attention is back on it, a small grin creeping across her face as she types a reply.

"You're late," Mary informs Meesha. "You missed Scott's entire introduction."

"I'm actually exactly on time," Meesha says, not glancing up from her phone, her voice flat. "You just started this meeting freakishly early."

I sneak a glance down at my neon-green rubber watch. She's right. She's exactly on time.

"If you're on time, you're late," Mary says. "How many times do I have to remind you girls?"

"Mom, maybe go easy on her," Melody suggests sweetly. "I mean, Mona isn't even here yet."

"Yeah," Meesha chimes in with what I'm quickly realizing is her typical almost-monotone voice, eyes still glued to her iPhone screen. "If being on time means being late, what does being actually late mean?"

"I don't have time for this nonsense. Josie Joon, sorry for the distraction. Let's get back to the meeting. As Scott was saying, nobody could do what I did," Mary tells me without a trace of sarcasm. "But if I hadn't got Farida"—she gestures at the woman sitting across the table from her—"to come on board, none of this would have been possible."

Farida, the executive producer and cocreator of *Making*

Mashad, is one of Mary's oldest friends. The two grew up together in Tehran, up until Farida moved to America at twelve. They lost touch until, according to Farida, "flash forward thirty-something years and I'm in a horrible, loveless marriage, bored out of my mind and throwing myself into working another mind-numbingly boring season producing on *The Bachelor*. And I get an email from Mary. She'd heard I worked in reality TV, and she wanted me to come create this show with her. We wanted it to be different, you know? We wanted to change the narrative of what the typical all-American family looked like. And I think we've done a damn good job at it."

"That's the magic of the show. These people are just like everyone else: They love their family, they get their hearts broken, they fight," Scott says. "The only difference is they look more beautiful, drive nicer cars, live in nicer houses, date better-looking people, and have more impressive wardrobes."

I catch myself staring at Mary for a second too long. I am sure countless creams and treatments that cost more than my entire college tuition have gone into this, but the woman really *is* beautiful. And maybe it's because I'm not used to being around so many Iranian people and the faces are sort of blending together, but I notice she shares a lot of features with my mom. The large almond-shaped hazel eyes. The dewy olive skin. The thick head of long jet-black hair, though Mary's is almost definitely dyed to be that way. I wonder if this is what my mom would have looked like if she had lived to see sixty. Okay, obviously no regular human could afford to look like *this*. But maybe, like, a normal-person variation of this.

Of course, after a certain point, the Mashad empire grew bigger than just the show. That's where Javier Martinez, the branding director at Mashad Lifestyle Group, came into play. "Javier is a branding genius," Mary explains. "About two years into the show, when things were just starting to really take off, I decided to open MLG—Mashad Lifestyle Group. MLG handles everything from paid social deals to the girls' product lines. I had the business savvy, but Javier is the one who really had the creativity."

"I saw what each Mashad could be, in terms of a brand," Javier tells me. "And what each brand would say about the family as a whole. I worked with Mary to flesh it all out, of course. But that's sort of the gist of what I do. Ideate the brand, make sure everyone sticks to it, and make sure we're all profiting off it."

"Speaking of which," Meesha cuts in. "Mom, Javier, I want to discuss the Zoloft deal you sent my way."

"Oh, yes!" Mary exclaims. "The Zoloft deal! Great terms, right? A *lot* of zeroes on that contract."

"Yeah—actually, Farida, I never got a response from you on that email," Javier says. "The clip of Meesha having a panic attack is included in the premiere for the upcoming season, correct? It would be great for the Zoloft partnership; we're offering them a complete ad takeover on the premiere episode."

"Um, excuse me." Meesha calmly raises an arm. "What if I don't *want* to turn my mental illness into a brand partnership?"

"Nonsense, Meesha Joon," Mary says. "Think of how many people you're helping!"

"The world watched me get my first period, they watched me come out, they watched the aftermath of me losing my *virginity*," Meesha retorts. "Could we just maybe keep the brand of medication I take to fight off my crippling depression private?"

Yikes. I know I could not be more out of the loop here, but even *I* see her point.

"This was supposed to be a compromise," Mary says with an exasperated sigh. "You didn't want to create your own line of calming cannabis gummies, which we *both* know would have been a cash cow. So why not this? You don't even have to start a company or anything. Just post a few Instagram ads and shoot a commercial or two."

"Because I don't feel comfortable doing this," Meesha maintains, her voice still shockingly calm. "How is that not enough of a reason for you?"

"I just don't understand what the issue is," Mary says with a shrug. "You already *take* Zoloft. The world already knows you have depression. Why not just get paid the millions of dollars they are offering you to do a few Instagram posts about it?"

Because she doesn't want to! And she already has enough millions to last her forty lifetimes! How could Mary not see that?

"You are unbelievable," Meesha says, turning her attention back to her phone. "Axe the deal or I'm using my executive producer credit to cut the panic attack scene."

"You are being ridiculous," Mary fires back, opening her mouth to say more before Melody stops her short.

"Mom, maybe you should just drop it for now. This meeting is supposed to be about Josie anyway, remember?"

Mary sighs. "Fine," she concedes. "I'm sorry, Josie Joonam. We keep getting sidetracked."

"Oh, um, it's okay," I mumble, deeply disturbed by the conversation that just unfolded right in front of me. Scott was right in that these people are richer and more beautiful or whatever, but is all of that worth it if you have to fight with your mom about whether or not you're going to be exploiting your depression for a profit?!

Mary checks the time and gives a long, exasperated sigh.

"Mona is officially fifteen minutes late," she announces. "This is unacceptable."

"Question," Meesha says, raising her hand, a small smirk on her face. "When you say she's fifteen minutes late . . . are you basing that number off the actual time the meeting was supposed to start or the secret early time when you really expected everyone to show up?"

Melody lets out a giggle and Mary rolls her eyes, ignoring Meesha's sass.

"Melody, try going on Find My Friends," Mary instructs. "Do you see her? She blocked me, that pedar sag."

"Uh, one second," Melody says, pulling out her phone and waiting for her sister's location to load. "Okay, I got it. It looks like she's in WeHo."

WeHo, which I only know means West Hollywood thanks to Lou's study guide, is pretty close to where we are in Beverly Hills. But considering it's rush hour, it will probably take

Mona about half an hour to get here . . . and that's assuming she's actually on her way.

Mary looks like cartoon characters do right before their heads explode. Her face is a deep red, and I'm pretty sure she hasn't taken a breath since Melody tracked her. She screams at Siri to "call daughter Mona," and it rings for a millisecond before going to voicemail.

"She's clearly screening your calls," Meesha chimes in, her demeanor as unbothered as her voice. "Let me step out and try calling her. You guys get started, and I'll try to get ahold of Mona."

Before Mary even has a chance to respond, Meesha has grabbed her phone and headed out the door.

"Uh," I nervously add. "I also don't mind waiting! Seriously. I've got nothing going on tonight. Just some homework I can do on the car ride back."

"Nonsense, Josie Joon," Mary says. "Meesha's right. This meeting is for you. She'll deal with Mona, and we'll get the ball rolling here."

First, we have to discuss the Mashad family *brand*. Because, Javier says, while they "are a family," this is, after all, "a business." They've got a twenty-seven-slide PowerPoint all about what it means to *Be a Mashad*, which really just turns out to be a more thorough version of Lou's study guide and ends with some details on how I'm going to fit into things. Without any consultation on my end, Javier says I am going to be the "awkward, relatable" sister.

I know I should be offended, but I'm not. I don't know

about relatable, but I *am* awkward, and, frankly, I'm pumped I don't have to pretend to be anything else.

"Honestly," Melody says. "Awkward is *so* in right now. I think people are just going to go nuts for your vibe."

"I agree." Javier nods enthusiastically. "People love awkward. And it's fun to work with. Think of all the great branding opportunities. Do you sweat a lot when you're nervous? I'm noticing you seem a little sweaty."

"Oh," I say, his comment only causing my evidently prolific sweat glands to produce more liquid above my upper lip. "I didn't realize I was sweating. Sorry . . ."

"No!" he exclaims. "Do not be sorry. This is great. We could do a partnership with Secret. They have been wanting to do something with us for a while now."

"Or better yet, she could roll out her own deodorant line," Mary notes. "Something strong—clinical strength."

"It could be a partnership with me," Melody adds, turning her attention to me. "Everything I make is organic and natural, and consumers are *super* into natural deodorant right now. It would be our first sister collab!!!!"

I gulp hard. Okay, yes. I signed up to come on the show. And no. I'm not a lawyer, so I don't know *exactly* what I agreed to when I signed that contract, but I definitely don't think I opted in to making a line of organic deodorant. I thought the deal was just do a season of the show and get out.

Melody must notice my brain spinning because she quickly adds, "Or not! Maybe we save all the branding talk for another time."

"Yeah," I quietly agree. "That would be great. I'm just sort of wrapping my head around the whole going on reality TV thing. I don't know if I'm ready to jump into branding."

"We should really be focusing on all the storylines!" Farida chimes in. "So much potential for great storylines. We've never really had the awkward, relatable type to work with before."

"Yes," Mary agrees. "Let's focus on the show for now, starting with how we're going to intro you to our audience. We already recorded the episode where I reveal you're coming on the show—so we've got the drama covered. I'm thinking now could be time for a fun reveal. Josie, I know this is your first time in a production meeting, so why don't you just observe for now. Okay?"

LOL. As if I was about to be chiming in left and right with ideas. Did she already forget I'm the awkward sister???

Scott is the first one with an idea, suggesting they have my sisters come pick me up at school. Everyone shoots that one down *real* quick.

"If anyone in Josie's circle—other than her father and her best friend Louise, who have already signed NDAs—gets so much as a *whiff* of what's going on, it's over," Mary warns everyone. "Our numbers are shot. Her existence *has* to remain an absolute secret until the show officially airs. So no, we can't have the girls going to pick her up from school, alerting all one thousand kids at Valley High School of what's going on. Ridiculous idea, Scott."

That's when Farida suggests they make my introduction at Mary's Persian New Year party on Saturday. "It's perfect," she tells Mary. "It will be here, where you know everyone has signed NDAs. Nobody *can* have phones, so you don't have to worry about people leaking pictures to the press. And it's a big enough event that it will be fun to film. Everyone who's anyone will be there, and Josie will have a chance to mix with your whole circle. Plenty of opportunity to film some hashtag AwkwardJosieMoments, which, by the way, we should really try to get trending when the show airs."

"Great call," confirms Javier, taking note of it on his phone. "Definitely."

"Josie." Mary turns her attention toward me. "Did you celebrate Nowruz growing up?"

"Um, yeah," I say. "I still sort of do. Matt and I usually just go to a Persian restaurant by our place for some sabzi polo mahi."

"Matt is her adopted father," Mary explains to the rest of the room.

"Yep." I nod. "He's been my adopted dad since I was five."

"You should bring him to the Persian New Year party!" Melody excitedly suggests. "Right, Mom? We don't want to pull them apart and ruin their Persian restaurant tradition."

"Sure," Mary says with a shrug. "He already signed the NDA. And his presence could add an interesting element to the storyline."

"Okay," I say, the thought of having Matt there instantly reassuring me a bit. "I'll see if he can get off work."

"Yay!" Melody squeals. "Josie, I promise you two are going to have a blast. Not to sound all *Bridgerton*, but the party my mom throws is, like, the event of the season. Everyone who's anyone always shows up. Politicians, billionaire business moguls, athletes, fashion designers, supermodels, pop stars, actors. You name it, they're there."

I think she notices the look of sheer terror that must be plastered across my face because she quickly adds her own, new suggestion. "Farida Joon, why don't we make Josie's initial intro on the show a bit more mellow? Maybe she can come for Friday night dinner, spend the night here—Mona obviously lives here, but Meesha and I can plan on spending the night, too. We'll do a real sisterly slumber party, and *then* the next morning we'll all get ready and go to the party together and her dad can come meet us."

"Oh, this is a great idea." Mary nods enthusiastically. "Especially if her father is coming the next day. The audience needs to see Josie on her own bonding with you girls. Josie, I assume that works for you?"

Yes, Melody's suggestion is slightly less horrific in that it gives me a chance to get more familiar with everyone before Matt and I are thrust into the middle of an A-list Hollywood event. But her plan would also involve me spending my first Friday night without Louise since the day we met in preschool.

"I know this is kind of weird," I say, trying to ignore the salty beads of nervous sweat dropping from my upper lip into my mouth as I speak. "But, um, could my best friend Louise maybe come, too?"

"No," Mary shoots back quickly. "This is sister bonding time. Your father is already accompanying you to the party, assuming he will say yes. But let's keep Friday as just family.

Louise can join us later on, once the four of you have really bonded. Remember, Josie Joon. This is what your father wanted."

"My biological father," I mutter under my breath, trying to blink away the tears.

"So awkward." Javier giggles to himself as he watches my breath get tighter and tighter. "This chick is *made* for television."

"It will be fun," Melody reassures me, rubbing a hand on my shoulder. "Promise."

I know that in the grand scheme of life this is no big deal. It's one night. Louise probably won't even care that much. She could spend the night with Grant. But to me, the change in my almost fifteen-year-long routine feels cataclysmic.

"I'm sorry," I say. "Do you mind if I use the bathroom?"

"Go ahead, Josie Joonam," Mary says. "Closest one is toward the end of the hallway, to your right."

Mary's instructions sound simple enough, but they're suddenly way more complicated as I realize the right side of the hallway has about fifteen doors to choose from. To make matters worse, *all* the doors here are closed. Melody told me on the tour that's just how Mary likes it. Keeps the crisp white halls looking clean and uniform. So I'm stuck cautiously opening each door, one by one.

I cannot tell you how many random people I walk in on, from the PR lady taking calls in one of the offices, to the housekeeper cleaning the gallery room with their family photos, to the masseuse setting up in the "mini spa," but, finally,

I'm at the very last door on the right side of the hall. This *has* to be the bathroom.

I pause at what I'm, like, 99 percent sure is the bathroom door. I feel a little weird just opening a bathroom door without knocking, but that seems to be what people do around here. Melody even said it herself on the tour: "Feel free to let yourself in wherever—if you're not wanted in a room, it'll be locked."

So I swing the door open, excited to finally rest my butt on a toilet and *breathe* for a second, and, oh GOSH. I wish I'd knocked.

Chapter 9

"And you're *sure* it wasn't Bunny?" Lou asks for what must be the thirtieth time as we place our lunch trays down on our table in the cafeteria annex. "You know what Bunny looks like, right?"

She pulls up Bunny's Instagram page, which is filled with pictures of the pink-haired pop star dressed in all sorts of crazy outfits, like bedazzled bikinis and massive gowns with one-hundred-foot-long trains. I carefully examine each picture, wanting so badly for who I saw in the bathroom to be her. But it's not. It's just not.

"No," I confess. "It's definitely not her. Louise, I'm telling you. It was a *guy*. Like, a big man. Really big! Well, not the size of Mary's security guards—those guys are so big. I wish I could show you a picture. They're *huge*. I wonder if they used to be bodybuilders?"

"Josie." Lou snaps her fingers in my face. "Back to the intensely juicy piece of gossip you just dropped. Who was in the bathroom with Meesha?!"

I cringe at the memory, wishing I could erase what I saw from my mind entirely.

"I don't know! You know I don't keep up with this stuff," I tell her. "All I know is that he was really, really big and had a bunch of tattoos all over his back . . . and one tiny one on his butt."

I'm genuinely worried Louise's eyes might burst out of her head. "Wait a minute," she says. "You saw his *butt*?! You didn't tell me they were NAKED!!!"

She really is the worst listener sometimes. "I told you I walked in on them hooking up!"

"Yeah, but *naked* hooking up is so much more intense than just clothed hooking up," she says as she takes a large bite out of her turkey sandwich. "I was thinking they were in there having a quick peck. Or maybe even a little dry hump. But *naked*? With the door unlocked in a bathroom at her mom's house during a professional meeting?! This is so SCANDALOUS."

"And so *secret*," I remind her in a near-whisper. "Stop being so loud!!! I'm only allowed to tell you because you technically also signed the NDA."

"I know," Lou says, dropping her voice to match mine. "I'm sorry. I just can't believe this. I think I'm kind of heartbroken, honestly. Bunny and Meesha were such a cute couple!"

"Maybe they were on a break?"

"No chance," Lou says, once again pulling out her phone. "Look. Bunny literally posted this yesterday while you were at your meeting."

Lou clicks on Bunny's Instagram page and shows me her

story from seventeen hours ago. The caption *can't wait to see my babyyyyyyy @Meeshamash* accompanies the picture of a private jet she was presumably about to board.

"Okay," I say. "So they weren't on a break. Maybe they're in an open relationship?"

I notice myself exhausting all the same possibilities I used to explain my mom's tryst with Ali. If there's one thing I'm taking away from the past few days, it's that relationships are complicated.

"I don't think so," Lou says. "They agreed to be exclusive last season. Plus, Meesha's supposedly a lesbian! Oh my God, you don't think her coming out was a publicity stunt, do you?"

"To be honest, I wouldn't put it past Mary," I admit. "You should have *seen* her trying to push Meesha into becoming a Zoloft spokesperson. But I don't know, it really doesn't seem like something Meesha would do for publicity. I know I only met her for a bit, but she seems pretty genuine."

"It just seems fishy that she would come out on national television only a year ago," Lou says, "and now she's hooking up with giant dudes in her mom's bathroom?"

"Louise! You were at the same Diversity Day assembly as me," I remind her. "You know that sexuality is a spectrum. And who knows? Maybe the person I saw doesn't identify as a man."

"Yeah," she says. "You're right. This is honestly just shocking. Bunny and Meesha really do seem so in love. So, what did she say when you walked in on them? Did she even see you?"

"Yes," I say, shuddering at the memory. "She DEFINITELY saw me. We made eye contact as soon as I walked in, and I just stood there frozen until she finally whispered, 'What the *fuck* is wrong with you? Leave!' Then she shut the door in my face."

"She dropped an f-bomb?!" Lou exclaims. "That seems unnecessary."

"I mean, I *was* just standing there staring at her naked body wrapped around a person who was by no means her girl-friend," I remind her. "I see why she might have been peeved."

"I still can't believe you're a Mashad," she says, carefully examining her sandwich before taking another bite. "This is just too much. It might genuinely take me years to fully process."

"Honestly, same," I say. "It's so weird. It's hard for me to believe I share a planet with these people, let alone a genetic code. I just wonder where my mom even met them. The whole time I was there I kept trying to picture her in Mary's giant compound, and I just couldn't. How do you think she even crossed paths with Ali?"

"Didn't she used to cater before she opened the restaurant?" Lou asks. "Maybe she catered an event he was at."

"You're right. That could totally be it." I try to paint the picture of the scene in my head. "I just can't imagine what she would have even talked about with these people. Everything about them is the opposite of her."

"Well, it wasn't *them* that she fell for," Lou reminds me. "It was him. And you never knew him."

"I guess that's true," I say. "But could he have really been *that* different? The paper he wrote the letter to me on had a watermark at the bottom indicating that it was handcrafted in Milan."

"Maybe she saw something under the fanciness," Lou says. "That's what everyone loved about him—about all of them. There's something there. Under all that other stuff."

"Yeah," I say, remembering Scott's line from the meeting about them essentially just being glittery versions of the rest of us. "But anyway, I feel like we've only been talking about me. What's up with you? I meant to tell you—I know you were bummed Santa Clara didn't have anything fashion design related for you to major in. But! Have you looked into their Retail Management Institute? It's apparently a great program. I think you'd thrive."

"Oh, I'll be sure to look into that," she says, her eyes hyper-focused on a strand of her hair as she delicately pulls apart a split end.

"I truly cannot wait, Lou. It's all working out! Us just thirty minutes apart," I continue. "It's going to be perfect. Did you confirm your dorm choice yet?"

The Bay Area. That's what I need to focus my attention on. I just have to get through shooting this dumb season, then Lou and I can move on with our lives in Silicon Valley.

"Yeah." Lou nods. "We're living the dream. But, um, no. I haven't gotten to the dorm selection yet. I've just been so busy with Grant, you know?"

The truth is I don't know. So she has a boyfriend. What does that have to do with slicing twenty minutes—maybe even less!—out of her day to select a dorm? I already looked into it. Swig is absolutely the best fit for her. And everyone knows a freshman dorm can make or break your college experience. If she waits too long she might have to pick a bad dorm, and then she'll hate Santa Clara and transfer somewhere way too far from Stanford.

But then again, what *do* I know? I've never had a boyfriend. Maybe they really are so time consuming that you don't even have twenty minutes to spare for the most important decision of your life.

"Yeah, I can imagine," I say. "Anyway, um, how are things with Grant?"

"So great. I know *nobody* is perfect. But I swear I think he might be. Like, every morning, I wake up to a text from him that says 'good morning, beautiful' with that little smiley with the hearts all over it," she gushes. "You'd never expect it from a jock guy like him, but he is *so* sensitive."

"Wow, that really is cute," I admit. "You've always wanted a boyfriend who sends you good morning texts!"

"I know," she says. "It's literally been my dream forever. And now it's happening! Plus, he's so good about including me on everything with his friends. Speaking of which . . . Grant said Oli Blair's having another party on Friday. I *know* the last one wasn't the best experience for you, but would you be down to come? I mean, I obviously won't go if you don't want to. Duh. But just, like, if you were down, I thought it would be fun!"

Oh gosh. Here it comes. The moment I have to tell sweet,

loyal Louise that her best friend is an evil backstabber who let the Mashad family throw away our longest-standing tradition without so much as a fight. I was hoping I could at least postpone this until the end of the week.

"Oh! Well, that sounds fun, but . . . actually, I kind of already told—"

Before I can make my confession, Grant's voice comes blaring out of the loudspeaker. "ATTENTION, WILDCATS," his too-deep voice booms across the cafeteria. "IT'S YOUR PRESIDENT, GRANT MILLER, SPEAKING."

"OMG," Lou squeals, as if he doesn't make announcements literally every single day. "Doesn't he sound so *cute*?!"

I feign excitement as Grant drones on about the details for our senior prom, which I cannot believe is coming up in a few weeks. And I know it's early, but it's not looking like I'm going to get a date . . . meaning I very well may be graduating high school having never had a date to *any* of our dances. Classic me. Josie "Awkward Sister" Lawrence.

"Yeah! He sounds so, uh, *official*," I respond to Lou. "Like a real JFK."

"Yeah," Lou dreamily agrees. "And *I'm* his Jackie."

"Well, I hope not," I mumble. "Jackie had a real drug problem. And JFK was infamous for his extramarital affairs."

"AND THE THEME IS GOING TO BE 'THE CITY OF LOVE,'" Grant announces, spurring inexplicable cheers from across the cafeteria. This morning he announced our retired biology teacher Mr. Ricci won a Nobel Peace Prize and nobody even flinched. But "City of Love" merits fist pumps and high fives.

"OMG," Lou gushes again. "He really is so romantic."

"Well, I don't think he chooses the theme on his own," I remind her. "Isn't that the Spirit Commissioner's job?"

Listen, I'm not trying to yuck Lou's yum here or anything. But, I mean, the guy is not exactly the second coming of Christ. Let's be a little realistic here.

Grant continues. "SPEAKING OF LOVE, I'D ACTUALLY LIKE TO ASK A SPECIAL SOMEONE TO STAND UP RIGHT WHERE I KNOW SHE'S SITTING IN THE ANNEX NEXT TO HER BEST FRIEND JOSIE. LOUISE? CAN YOU STAND UP, BABE?"

Louise excitedly jumps out of her seat, and, as soon as she does, the lights shut off. She reaches a hand down toward me and I give her a supportive squeeze.

"Oh my gosh," Lou whispers. "This is so cool! What do you think he's doing??"

"I don't know," I whisper back. "Maybe the power went out. Remember when that happened freshman year? We got that whole week off?"

Suddenly the lights come back on, and Oh. My. Gosh. The cafeteria has been entirely cleared out so that it's filled with just the basketball team, Isaac included (and, yes, he looks exactly as adorable as he always does). The Train song "Marry Me" is playing over the loudspeakers, but instead they've somehow remastered it so that it's saying "Prom with Me" and the boys are DANCING IN A FLASH MOB. I can't believe no one else is in here. I can't believe I'm the only one who gets to witness this firsthand. Shoot! Should I be filming? I should be filming.

I pull out my phone as quickly as I can and film as, one by one, each of the twenty guys twirls toward Lou with a red rose in hand until finally Grant makes his way over to her with the most gigantic bouquet of roses I've ever seen. "Hey, babe," he says, with literal *tears* in his eyes. "You wanna be my prom date?" I know I'm supposed to be a supportive best friend and all that, but come on. *Tears?!*

"Of course!!!" Lou exclaims, dropping all the flowers on the ground as she jumps into his gigantic arms.

Aaaaaaand now they're sucking each other's faces off.

I hit pause on my recording and get down on my hands and knees to clean all the flowers off the cafeteria floor. Lou loves flowers. I know she'll want to save these. For the next week, her mom's gonna be complaining about her allergies as Lou fills their entire house with roses her class president boyfriend had the entire basketball team serenade her with.

Okay, fine. I admit I was being kind of salty earlier, but I've gotta say, my whole body feels kind of warm and fuzzy for Lou right now. Lou is, like, the best, most loyal, perfect, loving, wonderful human being on Earth. Grant may be a cheeseball who cries during prom-posals and forgets to specifically invite me to parties, but if he's really willing to go this over-the-top to make Lou happy, then consider me 110 percent Team Grant. Also, did he say he *loved* her earlier? In that announcement? I don't think he overtly said it, but he implied it, right? I make a mental note to discuss that with Lou later.

That and the dyslexia thing. I keep forgetting about that.

Chapter 10

I ran into Meesha and Mary (like, I literally, physically bumped into them—it was so awkward) when I first entered the house today, and they each greeted me with big hugs, which I *thought* was a great sign. But when Meesha wrapped me in her bony arms, she leaned in and whispered in my ear, "Don't you *dare* tell anyone what you saw."

It was, by far, the most terrifying moment of my life. Truly bone-chilling.

So now I'm in one of four glam rooms in Mary's house, letting a woman named Becky put on my Melody Mashad–brand organic eye shadow and a guy named Alfie blow my hair out as I imagine all the different ways Meesha Mashad would murder me.

"Josie, babe," Becky interrupts as I envision Meesha casually dumping my lifeless body off a yacht into the Pacific Ocean. "Can you pucker your lips for me a bit? I want to put this lipstick on."

"Speaking of your lip," Ernesto, the dermatologist on staff, chimes in, pulling a needle out of his neon-pink Moschino fanny pack. "What do you say I give you a quick little plump?"

"Oh!" Becky exclaims before I can fully process the question. "That would be *amaze*."

I stare at my lips in the mirror. Listen, I know they're thin. But is that really such a bad thing? I look around the room, dozens of pictures of my half sisters' perfectly plumped lips smiling down at me. *Maybe to these people it is.*

He turns to the small beauty fridge in the back of the room and finds a vial of something else. "And maybe some Botox? I know you're young, but it's preventative, you know? Helps *keep* you young."

Botox??? I'm eighteen! Are these people nuts?!

"Yes," Becky muses. "Now that I think about it, Ernesto, she has a zit coming up on the right side of her forehead here. What do you think we just give her a quick cortisone shot to calm that puppy down?"

I lean my head in toward the mirror, squinting to try to find the zit Becky is referring to. I see nothing. Okay, this confirms it. They're nuts.

"Yasssss, that would be fab," agrees Alfie. "And . . . this might be tough to pull off before we actually have to be on camera, but I think I could swing a quick balayage on her hair. We'd go a little more golden blond around her face; it could really brighten up her complexion."

"Yes!!!!" Becky and Ernesto squeal in perfect harmony. "Makeover!!"

Blond?! So Genevieve can think I'm copying her?! Absolutely not.

"NO!" I accidentally yell. We all stare at my reflection in the mirror, collectively stunned.

"Uh, sorry. I—I didn't mean to yell," I stammer, this time in a too-quiet voice. "I just . . . well, it's important to me that, if I go on this show, I look like *me*. I didn't even want to do the makeup or the hair. No offense, Becky or Alfie. It obviously all looks great."

"Well, thanks, sweetie," Becky says, wiping the hair out of my face so she can admire her work.

"It's just that I'm not the girl who gets blowouts and Botox and fancy shots to get rid of my zits," I continue. "I know I'm not winning any beauty pageants anytime soon. But I like the way I look. Well, *like* is a strong word, but I'm okay with it."

"So," Alfie says, "not even a quick highlight . . . ?"

"Not even a quick highlight," I repeat, frankly shocked by how crystal-clear my voice is coming out now.

"I can't believe this bitch just turned down free Botox." Ernesto shakes his head in solemn disappointment. "You sure you a Mashad?"

"Honestly, not really," I say. And I mean it. All I got was a stupid letter and a visit from Mary Mashad. There's no DNA test to prove I'm related to them, though I have a hard time believing Mary would let me anywhere near her family without having done her due diligence beforehand. But these people feel like an entirely different species than me.

I look around the room, three of its four walls adorned by what must be hundreds of framed magazine covers featuring images of my so-called sisters with words like SEXIEST WOMAN ALIVE, AMERICA'S SWEETHEART, and A NEW KIND OF MOGUL sprawled across their photoshopped bodies. I stare at a picture of Mona gracing the cover of *Cosmopolitan*. We're practically the same age, but while my body resembles that of a prepubescent tween boy, Mona's looks more like that of a Victoria's Secret Angel before they got into body inclusivity.

I have to admit our faces do look similar, probably more so than with either of my other half sisters. But Mona sort of looks how I imagine I would if I let the Ernestos, Alfies, and Beckys of the world have their way with me. Where my big brown eyes are surrounded by short, stubby lashes, hers are highlighted by lashes so long they look like they could easily get tangled in her eyebrows. Where my olive skin is blemished by a smattering of zits, Mona's looks silky smooth. Where my long black hair puffs with curls and frizz, Mona's sits in perfectly glossy waves.

"Is this hair and makeup stuff just for, like, filming the shows and for magazines?" I ask the stylists, my eyes stuck on the picture of Mona. "Or do they actually do this every day?"

"Of *course* they do it every day," Ernesto replies before Becky has a chance. "Those fine ladies are committed to *staying* fine . . . unlike some people."

I ignore his dig, trying my best to visualize the four of them not looking so perfectly *done*. The other day in the meeting, it didn't seem like Meesha had any makeup on. But something about her still looked so perfect. Like even the out-of-place hairs were *supposed* to be falling that way.

"But why?" I ask. "It's obvious they're all naturally pretty. They don't even need any of this stuff."

"I can't with her." Ernesto sighs with exasperation, throwing his hands in the air and storming out. "I'm out."

"Oh, sorry," I say, my cheeks growing hot. "I didn't mean to—"

"Completely disrespect our life's work?" Alfie asks as he carefully curls another strand of my hair. "Sure you didn't."

"Go easy on her, Alf. She was just asking a question," Becky says, a gentle smile making its way across her face. "Josie, honey, don't pay attention to Ernesto. He's a drama queen. The answer to your question is that the Mashads are doing more than just looking pretty. They're upholding the brand."

I instantly think of Mary's third rule, the one that comes after putting family first and maintaining an unfailing level of professionalism: *Uphold the family brand in all realms of your life.*

"The Mashads aren't going for *naturally* pretty like some basic girl next door," Alfie explains. "They're going for other-worldly. So gorgeous that their beauty slurps up every last bit of oxygen floating around in any room they walk into."

"Huh," I say, musing over his point. "I think I actually get that."

Honestly, it sounds dramatic, but that *is* undeniably the effect of their looks. They don't just look beautiful. They look so beautiful that it's almost powerful.

"So does that mean you're down for some highlights?" Alfie asks, an eyebrow raised in excitement. "Come on, babe. You're a *Mashad*."

"I could get Ernesto to come back right now," Becky says, putting the setting spray bottle down on the counter and pulling her phone out. "I told you. He was just being dramatic."

This has all already felt like such a betrayal to my mom. Morphing myself into some sort of wannabe Mashad lookalike feels like it would be the final fatal stab in her back. *Josie Joonam*, I remember her saying when we'd see these same magazine covers at the grocery stores. *This is fake. It's all fake. This is not what real women look like. We are what real women look like. We are beautiful.*

"Um," I say, considering my reflection in the mirror as her voice rings in my head. "I really actually think I'm good."

I spend the rest of my glam session sitting in an awkward silence as an obviously annoyed Alfie and Becky complete the finishing touches on my hair and makeup. With the amount I've experienced, I really should be getting used to awkward silences. But all this one is doing is giving me more time to think about the fact that this is really happening. I, Josie Lawrence, am about to film a scene for the most-watched television show in the *world* in less than an hour. I take a deep breath, hoping it will nullify the wave of nausea that's just hit me. *Chillax, Josie. Chillax.*

I try to visualize Matt. His club. Stanford. That's what I'm here for. Eyes on the prize.

"All set," Becky says, blowing on my eyelids.

"Yep," Alfie says, squeezing a pump of some shimmery oil into his hand and running it through my admittedly gorgeous hair. "You should be good."

What the heck do I do now? Am I supposed to know?

"So . . . do I just go to the dining room?" I ask, looking in the mirror to check the time on the clock above the door behind me. "Dinner starts in ten minutes, right?"

"Yeah, sweetie," Becky says, and I'm grateful to hear she's still calling me "sweetie," even after I seemingly disappointed them all so deeply. "Just hang tight here for a second. The PA is gonna come here and get you set up with your microphone."

Becky and Alfie are barely gone for a second before I hear a knock on the door. I really wish Melody would have told me people definitely *do* knock around here.

"Come in," I say, and in walks a surprisingly normal-looking boy who seems to be around my age. By "normal-looking," I mean that nothing about his slightly acne-prone skin looks like it's been spray tanned or lasered, his teeth aren't so white they could blind me, his outfit doesn't look like it was tailored by a professional, and his body looks like he has other things to worry about. His chocolate-brown eyes are kind of squinty, and he's got little dimples around his mouth that make me think he must smile a lot. Something about him is almost overwhelmingly comforting to be around. Like chicken soup personified.

"Hey," he says, reaching out his hand. "I'm Timmy, the PA. I'm here to get your mic set up."

I remember Timmy from the call sheet. He's a production assistant whose email is timmy@yaynetwork.com. I remember because I was shocked he was able to snag such a simple email without having to add a last name or anything. I mean, is there really not *any* other Timmy at all in Yay! Network? They have to have, like, thousands of employees.

"Hi, Timmy," I say, clinging to his slightly sweaty hand like it's a life raft.

"Firm grip," he jokes. "You nervous?"

"Nervous doesn't even begin to describe it," I blurt out. "I'm pretty sure the whole glam team already hates me. Except maybe Becky. I can't quite get a read on her. And I don't think I got off on the right foot with one of my sisters. Also, there's the overarching issue of my not even slightly being cut out for this. You know what happened last time I had to give a presentation in front of my class? I fainted. And that was only in front of twenty-two people! And I had *note cards*! Now I have to go 'be myself' in front of a camera recording footage that will ultimately be shown on every television in America?!"

The magnitude of it all hadn't really hit me until now, and I think I feel lightheaded just thinking about it.

Timmy doesn't say anything. He must think I'm a total freak. Who do I think he is, spilling my guts like that? Louise? He's a stranger, for Pete's sake.

He just stares at me with a crooked smile a few moments longer, before finally asking, "Jim Gaffigan?"

"What?" I ask. "What does Jim Gaffigan have to do with anything?"

Did he not hear me? I do have a bad mumbling habit. But I really don't think anything I said rhymed with *Gaffigan*.

"Your shirt," he says. "That's a Gaffigan quote, right? From *Comedy Monster*? I love that one."

I look down at my shirt, which says LET'S JUST SAY I DIDN'T DO A LOT OF RUNNING. He's right. Matt gave it to me after Gaffigan performed at his club one time.

"Yeah! It's one of my favorites," I say. "Especially this line. The whole bit about the playground was so funny."

"As a fellow guy who absolutely was not chased by girls on the playground, I think I related to it on a personal level," Timmy says with a chuckle. "I definitely know where I stand."

"Same," I agree. "Well, I'm a girl. So, not *same*. I just mean I get the principle as someone who would not have been chased on the playground if I was the gender that got chased, you know? Not that I believe the chasing on the playground has to be a gendered thing! I think I've lost the plot here...."

He laughs. And I can tell it's not *at* me. He's laughing with me. "You might have," he says. "But I get what you're saying. Though I do have a hard time believing *nobody* would have chased you. You seem pretty cool."

My face turns red. Was that flirty? No. This is clearly friendly. Or maybe he has some sort of learning disability? I don't think anyone has ever identified me as cool. I'm the awkward sister, remember?!

"But," he continues, changing the subject, "you shouldn't be worried about tonight. They really are super nice. And if the cameras start to make you feel uncomfortable, just look at me and I'll ... hmm ... I'll make a funny face?"

"Huh," I say, considering his proposition. "I guess it depends on how funny the face is."

"Yeah, true," he says, raising his dark bushy eyebrows up

so high they almost touch his hairline and folding his lips so they're tucked all the way inward as he forces a smile. "How's this?"

I'm genuinely shocked that Mary Joon hired someone so . . . goofy? He must have slipped through the cracks. It's the only explanation.

"I guess that does put me at ease," I say through laughter as I stare at his distorted face. "But how will you know if I need you to make the face?"

"Great point, Josie. Great point," he says as he lowers his eyebrows and untucks his lips. "Honestly? I have a feeling you and I are cut from the same cloth. I'll know."

"But maybe we should make some sort of signal," I insist, feeling my nerves flooding back in. "Just to be sure."

"Okay," he says. "For the entirety of this season, if you feel uncomfortable, you can just clasp and unclasp your hands a few times. That will be our signal."

I try it out, taking my left hand in my right, then my right in my left. "Like this?"

"Yep," he says. "You're a natural. Okay, now I gotta be honest. We usually have a woman do this, but the two girl PAs for some reason bailed today and I feel creepy clipping this thing onto you, so I'm just gonna give it to you. It's pretty simple. You just . . . clip it onto the back of your pants or bra, then there's a wire you're going to want to thread up your top so it sits closer to your mouth. I'll, um, give you some privacy while you figure it out."

He turns his back toward me as I take the bulky mic out of his hands and carefully follow his instructions.

"Uh, I think I got it," I say, giving him a tap on the shoulder. "This right?"

"Would you look at that," he says, turning around as the same crooked smile makes its way across his face again. "Clipping that mic like it's no big. You were *born* for stardom."

Chapter 11

"So, do you have a best friend at school?" Melody asks me.

It's the third question she's asked me since the cameras started rolling a few minutes ago and it's a total softball (duh). I think that's why she asked it. I already mentioned Louise in the meeting, so she knew I had a best friend. It *should* be easy for me to talk about. And, under any other circumstance, it would be. I mean, normally I can talk about Louise for days. Months! Years! People don't even ask me, and I find myself unnecessarily working her into conversations.

But now nothing comes out. I've been silent for the past five minutes. Like, literally silent. At first it was okay, because nobody was really talking to me. By the time I sat at the table, Mary and Melody were deep in discussion about exactly how Persian they are going to make the Persian aghd she's having for her wedding ceremony. Then the conversation shifted toward me, and that's when things went south. Melody and Mary and even Meesha have been trying to make conversation with me, and trust me, I *want* to engage, but it's just . . . not happening. The thing is, every time they ask a question, the camera operators, Zadie, Jasmine, and Leah, turn all THREE of the giant cameras in my direction, and I go silent. Then Farida gives me this look that's like, *SPEAK! YOU IDIOT! SPEAK!* Her already big brown eyes expand to the size of quarters behind her red-framed glasses as she frantically gestures in a circular motion to urge me to keep the scene moving. "I thought you mentioned someone," Mary presses. "At the meeting, right? Your best friend."

I try giving Timmy the signal, but it's no use. My hands won't move from their spot on my lap. My whole body, from my mouth to my toes, is now frozen. It's exactly like one of those nightmares when you're being murdered, and you can't scream or move. Only this time I am awake and, instead of being murdered, I'm being filmed for the number one television show in the country.

I try my best to do some breathing exercises, but I can't. I'm consumed by these cameras. They're all I can focus on. They're all I can see, and the more I stare at them, the more I feel my chest constricting, tighter and tighter. Just when I think it's about to get so tight that it'll smush my heart, Melody reaches under the table and grabs my hand.

She keeps rubbing it in a very specific rhythm, and I don't know what sort of magic she's doing, but I feel myself almost immediately breathing more easily.

"So," she says, still rubbing my hand in the same creepy magic motion. "What are you into, Josie? Any extra-curriculars?"

I open my mouth, and, much to my total and complete

surprise, words come out. "Well, yeah. I do a ton of extracurriculars. I'm the chair of the Antiracist Book Club, Environmental Action Club, and Girl Up Valley High—that one's all about lifting up women in our school community. Actually, what you guys do here—you know, putting on such a female-centric show—is very Girl Up. But anyway, I'm also the founder of the Shakespeare Club," I say. "I founded it after I read *The Merchant of Venice* in English freshman year. See, I've always loved comedy. You know, Matt owns—er, owned—a comedy club. And that was always kind of our thing. It's interesting because *I'm* not necessarily that funny. But I appreciate humor, you know? And, obviously, with my dad's line of work, a lot of the comedy I grew up on was more modern. But after reading *The Merchant of Venice*, I realized Shakespeare really was the original comedian. And I just couldn't get enough of his stuff. So that's how I started the Shakespeare Club. I really just wanted to create a space where people could come to discuss his works in a more nuanced way than we would in, say, English class. Not a ton of people have been interested in joining, sadly. Right now, it's just me and Lou—oh, by the way, when you asked earlier, Louise is my best friend. . . ."

I honestly think Melody might be a witch who cast a spell on me because I'm looking at the clock now and seeing that I've been blabbering on for ten minutes. I don't even know what I'm saying at this point. The words are just flowing out of my mouth with no end in sight. Meesha looks like she might fall asleep. Melody is so bored she's stopped even bothering with the hand voodoo, probably hoping it might shut me up. Mary is just looking at me with . . . pity? I can't get a read on her, but I think it's the closest I've seen to pity on her face since I've met her. Is this . . . worse than my silence? It might be. I think me talking is actually more boring than me potentially dying of an anxiety attack on camera.

Finally, I catch a glimpse of Timmy behind Zadie. Without me even giving him the signal, he shoots me a funny face. But this one is even funnier than the expression he flashed me in the glam room. Rather than flipping his lips inward, he's now flipping them *out* while he crosses eyes and scrunches up his nose. He sort of looks like a demon. But, like, a funny demon.

And I just *lose* it. Like, I absolutely lose it. My monologue is interrupted by an absolute fit of uncontrollable laughter. I laugh so hard that I snort multiple times. I laugh so hard that the water I take a sip of to calm me down winds up coming right back up my nose. I laugh so hard I nearly fall out of my chair and onto the floor. That's right. I literally almost ROFL'd. At this point, I don't even know why I'm laughing anymore. I mean, the face was funny. It just wasn't *that* funny. But the more I look into the cameras, and the more I look at Mary, Melody, and Meesha's increasingly concerned-looking facial expressions, the harder I laugh. It's like all the tension that's been building up over the past twenty minutes has bubbled up into this absolute fit of uncontrollable laughter.

"Um, Josie?" Melody interrupts. "Are you . . . okay?"

This only spurs me to laugh more, and the more uncomfortable I become at this truly bizarre reaction I seem to be having, the more my body seems to propel it. I keep laughing and laughing and laughing until, suddenly, Mona Mashad bursts into the formal dining room where we're seated, now twenty-five minutes late for filming.

All eyes and cameras in the room are suddenly off me and onto her and, for the first time since I stepped in here, I feel like I can catch a deep breath. I hear my mom's *cheelax* in my head and manage a long inhale. And then out. In. And then out.

"You're late," Mary says. "Almost half an *hour* late. Do you have any idea how rude that is? Where have you been?!"

"Oh, whatever. I'm here, aren't I? Besides, I'm not here for you treacherous people," Mona replies to Mary, gesturing toward her mother and sisters. "I'm here for my new sister!!!"

Aaaaand the cameras are back on me. Great.

"Well, well, well. If it isn't Josie Lawrence," Mona says, making her way over to my seat at Mary's long, sleek marble dining room table. "Get over here, bitch!!!"

"Mona," Mary warns. "*Language.*"

Mona rolls her eyes and corrects herself with a laugh. "Excuse me. Get over here, *you.*"

Before I know it, Mona has literally picked me up out of my seat and lifted me into the air.

Mona is less than a month younger than me, but she comes across as ten years my senior. And much, much, *much* cooler. Except for the faint trace of alcohol that I detect on her breath, she smells amazing—sort of like the candles in that one SoulCycle class Louise made us do for her birthday last year. But better. Definitely better. Like, the SoulCycle candle minus the sweaty undertones. There's just something very *refreshing* about her, not only in her scent but in her energy. She's fun, she's loud, and she very obviously could not care less what anyone else thinks. Pretty much exactly how Louise described her in her study guide.

"All right," she says, placing me down on the ground and taking a seat next to mine. "Let's get this snooze fest over with. Josie, how much have these three losers been boring you? Ugh, I wish you could have met Dad. He was sooooo much more interesting than these yawns."

"Oh," I say, turning my attention to Mary, Meesha, and Melody, who seem to be totally unfazed by Mona's direct attack. "They weren't boring me at all! They've actually been super nice. If anything, I was boring them, I went on this long rant about Shakespeare. . . ."

"Shakespeare is suuuch a vibe," Mona says. "That's not boring. Boring is not having any *interests*."

I'm pretty sure this is the first time anyone has ever described Shakespeare as "a vibe" and I have a *strong* feeling Mona's never read any of his works, but I appreciate the effort.

"Thanks," I say, doing everything in my power to look at her and not the cameras. "So, um, you must be a senior, too, right? Do you do any extracurriculars?"

"Let's see. Drinking, doing drugs in grimy club bathrooms, and . . . having sex with guys who never speak to her again," Meesha interjects. "I think that pretty much sums it up as far as Mona's *extracurriculars* go. Right, Mel?"

Um, okay. Not the response I was expecting. I cannot believe she just put her sister on blast like that on TV, like it was absolutely nothing. Maybe having their dirty laundry aired on TV *is* absolutely nothing to them. Melody winces as Meesha looks to her for backup. And Mary gets that angry cartoon look on her face that she got in the meeting. Oddly enough, it's only Mona who seems to be totally unbothered.

Before anyone addresses Meesha's jab, the caterers step in to serve us our first course: salmon sashimi prepared fresh in Mary's kitchen by the head chef at Nobu Malibu.

"Meesha Mahsa Mashad," Mary finally says once she's been served her raw salmon. "Do *not* speak to your sister like that. And Mona, I *hope* your sister was lying about everything she just mentioned."

"Are you kidding?!" Meesha screams—well, as much as someone as calm and cool as her can. "You always end up taking her side. It's ridiculous. *She* is the one who strolled in late reeking of vodka. And what? Now she's Josie's number one fan? She didn't even show up to the meeting! Mona gets away with everything just because she's the youngest. It's absurd. I'm done putting up with her shit! Melody feels the *same* way. She's just too wimpy to say it."

"Do you, Mel?" Mona asks in a much gentler voice than what she's been using up to now. "Just say it. If you have a problem, say it to my face."

"Well, yeah . . . sort of. I mean, you like to have a good time. That's what we all love about you! It's not a *bad* thing, necessarily," Melody says slowly, choosing her words like she's carefully selecting colors for her next organic eye shadow palette. "But! I don't think it's your only interest. You're also great at pottery. Do you still do that, Mona?"

The tension in this room is so thick a knife couldn't even cut it. You'd need a chain saw.

"That wasn't the question," Mona says in a disturbingly calm voice. "Are you or are you not done putting up with my 'shit'?"

"Girls," Mary interrupts again. "Language!"

"Oh my God, Mom," Mona groans. "They bleep it out! Who cares?"

"*I* care," Mary maintains. "You are Mashads. And Mashads don't speak like truckers."

"Ugh, whatever." Mona sighs, turning her attention back to Melody. "Just answer the question. It's a yes or no."

As if on cue, the caterers are once again back in the room. After collecting our sashimi plates, they serve us the miso cod Mary told me "everyone goes to Nobu for." I take one bite of the cod and immediately get why. This stuff is amazing. It's like butter. Flaky, sweet butter that's melting in my mouth. I wish I could have five hundred pieces. Like, it's so delicious that if someone told me I would have to sit in this room every night for the rest of my life and have these stupid cameras in my face *but* I would get to eat this cod, I'd do it.

"What is it, Melody?" Mona presses. "Have a backbone and say it to my face."

Just focus on the cod, I remind myself as the pressure in the room grows closer and closer to a boiling point. *Tune them out and focus on this buttery deliciousness.*

"Fine! I hate that you didn't come to my bachelorette party," Melody bursts out, now fully sobbing. "And I hate that you threw up on me at my engagement party. And I hate that you never even congratulated me on my engagement. Sometimes I feel like you resent me. And it's not just about the wedding stuff. It's everything. I know I'm the oldest and I should rise above it, but I hate that I had to spend the entire Met Gala last year in the bathroom taking care of you. I hate that you didn't show up to the ceremony when *Glamour* named me woman of the year. I just . . . I know you have been dealing with a lot, but I wish I could rely on you."

I carefully study Melody's face, drawing from what I learned in AP Psych last year to search for clues that she might just be upping the drama for the cameras. But I can't find any. She seems genuinely upset. And, if what she's saying is true, I can't say I blame her.

"See?" Meesha nonchalantly says, taking a triumphant bite of her cod. "I told you."

I look over at Mona—her jaw clenched tightly, eyes transformed into glossy daggers—and I have to actively resist the instinct to run out of the room for safety.

"But," Melody continues, her voice calmer now, "I've talked about it with my life coach, and I know it's not right of me to expect you to be someone you're not. True peace is achieved when we accept people as they are, and I'm working on that."

I hold my breath as I watch Mona, looking like a human missile about to go off at any second, silently process Melody's peace offering.

"So you're saying I just *am* an unreliable mess," Mona finally says, a small pool of tears gathering in her eyes. "And now it's your burden to deal with me."

"No," Melody interjects. "That's not what I meant—"

"I think that's exactly what you meant," Mona says. "Well, then let me spare you the *burden* and leave."

Aaand the missile is off. Honestly? I cannot believe anyone watches this for *fun*. One live showing, and I think I might have a heart attack.

Mona slams her napkin on her chair and angrily marches toward the door.

"MONA JOONAM," Mary yells after her. "Where are you even going?! You live here."

But it's too late. Mona storms out of the room.

"AND CUT," Farida yells. "Nice work, everyone."

We all sit there quietly for a moment until Mary finally turns her attention to me. "Josie Joon. Do you want Mona's cod? She didn't touch it."

Chapter 12

"Wow, you were *so* good," Timmy says as he waits for me to clip the mic onto the plush white terrycloth robe Mary told me to put on over a bathing suit for our slumber party spa scene. "Are you pumped?! Best-case scenario for your first scene."

"Pumped?" I ask. "Are you kidding?! That was horrible! I was silent. Then I couldn't stop talking. Then I couldn't stop *laughing*, no thanks to you. . . ."

"Yeah," he agrees. "We should probably come up with a new emergency plan."

"Everything that could possibly have gone wrong went wrong," I lament. "This is a total disaster. And don't even get me started on that fight. That was terrifying. Do you think they're going to expect me to get in big blowup fights like that? Because I genuinely don't think I'm capable."

Just the thought of having to come for *anyone* the way the three of them came for each other tonight launches my stomach into a full-on gymnastic routine.

"Definitely not," Timmy reassures me. "They already have enough great fighters in Mona, Meesha, and occasionally Melody. Not to mention the world-class champion, Mary. Everyone's going to love that you bring something different to the table. It's refreshing."

"But did I even deliver on being refreshing?" I ask. "I was just an awkward mess. You know, Mary can technically terminate my contract at any given moment! Even before I earn out the money, which was honestly the only reason I even agreed to do this. I *need* the money to help my dad and pay for Stanford, and I'm pretty sure I just blew it."

"Nah," Timmy says with a smile. "What I saw today would make for *great* television. Besides, like you said, everything that could possibly go wrong has already gone wrong."

"And . . . that's supposed to make me feel better?"

"Yes!" he exclaims. "Don't you get it?! Everything that could have gone wrong *already* went wrong, so *now* what do you have to be afraid of?"

"Huh," I say, after carefully considering his point. "I guess you do sort of make sense. The worst happened. And I'm alive . . . ? Mary didn't even fire me! She just gave me more cod. If anything, it's Mona I'm worried will get the axe, which would really be a bummer because I liked her a lot."

"Mona will not get the axe," Timmy says with a laugh. "I can promise you that. She has done much worse than fight with her sisters at the dinner table, and she always gets away with it."

"She's kind of an inspiration," I admit. "Do you think she's afraid of literally anything?"

"Josie Joon," Farida interrupts, walking into my glam room before Timmy has a chance to respond. "Come on, it's time to head to the spa. And Timmy, we need you in there setting up!"

"Sorry, Farida," Timmy mumbles as we shuffle out of the room behind her. Farida leads us out of the main house, alongside the pool, and over to a cottage on a section of Mary's expansive property that Melody must have missed on her tour the other day. When I saw on the call sheet that this scene would be filmed in "the spa room," I assumed it would just be a room with maybe a few massage chairs in it.

But no. This modern wooden cottage looks like a miniature version of Mary's main home and is still absolutely twice the size of the house Matt, Mom, and I used to live in. This space could very well be its own standalone spa. I enter into a giant open-concept room lined with beautiful glassy mint-colored tiles and marble floors, which Farida tells me are intentionally kept hot in lieu of steaming the entire room. "Steaming the entire room is horrible for filming," she explains. "Besides, this is how they keep their hammams warm at the famed Royal Mansour spa in Marrakech."

I don't really know what she's referring to, but I nod along anyway, doing my best to take in this space. Unsurprisingly, Mona was *not* up for filming with us. So the scene is just going to be me, Melody, and Meesha. But Meesha doesn't seem to be too interested in hanging out with us, either. Instead, she's stationed in an alcove on the opposite side of the cottage getting a massage. I try to say hi and—shocker—she ignores me.

Apparently, I'm supposed to be getting mani-pedis with Melody in a separate little alcove, which Timmy is currently carefully lining with giant candles. This is our chance to have a "heart-to-heart," says Farida as she carefully walks past the cold plunge and the mineral bath over to where our mani-pedi stations have been set up. "Josie Joon, this one should be easier for you," she says, a warm smile flashing across her face. "You are going to be so relaxed that you are going to forget the cameras are even here! Jill, the nice lady over there, will be giving you a mani-pedi with some organic Melody Mashad–brand nail polish while you girls chat. Easy, right?"

"Right," I lie, a frenzy of thoughts about what in the world I'm supposed to chitchat about on national television wringing any trace of Timmy's pep talk right out of my brain.

"Don't worry, Jos," Melody, who I'm starting to think might be psychic, cuts in as she enters the spa wearing her own plush white robe. "I'll lead the convo. It'll be fine."

"You see that?" Farida says as she pulls the two of us into a group hug. "*Sisterly* love. So sweet."

By the time Farida yells "ACTION," Jill is already gently placing my feet into a small glass tub filled with fresh rose petals and hot bubbling water.

"I actually have been working on a little surprise for you," Melody announces the minute the cameras start rolling.

"For me?" I ask. "What . . . what is it?"

Oh gosh. An on-camera surprise?!?! This has already been terrifying enough even when I somewhat know what's coming.

"Mona, Meesha, and I teamed up with a bunch of the producers to go over our old home movies and clips from the show, to make a highlight reel of the scenes we thought described Dad best," she explains. "I know there are plenty of

Ali Mashad highlights and memorial tributes on YouTube and stuff, but we wanted this one to be more . . . personal. So you could see him how *we* saw him. Not how the world saw him."

Before I can muster a response, a movie theater–style screen cascades down from the ceiling in front of us. Melody pulls a remote from the pocket of her robe and powers it on, the screen immediately filling with the words *Our Dad*, sprawled in cursive over a still photo of Ali twirling his three girls on the dance floor. Oh.

"So, uh, what do you think?" Melody asks, seemingly just now noticing I haven't said a word. "Should I press play?"

I cannot think of a single thing I want to do less than watch an entire highlight reel of Ali Mashad being the wonderful man he refused to be for me and my mom, for the family he chose over us. Like, Jill dunking this tub of hot feet water over my head sounds like a more pleasant experience.

I open my mouth to politely suggest maybe we do something else but have to shut it the minute I look into Melody's eyes. Her hazel eyes are brimming with so much hope she looks less like a human and more like Bambi. *Ugh.* I'm not getting out of this.

"Sure, yes, play," I say through gritted teeth. "This sounds so . . . special."

She presses play, and there it is . . . scene after scene of Ali Mashad, Superdad. Ali cheering the girls on at their soccer games. Ali dancing with the girls in the living room. Ali smothering the girls with kisses when they wake up in the morning.

"He would always wake us up in the morning," Melody tells

me as the morning kisses transition into scenes of him braiding their hair into perfect little French braids. "No matter what. He would rarely go out of town without us, but even if he did, he would have Mom wake us up with a note he had written to start our day."

The movie seems to catch Meesha's attention, because she saunters over from where she was getting her massage, sinking into the plush leather seat next to Melody's. "He was *obsessed* with writing letters," she quietly adds with a small laugh once she's settled in her seat. "Even the smallest milestone warranted a sentimental letter."

Her laughter grows silent when the scene flashes to him presenting her with flowers after a school play, and I watch as Melody gives her hand a tight squeeze. They don't need to tell me what they're feeling, because I know. It's how I feel when I start thinking about my mom too much. Like you miss them so much it might actually kill you.

"I think Josie got a good enough idea of him," Meesha finally says, switching the channel. "The Warriors game is on. We should be cheering for Pete."

"*Meesha,*" Melody scolds. "This was supposed to be for Josie. We don't even know if she likes basketball. Sorry, Josie, Meesha's best friend just got drafted to the Warriors."

"Wow, that's so cool," I say, thrilled to be watching literally anything else. "My crush at school actually plays basketball." The words fall out of my mouth before I remember this tender moment is being captured for millions of viewers across the globe. Millions of viewers including Genevieve. Oh no.

"A crush??? OMG!!! I want every detail," Melody excitedly

demands. Then, seemingly noticing my panic, she adds in a hushed tone, "Don't worry, we'll cut anything you don't want on TV."

I let out a sigh of relief. "Well, his name is Isaac, and we have this great connection in math class," I begin. "But he's dating my archnemesis."

"Oh no!" Melody exclaims. "How long have those two been together?"

Honestly, with the privacy concern out of the way, it feels refreshing talking about Isaac with someone other than Lou.

By the time Farida yells cut, the Warriors have won, and I've fully filled Melody in on the entire saga that is me, Isaac, and Genevieve.

"Josie, that was *intense*," Melody says as we get up from our seats. "But don't worry. I think Isaac is going to come around. Boys always do."

"Thanks," I say, wanting to believe her maybe more than I've ever wanted to believe anyone.

"I'm tired," Meesha says, letting out a loud yawn as she shuts the TV off. "I'm gonna head up to bed."

"And actually I told Axle I would call him before bed," Melody tells me as Meesha walks out. "You know how to get to your guest cottage, right?"

"Oh, uh, yeah," I lie. "I've got it. You go talk to Axle."

I look around the spa nervously as Melody makes her way out. Yes, Mary showed me where the guesthouse was. But this compound is massive. How am I supposed to remember how to get there??? Plus, I'm not really even that tired. Ugh, I wish Lou was here.

Just as I start to make my way out the door, I feel a light tap on my shoulder.

"Hey," Timmy says as I turn around to see him standing on the step below me. "What do you say we go celebrate your first night of filming with some ice cream?"

Chapter 13

"Okay, so where are we going?" I ask as I follow Timmy past Mary's basketball court. "Are we allowed to leave the property? Should we ask Mary? I don't really want to be breaking the rules."

"Well, first of all, I feel like I should remind you that this is not a hostage situation, and that you are free to leave," Timmy says with a laugh. "Second, as much as you strike me as the rebellious type, no. I am not taking you to break any rules. I'm just taking you for the best soft-serve ice cream in Los Angeles. Maybe even in the world."

"But *where*?" I ask, following him through the back entrance to the main house.

Have I not had enough surprises tonight?!

"Right here," Timmy says, making a sharp right and opening the door to Mary's staff-only kitchen. "Come on, follow me."

"Are we allowed back here?" I ask, bracing myself for some sort of alarm to go off. "It says staff only!"

"I work on the show!" Timmy says, entering the massive restaurant-grade kitchen. "I am staff. And technically, as a star of the show, you are also staff."

"I guess you're right," I admit, taking in yet another gigantic room Melody left off her tour. "This is wild. Why would anyone need a kitchen like this in their *home*?"

"Honestly, I would have thought the same thing," Timmy tells me as he makes his way over to a door leading to a pantry the size of a small Costco. "But it sort of makes sense for Mary. She entertains so much, and a normal kitchen doesn't really do the job for the size of parties she hosts. Like tomorrow, for example, Mary is expecting two hundred and fifty guests. Instead of getting all that catered, she can have her private chefs prepare all the Persian dishes in this kitchen."

"I guess," I say, still trying to wrap my head around all of this. "Do her chefs come in every day?"

"She has two, Gina and Lenny, who do," he explains as he enters the pantry and returns with two waffle cones. "They're usually here from five in the morning to nine at night, seven days a week. Then she has a larger team of people she brings in for big events. A bunch of them were here earlier in the day prepping for tomorrow, and they'll probably be back early in the morning."

"My mom was a chef," I find myself telling him. "I spent so much of my childhood with her in kitchens like this." The nostalgia washes over me like a wave as I brush my hand across the stainless-steel countertop on the large island in the center of the kitchen.

"Wait," he says, pausing in front of one of the seven refrigerators, also stainless steel. "I forgot to warn you. This is just regular ice cream. You're okay with that, right?"

"What?" I ask with a laugh. "What other sort of ice cream would I be expecting?"

"I don't know," he says. "Oat milk ice cream, low calorie Greek yogurt ice cream, coconut milk ice cream . . . This is LA! The low-cal and dairy-free options are limitless."

"I tried oat milk ice cream once, and I have to admit it was really delicious," I say. "And I read once that Middle Eastern women are more likely to develop dairy intolerances later in life than other groups, so maybe I should be paring down the dairy. But no. For now, I'm good with regular ice cream."

"I'm telling you—even if you were intolerant, this soft serve might be worth the stomachache," Timmy says, opening the door to the refrigerator to reveal an interior lined with soft-serve dispensers. "What flavor do you want? Chocolate? Hazelnut? Vanilla? Butterscotch? Strawberry shortcake is my personal favorite."

"Hmmm," I say, carefully reading the labels denoting each of the flavors. "I'll go with white chocolate blackberry."

Timmy pauses for a beat, seemingly surprised by my order. "Really?" he asks.

Oh no. Bad order.

"Shoot," I say. "Is that a bad one? It just sounded good. I can get chocolate."

"No, no, no," he quickly reassures me, topping my waffle cone with a dollop of lilac-colored ice cream. "It's a *great* one. The best. You'll love it."

"You're sure?" I ask, skeptically staring at my cone after he hands it to me. "You seemed weird about it. I won't be offended if it's a bad one!"

"I'm sure," he says, smiling. "Just take a lick."

I stick my tongue out less than a millimeter to get the smallest taste I can manage, just to be sure.

"Oh my *gosh*," I say as Timmy finishes off his own waffle cone with a pink dollop of the strawberry shortcake flavor. "First the cod, now this?!"

"I told you," Timmy says, taking a seat on one of the two chrome stools available by the kitchen island and gesturing for me to sit in the other. "The best ice cream in the world. Right here, in Mary Mashad's staff-only kitchen. But anyway, I'm sorry I cut you off with my ice cream question. Your mom worked in restaurants?"

I pause for a minute, looking into Timmy's eyes staring intently back at me. I don't know how, but I can just tell he's not just circling back to be polite. He actually cares.

"Well, sort of," I say. "She was a caterer for a long time. Then she briefly worked in restaurants until she opened her own little breakfast café in Van Nuys. The kitchen wasn't *just* like this, it was more a mini version. And I would spend my time sitting on a stool like this doing my homework in the corner."

"Do you guys still have the café?" Timmy asks. "You and your dad?"

"No. Matt tried to keep it afloat for a bit, but you can't really have Sharzad's Café without Sharzad, you know?" I say with a light laugh. "It sort of just stopped working."

"Do you miss her cooking?" Timmy asks, licking a large drip off the side of his cone. "I feel like that would be the hardest part of losing a parent who was a chef."

"Yeah," I say, another wave of nostalgia hitting me like a tsunami. "I crave her cooking all the time. It's weird, because it started off as a totally separate thing from missing her. Like, I always craved her cooking. Even when she was alive. But now when I crave the chicken schnitzel she used to make on my birthday or the sabzi polo mahi she would make on Persian New Year . . . it's all just a reminder that she's not here to make them for me."

Timmy pauses for a few seconds before finally saying, "Sorry, I'm just trying to think of the right thing to say. I was going to go with 'I'm sorry,' because I really am. But that feels sort of obvious, right? Like, how could I possibly not be sorry? And you probably get that all the time. So then I was considering a variation of 'That sucks.' Because it does. But that still feels like a bit of an understatement. It more than sucks. And now I'm just thinking maybe there's no right thing to say when someone loses a person they love."

I laugh, his maybe too-honest response disintegrating all the heaviness that had built in the room. He's right. There is no right thing to say. And maybe admitting that *is* the only right thing to say.

"It's okay," I say. "I think you might be the only person who rambles as much as I do."

"Oh, I am by no means athletic or very smart," Timmy says. "But I am a *champion* rambler."

I take another lick of my ice cream, trying my best not to gobble the whole thing in one bite.

"This legitimately might be the best ice cream I have ever had," I say. "How does she get it so . . ."

"Creamy? Delicious? Flavorful?" Timmy asks, taking one last lick of his own cone. "It's a simple rule of thumb. Mary Mashad has the best of everything in this home. From ice cream to spas, you are going to be having the world's best version of it under her roof."

"Why would she even leave?" I ask, nibbling the remains of my waffle cone. "I would lock myself in here forever."

"She does spend a *lot* of time here," Timmy says. "Leaving the house is just such a hassle for her. The girls, too. And Ali, when he was alive. They're too famous to just casually go out like you or I can. It's always this huge ordeal, with security and paparazzi and all of that."

I remember the sight of Mary in Mr. Schwartz's office, how out of place she looked. Maybe that's the curse of their *otherworldly* beauty. It bars them from doing anything of this world.

"Can I ask you a question?" I ask, wiping my hands on a napkin after finishing the last bite of my cone.

"Shoot."

"You seem to know them all so well," I say. "Did you know . . . you know, my biological dad?"

"Ali?" Timmy asks. "Yeah, I knew him well."

"What was he like?" I ask. "And not just the TV version. What was he really like?" I'm not sure why I trust Timmy on this, but I do. Something about him seems like he might process the world like I do.

"Honestly? He was great," Timmy says. "He was super warm. You know how Mary can be kind of . . . icy? Well, Ali was the opposite of that. First of all, he was super fun. He was the life of the party. He loved a good martini. And he *loved* to dance. He was by no means good. But he was always the first one on the dance floor."

I hate how disappointed I am by Timmy's rave review. It's nice that Timmy had this wonderful impression of the man. I don't want to take that away from him. It's just . . . can't *one* person have something negative to say about this guy? Or was he just wonderful to everyone except me and my mom?

"He and Mona loved old early 2000s rap hits. That was their thing," Timmy continues. "Every year he had a special 'Mona's Birthday' playlist he'd blast in the morning to wake her up on her birthday. He would get it going on every speaker, then burst into her room to wake her up with a little two-person dance party. It was a cute little tradition they had."

"Lou, my best friend, keeps telling me he reminded her of me," I say. "But I don't think I get how. I mean . . . maybe it's that we were both bad dancers? But, other than that, I don't see it. Like, I can pretty positively say nobody has ever described me as the 'life of the party.' If anything, I might be the death of the party."

"Well, Ali wasn't just the life of the party," Timmy says. "He had other sides to him, too. Like, when he was talking to you, he always made you feel like you were the most important person in the room. It didn't matter if you were the janitor or the CEO of a company. Ali would give you his undivided attention. And he was an amazing friend. So loyal. If you were friends with Ali, he had your back for life. A lot of the people who work around here are friends and distant relatives of his from Tehran. He was always taking care of people."

I want to bite my tongue, but I've been doing that all night and I just don't have it in me anymore. I have to ask.

"That's the part that makes no sense to me," I say. "How could he have been this amazing, loyal person and ditch my pregnant mom?"

"I honestly have no idea," Timmy says. "Leaving a woman pregnant with his child feels out of character from everything I knew about him, I can tell you that much."

"It just feels so weird that this guy was the villain in my mom's story—not just hers, but mine, too!" It's like I'm thinking out loud. "He most likely lied to her, then left her pregnant and alone. And now I'm just casually in his home eating his ice cream, getting manicures in his spa, listening to a whole new group of people describe him as the hero in their stories. I'm just kind of torn. Like, do I want him to be the villain? If he was the villain, then 50 percent of *me* is villain. That's part of my genetic code! And study after study shows that nature does play a very pivotal role in a human being's character, no matter what the nurture. But, then again, choosing to see him as anything other than a villain feels like a slap in the face to my mom. . . . Oh gosh, I'm sorry. Now I'm rambling again. And it's way too personal. You just met me."

"Want to hear something funny about you and Ali?" Timmy asks, completely ignoring my apology. "I wasn't going to tell you, because I wasn't sure if you really felt like talking about him, but now it feels like maybe you might, so . . . the reason I paused when you asked for the white chocolate blackberry is that they didn't use to have it until Ali tried that flavor while visiting a friend in Cape Cod once and loved it. The doctor told him a thousand times to cut down on dairy, but at least once a week, he would sneak into this kitchen and get himself a dollop of white chocolate blackberry ice cream. He loved it too much to resist. Nobody else ever wants it, but Mary keeps it stocked in his memory."

"Oh," I say, not sure what to make of this random connection with him. "Huh."

"I know it's kind of a stupid thing to have in common," Timmy says. "But I don't know. I think it sort of humanizes him, right? Instead of all these stories about how good he was or how evil he was. Maybe he wasn't a hero or villain. Maybe he was just a regular guy who did some things right, did some things *very* wrong, and liked the same ice cream as you."

I nod politely. But, no matter how hard I try, I can't see him as anything other than the man who lied and left us.

Chapter 14

"HAPPY NOWRUZ," Mona exclaims, bursting into my guest cottage and leaping on top of my bed.

"Mona?" I ask, still half asleep. "What time is it?"

"Six," she says, her fresh SoulCycle scent immediately filling the room. "I'm a morning person. I'm *always* up by five thirty. No matter how late I go to bed. Nobody else in the family is up when I am. I mean, except Mom, but I'm not trying to start my day listening to her scream at God knows who on the phone."

I stare at her for a minute before I fully rule out the possibility that I'm still sleeping and this is all a dream. *Nope. This is really happening.*

"Yeah, that sounds . . . intense," I say, stacking my pillows so I can sit more upright. "Are you feeling better? You seemed so upset last night."

"It's whatever," Mona says with a shrug. "Meesha has just been a raging bitch lately. I don't even get why! Like, I got it when she was a starving depressed model stuck in the closet.

That sucks. But what's her deal now? We don't care that she's a lesbian. She quit modeling. She's got meds for her depression. And she's, like, super in love with the hottest woman in the world. Seriously. What the fuck is her deal?"

I have a feeling I know what her deal is, but I know I can't say anything.

"Maybe her medication is taking a while to settle into her system," I suggest. "I read it can take months sometimes."

"You seem like the type of person who would read studies and stuff. So I'll take your word for it," Mona says, pausing before lifting the corner of my plush white duvet. "You don't care if I get under the sheets with you, do you? It's freezing in here."

"Not at all," I say, instinctively scooching over. "This bed is so massive. I probably wouldn't have even noticed if you didn't say something."

I know we have only met one other time, but the weirdest part of this early morning exchange is how *not* weird I feel right now. Maybe it's the fact that we share DNA. Maybe it's that she's the closest in age to me. Or maybe it's just the undeniable level of confidence she carries herself with. But something about hanging around Mona just feels sort of natural.

"Cool," Mona says, seamlessly slipping under the covers next to me. "So, anyway, Meesha has been a raging bitch, and Melody is taking her side, which is so annoying. Like, do you know how much I've done for her wedding?!"

I shake my head no, though I'm sure she would tell me either way.

"I have planned pretty much anything fun having to do with

it," she says. "Okay, yes, I might have dropped the ball here and there. But the bachelorette was nothing short of iconic. Like, *Betches* did a feature on it and literally called it 'iconic.' Who do you think planned it? Meesha, the most boring human alive? No, it was *me*. I know I wound up bailing, but is that really a big deal when I fucking killed the planning process?"

"I'm sure you did a great job planning it," I try, knowing she needs to hear the words. "I bet Melody loved her bachelorette party."

"Oh, I *know* she did," Mona says, pulling up a video of a drunk Melody diving off the stage at a packed nightclub and surfing the crowd. "This is, like, the most fun I've seen her have maybe ever."

"I might not be your best audience here, because the thought of crowd-surfing genuinely terrifies me," I say. "But I will say, it definitely looks like Melody is having fun."

"Right?!" Mona exclaims as she puts her phone back in the pocket of her sweatpants. "But that's enough complaining about our sisters for one morning. I mostly just wanted to break into the guesthouse because I was sort of bummed we didn't get to hang more last night."

"Don't worry about that," I say, feeling a sad shift in her energy. "We have the whole rest of this season to hang out."

"I'm kind of excited to have a sister my age," Mona says, her voice a little quieter than usual. "I know this sounds so lame, but . . . I was hoping we could be friends? I know we're technically sisters and, like, biologically have to love each other. But I just thought maybe we could be friends, too? I . . . don't really have a ton of friends."

"Really?" I ask, remembering the many pictures Lou included in my study guide of Mona out and about with other Hollywood starlets. "I feel like you're the most popular girl in Hollywood."

"I have a lot of *acquaintances*," she says with a sigh. "Like, right now. There's probably fifty people I could text who would be down to come do whatever I wanted. But that doesn't feel the same as having a real friend, you know? Like, people I can actually tell my secrets to without worrying that they'll sell them to TMZ."

"Yeah." I nod. "I guess I have the opposite problem. I have one best friend, Louise, who is definitely a real friend. But that's pretty much it. I don't think I even have fifty people in my contacts."

"I guess I have Meesh and Mel, too," Mona says. "Even when we fight and stuff, I *do* know I have them, and I can trust them with anything. But they're older. To them, I'm always the little sister . . . which is extra annoying considering Meesha is, like, barely a year older than me."

"That would be super annoying," I say with a laugh. "But it is nice you have them."

"Yeah." She nods. "It is. You know what I can't stop thinking about?"

"What?"

"Last night, Melody said she feels like I resent her," Mona says. "And honestly? Maybe I do. I swear I'm happy for them for the most part, but it just sort of sucks having her and Meesha both in relationships. I feel like they're being taken away from me."

"I know that feeling," I say, thinking of Lou and Grant. I'm lost in my thoughts for a minute until I feel Mona wrap her arms around my shoulders.

"It sounds like we came into each other's lives at the perfect time," she says with a smile, pausing for a beat before changing the subject. "Hey, so are you excited for the party today?"

I gulp hard.

"You know when you agree to doing something and you just sort of think that the day will never actually come?" I ask. "That's kind of how I feel about this party. This all just feels like it's happening so fast. Last weekend I was spending my Saturday night as Lou's plus-one to a garage party with twenty kids who barely know I exist, and now I'm attending, like, the hottest A-list event in Los Angeles?!"

"You'll be fine," Mona reassures me. "You already know me, Meesh, and Mel. Not to mention Mom, even though she is always a *nightmare* today. Just stick with us."

Chapter 15

I crane my neck to find Matt's old Hyundai inching up Mary's winding driveway behind a long line of Rolls-Royces and Bentleys. Just the sight of his beat-up car amid all of this is an instant comfort. Something *normal*. I wonder if any of the other cars in this lineup have even seen the inside of a mechanic shop.

"That him?" Gene, Mary's valet, asks.

"Yep," I confirm, nervously biting the inside of my cheek. "That's him."

I crane my neck even farther to try to get a look at Matt's face. Matt has one of those faces that tells you everything about him in an instant. If he's feeling overwhelmed by all of this, I'll know just by looking at him because his eyebrows will be raised so high, they'll almost touch his hairline and his chest will be puffed out like he's taking a giant deep breath in. But Matt is so far down the miles-long driveway I can hardly make him out in the driver's seat.

Ugh. But I have to see him! If I can just see his face, I'll know how he's feeling, and I can chill. I stretch my neck out farther and farther until I lose my balance and almost trip into one of the massive columns in Mary's entryway.

"You good, hun?" Gene asks with a laugh.

I look up at Gene, who I just met about five minutes ago, but who for some reason reminds me of Matt.

"Hey, Gene?" I say. "Can I ask you a question?"

"What's up, kid?"

"Do you think my dad will like all this?"

Mary's compound is always over-the-top. But things have reached new heights for this Persian New Year party. The driveway alone has been lined with what seems like miles and miles of hyacinths, the Persian New Year flower. And, when you finally reach the top, a line of escorts dressed in tuxedos are ready to serve you a cup of Persian jasmine tea or a Persian martini (a mix of Grey Goose and fresh pomegranate juice with just a dash of angelica powder). Once guests have their beverage of choice in hand, their escort gives them a golf cart tour of the property ending at the party, which is currently roaring in the backyard.

"Beats me," Gene says with a casual shrug. "I don't know the guy."

Duh, Josie. Why would this stranger know if Matt will like this? Just because they're two middle-aged white men who vaguely resemble each other???

"I know," I try one more time. "But . . . if you were just a regular stranger coming into all of this, what would you think?"

"Why don't you ask him yourself?" Gene nods toward the driveway as Matt finally pulls up to the front of the line.

"Matt!" I exclaim, my heart rate instantly decreasing as I take in his face. Mouth slightly turned upward in a relaxed smile, forehead just creased a smidge. He's cool as a cucumber. I smile, remembering how this quality of Matt's was one of my mom's favorites. "You know, some big celebrities come to that club," she would tell me when I was way too young to fully get what she was trying to say. "Even Jerry Seinfeld came in to do a set once! During the height of *Seinfeld*! Most club owners would be bending over backward trying to impress him. But not Matt. Matt treated him like any other comic at the club. He is so *confident*. That's the key, Josie Joonam. *Confidence.* Insecure men require too much of our time and energy." With everything that's gone on in the past few years, it's been a while since I've had the chance to see *that* version of Matt. The one who is intimidated by no one. But here he is again, this time strolling into his late wife's late ex's palatial home, exuding that same trademark confidence. *This is what he looks like when he's relaxed*, I realize. *When he's not exhausted from working double shifts or scrambling back to work.* Maybe when I get the money, he can go back to being this guy all the time.

"Well," Matt says, straightening his old Men's Wearhouse suit as he strolls away from the car. "This sure beats a shift at CPK."

"I am *so* happy you're here," I say, giving him a giant hug. "I can't wait to introduce you to everyone. They're actually pretty nice. I think you'll like them."

Matt barely has a chance to get his tea from a tuxedo-clad guy named Nima before Farida comes rushing over to us.

"Matt! Hello!" she exclaims. "Happy New Year!"

"Eid eh showmah mowbarack," Matt says with a smile, before taking a sip of his tea. "This is good stuff. It's gotta be Sadaf, right?"

"Wow, someone knows his Farsi," Farida replies, impressed. "Now, before you enter the party, we're going to need to go inside to get you miked."

"Miked?" he asks, an eyebrow raised. "I thought I was just here for a party."

"Well, yes," she says, nodding along quickly. "But we are also filming. Your daughter is a central part of the show. And you are here as her guest."

"Does he really have to?" I ask, my heart picking up speed again at the thought that he might leave if he does. "Maybe we can just keep him out of scenes?"

"It's fine," Matt says, sensing my nerves. "But just this *once*."

The two of us follow Farida into the foyer, where Timmy is standing ready to get Matt set up.

"Hi, Mr. Lawrence," Timmy says, reaching out a hand to him. "I'm Timmy. I'm a production assistant on the show."

"Timmy liked the Gaffigan shirt you gave me," I tell Matt. "He's into comedy, like us."

"Really?" Matt asks, raising his arm as Timmy clips the mic onto his belt. "Well, I have more of those shirts if you want one. And a bunch of others, too. Who are your favorite comics?"

"Well, I'm a huge Gaffigan fan," Timmy says. "And I really did like Chappelle's earlier stuff, before . . . you know. I like old John Mulaney stuff, too. Then Jerry Seinfeld. Adam

Sandler. Amy Schumer. And I'm a huge fan of his movies, so I'm biased here, but I also loved Judd Apatow's Netflix special."

"You know I had almost all of those people at my club back in the day," Matt says. "You have good taste, my friend."

I stare at Matt's face intently. Gentle smile, one eyebrow slightly raised. He's impressed.

"Wait, no way!" Timmy exclaims as the three of us follow Farida out to the party. "That is awesome. Which club did you own?"

"Crickets," Matt replies. Then he adds with a sigh, "You probably haven't heard of it. But it was a good spot back in the day."

"Heard of it?!" Timmy asks. "I've been! My mom snuck me in there once with her when I was eleven. We saw Sarah Silverman do a set."

"Wow, you were there for the Silverman set?" Matt asks. "You know, Jos was there, too. The only two minors in that club. I'm surprised you two didn't cross paths."

"Really?" Timmy asks. "You were there?"

"Yep," I say. "Matt and my mom made me go *every* time there was a female comic headlining."

"It was important for you to see!" Matt exclaims. "There are too many male comics out there. We wanted you to know women can do anything men can do, and most of the time even better."

"Timmy," Farida says, making eye contact with Zadie across the backyard as soon as we enter the party. "I think something is happening with the sisters. We've got to get over to where they're standing by the Persian martini bar."

The two of them rush over to where Mary has waiters serving more of the pomegranate juice and vodka concoctions in crystal martini glasses, leaving Matt and me to take in the party on our own.

"You know, this is all nice," Matt says. "But nothing will compare to your mom's Persian New Year spreads."

When my mom was alive, celebrating Persian New Year meant we would set up a small haft sin on the coffee table, then spend the day eating sabzi polo mahi while we blasted Googoosh songs. At the end of the night, she would give me a two-dollar bill as an eidee and tell me to save it in my wallet as good luck for the year, and that was pretty much it. This is that on steroids.

While I was still getting ready, Mary and Farida each stopped by to give me crisp one hundred–dollar bills as eidees. A hundred dollars!!! As *good luck* money. To decorate the party, there is a giant haft sin set up on a white marble table by what is the largest of the many infinity pools throughout Mary's palatial estate. There are waiters passing around small Persian bites of cotelet and kookoo and kabob kubideh wrapped in lavash bread. Off to the left of the yard, there is a giant Persian food station. In addition to the gigantic platters of sabzi polo mahi, I can see Mary's chefs grilling fresh skewers of chelo kabob and joojeh kabob in a giant wood-burning oven to serve with zereshk polo and tahdig. As for the entertainment, Mary has turned this event into a concert, with every legendary

Persian singer alive performing their own complete set.

"Yeah," I say. "And that full food spread? She would freak out if she knew anyone was eating anything other than sabzi polo mahi on Nowruz."

"She really would," Matt agrees, letting out a laugh. "Before we knew it, she would be back there telling all the caterers what they *should* be making."

We both pause for a second, quietly remembering her, before Mary interrupts.

"Matt Joon! Salom!"

"Mary!" Matt exclaims. "Say-lom. You'll have to forgive me. My Farsi is a little rusty. But it's good to meet you in person."

"Pleasure to meet you as well," she says, before gesturing around the party. "So, what do you think?"

"It's definitely . . . different from what we're used to," Matt says. "Very extravagant."

"Yes." I nod. "Extravagant, but in a good way!"

"Thank you," Mary says. "You know, back in the day, we would try desperately to tone down the *Persian*-ness of it all. I was so worried it wouldn't appeal to wider audiences. That all of a sudden we would be categorized as a niche show for minority demographics. But now everyone loves diversity! Not a single white person won an Emmy last year, did you know that?"

Matt and I both shake our heads that we didn't.

"Well, it's true," Mary continues. "Not one white person! You know, Persians are technically considered white. But I figured playing up the diversity could be worth a shot to secure a win this coming year. I told the planners this year to go *all* in. Don't hold back a single thing. That food station over there? You can't fully see it from here, but we are serving every single Persian dish. All of them! From salad olivier to khoresht eh badem joon. And, oh, you *have* to see the Persian dancers—they're performing by the firepit."

We look over at where the dancers are performing, and, slightly to their left, I spot Meesha, Bunny, Melody, Mona, and a few other famous people whose faces I unmistakably recognize but whose names I can't remember for the life of me standing in a circle. "Josie!" Melody gives me a welcoming wave as our eyes meet. "Get over here!"

"You wanna come meet my half sisters, Matt?"

"Before he does," Mary cuts in. "Let me introduce him to Scott Sanderson. He just got here, and I think it's important your father meets the president of the network you're now technically an employee of."

"Seems fair enough," Matt says with a shrug. "Josie, you go hang with them, and I'll catch up with you later, okay?"

"Josie!" Mona exclaims as I sheepishly make my way into their circle. "Whoa, you look great."

"You *really* do," Melody echoes. "Mona, it kind of reminds me of what you wore to the VMAs last year. That Valentino jumpsuit. Do you still have it?"

I awkwardly look down at the formfitting black jumpsuit Mary's stylist Mauricio picked out for me this morning. I can tell that *other* people think it looks good—Mona and Melody aren't the first to have commented on it today. And a few guys at this party have looked at me with the googly eyes boys usually save for Louise. But rather than the almost cosmic confidence my half sisters seem to derive from rocking this sort of look, the newfound attention just makes me want to go into hiding.

"So, Josie, the jumpsuit is so chic. Who's it by?" Mona asks, the cameras zooming in on her as she purposely makes a point of ignoring her sister. "It literally looks like it was tailor made for you."

I know the question was meant more to snub Melody than it was to actually engage with me, but I figure I should answer anyway.

"Thanks, you guys," I say, trying my best to ignore the tension. "Um, I think Mauricio said it was designed by someone named Alaïa? It's honestly kind of a pain when I have to pee."

"Girl, I know how you feel," Bunny says. She's dressed in a latex pink jumpsuit that matches the exact shade of her bubblegum-pink hair. "Wanna be pee buddies? We can unzip each other."

"Oh, uh, sure," I say, sweat dripping down my forehead as Meesha stares daggers at me. "Bunny, right?"

Shoot. Was that creepy? How are you supposed to not creepily react when someone is so obviously famous?

"Yes, I'm Bunny," she says with a laugh, before nudging Meesha. "Meesha's girlfriend."

"Oh yeah," Meesha says. "Sorry, babe. This is Josie. My new . . . sister."

"And you want to give *me* shit?" Mona snorts, glaring at Meesha. "You are the coldest human alive. Have you even said more than two words to Josie since she's been here?"

"Josie is our sister, and we *love* her," Melody tells Bunny, ignoring Mona's comment. "Now, Josie, come here. I have to introduce you to Axle!" She wraps an arm around me.

"Axyyy," Melody coos at her fiancé, who's standing at the other end of the circle chatting intensely with another glittery-faced stranger. "I want you to meet someone *extremely* special."

When he turns around, I'm absolutely *floored* that this is the guy Lou described as having "soulful, sexy vibes, like Shawn Mendes and Harry Styles morphed into a sweet, sensitive superhuman."

"Axy" has long, jet-black hair down to his hip and smells like a mix of patchouli and armpit sweat. It's eighty degrees outside, but he's wearing a floor-length purple velvet coat over a fishnet tank top that shows off his very skinny, yet also very chiseled body. He also has on not one, not two, but *three* scarves, along with silk sweatpants that I can tell are from his fashion line because they're printed with images of babies and, according to Lou's study guide, that's "his thing." Each one of his fingers is adorned by at least three different chunky rings, and—this is neither here nor there—his eyebrows have been waxed to sheer perfection.

"Well, hello there," Axle says, clasping my left hand in both of his perfectly manicured ones. "Amazing to meet you, Josie. Absolutely amazing. From what Melody's told me, it really sounds like you have a lit soul."

He's intensely gazing into my eyes in a way that makes me think he's trying to stare into my soul but kind of missing.

"Uh, thanks," I say, searching for something more comfortable to look at and settling on Timmy, who's standing behind Jasmine as she films us. "It's so nice to meet you. Are you excited about the wed—"

"Nah, ah, ah." He puts his delicate fingers to my lips. "Hush. It's not the ceremony we rejoice about, it's the union."

"Isn't he so *romantic*?" Melody gushes, wrapping her arms around his lean, slightly smelly body. "Axy, tell Josie about the new collection you made."

"Ah, yes," he says. "My new bracelet collection, entitled LOVE. Inspired by *my* love, Melody Mashad. It's a series of beaded bracelets, hand beaded by myself with the help of my former nanny, Sylvie."

"Oh! That's nice," I say. "Can I see some?"

He pulls up one of his velvet sleeves, exposing his forearm, which is covered all the way up to his elbow with dozens of bracelets. They sort of look like the ones you'd make at summer camp. You know, like with the letter beads? For each bracelet, he's strung the letter beads onto a neon-colored piece of string to make a different word. SUNSHINE, one reads. DARKNESS, says the one right above it. And below that, GODDESS, DEVIL, SEX, and CHASTITY.

"Aren't they magnificent?" he asks me. "Each is a word that makes me think of my sweet, disgusting, beautiful, hideous, amazing, boring, perfect, flawed, insufferable, lovable, infuriating, calming, bewildering, simple Melody."

"Wow," I say. "Um, yes! Yes. They're really . . . something."

"They're only three thousand dollars each, if you'd like to purchase one," he says, taking a mini cucumber sandwich off the hors d'oeuvres platter the caterer has been passing around and shoving it in his mouth whole.

"Axyyy," Melody says. "Josie doesn't have to *pay*. She's family! She—"

Before Melody can finish making her point, Axle spits the cucumber sandwich onto the ground, upchucking the whole thing out of his mouth, completely unchewed, with the loudest *bleh* sound I've ever heard. "DISGUSTING!" he screams. Literally screams. "Melody . . . don't tell me your mother purchased nonorganic cucumbers."

Everybody stops and stares at him. The scream was so shocking that even Persian pop star Leila paused during her performance.

"What? She would never," Melody reassures him, turning her attention to Mary, who's standing across the pool from us. "Right, Mom? You know Axy is allergic to nonorganic vegetables."

"Axle Joon, this is all organic," Mary reassures him. "Fresh from our vegetable garden."

"No," he says, shaking his head. "It's not. I can *taste* nonorganic. And I promise you, that was *not* organic. My tongue is going numb. I'm going to be ill."

I swear I see a tear well up in Axle's left eye as he rolls his velvet sleeve back down and starts making his way out of the party.

"Axy," Melody says, rushing after him. "It will be okay. Remember what you told me when we did molly at Coachella and it was accidentally laced with meth? Our minds can conquer all toxins."

"You're right, my goddess." He nods, stopping in his tracks. "The mind can conquer all. But you know my stomach is incapable of digesting pesticides."

"I know," she says, giving him a kiss on the forehead. "Do you want to go see Dr. Juniper? Would that make you feel better?"

A sniffly Axle nods yes.

"Okay, sweetie." Melody nods enthusiastically. "Go see Dr. Juniper. Do what you have to do."

Just as she leans in to give him a kiss goodbye, Axle pulls away and screams—just as loudly as he did the first time, maybe even louder now—"NO!"

Melody stares back at him, stunned, before he gently explains, "My lips are tainted. With the pesticides. I can't have them touching your soft, innocent, seducing pillows of heaven." With that, he inhales deeply with his nose pressed to the top of her head, then tearfully walks out.

"Um, I'm sorry, guys," Melody sweetly says as everyone stands staring, trying to process whatever it was that we all just witnessed. "He's just really sensitive."

Everyone, like all two hundred and fifty fancy people at the party, silently stand there for a few seconds too long, unsure of how to react.

Then, out of nowhere, Mona intervenes. "WHAT THE *FUCK* ARE YOU ALL LOOKING AT?" she exclaims, rushing from her spot by Meesha and Bunny over to Melody. "Are your own lives all so boring you have to stand there gaping at her like she's an exhibit at the fucking zoo?! So her fiancé is a freak! Like you people are normal??? Get over it!"

"Well, all right then," Leila says into the microphone, before launching back into her hit song "Boro Oon Ja."

"Come on, Mel," Mona says, wrapping her arm around the sister who she was ignoring, like, twenty minutes ago. "Let's go inside." The sisters head inside Mary's house, Farida, Zadie, and Jasmine following with their cameras as Timmy trails closely behind with his laptop.

And now I'm standing here, awkwardly scanning the crowd for someone I can at least pretend to be talking to, until I spot Matt making his way over toward me. "You hungry?" he asks when he finally reaches me. "Because there is *plenty* of food to be had here."

We make our way over to the Persian food station, where two crystal bowls at the end of the table instantly catch my eye. One contains a reddish soup, another a mashed-up meat and bean puree sitting next to some sangak bread and a smaller bowl of torshee. I immediately recognize it as ab goosht. My mom would make me ab goosht whenever I was feeling sad. It was the ultimate comfort food. She would mix the soup with the puree, add some torshee, tear up a bunch of sangak bread, then bring it to me on the couch, where we'd spend the rest of the night slurping it up while watching old reruns of *The Fresh Prince of Bel-Air*.

Other Persian dishes, like the rices and the kabobs, are easy to come by. Especially in LA. But ab goosht isn't as common. I mean, I'm sure there are some places that serve it, and I just haven't looked hard enough. But for the most part, it's one of those dishes that has to be cooked at home.

"It reminds me of her, too," Matt says, noticing the tear that escaped my eye as I stare at the delicious bowl of soup. "You know she made me ab goosht on our third date?"

"No, you never told me that," I say, letting out a slight sniffle. "She must have really liked you. Ab goosht used to take her *forever* to make, remember?"

"Yep," Matt says with a nod. "She would wake up early if she wanted to have it for dinner that night. It was the only thing she would wake up early for on her days off."

"I didn't expect this part," I tell him. "Like, all the Persian stuff. The Farsi, the Persian food, the music . . . I didn't think about how it would make me feel, being around all this again. It's like when she died that part of me sort of died, too, and now it's slowly coming back to life around me and I don't know how I'm supposed to feel about it."

"What do you mean how you're *supposed* to feel?" Matt asks with a laugh. "What kind of a question is that? How *do* you feel?"

"I don't know," I say, staring down at the soup. "Confused?"

"Then I guess you're supposed to feel confused," Matt says, wrapping an arm around me. "Now, what do you say we have some ab goosht?"

"I . . . I don't know," I say, tentatively staring down at the bowl. "We haven't had it since she died. What if it's too sad?"

"How about I make a bowl and you have a bite?" Matt suggests. "I'll make it teeleet style, just how you like it."

"You guys eating?" Timmy asks, making his way over to us from inside Mary's house. "This stuff smells phenomenal."

"Yep," Matt says, carefully stopping at each bowl to mix it

up for himself just the way my mom would have. "So, according to my late wife, this isn't really the traditional way to eat it. She used to tell me that the construction workers in Tehran would eat it this way. It's called *teeleet*, and basically you just mix everything together with torshee—these pickled vegetables—and sangak bread. You want a bowl?"

"Sure, if you don't mind," Timmy says. "It smells amazing."

"It's really good," I tell him. "It used to be one of my favorite foods."

"Ah, I see." Timmy nods. "One of those cravings you were telling me about?"

"Yeah," I say. "But this one is so weird because I almost forgot about it. It was one of my favorite foods growing up, and I haven't craved it in years."

Matt hands Timmy the first completed bowl, and we nervously watch as he takes his first bite.

"Holy crap!" he exclaims. "This is incredible! Why are more people not talking about this stuff?"

"I don't know, man," Matt says, turning to complete the second bowl. "Now, Jos, what do you say? Want to have some?"

I stare at it nervously, terrified that just a single bite might turn me into the sobbing, blubbering mess of a person I was when I would listen to her voicemail that whole first year after she passed. But also, it smells so good. And I haven't had it in years. I wonder if there's something in Iranian people's genetic coding that just *needs* a hot bowl of ab goosht a couple times a year for the body to function optimally. What if my body is ab goosht *deficient*?!

"Okay, I'll have a bite," I say, taking a spoon and pausing before I dip it into Matt's bowl. "What if it doesn't taste like Mom's?"

"You know what? It probably won't," Matt says. "Hers will always be better. And there's some freedom that comes with accepting that."

"I know my word means nothing here," Timmy says, slurping down the last sip of his already. "But this really is *very* good."

"Fine, I'm going to do it," I say, before turning my attention to Matt. "You're having it, too, right? We're having it together?"

"You know it," he confirms. Then he smiles. "You and I are always in it together."

We clink our spoons together as a sort of cheers and each dig into the soup. I pause for a second as the delicious flavor fills my mouth, and wait for something bad to happen. Like maybe a stroke of lightning will knock me out for treasonously trying someone else's ab goosht. Or maybe, more likely, the familiar taste will spark such emotionally overwhelming memories that I'll keel over in tears. But . . . nothing happens. No tears, no lightning. I'm just standing here eating a soup I always loved, its hearty flavor actually providing the same comfort it did for me when she was alive. I can practically hear Lou's voice in the back of my head: *See? You can eat your mom's favorite dish and it won't kill you!!!!*

"Oh no." Timmy shakes his head. "You hate it."

"Nope," Matt says, a smile breaking out across his face. "I know that look. She likes it."

"Yeah," I say. "It's obviously not as good as hers. But it's pretty dang good. Matt, you mind if I keep this bowl?"

"You've got it," he says, turning around. "I'm actually going to go check out the kabob situation over there. I'll be right back."

"So, how you holding up during your very first Mashad party?" Timmy asks me.

I wonder if I would find Timmy this comforting under any other circumstance. Like, at Valley High, he would just be another boy in my class. I probably wouldn't even register his existence. He *definitely* wouldn't register mine, considering nobody at school does. But something about having a normal boy like him here, in this world with all these terrifyingly glamorous people, immediately puts me at ease.

"Oh, man," I say. "I'm not sure I really know where to begin. Maybe Mona and Melody? I didn't expect Mona to ice Melody out forever, but I thought their fight would maybe last more than twenty-four hours."

"Nah," he says with a shrug. "When push comes to shove, she's always gonna have her sister's back. They're all like that. Very loyal."

"That's nice," I say, wondering if they'd ever show that kind of loyalty to me. Not that I expect it from them. Lou has my back, and, trust me, that's *more* than enough. I just . . . I don't know. I know I'm biologically their sister, and I know they've all been welcoming so far (well, except for Meesha), but I can't help but wonder how they *really* feel about me.

"How about Axle?" Timmy asks. "Quite the character, huh?"

"Yeah," I say. "To say the absolute least. I don't really . . ."

"Get it?" Timmy finishes my sentence. "I know. Same. Sometimes I feel like I'm living in a parallel universe. You know that guy was named *People*'s sexiest man alive last year?"

"What?!" I exclaim. "I guess my best friend, Lou, thought he was really hot. And it's not that he's not. It's just . . . well, his personality."

"Yep, his personality is definitely . . . something," Timmy says. "The first six months of knowing him I couldn't tell if he was doing a bit or if this is actually what he's really like."

"It does really feel like he's doing a bit," I say. "Honestly, he reminds of the lead in this weird British mockumentary I love about an eighties rock band."

Timmy just looks at me for a second, his eyes wide. "You're not talking about *Island Rock*, are you?"

Now my eyes are wide. I've never met another human who's seen the three-hour-long comedy about a group of British has-been rock stars who form their own band after getting stranded on a remote island together.

"You've seen *Island Rock*?! Nobody has seen *Island Rock*. I'm always trying to get Louise to watch it with me, and she refuses. She says she 'hates' old movies. And I'm like, it's not even that old!"

"I know," Timmy agrees. "I have the same issue with my brother."

"Well, their loss," I say. "*Island Rock* rules. I've probably seen it, like, two hundred—"

"Josie!" Scott Sanderson, the Yay! Network CEO, jumps into our conversation before I can finish. "I just met your dad earlier. What a great man. Did he leave already? We were cut off in conversation, and I was so enjoying hearing his stories about the club."

"Oh no. He just went to get some kabob," I say, gesturing to where he's standing in line. "He'll be back here in a minute."

"Ah, well, I will wait for his return," Scott says, before gesturing to Timmy standing by my side. "And I see you've met my son!"

"Hey, Dad," Timmy says nonchalantly.

"Wait, what?" I ask, before I can think better of it. "You're . . . his . . . what?"

"Yes," Scott says with a laugh. "Believe it or not, he's my son. How else do you think this knucklehead with *nothing* on his résumé scored a PA job on the most popular show in reality television history as a nineteen-year-old fresh out of high school?"

"Thanks, Dad," Timmy retorts sarcastically. "Really appreciate the support."

"So . . . you guys . . . the two of you . . . Timmy, you're . . . ?" I say, my brain apparently still not capable of processing what these people are telling me.

"His son?" Timmy asks. "Yeah, believe me. I often find myself being just as shocked as you are."

I guess that explains the whole Mary hiring this normal-looking goofball thing. Because he's *not* normal at all. He's one of them. I'm so dumb. He's just a nineteen-year-old PA, and he knew all those intimate details about Ali. It's not like he's been working with them for decades. Obviously, he had to be

intimately involved with them. How did I not catch that?????
Why on Earth would I just *assume* he's like me? Nobody in
this absurd world is like me.

"Hey," Scott says, putting his arm around his son. "I tell
you, this kid has *no* family pride. Did he even tell you about
Pete? He never talks about Pete—his own brother! A famous
basketball *sensation* . . ."

"Okay." Timmy rolls his eyes. "*Sensation* is an exagger-
ation."

"I bet you didn't even mention your brother once," Scott
retorts. "Did he even mention him, Josie? Did he mention *any*
of his family members?"

My brain is whizzing too fast for me to formulate a
response, but it doesn't seem to matter because Scott is
already pulling out his phone and showing me a series of
family photos. There's a shot of the four of them. Scott, his
wife and GRAMMY AWARD–WINNING singer Susan
Sanderson, Timmy, and Timmy's PRO ATHLETE brother,
Pete, all on a yacht in the South of France a couple summers
ago. A childhood picture of them at Christmas dinner with the
Mashads, my birth father included. A picture of them skiing
in Switzerland last winter. A picture of them and the Mashads
at a Fourth of July barbecue at their place in East Hampton.

Timmy is, without a doubt, one of *them*. Not just one of
them, but maybe even more fabulous than them. His dad *made*
half the people at this party. His mom is a singing legend—*my*
mom used to have every single one of her albums on vinyl. But
his brother is the one I can't stop staring at in all these pictures.

"I know you mentioned he's a basketball player, but would I

know Pete from anywhere else? Like, does he do commercials or something?" I ask as Scott swipes through what must be the fiftieth photo of his family on a lavish vacation, this time riding camels in Morocco. "He looks *so* familiar."

"Well, I wouldn't say he's got any major brand deals yet, but if you follow basketball, you have definitely seen him on TV," he says, pulling up an album on his phone entitled *Petey B-BALL*. "He just got drafted by the NBA last year. He's playing for the Warriors. We're really proud. That's where his mom is today, actually. Over in San Francisco helping him move into his new place."

Is that where I recognize him from? From watching the game with Meesha and Melody last night? This was clearly the Pete Meesha wanted to watch for. But that can't be it. I was hardly paying attention to that game at all.

Scott continues to scroll through the hundreds of photos of him on the court, finally showing me a shot taken from behind as Pete scores a slam dunk.

Oh my gosh. The tattoos on his shoulders. Everything clicks into place as I look over to Meesha, who's been watching my conversation with Scott like a hawk.

I know exactly where I recognize him from.

Just as I'm about to faint right into Mary's infinity pool from this absolute overload of new information, Melody borrows the microphone from Leila to make an announcement.

"Hi, everyone," she says, her sweet voice booming through the giant yard. "First off, I just wanted to thank you all for being here. My sister Mona and I were just talking about our dad. You know, this day was his favorite. It meant the world to him that one day a year we could all get together here and celebrate the culture he loved so much. This year, we've had a particularly special reminder of our dad, as our sister Josie has made her way into our lives. She's right there, standing by Uncle Scott and Timmy. Josie, can you give everyone a wave?"

Uncle Scott?! TIMMY IS BASICALLY FAMILY TO THESE PEOPLE, which means Pete is basically family to Meesha?!

"Josie?" Melody repeats into the microphone. "A wave?"

I close my eyes tight as every eyeball and camera in the yard turns toward me and jerk one flailing arm up in the air.

"Nailed it," Timmy whispers with a laugh, giving me a pat on my sweat-drenched back. Normally that would make me laugh, but I still haven't fully swallowed the he's-bona-fide-Hollywood-royalty-and-also-the-little-brother-of-the-extremely-close-family-friend-Meesha-is-having-a-super-secret-affair-with pill.

"Anyway," Melody continues. "Josie, we all want you to know how grateful we are to finally have you in our lives. I'm so happy we could fulfill one of Dad's greatest desires—for *all* of his girls to be sisters. So I thought today, on his favorite day, in front of so many of his favorite people, I'd ask . . . will you do me the honor of being a bridesmaid at my wedding alongside Meesha and Mona?"

Chapter 16

I'm so excited to be with Lou, I could just burst. We were supposed to have a school-night sleepover last night to catch up, but it was her "one-week official" anniversary with Grant, and he wanted to celebrate. After my conversation with Mona, I realized maybe I was actually a little resentful of Lou's new relationship. But that ends now. Lou has always been my biggest cheerleader; the least I can do is return the favor.

So I told Lou I was cool with it. Besides, I had a ton of homework to catch up on after having spent the entire weekend in Mashad World.

But now it's lunchtime, which means we finally have a full forty-five minutes of uninterrupted hang time.

"SHUT UP," Lou practically yells as we make our way through the cafeteria line. "Josie Farrah Lawrence. You cannot be messing with me right now."

"I'm not!" I exclaim. "I'm dead serious. Melody asked me to be a bridesmaid in front of everyone—it was mortifying. I obviously said yes, because how could anyone not when someone asks you something like that in front of, like, half of Hollywood? Then afterward she invited Matt. And I figured I would ask if you could come. Mary said no, but Melody is just literally the world's nicest human. She insisted it's her wedding, and any friend of mine is a friend of hers. So . . . we're both invited, with plus-ones."

"Holy shit." Lou shakes her head as we inch our way to the front of the line. "Holy freaking shit. You're telling me we're going to be at Melody Mashad's wedding to literally the sexiest man alive, Axle Wilder?! Oh my God. What do I even *wear*?"

She pauses for a second, seriously considering her own question.

"I feel like I should make something myself, right?" she asks. Before I can respond she continues, her tone more hushed this time. "No. Who am I kidding? I've made *one* outfit. I'm not ready to be making clothes that, like, every single iconic name in fashion is going to see. I'll go with something simple. Maybe a chic slip."

"Are you kidding?" I ask. "Lou, look at yourself right now. Your outfits always kill it. There's a reason you're literally getting Best Dressed in our yearbook."

Lou nervously bites her lip as she looks down at the suede camel-colored micro skirt she's paired with a fitted black top, chunky loafers, and a matching oversized camel suede coat.

"Getting Best Dressed in a public high school yearbook is nothing compared to an A-list event. But you're right. I'll figure something out. Okay, moving on from my fashion emergency, when is it? Oh my God. Oh my *God*. And we get plus-ones? I can't wait to tell Grant. He is going to freak."

"It's the week before prom. And you *cannot* tell Grant until after school. We can't risk anyone hearing! Plus, he has to sign this NDA before you can even tell him about it," I say as I rifle through my old Kirkland-brand backpack to find the sheet of paper Timmy gave me before I left the party.

"Of course, of course." Lou aggressively nods as she shoves the paper into the vintage Louis Vuitton book bag she saved eight years' worth of birthday money to buy. "Ah! This means I get to tell him about you. Honestly, it's been *so* hard keeping a secret from him. We're just so close, you know?"

"Yeah, totally," I say, giving my best go at my new role as Supportive Best Friend. "You guys really have something special."

"We really do," Lou says, smiling to herself for a minute before adding, "Anyway, who are you going to take as *your* plus-one? Why don't you go with Timmy?"

"Timmy is most definitely also invited, so I'm not sure that counts as a plus-one," I note as I plop a scoop of mashed potatoes onto my lunch tray. "Not to mention the fact that, even if he weren't, I'm not sure the son of the two most powerful humans in maybe the entire world would be dying to be my date to anything."

"I blame myself for the Timmy snafu." Louise sighs as she tosses a few chicken fingers onto her plate. "I should have included him on the study guide. I just didn't know he worked on the show! You know, there are, like, Instagram fan pages dedicated to him. They call him the hashtag NormalSanderson. There are girls who would *kill* to date him, just to get in with his family. But no one can even track him. I mean, to be fair, the guy does keep an extremely low profile. No social media, barely anything about him online. Only reason people know what he looks like is when his family or the Mashads post group pictures that he happens to be in. But the rest of his family is, like, insanely A-list. You know, his dad was, like, your birth dad's best, best, best friend. Kind of like me and you, if we were superpowerful Hollywood men."

"Oh, trust me," I say. "I know. They literally call him Uncle Scott! I saw the hundreds of childhood pictures of their families on five-star vacations together."

"I guess that makes it kind of sweet that Meesha and Pete have something going on," Lou muses. "Pete really is so hot. Wow, I can't wait to see him in person at the wedding. Oh my God. I'm sorry, Jos. I'm trying my best to play it cool, but I truly can't get over this. *We* are going to be at Melody Mashad's top-secret wedding. And I get to bring Grant! The hottest A-list event of the decade with my best friend *and* the love of my life. I just can't believe it. It's like a dream come true and a half."

"I know." I smile. "I thought you'd be excited. That's why I asked if you could come! Well, that and the fact that I'd probably die of a nervous breakdown there without you."

"Oh, don't you worry. There will be no nervous breakdowns on my watch," she reassures me. "Wait, so do you have to do anything as a bridesmaid? What is she having you wear?!"

I take a deep breath. "I can't believe this is a real sentence that's about to come out of my mouth," I tell Lou. "But she wants me to fly to Paris with her next weekend for her final wedding dress fitting."

Louise sets her lunch down and pauses, holding the entire lunch line up.

"You're going to *Paris* next weekend?!" she squeals as much as she can while still whispering. "*How* is this not the first thing you mentioned?!"

I look around. Nobody seems to have heard or noticed, but I'm still panicked. "Can you not stop the entire lunch line to discuss this?" I whisper back as I push her along. "The last thing we need is people at school getting suspicious."

"Fine," Lou says, resuming her pace. "But seriously. Why would you not tell me this immediately?"

"Maybe because I was hoping that if I didn't say the words out loud, it wouldn't actually have to happen," I say, nervous beads of sweat dripping down my forehead. I lower my voice as much as I physically can before adding in Lou's ear, "You know I don't like flying. And Melody was insisting we take her private plane, which is extra terrifying."

I raise my voice back to a normal level and continue, "Did you know they have two hundred times the fatality rate of commercial airliners? Not to mention the fact that they are *destroying* our planet."

"Yep," Lou says. "I am *very* familiar with your stance on private planes. You dragged me to that five-person protest outside Van Nuys Airport, remember?"

"Oh yeah," I say. "Well, anyway, I tried to get out of this trip a few ways. First, I tried telling her I had school. But then

I remembered we have a teacher conference day next Friday. So then I just told her I'm not comfortable flying private."

"You *would* tell a Mashad you're not comfortable flying private," Lou whispers with a laugh. "For someone so terrified of everything, you really have some guts every once in a while. How did Melody react?"

"She's too nice," I say. "She just said she totally understands and had her assistant buy out the entire first-class cabin on the earliest Delta flight to Paris next Friday morning. So now I'm stuck."

"Yep," Lou says. "There's no getting out of this. But it's *Paris.* You've never even left the country! This is going to be amazing. Who else is going?"

I look around cautiously before answering her question. Seems like my practically near-invisible social status at school is coming in handy for once. Not one person in line is even remotely paying attention to us.

"I think it's just going to be me, Melody, Axle, Mary, and some of the crew," I quietly tell Lou. "Mona and Meesha are both going to be at Coachella, since Bunny is headlining."

"Kind of a blessing you don't have to deal with Meesha in Paris, right?" Louise says.

"Definitely," I say. "The girl might be the scariest person I've ever met."

"It's weird," Lou says. "You'd think she'd be extra nice to you if she wanted you to keep this huge secret she has."

"I think the approach she's going for is more to terrify me out of ever mentioning it," I say, grabbing a chocolate chip cookie before we check out. "And, I have to say, it is definitely working. Not that I would have said anything in the first place. It's her business! But whatever. I just can't believe Timmy is Pete's *brother*. He seemed so . . . normal?"

"I feel like Timmy is into you," Lou says as she gives the lunch lady her student ID card to check out. I resist the urge to completely laugh in her face. Is she for real right now?

"Louise," I say once I've checked out with the other lunch lady. "There is truly no possible way he has even the slightest interest in me. It would be more likely that Isaac stops me right here in the middle of the cafeteria and starts making out with me. . . . And speaking of Isaac, you know, if he's single, I was thinking maybe I could ask him to come with me to the wedding? Even if he's not! Maybe I could just ask him as, like, friends?"

"Josie, you're literally the smartest person I know," Lou says, rolling her eyes. "How can you be so stupid when it comes to boys? Isaac. Is. A. Jerk. But *Timmy*. Timmy sounds like a nice guy who actually likes you! This seems like an obvious choice."

"Lou, are you kidding? Stop pretending like Timmy is just the sweet boy next door in a nineties rom-com." I lead the way toward our go-to table in the annex. "You said it yourself. The guy has FAN PAGES on Instagram. His family is 'insanely A-list'—*your* words—"

"Um, actually," Lou interrupts, her voice uncharacteristically timid. "Would you mind if today we sat with Grant and his friends?"

"What?" I ask, genuinely stunned. "Like, at the popular table? With Isaac? And Genevieve? And her minions?"

"Well, yeah," Lou says. "Grant just thought, you know, now that we're official, it's sort of weird for us not to be eating at the same lunch table. He obviously invited you, too! Like, for real. I can show you the text."

"It's fine. I believe you," I lie. "Can he not just sit with us in the annex?"

"Well, he would," Lou says. "But, since we're going to pre-prom with his crew, I thought maybe it would be good for us to hang with them a bit. You know, so it's not awkward."

"Oh," I say. "Um, well, okay."

"Aww, you guys," Genevieve says as we place our trays down at the table I've spent the last four years of high school avoiding like the bubonic plague. "Look! Chewy and her slutty little sidekick thought they'd sit with the cool kids for a day."

"Genevieve, you are the human equivalent of the poop stain that doesn't wash out of the toilet no matter how many times you flush," Louise fires back.

"Remind me who you are again?" Genevieve asks. "Oh yeah. That's right. The whore who managed to sleep her way up to the top of the social ladder."

"What is this, 2002? Who still slut shames?" Lou rolls her eyes, turning her attention to Grant, who's been too busy talking about sports stuff with Isaac and the other guys to notice Genevieve attempting to verbally decimate his girlfriend. "Hi, babe."

"Hi, babe," he parrots back. "How you doin'?"

The two start catching up on their days, and Lou tries to

include me in the conversation as much as she can, but there's only so much she can do when Grant pretty obviously seems like he has no interest in talking to me. It's okay, though. I get it. They're a couple. That only leaves room for two. Grant wanted to date Lou, not me. So I try to focus on my fried chicken and mashed potatoes as I let them chat.

I spot Alicia Saraki sitting across the table next to Genevieve. "So, uh, Alicia," I try. "You have any ideas for promoting next week's clothing drive?"

"Yeah, I have a few," she says, barely making eye contact with me before turning back to gossip with Genevieve and her crew.

All right, well, I guess I can say I *tried* to bond with Grant's friends. Isaac is sitting on the other side of the table chatting with Oliver Blair, so I can't even distract myself by gazing into his gorgeous hazel eyes. No, all I have to keep me company is the quickly diminishing plate of cafeteria food. Honestly, the invisibility is kind of nice. Especially after this weekend. It's kind of meditative. I just have a chance to sit here and be me, with no camera shoved in my face.

I'm swirling the food around on my plate, trying to avoid taking the last bite and leaving myself with nothing to focus my attention on when my phone buzzes with a text from a 310 number I don't have stored.

The text is a *Vulture* article announcing AXLE WILDER COMES OUT WITH NEW PODCAST: "HOW TO BE LIKE ME." Then, almost immediately after, my phone buzzes again with a GIF of Sid Slasher, Axle's ridiculous doppelgänger from *Island Rock*, captioned with his best line from the movie: *What the world needs is more of . . . me.*

I burst out laughing a little too loudly, but it doesn't matter because nobody even notices I'm sitting at this table. Before I can craft a response, my phone lights up with a third text:

It's Timmy Sanderson, btw, hope you don't mind I got your number from Mary.

Then another:

Well, first I tried texting your number on the call sheet, but after two bounced back texts I realized it was your home phone number . . . you should probably get that updated.

I didn't expect it to, but my heart does a little cartwheel as I see my phone immediately replace his number at the top with Maybe: Timmy Sanderson.

Haha, sounds like you went to great lengths.

I send the text, then quickly change his contact name to Dad's Friend Bob in case anyone catches a glimpse of my phone.

So weird coincidence but . . . there's an Island Rock cover band playing a concert next Wednesday and I've got two tickets. I figured you might be the only other person on Earth down to join me?

I stare at his text for a beat. Over a day ago this would have been no big deal. Just an invite from my pal Timmy. But now Timmy is no longer my pal Timmy. Timmy is Timmy *Sanderson*, bona fide Hollywood royalty, casually inviting me to hang on a school night.

"Lou!" I whisper-yell, giving her a light nudge under the table. "Look at this text."

Lou pauses her conversation with Grant to look down at my phone.

"Matt has a friend named Bob?" she asks. "Ew, wait. Why is Matt's friend asking you out?"

"It's not actually my dad's friend Bob," I tell her. "It's a cover name I made up on the spot. It's Timmy. And he's not asking me *out*. He just wants to bring me because we both love *Island Rock*."

"Why wouldn't you just change his name to Timmy with a different last name? Like Timmy Smith? That way people won't look over your shoulder and think you're creepily texting with your dad's friend."

"Oh, that's a good call," I say, quickly changing the contact name. "So, what do you think? Should I go?"

Before she can reply, another text from Timmy comes in:

I totally get if you're not up for it. I know we have to leave for Paris that Friday—no worries if you'll be too stressed!

"Wait—*we* have to leave for Paris," Lou quietly says, continuing to read my texts. "As in he's going to be there, too!"

"I guess," I say with a shrug, though I would be lying if I said part of me hadn't been hoping he would. I lower my voice as much as humanly possible, then ask, "But what do I do about this? You know an *Island Rock* cover band is, like, the most up-my-alley event possibly ever. But this whole Sanderson deal makes things so weird! You know, Scott Sanderson is technically my boss. Do you think it's an HR violation if I hang out with his son outside of work?"

"Do *not* overcomplicate this," she whispers back. "Josie, it's nothing short of a miracle that you found a guy our age who has also seen that godforsaken movie. Let alone enjoys it. You have to go on this date!"

"Why do you keep calling it a date?" I ask. "He just asked me as a friend."

Lou grabs my phone and shows it to Grant, who's heatedly debating something football-related with his friends.

"Babe," she says. "What do you think this text means?"

"Did someone ask you on a *date*?!" Grant asks. "Who is he? I'll kill him!"

"Oh my God, babe," Lou says with a giggle. "Chill. Nobody asked me on a date. Someone texted this to Josie. And she is swearing it's not a date."

"Nah, that's definitely a date," Grant says, offering me a fist. "Nice, Jos! Pound it."

"It's *not* a date," I tell them, ignoring his pound and taking my phone back. "He just couldn't think of anyone else who would want to go."

I look over to see if Isaac is paying attention to this debate about my suddenly interesting love life, but no. Genevieve has slipped onto his lap and is covering his face in disgusting little kisses. I resist the urge to puke right onto the lunch table.

"Okay, well, date or not, I think you should go," Lou tells me, her eyes catching the same repulsive interaction.

"You're *sure* I'm not in over my head here?" I ask, lowering my voice to a whisper again. "Even though he's—"

"I'm sure," she says, cutting me off. "Do you need me to send the text for you?"

"Sort of," I say, handing her my phone but snatching it back as soon as I see her typing Down! XX.

"XX? Who texts like that?!" I ask, deleting what she wrote and replacing it with a simple I'm in!

"I dunno," she says with a shrug. "I heard British people use it in all their texts and I thought it might make you look cool and worldly."

"He would literally think I was abducted by British aliens," I begin to tell her, but it's no use. Her attention is already back on Grant.

Timmy responds immediately:

Awesome! Not to be creepy, but I already have your address from work. So just be ready outside around 6:15? I'll pick ya up.

I agree, and we spend the rest of the lunch period ping-pong texting each other back and forth until, finally, the bell rings and Lou turns her attention back over to me. "So, Jos," she says. "Grant and I were thinking maybe we'd go prom shopping soon? You in?"

My heart sinks as I remember I promised Farida and my sisters we could devote an entire episode to shopping for my prom dress. How could I have forgotten to warn Lou?

"Oh," I say. "Thanks, Lou. I actually think I have to go with—"

I stop myself short, realizing all these people I don't trust might be able to hear me.

"Them," Lou says, immediately understanding. "Got it."

"Yeah," I say. "You don't mind, right? I thought, if anything, it would be nicer for you guys to be just the two of you."

"Oh! No," Lou says. "Of course not. I just assumed we'd go together, since that's what we've done for every other dance. But it's not like that was a tradition set in stone."

"Yeah," I say. "Right. And we're still, like, getting ready together and stuff."

"Of course," she says, her voice sounding strained. "Obviously, it's good you're spending time with them. I'm happy for you. And, yeah, I'm sure it would have been boring for you to watch Grant changing tuxes anyway."

"Right," I say, forcing a smile. "Well, not *right*. Everything is fun if we're together. But you know what I mean."

"Yeah," she says. "Totally . . . Well, I've gotta get to Spanish."

"And I'm headed to chem," I say. "Opposite directions."

"Yep," she says, standing there a second longer. "So . . . I guess we should get going or we're gonna be late."

And with that, Lou heads downstairs toward Spanish with Grant, and I head upstairs alone toward AP Chem.

Chapter 17

"Uh, Jos," Matt says, knocking on my bedroom door. "I think your date is here."

"First of all, it's not a date," I tell him as I make my way out into the living room, willfully ignoring a text I just got from Mona asking why I didn't tell her about my "date" with Timmy. "Second, are you sure? Timmy isn't supposed to be here until six fifteen."

"Yep," Matt says, pointing toward the street outside our living room window. "I mean, that's gotta be him, right?"

My eyes follow Matt's index finger until I see exactly what he's talking about. *Oh. My. Gosh.* Yep. Timmy's a Sanderson, all right.

"I'm sorry about the car," Timmy says, his face bright red as I strap into the plush white leather seat of his Rolls-Royce. "I bought myself a used Toyota Camry this year with my money from the show, and it keeps breaking down."

"Honestly, I was a little weirded out when I saw it," I admit. "But I can't lie. This car is pretty sweet. I can't believe your dad just casually drives this around. Like, I'm pretty sure I just saw a shooting star," I say, looking up at the dozens of little lights made to look like a celestial constellation in the ceiling.

"Me neither," Timmy says. "But, alas, he does. Sometimes I wonder if we have anything in common at all."

I stare at him, confused. Is this, like, a weird rich person rebellion? Pretending you don't enjoy stuff like this? I typically could not care less about fancy things, but even I must admit this car is like heaven on wheels.

"Come on," I say. "You're telling me you don't think this car is incredibly cool?"

"Honestly? I like my Camry better," Timmy says. "The stars are distracting! It's a safety hazard!"

"I could see that," I concede, my heart rate picking up speed as I envision a shooting star–induced car crash. "Is there a way to turn them off?"

"One step ahead of you," Timmy says, gradually decreasing the brightness of the stars until they're off completely. "It's better this way, right? Feels *almost* like a normal car."

"Almost," I say with a laugh, rubbing my hand against the supple leather seat. "But maybe not quite."

"Wait," Timmy says, looking over at me as we pause at a red light. "I can't believe I didn't notice your outfit earlier. Is that . . ."

"An exact replica of Sid Slasher's studded Hawaiian shirt from the 'sensual luau' scene?" I ask, thrilled he noticed. "Yep."

A proud smile makes its way across my face. Lou tried her best to convince me to wear something *cuter*, but I knew this was really the only option for tonight.

"No way!" Timmy exclaims. "How did you even find that?!"

"I knew I needed a good Sid outfit when you invited me, so found this on Etsy earlier this week," I tell him. "There were a bunch of vendors who sold replicas, but one of them was based in LA and got it to me in twenty-four hours. All for twenty bucks. Can you believe it?"

"No way," he says, still staring at me dumbfounded. "That is the greatest deal of all time."

"Thanks," I say, happy I trusted my gut on this. I *knew* he would get it. "Do you think anyone else there will be dressed up? I have the YouTube clip of the scene queued up on my phone just in case anyone doesn't remember."

Timmy laughs. "I love the preparedness. And, as much as things totally get *way* funnier when you explain them with a YouTube clip, I have a feeling this might be the one place on Earth where every single person instantly gets what you were going for."

When we enter the tiny venue, I realize Timmy was right. There are at least ten other people here dressed in the same outfit as me, and dozens in some of Sid's other iconic looks— including a wide array of feather-trimmed robes thrown over colorful silk sets, and even a few of Sid's signature too-tight bedazzled Speedos that would make me uncomfortable in almost any other setting.

Timmy gestures to his totally normal outfit of jeans and a hoodie.

"This is wild," I say. "There have to be, like, fifty people here. I can't believe there are fifty other people who have seen *Island Rock* in the greater Los Angeles area."

"I know," Timmy agrees, looking around the crowd. "We've found our people."

I smile. "I guess we have."

"Man," he whispers to me as we make our way over to the bar. "I feel like a loser dressed like this."

"No," I say. "You're a good foil."

"Huh?"

"You know, a foil," I tell him. "Like God and Satan. One only packs the desired punch when juxtaposed next to the other."

"Um, am I supposed to be Satan in this example?!" Timmy exclaims. "I take *serious* offense to that."

"No," I say with a laugh. "Well, yes, I guess technically in that example one of us would have to be Satan, and it would *not* be the one dressed in the fantastic costume. But, in this case, your normal outfit is just highlighting how *not* normal the rest of us are. And, honestly, none of our outfits would be as funny if there wasn't one person here dressed normally."

"If you think about it," Timmy muses, "the fact that I'm *not* in costume might make me the funniest person here. Like, in the outside world, this would be a normal outfit. But here, *I'm* the weird one."

"Honestly, that's a good point," I agree. "This isn't just a hoodie and jeans. It's a brave comedic choice."

"Thanks," Timmy says with a smirk. "That's exactly what I was going for."

I follow as Timmy finds a small open spot by the bar in the corner of the room, which has been decorated to look like an exact replica of the makeshift bar they create in the movie.

Wait. Does he think we're going to drink? I hope *he* isn't thinking of drinking. He's driving! And I obviously can't drive us—after my mom's accident, I just never learned.

"Uh, Timmy?" I ask, mentally calculating how much an Uber from this venue in Culver City back to my place in Van Nuys would cost. "I, um . . . I actually don't drink."

"Neither do I," Timmy casually replies, pointing to a frozen white drink slushing around behind the bar. "I just saw they had a virgin piña colada, and I thought it would be fun to get in the spirit. You want anything?"

"Oh, awesome," I say, my eyes shifting up to a frozen pink drink next to the white one. "How about that one? The frozen virgin daiquiri?"

"*Great* choice," Timmy says, ordering both of our drinks.

"Here," I say, pulling cash out of my pocket. "This should be enough to cover mine."

"No, I invited you!" Timmy insists. "If you didn't come, I would be stuck here alone. The least I can do is get our drinks."

"Okay, fine," I acquiesce. "But only if you let me treat you to a pizza or something after this. Maybe we could pop by CPK? Matt would love to hang with us after his shift."

"Deal," Timmy says. Then he adds, with an eyebrow raised, "Although I'm pretty sure you're entitled to a family discount there. Is that really a fair trade-off?"

"Oh, there is *no* such thing," I tell him. "The manager Gemma is a real stickler about that stuff. Sometimes Matt covers my bill, but I usually pay full price."

"All right," Timmy agrees, sliding me my strawberry drink

as he takes the first sip of his. "If that's *really* true, I think we've got ourselves a deal."

Splitting bills evenly and fairly and topping the evening off with a hang sesh with my dad? *So* not a date. I quickly send the update to Mona and Lou under the bar. A triumphant smile creeps up on my face when Lou texts back:

Hanging with Matt? Okay, you might be right. Def not getting date vibes

Then, five seconds later, Mona texts:

Huh. Weird. I was at the Sandersons earlier today and he tried on THREE different outfits for tonight. Maybe Timmy is just a low-key diva 💁

I take another look at Timmy's jeans and hoodie, suppressing a smile as I try to imagine him meticulously selecting the perfect outfit for tonight.

"Did you notice these drink glasses are exact replicas of the ones from *Island Rock*?" Timmy asks, pointing my attention to the curvy contraptions holding our drinks. "They curve in the same way."

"Oh, I fully noticed," I say, taking another sip of my slightly too-sweet drink. "They even have the same fun colorful straws with the disco balls at the ends!"

"I know," Timmy excitedly agrees. "I feel just like Sid's brother, Jeremiah. Well, a sober Jeremiah."

"So, do you never drink?" I ask. "Or are you just not drinking tonight because you're driving?"

"I never drink," Timmy says matter-of-factly. "When I was a freshman in high school, my brother Pete took me to a party, and I had one jungle juice and spent the whole night puking. That was pretty much it for me and alcohol. So what's your deal? Have you never drank before?"

Before I can fill him in on the horrors of Oliver Blair's party, a pretty blond girl dressed as one of Sid's groupies in a neon-green bikini comes up from behind and gives Timmy a tap on the shoulder.

"Uh, excuse me," she sweetly interrupts. "I hope I'm not bothering you. But, um, are you the hashtag NormalSanderson? Pete's brother?"

Oh, wow. So this really is a whole *thing*.

"Ah, no," Timmy says, his face turning bright red. "Think you've, um, got the wrong guy."

I notice large beads of sweat gathering on his forehead, his subpar lying skills on full display.

"Aw," she says with a frown. "You really look *just* like him."

"Yeah, uh, sorry," Timmy says, his eyes now glued to the floor. "But you've got the wrong guy."

"Well, that's a real shame," she says, lifting his chin up so that his eyes meet her piercing blue ones. "Because I have a *huge* crush on the NormalSanderson."

I gulp hard. Should I be doing something here? Like, do I need to step in?! Timmy looks like he's one flirty comment away from a heart attack.

"Well," Timmy says, using his visibly shaky right hand to gently remove her hand from his chin. "Like I said, you've . . . got the wrong guy."

"Okay," the girl says, finally relenting. "I believe you."

"I'm so sorry about that," Timmy says to me as she walks away, his face still so red it could work as a stoplight. "I feel like a jerk lying, but I've tried not lying when stuff like that happens, and trust me, things just get way weirder."

"Well, I could definitely tell lying isn't your strong suit," I say with a laugh. "But it's not mine, either. So no judgment. Do girls . . . just come up to you like that all the time?"

"Not all the time," Timmy says. "But yeah. Every once in a while, I'll get someone coming up to me. Luckily that girl was relatively chill. It only gets *really* bad when someone starts screaming my name, then it draws an actual crowd and becomes a whole god-awful thing."

"I can't imagine," I say, shuddering. "That sounds horrible."

"Right?!" Timmy exclaims. "I hate the attention. But the rest of my family thinks I'm nuts for hating it. Even the Mashad girls don't mind it the way I do. And they have it a billion times worse than my entire family combined."

"I just think it would be so weird to get that sort of attention from *strangers*," I say. "They don't even know you. How could they possibly like you for who you really are?"

"Exactly!" Timmy exclaims, his chicken soup smile breaking across his face. "I feel like you're the only person I've ever talked to who gets what I'm trying to say. My family just thinks I'm being ungrateful. Like it's some sort of perverted blessing that these strangers semi-stalk me no matter how private I desperately try to keep my life."

"I don't get how the rest of them are so comfortable with it," I say. "Especially Mona, Melody, and Meesha. I feel like it would be so overwhelming, with how famous they are."

"Well, to be fair, Meesha complains about the attention sometimes," Timmy admits. "Especially before she came out. She was pretty depressed, and the paparazzi was so insensitive when it came to just giving her some space. And Mona was really down when the media was skewering her after her breakup. It's still happening a lot, actually. You know her ex is engaged to that supermodel Chya? They're always finding super-unflattering pictures of Mona and comparing her to Chya in these awful memes."

"Yeah," I say, realizing even I have seen some of the memes comparing them. "I guess they deal with so much negative attention that the few positive encounters must come as a welcome change of pace."

"I don't even know if the positive attention is that much better, though," Timmy muses. "Take Melody, for example. Yes, she's America's sweetheart. But the pressure to be perfect all the time gets to her. So, no matter the case, they all have to deal with much worse than my few and far between 'fan encounters.'"

"I guess that makes sense. Their level of fame just seems terrifying—and I feel like they just keep getting *more* famous, if anything."

"Josie," Timmy says, a look of genuine concern taking shape

on his face. "You get that you might experience a level of that when the show airs, right? Your face is going to be on those billboards, right there next to theirs."

I know it sounds obvious when he puts it like that, but the comment still catches me off guard. I stare at Timmy for a moment, silently willing my brain to conceptualize the reality of what he's saying. I was so focused on the money and Stanford that I hadn't yet considered what it would be like when the show airs and the world suddenly becomes aware of who I am.

"Honestly," I say, trying my best to imagine my alternate life as a celebrity, "I'm a borderline professional worrier, but the possibility seems so far-fetched it's kind of hard to even fathom it as a real concern. Like, people in my high school barely know who I am."

"I don't want you stressing about it, obviously," Timmy says, flashing me another one of his patented smiles. "Just don't want you blindsided, either."

I consider his point, a mild panic rising as I envision myself getting swarmed by masses of fans. But the vision evaporates almost immediately. I just . . . can't fully see it.

"Here's the thing," I tell Timmy. "I've been in rooms with them. I get the hype. I get why people freak out and fawn over them. But just look at me. I'm not like them. Even if I do one quick stint on the show, there's no world in which someone like me will ever garner the level of intrigue they do. I'm just . . . boring."

"Well, I don't know about *boring*," Timmy says, flashing me a shy smile. "I actually think you're pretty cool."

I'm flattered by the compliment, but I don't buy it. Listen, I'm not confident in many things. But if there's one thing that I am certain about, it's my ability to be forgotten.

"Um, excuse me." The Sid Slasher impersonator interrupts our conversation from where he's standing onstage. "You, over there."

"Oh my God," Timmy whispers. "It's *you*, Josie. He's talking to you."

"No," I whisper back, looking around us. "It can't be me."

"You!" the impersonator exclaims again, this time pointing directly at me. "Your outfit is incredible. What do you say you come join me onstage?"

I look over at Timmy, who stares back at me with his eyebrows raised in excitement.

"No, I can't do it," I whisper, taking a deep breath before blurting, "I was avoiding telling you this because it is a lot to take in, even for an avid *Island Rock* fan. But I was so into the movie that I literally did a rendition of Sid's 'The Me Within Me' at my fifth-grade talent show and, um, it was a disaster. Like, I still have nightmares about it."

"Well?" the Sid impersonator chimes in again. "You coming up here or what?"

Timmy puts his hand on the small of my back, setting off a teeny firework inside me. Wait. What was that? Do I *want* this to be a date? No. Timmy is just my friend. He's just comforting me like any *friend* would. That was just a friendship firework. Those are a thing, right?

"Come on," he insists. "This is a once in a lifetime opportunity to vindicate fifth-grade Josie. I'll come with you."

He flashes me a hopeful smile, and the urge to vomit suddenly feels a little less strong.

"Really?" I ask. "You'd go onstage with me?"

"If it means you'll go up there, then yeah," he says with a shrug. "We've got this."

I'm not one to ever think I've "got" anything. But something about the way Timmy says it makes me feel like maybe I do.

"ALL RIGHT," I yell back at the Sid impersonator as Timmy grabs my hand, another tiny firework going off as he guides us through the crowd toward the stage. "WE'RE IN."

"I cannot believe that just happened," I say, still laughing as we get back in the Rolls-Royce. "We performed my fifth-grade talent show rendition of 'The Me Within Me' onstage with a Sid Slasher impersonator."

"And you got a standing ovation!!!!" Timmy excitedly reminds me. "Can you believe you almost didn't do it?! That would have been a lifelong regret."

"Well, to be fair, if you didn't get up there with me, I would have just stood there frozen," I admit. "So it's all very circumstantial."

"Good point," Timmy nods. "Thank *God* I am such a good interpretive dancer."

"Seriously." I nod solemnly. "And even with your hoodie scrunched up so tight you could barely see!"

Timmy laughs. "Yeah, it was a challenge. But I couldn't risk any viral 'hashtag NormalSandersonTakesTheStage' videos leaking, so figured I might as well cover my face as much as I can."

"Well, you are a *very* talented dancer, either way," I joke, remembering him tripping over himself as he leaped around onstage behind me. "You should quit working on the show and consider taking up dance professionally."

"I'll look into it," Timmy says. "Maybe Pete could hook me up with a spot as a Laker girl."

"Doesn't Pete play for the Warriors?"

"Oh, yeah," Timmy says. "Well, they probably have dancers, too. If you can't tell, I'm not much of a sports guy."

"Yeah, I'm getting that," I say with a laugh, before checking the time. "Shoot, it's eleven."

"Oh no," Timmy says. "Did you have a curfew or something?"

"No, it's just CPK is closed," I say. "It doesn't look like we'll get to see Matt. He's probably passed out on the couch by now."

"Maybe we can go next time we hang out?" Timmy asks. "I really do love CPK. And Matt is awesome."

"Sure," I say, already excited that there's going to be a next time. "Although I'm not sure a night at CPK will top this."

"I don't think anything will top this for as long as we live," Timmy says. "And I think the sooner we accept that the better."

"Agreed."

The two of us sit in comfortable silence until Timmy pulls up to my building.

"Wait," I say as he parks in front of the laundromat in the

strip mall across the street. "If I didn't pay for CPK, that means you got all our drinks and paid for the tickets! Let me at least pay you back for my ticket. How much was it?"

"Don't worry about it," he says. "Honestly? My dad gets free tickets to concerts and stuff all the time. I didn't even pay."

"You sure?" I ask. "I feel bad."

"Don't," Timmy says, unbuckling his seat belt. "If we didn't use these, he would have just thrown them away. If anything, we saved these tickets."

I sit in the car for a few more seconds, not really wanting the night to be over.

"Okay, well, I should probably head up," I finally say. "It's getting late."

"Let me walk you up," Timmy suggests, rushing out of his seat to open my door.

I argue, but he insists, which I will admit is pretty date-like behavior, but also the weather is great tonight and maybe he just wants to get some fresh air.

"Thanks again," I tell him when we reach my front door. "I don't think I'm even exaggerating when I say this might have been one of the best nights of my life."

"Same," Timmy says, his hand resting on the door above me. "See you in Paris?"

I feel him inching closer to me, another series of tiny fireworks exploding inside me as he does.

"Y-yeah," I say. "See you in Paris. I'm really happy you're going to be there."

He leans in closer, a not-so-tiny firework going off as he

reaches down and grabs my hand. Okay, that was not a friend-ship firework. Even I know that.

"Josie, do you mind if I . . ."

Oh my gosh. Is he going to try to kiss me?! And do I *want* him to kiss me?

"Um, I should probably get inside," I say, reflexively pulling my hand away from his. "It's getting late."

Josie Farrah Lawrence, what in the WORLD is wrong with you? You realize you want to kiss a guy for the first time ever, so you pull away like an awkward freak and make up some pathetic excuse to go inside?????

"Oh," he says, his face falling. "Got it! Okay, well. Um, I'll see you Friday."

"See ya," I say, forcing an awkward smile as my heart plum-mets down to my feet. "And, um, thanks again for tonight."

"Of course," he says, flashing me an awkward smile of his own before making his way back down toward his car.

For a millisecond I consider chasing after him, rom-com style. But I know it's too late. I blew it.

Chapter 18

"But *why*?" Lou asks as we weave our way through senior hall on Thursday morning. "I just don't get it. You clearly wanted to kiss him. And he wanted to kiss you. Why would you not just kiss him?"

"I don't know!" I exclaim, the memory making me want to burst into tears. "I just freaked out. You know I've never kissed anyone before. What if I'm like . . . bad at it?"

"Well, you'll never know if you're a bad kisser if you keep *not* kissing," Lou says. "Besides, nobody is great their first time. It's no big deal."

"Maybe it's better Timmy and I are keeping things in the friend zone," I say, trying to convince myself more than anything else. "I mean, yes, he took me out for the best night of my life. And yes. His touch set off fireworks inside me on multiple occasions throughout said night. But Timmy and I have a great friendship. And this whole Mashad World is scary and new for me. Maybe it's for the best I didn't mess with the one stable thing I have in that world."

"Okay." Lou slowly nods as we stop outside my math class. "Then maybe you just give it some air. Don't acknowledge the friend zoning happened and just hope that you didn't bum him out too much to ruin the friendship."

"What???" I ask, horrified. "You think this could be a big enough deal to ruin the friendship?!"

I know I've only known him for less than two weeks, but Timmy somehow already feels like an integral part of my life.

"You never know," Lou says with a shrug. "Remember how weird Brett Farber was when I told him I wouldn't make out with him after Junior Prom?"

"Oh no," I say, remembering Brett's dramatic refusal to be Lou's lab partner ever again. "You don't think Timmy will stop talking to me, do you?"

"I don't know," Lou says. "I'm just trying to mentally prepare you. Boys are weird."

"Maybe I should text him an inside joke or something," I suggest, my heart sinking at the thought of losing him entirely. "Just to make sure he knows I really did have a great time."

"Well, have you thanked him yet?" Lou asks. "Maybe you could send a thank-you text. For such a great night."

"I already thanked him a bunch in person," I tell her. "But you're right. Maybe a text will be good."

"Yeah, perfect," Lou says. "That way we can see how he responds and assess the damage from there."

We stand paused outside Mrs. Lopez's classroom as I write up the text:

Hey, just wanted to say thank you so much again for last night!!!! CPK on me next time, I promise.

"What do you think?" I ask, giving Lou the phone. "Friendly enough to dilute a friend zone?"

Lou squints, carefully scanning the text like it's a forensic file before handing the phone back to me.

"Yep." She nods. "Send it."

"Yo!" Isaac cuts in just as I hit send. "Two of my favorite ladies!"

Lou rolls her eyes dramatically as my heart dissolves into mush.

"Hey, Isaac," I say, quickly shoving my phone in my backpack. "You ready for our quiz?"

"Not really," he admits. "Louise and I were out late last night with the rest of the crew. Where were you, Jos?"

Um . . . did he just imply that I'm part of his *crew*? Any thought of Timmy and the friend zone makes its way into the crawl space of my mind as the rest gets filled with thoughts of Isaac roaming around last night's party hoping to see me.

I'm too busy daydreaming about a mopey Isaac drafting and deleting *Wish you were here* texts to me to say anything before Lou interjects, "Josie was actually too busy to come to the party because she was on a *date.*"

I shoot her a death glare, but she just smiles and shrugs, adding, "Anyway, I'm going to be late to class. But you two have fun catching up."

"So, a date, huh?" Isaac asks as we take our seats in class. "Who's the lucky guy?"

"Oh, you don't know him," I respond, a little too quickly. "He doesn't go here. And, honestly, I'm not even really sure it was a date."

"Well, what did you guys do?" Isaac asks. "Maybe I can help you figure it out."

The thought of my lifelong crush trying to help me figure out a situation with my potential new crush (or friend? Ugh, I don't know) simultaneously thrills and terrifies me. On the one hand, mixing the two makes me feel like the evil adulteress in one of the soaps Lou and I occasionally watch with her grandma. On the other, Isaac *wants* to help me figure this out. . . . Why does he care? Is he jealous???

"We went to a concert together," I tell him, willfully choosing to leave out the whole *it was the best night of my life* detail.

"Sick!" Isaac exclaims. "What concert was it?"

"Uh, have you seen the movie *Island Rock*?"

"No." Isaac frowns, the expression on his face totally confused. "Wait, did you go to a concert or a movie?"

"A concert," I reiterate, suddenly longing for the way Timmy just always knows what I mean. "But there's this movie called *Island Rock* that we both love. And it's about this group of totally ridiculous rock stars. And we went to see a cover band doing a concert as the band they create in the movie."

"Huh," Isaac says, visibly losing interest. "Sort of like *Inception*."

"Uh, yeah . . . sort of."

"And you both were down for this movie concert thing?"

"Yeah," I say, my heart skipping a beat as I feel my phone vibrating against my calf. "One second."

One new message from Timmy. Fast response. That must be a good sign, right??

I quickly slide the text open to find . . . he hearted it. I turn my phone off and on, hoping a refresh might show some follow-up text that might not have come through. But nothing. That's it.

I take a screenshot and quickly send it to Lou, who immediately replies:

Yikes.

Then, a few seconds later:

I told you boys are sensitive!

Then:

At least it was a heart? Thumbs up would be devastating.

Yes. Lou is right. It was a *heart*. Like he literally *hearted* my message. A symbol for love! This is good. We can work with this.

"Miss Josie," Mrs. Lopez announces as she takes her spot in front of the whiteboard. "Put your phone down immediately before I confiscate it."

"Going on weeknight dates with mystery dudes and texting

in class?" Isaac whispers, leaning in so close that I can smell his Axe body spray. "I have to say, I'm liking this new wild Josie."

Was that flirty? That was flirty, right?!?! Did he and Genevieve break up again? Is this *him* low-key building up to asking me on a date? Maybe that's what was missing. He didn't see me as a sexual being, because nobody else saw me as a sexual being. But now that someone else sees me that way, he can, too. Well, not that Timmy sees me as a sexual being. I still don't think it was definitely a date. Maybe the whole friend zone thing was just in my head. Or maybe the heart really was a snub. My heart sinks at the thought of Timmy actually being mad at me. It sinks even further when I remember how badly I actually wanted to kiss him.

We're better as friends, I remind myself. This is for the best.

"Hey, by the way," Isaac adds, his minty-fresh breath sending a literal chill across my desk. "It's cool if I scan some of your notes before the quiz, right?"

"Oh, yeah," I say. "Totally cool."

Chapter 19

I take a deep breath before entering the fancy, rich-people ter-
minal at LAX. *Josie Joonam, chillax,* my mom's voice instructs
in my head. She's right. I need to chill. This will be fine.
Timmy can't *hate* me.

I look down at a text from Lou, who must have telepathi-
cally sensed my terror from miles away:

You will be so fine. Seriously!!!

What if he hates me?

Then honestly he's a pathetic jerk who didn't deserve
your first kiss anyway.

Before I can type back, I feel a friendly pat on the shoulder
and turn to see Timmy standing behind me.

"You ready for Paris?!" he asks. "It's your first time out of
the country, right? *Very* exciting."

I stare at him, confused. Of all the hundreds of possibilities I had played out in my head for how our encounter would be today, I somehow completely forgot to prepare for him being totally . . . fine? If anything, he's being friendlier than ever. Did I make that whole thing up in my head? Maybe he wasn't trying to kiss me. Maybe I just wanted to kiss him.

"Uh, Josie?" he asks, waving a hand in front of my face. "You good?"

"Oh!" I exclaim a little too loudly, his question jolting me out of my head and back into the moment. "Yes. Totally good . . . pal."

Pal? What was that?

Timmy cracks up, my heart turning into a puddle as he flashes me what might be the most comforting grin smiled by any human.

"Here," he says, reaching down to grab my suitcase. "I'll get your bag. Let's head in."

As soon as we make it through the shockingly quick private security screening, Timmy rushes over to meet with Farida, Zadie, and Mary to discuss the logistics of shooting throughout the trip.

"Josie!!!" Melody calls out from where she's snuggled up next to Axle on the other side of the waiting area. "Come here! We're on FaceTime with Mona and Meesh."

"Hi, guys," I say into Melody's phone as I scooch into the seat next to hers. "Are you already at Coachella?"

"Yeah," Mona says as a makeup artist carefully pastes little rhinestones along her cheekbone. "Bunny played at the artists-only pre-show concert last night, and we were backstage for the whole thing. It was nuts. Right, Meesh?"

"Uh-huh," Meesha says as a hairdresser weaves neon-green hair extensions throughout her jet-black locks. "It was dope."

"And Pete came up to surprise us!" Mona exclaims, flipping the camera around to show Pete Sanderson lounging on the sand-colored linen couch behind their glam chairs. "How fun? It's so nice having *one* single friend here with us. Although, Pete, you could step up your wingman game a bit."

"What do you mean?!" Pete asks. "I spent half an hour laying down the groundwork for you and Jake."

"Yeah, but then you left!" Mona fires back, turning her attention back to the phone. "Can you guys believe it? Pete was being so antisocial. He literally had multiple Victoria's Secret Angels hitting on him, but he barely spoke to any of them. Then he wouldn't even go to any after-parties with me. Just went home early with boring old Meesha."

Even over FaceTime, Meesha still manages to shoot me a death glare so petrifying that it rocks me to my core. I don't get it at this point. What does she think I'm going to do? Blab about what I saw in the middle of this casual family chat? Plus, for all I know, that was just a one-time thing. Maybe Pete really did just go home with Meesha platonically. Though something in my gut tells me that's probably not the case.

"One, I'm not boring," Meesha says to Mona. "Two, Pete was tired because he's an athlete. It's normal for athletes to get tired and want some rest. Stop freaking out about it."

"Now it sort of feels like *you're* the one freaking out," Mona retorts. "But whatever."

"Yo!" Pete makes an obvious attempt to change the subject,

taking the phone from Mona. "Axle, we miss ya here, buddy. The king of Coachella."

Axle, who's currently dressed in an emerald-green velvet nightgown and adorned with at least seven different necklaces, deeply sighs, then clasps Melody's hands in his.

"Alas, the king has been dethroned by his beautiful queen," he says, his eyes gazing so deeply into hers that I feel like I should maybe scooch another seat over to give them some space. "The City of Love with my love. As she tries on the gown that she will wear on the day we become forever one. What a journey. What beauty."

"All right, cool, man," Pete says, laughing off the Shakespeare scene that just played out in front of us all. "Hopefully next year! Hey, is my little brother with you guys?"

"Timmy!" Melody calls out, giving Axle a gentle kiss before breaking her face away from his. "Stop talking business for a minute and get over here! Your brother's on the phone!"

"Hey, guys," Timmy says into the phone, taking a seat on the floor by Axle's bedazzled sandal–clad feet. "Pete, I didn't know you were going with them to Coachella. Don't you have, like, games and stuff?"

"Oh, Timothy," Axle says, grazing Timmy's cheek with his hand. "One must never presume to know all."

Timmy starts to look at me, but I quickly divert my eyes down to the floor. There is no way Timmy and I could make eye contact as Axle caresses his cheek in the most Sid Slasher way ever without both bursting out into uncontrollable fits of laughter.

"Glad to see you're paying attention to my 'games and stuff.'" Pete snorts, ignoring Axle. "But no. We finished the regular season as the one seed last week, so our coach is giving us the weekend off until eight seed is decided in the play-in games."

"I have no idea what you just said," Timmy responds, echoing my exact thoughts. "Was that even English?"

"I think it just means he's really good," Mona chimes in, taking the phone back to carefully examine the now-completed constellation of jewels splattered around her face.

"Her words, not mine," Pete says, blushing. "But basically, I have a break until Monday, so Meesh convinced me to fly out."

I notice Meesha's lips curve upward in a shy smile as his face brightens when he mentions her name.

"You have to play again Monday?" Timmy asks, visibly stressing. "Aren't you worried you'll be tired? Or hungover? Doesn't your team depend on you or whatever?"

"You're one to talk," Mona scoffs. "Weren't you out late at a concert with Josie just two nights before this big work trip?"

I gulp hard as both our faces turn increasingly bright shades of red.

"Well, that's not really the same thing at all—" Timmy starts to say before Melody cuts him off.

"Wait, what?!" Melody asks. "How is this the first I'm hearing of this? You guys went on a date?! This is so exciting! I'm already thinking of couple names. Tosie? Jimmy?"

"This does seem like a divine pairing," Axle says, squinting as he waves his arms between Timmy and me. "I sense an energetic alignment between you two."

I open my mouth to speak, but it feels like my throat has been stuffed with cotton balls.

"I know," Mona agrees. "It's, like, low-key incest. But cute, right? They weirdly work."

"I don't think it's *incest*," Meesha jumps in, a bit too passionately. "Yes, we grew up with them, and Dad and Uncle Scott regularly referred to each other as brothers. But we aren't actually related to the Sandersons. There's no blood tie here. Like, obviously, I'm not trying to date Timmy, or Pete, or whatever. But if any of us were to date or even just casually hook up, it wouldn't be *that* scandalous."

"Okay, chill, weirdo," Mona says. "It was just a joke."

"Anyway," Melody continues, ignoring her sister's minor outburst. "Josie, Timmy. We need details on this date!"

"Yes," Axle adds. "Tell us about your blossoming love. There is no story as beautiful, as serene, as magnificent, as genuinely awe-inspiring as a story of love found."

I stare at Timmy, hoping he'll take the lead here.

"Oh, it wasn't a date," Timmy says nonchalantly. "And we're definitely not in love or anything. We just were hanging out as friends. Right, Josie?"

"Right!" I agree, my voice coming out about two octaves too high. "Just two friends hanging out at a very niche concert."

Huh. So I guess it really was all in my head.

"So boring," Mona groans. "I can't believe you guys didn't at least make out."

"Aw," Melody says, her perfectly shaped brows drawing together. "Well, it sounds like you guys have a great friendship. And you know what? Good friends are hard to find. Arguably harder than love!"

"Not all can enjoy the passionate blend of ferociously erotic attraction and deeply intimate camaraderie," Axle says, nodding in agreement. "Some must settle for platonic companionship because they cannot *handle* a love that burns so fiercely."

"Ew," Mona and Meesha both respond in unison.

"Our love is not *gross*," Melody tells her sisters. "It's beautiful and rare. And *so is* a genuine, pure, romance-free friendship like Timmy and Josie's."

"Yep." Timmy nods. "Lucky us, I guess."

I quietly pull up my text thread with Lou and add a message under the picture of the bougie security I sent her five minutes ago:

Timmy confirmed—not a date.

She immediately writes back:

Amazing!!!

Then:

Wait, we're happy about this, right?

I start to type *yes* in response, but then delete it. I was right. Not a date. Just two "lucky" friends hanging out. Exactly what I was hoping for. So why *don't* I feel happy about this?

"Come on, everybody," Mary cuts in, walking over with her eyes still glued to her phone. "Enough chitchat. The car is here. It's time to board."

Chapter 20

After a flight so smooth that Mary legitimately tried to poach the pilot to come work for her own private plane, we land in Paris on Saturday morning to find two Range Rovers with tinted windows waiting fo us outside the plane. The luxe cars swiftly take us straight from the airport to Mary's place, which . . .

According to the call sheet, Mary's "place" is supposed to be an apartment. Obviously, I went into this experience knowing it wouldn't be just *any* apartment. It would be Mary Mashad's apartment. Even Lou warned me that her place is "wild," but, at the end of the day, an apartment is an apartment. It can only be so nice, right?

Wrong.

Mary's apartment is not "just an apartment." It's a ten-bedroom penthouse on Avenue George V, which Mary wasted no time telling me is the *most* prestigious street in Paris. With its grand winding staircase in the foyer, claw-foot bathtubs in every restroom, and delicate crystal chandeliers dangling from all the intricately painted high ceilings, it looks like a piece of history. Like somewhere Marie Antoinette would have hosted a dinner party, which quickly makes sense when I place my backpack on top of a dresser that Mary's housekeeper tells me was purchased directly from the Palace of Versailles.

"Okay," Mary begins as we all sit for brunch around her large antique mahogany dining table. "We must discuss safety. I have spoken to our security team and, as always, Melody, Axle, and I will have two security guards with each of us upon leaving the premises. I've already spoken to the door attendant, and they've ensured there are also going to be four armed security guards protecting the penthouse whenever we are inside, in addition to the two who are here at all hours. Now, Josie. The rest of the crew has grown accustomed to this, so they know the drill. But this will be your first time with security."

"Wait, I need security?" I ask, dipping my buttered bread into the dark orange yoke of the soft-boiled egg Mary's Parisian chef prepared to perfection. "Is that really necessary? Nobody even knows who I am."

"It is imperative," Mary says. "Not just for your own safety, but for ours. There have been two assassination attempts on me. Melody has thousands of stalkers, one of whom got so close to her during a trip to Miami three years ago that he chopped off a lock of her hair."

"Despicable," Axle says, shaking his head vigorously. "I hate that pervert with every fiber of my soul."

"It's okay, Axy," Melody says, giving Axle a reassuring kiss on the head. She explains to me, "It happened when I was promoting my organic hair care line. Some dumb internet article went viral saying my hair is worth more than most Americans' homes. Suddenly there were all these scary people trying to chop my hair off. And one of them actually managed to do it. Luckily, it wasn't the worst possible outcome. Nobody was seriously hurt, and I wound up rocking a cute bob for a bit, but it was just a reminder to beef up our security. Especially when we're out."

"Yes." Mary nods. "Luckily, when we are at home there is enough built-in security on the premises that there is no need for all of this. But it is a completely different story as soon as we leave the gates of our neighborhood. And that applies to anyone who is seen out with us, as well. We have been able to maintain a surprisingly low profile thus far on this trip, and, to keep you as a surprise twist for the show, we are going to try our very best to keep your presence on this trip hidden from the public. But all it takes is one stalker to follow you home after spotting you leaving Delphine's studio with us to put us all at risk."

I feel my body growing increasingly sweaty as I remember the stories Timmy told me about getting swarmed by crowds. This all suddenly feels much more tangible.

Timmy must sense my growing panic, because he flashes me a reassuring smile from across the table.

"The security really isn't that bad," he says between bites of his croque madame. "They're super nice. You'll like them."

"Even if you don't," Mary chimes in, "spending a day with someone you don't like beats being murdered, mugged, or raped, right?"

I gulp. "Yep," I say. "You're right."

Timmy and I talked about what they deal with in terms of public hate and adoration. I saw the exploitation Meesha has to deal with when she was discussing the Zoloft deal. But this? Threats on their *lives*? Creepy stalkers trying to chop their hair off? How is this at all worth it?

When we finish brunch, the rest of the crew leave with Axle and Melody to film as he surprises her with a "day of endless romantic intrigue," leaving Mary and I to just . . . hang out.

"So . . ." I try making conversation from where I'm seated across from her on these admittedly uncomfortable vintage couches. "Should we go out? See the Eiffel Tower or something? You know, this is actually my first time out of the country."

"Josie Joonam, I thought I made it clear during the safety protocol meeting," Mary says, her eyes glued to her iPhone. "We have to keep any possibility of you being spotted with me or the girls to a minimum. As much as I would love this to be a great vacation for you, remember that it's a business trip. We are simply here to shoot an episode."

"Right." I nod, taking a sip of the Sadaf jasmine tea her housekeeper brought us. "My mom used to have this tea every day."

"Most Iranians have this tea every day," Mary says, stifling a yawn before taking a sip of her own. "It's very common."

"So, do you have any other homes?" I ask, noticing the Sadaf talk isn't exactly getting much excitement from her. "This place is awesome."

"You know, I love a good hotel. But eventually, owning

places just became easier in terms of privacy and security and all of that," she says, placing her phone down for the first time since we sat here. "So, domestically, I've got the beach houses in Malibu and Hawaii and the lake house in Tahoe, but Ali and I had those long before the show began. Then, as things picked up with the show, we got a home on Star Island in Miami, a house with a *beautiful* view in San Francisco's Sea Cliff neighborhood, a waterfront estate in East Hampton because Ali just loved it there, a ski lodge in Aspen, even though Mona is really the only one of us who still enjoys skiing, and then Melody, Meesha, and I just purchased neighboring penthouses in Manhattan's TriBeCa. Don't tell Mona, but I purchased one for her, as well. She'll get it on her eighteenth birthday in a few weeks."

"Wow," I say, my jaw hanging so low it might be on the vintage Persian carpet on the floor. "That's, um, a lot of homes."

"Oh, I wasn't finished," she says with a chuckle. "Those were just the domestic properties! Of course, there's this one. Then a beach house in Saint-Tropez, a townhouse in London's Chelsea neighborhood, a villa on Lake Como, a couple of satellite apartments in Tokyo and Dubai, a ski chalet in Switzerland—even though, again, Mona is really the only one of us who still enjoys skiing—and I just went in on a private island with Melody and Axle. The one they'll be getting married on! But that doesn't quite count as a home."

"So which one is your favorite?" I ask, not really sure what else to say. "This one is awesome, but I bet the villa in Lake Como is pretty cool, too."

"They are all lovely," Mary says. "But nothing compares to this. For me, this is as close to home as it gets."

"You mean, like, Iran home?" I ask. "Or LA home?"

"Neither," Mary replies. "Paris will always be its own thing. Just *Paris*. Everywhere wants to be *like* Paris. But nowhere can be Paris but Paris. It's how I feel about our family, sometimes. Hundreds, if not thousands, of other families have tried to do what we did. But nobody can do it at our level. Nobody can be the Mashads but the Mashads."

"Got it," I say, her off-topic tangents reminding me of our chat in Mr. Schwartz's office. "So, uh, why does this feel so much like home for you?"

"When I was growing up in Tehran, my parents and I would come here all the time," she tells me. "It's how I learned to speak French fluently. And why it was so important for me to teach the girls."

I nod, suddenly understanding how Mary and Melody were able to chat with our flight attendants so seamlessly in French on the plane.

"A lot of my parents' friends and family members would send their kids to boarding school in Europe. Switzerland, mostly," Mary continues. "That was common in our circles. But my mother could never bear the idea of sending her babies so far away for so many months. So, instead, we would take family vacations to our favorite place in the world: Paris. My parents owned a place just up the street, a small flat."

"Wow," I say, wondering how Mary's definition of *small* would translate to normal-person speak. "Have you been there since you lost them?"

"I have tried," Mary says. "Farida and I even tried to do an episode with the storyline of me revisiting it, but the asshole who lives there now won't let me anywhere near the place. I even tried buying it from him! He won't sell it to me no matter how much I offer. Had the audacity to call me 'Hollywood trash.'"

"Well, that's rude," I say, incapable of wrapping my mind around the concept of anyone being brave enough to tell Mary Mashad off. "But at least you have this place."

"Yes," she says, looking out the window at her direct view of the Eiffel Tower. "I do love it here. Because, as I said, it feels like home. You see, I can never return to my *actual* home. Well, I could. I have friends who have. Farida's aunty still lives there, and she visits her once a year. But I can't stomach it. That place isn't the home I grew up in. The home I grew up in does not exist anymore. So this is the next best thing."

"I get that," I say, her story reminding me of my mom's similar ones of missing a no-longer-existent home. "Well, the next best thing is still *something*, I guess."

"You know, I was here when it happened," she tells me, clutching her Baccarat crystal teacup. "The revolution. Of course, there were murmurs of it brewing before things really took off. But my father refused to entertain the thought. He insisted that it was just a bunch of crazy fanatics revolting against our Shah—you know my father was good friends with the Shah. Very loyal."

I nod, trying not to dwell on all the not-so-great things I learned about that same Shah in my world history class freshman year.

"So, while many people fled as the revolution was brewing," Mary continues, "my family didn't. I was fifteen when it finally started. My mother was still too anxious to let me go to boarding school, but I had convinced her to let me come to Paris for a monthlong summer camp. I was at camp when an old neighbor called me in hysterics. Everyone was killed. My parents, my siblings. My aunts, my uncles. My grandparents. All our money dead with them."

I've heard dozens of stories like this from my mom about different relatives and friends from Iran. And I've even read some of Mary's own story before. But there's something about hearing it firsthand in the place where she got this devastating news that makes processing it a different experience entirely.

"So what did you do?" I ask, my eyes welling up even though I can tell Mary would not appreciate the display of pity. "Where did you go?"

"I asked my neighbor if I could come home to her house," Mary says. "Khanoom Hashemi. She was a wonderful woman. I loved her. And she loved me too but worried if I came, I would be in the same danger the rest of my family had been in. So I was sent to Los Angeles."

"What?" I ask. "With who? Had you ever even been there before?!"

"I had never set foot in America," she tells me. "But I had an aunt who lived in a small two-bedroom apartment in Westwood. She was a widow, and, after her husband had passed away, she and her daughter moved to America. They had been there for about three years when the revolution happened, and, when she heard about my situation, she offered to take me in."

"Were you scared?" I ask, eyes wide. "I would be terrified."

"Oh, I was petrified," Mary says. "I barely spoke a word of English. And, although they were my family, I barely knew my aunt or cousin. Not to mention the change in lifestyle. I went from having my own bedroom suite, complete with walk-in closet and bathroom in a large home with a full staff there to help my mother with household tasks, to sharing a twin bed with my little cousin while my aunt worked double shifts at the Nordstrom shoe department to make ends meet."

"Were they nice to you? Your aunt and cousin, I mean."

Mary thinks about this for a minute, taking a long sip of her tea, then finally answers. "Yes. They saved me when I had nothing and no one else. They became my surrogate mother and sister. Nice is an understatement. They were everything to me."

"So, where are they now?" I ask. "Do they live near you? Were they at the Nowruz party?"

"They died," Mary says, placing her teacup down. "Both of them."

How is it possible that someone this blessed is also *this* cursed? I think about the pain I felt when I lost my mom. Mary has experienced that ten times over. First her immediate family. Then Ali. Then her aunt and cousin?! How can one person stomach that much loss? Losing one person you love is traumatic enough.

"Oh no," I say. "I'm so sorry. How did they die?"

"Let's not dwell on all of this depressing stuff, Josie Joonam. People live, and then they die. It's how humanity works," Mary says, adjusting the gold *H* on her black leather belt as she gets up. "We should head over to Delphine's studio. Melody will be there any minute now."

Chapter 21

"Delphine, thank you so much again for doing this," Melody is saying, clutching the hands of the tiny French woman with the pin in her mouth, as Mary and I enter the studio. "I cannot believe this is happening. I feel like a princess."

Melody looks stunning. Breathtaking, even. Like, literally. I try to take a deep breath while staring at her and can't. It's like my body inherently knows my grimy, normal-person breath is not worthy of being anywhere near this perfect gown. It looks classic and bridal, but something about it still feels so . . . *Melody*. I can't put my finger on what exactly it is. Maybe it's the tiny flowers adorning the lace. Maybe it's the way the narrow train effortlessly flows behind her. But something about it just perfectly captures her.

"Delphine!" Mary exclaims, rushing over to the designer, who, even in her jeans and boxy white blouse, looks like she could easily grace the cover of *Vogue*. "C'est parfait."

Mary turns her attention to Melody, and I need to squint a little to make it out, but I swear I see a tear make its way down her face before she gives her daughter a big lipstick-staining kiss on the cheek. "Ghorboonet behram," she says, another set of words I haven't heard since my mom died. There's no real direct translation to English, but the phrase is sort of like a combination of *I adore you*, *I would die for you*, and *I will sacrifice myself for you*. Basically, it's like saying *I love you* but on steroids. I know that seems dramatic, but Farsi is kind of a dramatic language. Persian people say it all the time. Especially parents to their kids. "I wish your father could have seen you," Mary tells Melody, her voice cracking. "Me mord." *He would have died*. (In Farsi that's, like, a good thing. Again, dramatic!)

Zadie zooms her camera in on me as I stand awkwardly in the corner of Delphine's ultramodern Paris studio, unsure of what to do with myself during this tender moment. It's not just that it's a beautiful moment between the two of them. Well, of course, it's partially that. But also watching Mary and Melody share a moment I will never get to have with my mom is . . . harder than I expected it to be. I mean, not that my mom and I would have ever shared a moment anywhere close to resembling *this*. Who knows if I'll ever even get married? As of now, odds of that happening are seeming extremely low. But the intimacy. The lipstick-staining kiss on the cheek. The *ghorboonet behram*. That's what I miss so much that it physically hurts sometimes.

"Josie!" Melody shouts from across the room, what I'm now fully convinced is her psychic energy kicking in again. "Come here! You have to meet Delphine.

"Delphine, this is my new sister, Josie, who I was telling you about. Isn't it so special we get to have her here for this?"

Melody says, before turning her attention toward me. "Meesha and Mona were here to help pick this design. Now you get to be here for my final fitting. It's so special. A sister by my side every step of the way."

"Melody, it looks . . . *perfect* doesn't even begin to describe it," I tell her, still stunned. "Delphine, it's so nice to meet you. I can't believe you were able to create this!"

"Merci," Delphine says, her cool demeanor reminding me a bit of Meesha's. "You know, this is my first wedding dress. I don't do bridal, but when I heard Melody Mashad was getting married, I had to offer. She has been my muse for so many years. And my *friend*. One of the most wonderful souls. I wanted to make a dress that captured her spirit."

"And we are honored," Mary says, before looking my Stanford sweatshirt and jeans up and down. "Josie Joonam, I'm not sure how much you know about fashion, but Delphine is one of the absolute greatest designers of our time. She started her career designing for Chanel, then Celine, and finally launched her own eponymous label a decade ago."

"Delphine dressed me for my first Met Gala," Melody tells me. "We've been close ever since."

"Yes." Delphine nods, pulling up a picture of a teenage Melody on the pink carpet dressed in a delicate gown made entirely of pale yellow diamonds, the pattern almost making it look like a web of tiny bedazzled sunflowers clinging to her bare body. "This was our first baby together. Melody likes the California hippie, bohemian, free-spirited fashion."

"And Delphine knows how to elevate that and make it glamorous. But she always keeps it true to me," Melody adds, wrapping an arm around her friend. "So when she offered to do my wedding dress, it was a no-brainer."

"My competition was tough," Delphine tells me matter-of-factly. "Every major designer wanted to get *the* wedding dress of Melody Mashad. All of the big houses—Valentino, Ralph Lauren, Vera Wang, Givenchy, Oscar de la Renta. But I just knew I had to do it."

I try my best to nod along, pretending I know all the designers she just referred to.

"My mom's right," Melody says. "It was a major honor for us. *Lots* of major celebrities have tried to get Delphine to do their wedding dresses, but she refuses."

"I hate marriage," Delphine says, scrunching up her nose in disgust as she lights a cigarette. "I like to make clothes for women to celebrate their independence in, not clothing to commemorate the day they lose it forever. But Melody is my friend. And I've spent time with her and Axle. Their love is different. What they're going to have is special. It's not the boring, suffocating type of union most people are referring to when they speak of marriage. It is *exciting*—liberating, even."

I look at Melody, curious to see how Delphine's backhanded compliment landed, but she seems unbothered by the all-out attack on marriage. If anything, she looks touched.

"Aw, Delphine!" Melody says, wiping a tear from her eye. "We love you."

"I love you both, too," Delphine says, giving Melody a kiss on the cheek. "Where is Monsieur Axle?"

"Well, he's superstitious about seeing me in my dress before the wedding," Melody explains. "So, while we're doing this, he's over at Zegna doing the final fitting for his suit."

"Do you have plans tonight?" Delphine asks, waving her hand to include Mary, Zadie, Farida, Timmy, and me, as well. "All of you."

"I was going to have the new chef from the Ritz, Pierre, come over to my place to prepare dinner for us tonight, if you would like to join," Mary says. "We just can't do anything too public. We still haven't announced Josie as part of our family, and it's going to be a big shock to the world when they realize Ali had a love child, so we are trying to keep her presence with us under wraps until the show airs."

I smile self-consciously, feeling less like a human and more like an "Ali's love child" prop as Mary gestures casually in my direction.

"Americans are so fragile about these things," Delphine says, rolling her eyes. "I go to events with my partner and his wife, and nobody bats an eyelash. C'est la vie."

"Anyway, will you join us for dinner?" Melody adds. "You can bring your partner! And his wife?"

"No, no. I was going to invite you all to come to an exclusive dinner the president and her husband are hosting at the Élysée Palace," Delphine says, casually wafting her cigarette around. "But there are going to be lots of cameras. The British royals are apparently making an appearance, and you know the madness they stir up here."

"I *do* love Will and Kate," Melody says, before glancing at me guiltily. "But—"

"But we really should politely decline," Mary interjects, "considering we're trying to fly under the radar. Besides, we would never want to impose on a party without a formal invite from the host."

"Oh, nonsense," Delphine says. "President Laroux and I have known each other since we were in diapers. She's a close friend. Just come! It will be fun."

"I don't mind," I say, sensing Mary and Melody might both want to go. "Seriously! If you guys go, it might give me a chance to check out Paris a bit without worrying about pictures and stuff. Maybe separating wouldn't be the worst thing."

"But who will you hang out with?" Melody asks, her eyebrows scrunched together in concern. "This is your first time out of the country! You can't just roam the streets of the City of Love alone."

I look over to Majid, the beefy security guard Mary appointed to me just minutes before we got here.

"I won't be alone. I have Majid, remember?"

"Yes, but Majid is a security guard," Mary says. "I realize this is your first time having one, Josie Joonam, but they don't substitute for friends. Majid needs to be alert in order to properly protect you."

I look over to the corner of the room where Majid has been stoically guarding the doorway alongside the other five security guards. He definitely doesn't seem like the *chattiest* guy.

"Wait," Melody says, her eyes zeroing in on Timmy. "I have an idea. Josie, if we go, why don't you just hang out with Timmy tonight? Timmy, you hate this stuff. I know there's no way you'd come. And you guys are friends, right? Why not skip the event together?"

Oh *gosh*. First Timmy has to tell everyone he never took me on a date in the first place, and now he's being forced to take me on a pity friend hang? Kill me.

"No, really," I insist. "That's okay. I'm good on my own."

Mary looks between Timmy and me, most likely sensing the sudden surge of awkwardness in the room. "Interesting" is all she can muster.

"Melody's right. Unless it's a required work thing, I would rather not go to this dinner party. . . . No offense, Delphine," Timmy chimes in from behind the camera. He then adds, "So, Josie, I'm down to hang. But only if you feel like it! No pressure if you want to do something solo. Obviously."

Oh gosh. It's happening. He's pitying me.

"Oh no, I mean, it would definitely be better to do something with a friend," I say. "But I just don't want to force you to do anything lame and touristy with me if you already had other plans in mind."

"I didn't," Timmy says. "I was just going to sit in the penthouse watching old *Seinfeld* reruns."

"That's still a plan!" I insist. "Really, I don't mind—"

"Enough!" Mary inserts herself into the conversation before I can finish. "I can't watch this any longer. You know, for a WASPy American and a barely Iranian Iranian American, that was a lot of taarof-ing."

She turns to the camera to quickly add, "*Taarof* is this custom we have in Persian culture when two people insist on going back and forth on little polite pleasantries like this."

227

Then she turns her attention back to us. "Let me make this simple and say what you are both refusing to. Josie, Timmy would much rather spend his night seeing the Eiffel Tower with you than sitting at home watching *Seinfeld* in his pajamas. Timmy, Josie is thrilled to be spending the night with you. Everyone settled here?"

Chapter 22

"*Stop* it," Melody says, as soon as she enters the kitchen. "Is this for your date—er, hangout?"

My face is bright red as I turn to Timmy, whose face also seems to have grown a few shades pinker, and we look at each other's matching I ♥ PARIS T-shirts and berets.

"Not a date," we both blurt out too quickly, before Timmy adds, "I just saw these at a tourist shop after Delphine's. If I'm going to show Josie around Paris this afternoon, we might as well go full tourist, you know?"

"Right," Melody says, her yellow diamond teardrop earrings swinging back and forth as she solemnly nods. "Well, can I get a picture of you before you leave for this 'not date'? Meesha and Mona are going to die for these looks."

"Um, sure," I say, awkwardly inching closer to Timmy while consciously trying not to make any sort of physical contact with him.

"Oh, come on," Melody insists. "Get in closer!"

A series of those pesky little fireworks start going off inside me as Timmy tentatively wraps an arm around me and I subtly rest my head on his chest for the picture. *He's just a friend, Josie*, I remind myself. *Just a friend.*

"So cute," Melody gushes, quickly sending the picture to us in a group text with Mona, Meesha, and Pete. "I have to rush off to glam before this event, but you guys have so much fun, okay?"

"We will," I reassure her as she grabs a bottle of lemon water from the fridge and heads out. "You have fun, too!"

An awkward silence falls over the kitchen when she leaves, Timmy's arm still wrapped around me and my head still leaning on his chest.

"So, uh, we should probably get going, right?" Timmy asks, and a small feeling of disappointment washes over me as he shoves his hand back into his pocket.

"Yeah!" I exclaim a little too enthusiastically. "Let's go."

The first stop on Timmy's tour is the Arc de Triomphe, just a five-minute walk from Mary's penthouse.

"So if you look closely," Timmy tells me, bringing me up close and personal to the monument, "you can see they inscribed the actual structure with the names of the real people who died fighting for France in the French Revolution and Napoleonic wars. It's kind of crazy, right? To think that these were all real people on Earth, just like you and me."

"It's pretty special," I say, running my hand over the names. "To make a mark on the world like that. Like, they did something incredible with their lives and because of that people will honor them forever."

"I know," he agrees. "Obviously, I'm not trying to equate

being in the entertainment industry to heroically fighting in a war. But stuff like this is the only way I'm ever able to empathize with everyone around me caring so much about fame. I don't really have it, but I get the desire to leave your mark on the world."

"How many generations after us will remember the Mashads?" I wonder aloud.

"It's sort of hard to imagine a world without their impact at this point," Timmy says. "But who knows? I'm probably biased."

"I probably am, too, but I think I agree." In less than a lifetime, Mary might have managed to make her family immortal in their own way.

"Okay," Timmy says, walking back toward the street. "We *have* to get to the next stop before sunset."

When we arrive at the Eiffel Tower half an hour later, the sky has transformed into a pink-and-purple masterpiece. The whole scene looks like something out of a movie.

"Whoa" is all I can manage as I take it all in, my jaw practically on the grass beneath me.

"I know." Timmy's beret just barely grazes mine as he stands next to me. "Pretty awesome, right?"

"Extremely awesome," I say, nodding so aggressively my beret almost falls off.

"Well, we're just getting started," Timmy says with a laugh, flashing me his chicken soup smile. "After this we're going to walk along the Seine over to Le Marais, and *there* we will enter phase two of Timmy's Awesome Paris Tour: the food portion."

"I can't wait," I say, turning my attention back to the Eiffel Tower, then over to Timmy again.

We look at each other, and as his eyes linger on my lips for a few seconds too long, I could swear he's about to kiss me. And honestly? I sort of hope he does. *Don't be weird, Josie. Don't be weird. Just let it happen.*

"Uh, Josie?" he asks, his voice coming out smaller than usual as he inches closer. "There's something I've been meaning to ask you—"

Before he can finish, a brunette girl from what seems to be a group of American high schoolers on a field trip interrupts him with a tap on the shoulder.

"Excuse me," she says, giggling. "Um, are you Timmy Sanderson?"

Nervous beads of sweat break out on Timmy's face as he adopts a similar look to the one he had when he was recognized at the *Island Rock* cover concert.

"Who?" he asks, trying and failing to play it cool. "Sorry, you probably have the wrong guy."

"No," the girl insists, pulling up his pictures on her phone. "This *has* to be you."

"Listen, I appreciate your interest, but I'm really a private person," he pleads. "If you wouldn't mind—"

"OMG, it *is* you," she squeals, turning to her friends to yell, "YOU GUYS, IT'S ACTUALLY HIM. IT'S THE NORMALSANDERSON."

Almost instantly, I'm pushed to the ground as dozens of teen girls start swarming an increasingly panicked Timmy, each of them pawing at him like he's a doll they all want a chance to play with. Before I can pull myself back up to help him, Majid has lifted me up off the ground and secured me in the back of a black SUV with tinted windows. Moments later, Timmy's bodyguard Alesso opens the door and straps him into the seat next to mine.

"Date's over," Alesso announces while instructing the driver to take us back to the penthouse. "Sorry, kids. It's just not safe."

I reflexively open my mouth to remind everyone that it wasn't a date, but then I close it. Maybe it *was* a date. A date that got cut short by this mob of crazed fans. I stare at Timmy, who's still visibly shaken up, his beret missing and the I ♥ PARIS T-shirt slightly torn at the bottom.

"Are you okay?" I ask, my heart racing. "That was . . . terrifying."

"I'm fine," he reassures me, his chicken soup smile coming off a little forced this time. "It could have been worse."

I nod politely, but inside my heart is pounding so hard it could bruise my chest. *Worse? How?!*

"Um, excuse me?" I ask the driver, suddenly desperate for fresh air. "Would you mind putting the window down?"

"No can do," Majid says from the front seat. "Not safe."

Chapter 23

"I'm a little worried about your safety, hun," Matt says as we pull out of LAX Sunday morning. "You realize it's only a matter of time before you become just as famous as Timmy, if not more, right?"

Of *course* I realize that. How could I not after what I saw yesterday? It's literally all I've thought about for the past twenty-four hours. But Matt can't know how freaked out I am. The minute he does, he'll make me leave the show. And I'm in way too deep to give up now.

"You never know," I say, trying my best to emulate Meesha's cool, unbothered air. "I'm sure it's all gonna be fine."

Matt furrows his brow, not fully buying my response, and I pretend I don't notice.

"But, um, anyway," I say, desperate to change the subject. "I'm excited for us to hang out for the day. You're still up for a Netflix comedy special marathon, right?"

After the jarring experience I had yesterday, all I want is to just have a normal, cozy day at home with the person who makes me feel safest in the world.

"Oh, Jos, I'm so sorry," Matt says. "I'm happy to give you a ride if you want to go hang out with Louise or something! It's just I . . ."

"Took on an extra shift at work." I finish the sentence for him. "It's okay, I understand. I think Lou is hanging with Grant at Delaney's. I'll text her."

When I enter Delaney's, Lou and Grant are sitting on the same side of the table, with their chairs scooted so close that they've formed more of a bench. Grant's right arm is around Lou as his left hand feeds her bites of waffles, and Lou keeps giggling every time Grant "accidentally" smudges syrup on her cheek so he can lick it off.

"Ahem." I clear my throat loudly as I take the seat across from them, hoping the noise will maybe get Grant to quit licking my friend's face like a lollipop. "Hi, guys!"

"Josie!!! Hi!" Lou exclaims, pushing Grant off her before he has a chance to get the memo. "So sorry we didn't see you come in."

"I was just licking syrup off Lou's cheeks," Grant informs me as if the entire restaurant didn't see. "Did you know Lou has the softest cheeks in the world?"

"Well, I've never licked them," I say. "But she does take her skincare routine very seriously, so I can't say I'm surprised."

"I do not mess with my skincare routine." Lou nods solemnly. "But enough about me and my stupid cheeks! Tell us about Paris."

I shoot her my best SHUT UP RIGHT NOW look, but she rolls her eyes and adds, "We can talk about it in front of Grant now, remember? He had to sign the NDA to be my plus-one to the wedding."

"Yep, she told me everything a few nights ago," Grant says, feeding Lou another bite of waffles before taking one for himself. "Pretty sick, Josie! Lou told me the dude you're dating is Pete Sanderson's little brother. He's, like, my all-time favorite basketball player. Wait, have you *met* Pete?"

"Uh, sort of," I say, suddenly wishing he would just get back to feeding Lou waffles. "Just briefly on FaceTime."

"We don't care about Pete, babe," Lou says. "We care about *Timmy*. Josie, I fully think he was gonna kiss you at the Eiffel Tower."

"For a second I was hoping so, too," I admit. "But everything got so weird after the fan encounter. We were both so shaken up, and then we got home and Mary's entire PR team was there making sure no photos were taken featuring me. Everything got thrown off."

"I don't get it," Grant chimes in. "Lou, didn't you say she's not into this dude? Why does she seem so bummed?"

"Well, I *thought* I wanted to just be friends," I reply, ignoring the fact that the question was for whatever reason directed at Lou. "Mostly just because we work so well as friends, and I didn't really want anything to ruin it. But every time we hang out alone it just sort of leaves me wishing we were more."

"Well, Timmy obviously feels the same way," Lou says. "He's already taken you on *two* dates."

"Technically, neither were dates," I correct her. "He literally said the words 'not a date' multiple times. To be fair, so did I. But I was really just following his lead."

"But he tried to kiss you," Lou reminds me. "*Twice*."

"I really think the first time was definitely in my head," I say. "Seriously. He was so casual about it not being a date. There's just no way he thinks I rejected his kiss. And who knows? I could be wrong about the Eiffel Tower. Maybe he was just about to tell me I had a booger hanging out or something."

"He had to be trying to kiss you," Grant insists. "I mean, what kind of dude hangs out with a chick twice and doesn't even try to kiss her?" He looks genuinely perplexed.

"I don't know," I say, making a mental note to circle back to his sexist and heteronormative rhetoric later. "It's fine. Boys in the greater Los Angeles area clearly aren't working out for me. Maybe Stanford will be where I finally hit my stride in the love department. . . . Speaking of which, Lou, have you filled out your dorm preference form yet? I saw on this Reddit thread I joined that Swig is officially full, but—"

"Wait, have you not told her yet?" Grant asks Lou.

"Told me what? Wait, did you already fill out the form? Thank *God*. I wasn't trying to stress you out, but Swig really is the best fit for you."

"Wait, guys, Isaac is here!" Lou exclaims, the most excited I think I've ever seen her with regards to him. "Isaac! Over here!"

"Sup, everyone," Isaac says, taking the empty seat next to mine.

"Oh," I say, suddenly self-conscious about my greasy hair and gross postflight morning breath. "Hey, Isaac."

Even visibly exhausted and hungover in his sweats, the guy

looks like he was manufactured in some sort of elite hot boy factory. How could Lou not get what I see in him? Between his hazel eyes and perfectly chiseled jawline, his face is genuinely a work of art.

"Dude!" Grant playfully shouts, giving his friend a light punch on the chest. "I told you to meet us here an hour ago. Your breakfast is cold."

"I know, I know," Isaac says. "Sorry. I had a late start this morning."

"You must be so hungover," Grant says with a laugh. "You were *on* one last night."

"Yeah, I might have been a bit overserved," Isaac says, taking a bite of his cold eggs Benedict. "Then I had to re-ask Genevieve to prom this morning."

"What do you mean?" Lou asks. "Had you already asked?"

"I guess," Isaac says with a shrug. "She says I asked her when I was blacked out last night. So this morning, she forced me to ask her again so she could get it on her TikTok."

Lou and I quickly exchange *She is the absolute worst* looks before I turn my attention back to Isaac. "So how did you ask her this morning?"

"Gen loves old eighties movies, so I kind of went with a modern take on that famous scene from *Say Anything*," Isaac tells us. "I blasted Taylor Swift, 'You Belong with Me,' in her BMW stereo and stood outside the car with a giant poster asking her to prom."

Okay, that sounds like my personal hell. But come on. The guy is undeniably adorable and sensitive. How is it possible that someone this hot would also be this thoughtful and romantic??

"How did you get into her car?" Lou asks, clearly less impressed than I am. "And . . . why Taylor Swift?" She does have a point with that last question. We haven't been friends with Genevieve in years, but when we were kids, she *hated* Taylor Swift.

"Plus, is her car parked outside of her room?" I add, remembering the layout of their house. "Or was it in the garage? How did she see you?"

"I picked Taylor Swift because . . . I don't know . . . don't chicks like her music?" Isaac answers with a shrug. "And she parks her car in the driveway, facing her room. So it worked out because she's been wanting to debut the car on social for a while."

Okay, so not *as* romantic as I was previously thinking. But still! He tried. Isn't that all we can ask for?

"Sounds like you nailed it," Grant says, reaching his fist out toward his friend. "My man."

"Yep," Isaac says, pounding his own fist against Grant's. "And let's just say my efforts were *very* appreciated."

First Lou and Grant, now this repulsive sexual innuendo about my lifelong crush and my sworn enemy?! If there is a God, He will not be resting until I puke today.

"Enough about me," Isaac says, turning to face me. "Josie! Where have you been, dude? I've been seeing more and more of Louise and less and less of you."

"I told you at Oliver Blair's," Lou reminds him, giving Grant and me a look, before adding slowly, "she was at Stanford for a mixer with the other pre-med kids. Right, Josie?"

"Right," I confirm, my heart swelling at the thought of Isaac asking Lou about me. "It was . . . fun!"

"Sounds dope." Isaac nods. "You get to go to any frat parties?"

"Uh, no," I say, my voice quivering as I continue with the lie. "You know me. Not much of a partier. Just went to bed early."

"Got it," Isaac says. "So what wound up happening with that dude? You figure out if it was a date?"

"Wait," Grant says. "Bro, you know about that? You know he's—"

"A student at the new charter school down the street from ours," Lou quickly cuts in, giving Grant a swift kick under the table. "Super random. I've never met anyone else who goes there. Have you guys?"

"Nah," Isaac says. "So, Josie, was it a date or not?"

"It wasn't," I say with a sigh. "I think we're just going to be friends."

"Lucky him. You're a dope friend," Isaac says, before pulling his math binder out of his backpack. "Wait, actually, speaking of our friendship, did you already do your math homework? I straight up do not get it. Need your help so bad."

"Oh, uh, yeah," I say, looking over his familiar worksheet. "I did it on the plane home from . . . Stanford."

Yep, Stanford. That's where a boy might like me. I just have to hang tight until I get there.

Chapter 24

"Hey, by the way, Josie," Mona says as she riffles through the racks of dresses. "Since I don't go to a real school with proms and stuff, I'm going to have a prom-themed party for my eighteenth birthday at Melody's Malibu house. You *have* to come."

"Oh, um, that sounds so fun," I lie. "I'll check my schedule and get back to you." The truth is there's no world in which I'm going to go all the way to Malibu on a school night to attend a somehow even *more* intimidating prom than the one I already have to attend. But I have a feeling giving Mona a flat-out no will only make her insist.

"Wait, Josie," Melody interjects, pulling out a flowy mint-colored dress with butterflies embroidered all over it. "You *have* to try this Prabal Gurung one. The color would look so good on you."

"No, Melody," Mona replies. "That dress is so *you*. We need to find a dress *Josie* likes. Not something that *we'd* wear."

Before we came here, we were at Isabel Marant getting our custom flowy floral bridesmaid dresses fitted ahead of Melody's wedding. And I really thought it was the fanciest place I'd ever been to. That is, until we headed over to Vik to find a prom dress for me. Vik is *so* fancy that it doesn't have a sign on the door or anything. You just have to know it's here, almost hidden between the Chloe and Oscar de la Renta stores. I'm positive that if I came here alone, they wouldn't so much as open the door for me. But I'm here as a Mashad, and I'm quickly learning that means people just treat you differently. Including offering me multi-thousand-dollar dresses for free.

Ken is our producer today while Farida's busy working on some stuff with Mary. Ken's vibe is *entirely* different from Farida's. He's got pink hair, a cross earring in one ear, a pair of tan suede pants, and a matching suede button-down that's been left open to reveal his incredibly hairy chest. From what I gather, Ken is an old friend of Meesha's. They were in the fashion world together, and, when he wanted to make his way into production, Meesha begged her mom to give him this gig. His producing style is also very different from Farida's. Instead of pulling me aside before each scene to run through what's going to happen, he quickly introduced himself once I got here and said he'd just "hang back" while we did our "thang." Like, instead of yelling action, he literally yelled, "All right, queens, do your thang!"

In order to let us do our "thangs" optimally, Ken decided he needed to shut down the entire store. "It'll make for a less cluttered scene," he explained. "Also, Mary would lose her shit if I let people see you with the fam this early on, Josie." I've been holding in my pee for about an hour now, and I wonder if Mary would also "lose her shit" if I peed on the hardwood floor of this fancy store. Actually, on second thought—who am I kidding? She'd probably love that. Great content.

Mona keeps riffling through the racks of dresses. "I mean, Meesha, don't you agree?"

Meesha, who's spent the entire hour here silently plopped on the plush white bouclé couch in the corner of the store, looks up from her phone. "What?"

"I *said* we need to find something that suits Josie," Mona says. "That fits her personal style."

"Oh," she says, turning her attention back to her phone. "Cool."

"You've been so weird all day," says Mona. "Honestly, you've been so weird all *week*. Every time Josie is here, you get all emo and bitchy. What's your deal?"

"I don't have a *deal*," Meesha retorts icily. "I'm just busy."

"Busy doing what?" Mona asks. "We're literally in the middle of filming a show right now. What else could you possibly be doing?"

I brace myself for another blowout like the one at the dinner table, hyperfocusing my attention on the wide selection of designer dresses lining the rack in front of me. Honestly? At first glance, these fancy dresses look no different to me than the ones Lou and I usually sift through on the Macy's sales racks. It's when I feel the fabric that I notice a difference. Every dress here just feels so buttery smooth and undeniably luxe. I wonder if Mona, Meesha, and Melody's skin has ever contacted the itchy sort of highly flammable polyester most of my clothing is made of.

"Guys," Melody interrupts. "This is supposed to be for *Josie*. Can we all just relax for a second and focus on her?"

"That's what I am *trying* to do," Mona says. "I just wish our sister, who—mind you—is supposed to be the 'fashionable' one of the family, wouldn't ruin the entire vibe of the day by sulking in the corner glued to her phone."

"You know what?" Meesha asks, abruptly sitting up. "I just suddenly have to go pee."

She glides up from the couch, unclips her mic, tosses it on the couch, and storms into the bathroom in the other corner of the store. Well, it's not quite a storm. More like a stroll. Like she's totally unbothered. The bathroom door doesn't even slam behind her. It just quietly shuts.

"Oh!" I exclaim, a little more loudly than I intended. "I didn't realize we could use the bathroom while we filmed."

"Of course we can use the bathroom, Jos." Melody giggles. "Forcing us to hold it in would be pretty inhumane, don't you think?"

"Not that Meesha is *actually* using the bathroom," Mona adds. "She's just gonna lock herself in there doing God knows what on her phone until we're done filming. It's the oldest move in the book. Mom can't get mad at her for bailing, but she doesn't have to bother with filming."

"Mona," Melody says. "Did you *have* to keep pestering her?"

"Yes!" Mona shouts. "It's absurd she thinks it's okay to act like that. You have to admit, she's so weird every time Josie is around."

Ugh. The only thing more awkward than the iciness between Meesha and me is Mona and Melody *discussing* the iciness right in front of me.

"Yeah, I guess she could stand to be a bit friendlier," Melody admits. "Maybe she's just being shy! Remember how shy she used to be growing up? Her only friend outside of us was Pete Sanderson, and he's, like, basically family."

Oh gosh. Now we're discussing Meesha and *Pete*?! Please let this conversation be over. I frantically rummage through the designer dresses and try to focus my attention back on not peeing. But I guess now I know I technically can pee. I wonder if there's a bathroom outside of this store I could run and use while Meesha's in the one here.

"I mean, I think there's a difference between being shy and being straight-up rude. But whatever," Mona says. "Anyway, Josie, forget Meesha and her weirdness. What do *you* like in here? Well, more important, what's your date wearing? Are you guys gonna match?"

"Oh yeah!" Melody chimes in. "I didn't even ask! Did your crush end up asking you?"

"No," I say, suddenly very aware of the camera in my face. "He's still with that girl I told you about. But it's no big deal! Really! I'm just going to go solo, that's my comfort zone anyway. And, you know, I'll have Louise there. It's not like I'm going to be *alone* alone."

I watch as a look of pity flashes across Melody's face.

"Of course," she says, nodding a little too enthusiastically. "You're going to be *fine*."

"Wait, Josie. I need so much more detail," Mona presses.

"Who is this crush?! I didn't know you were holding out on us with this complex love life. I *love* it."

"He's just this boy I've been in love with forever," I say. "But he has a girlfriend. And she's evil. And it doesn't look like they're breaking up anytime soon. So I think I should just embrace single life."

"Yeah," Mona agrees. "You're much better alone than you would be with some idiot who can't see you're clearly better than literally anyone else out there."

"Yep," I say, appreciating her over-the-top support. "I think so, too."

"I've said it once, and I'll say it again," Mona says. "Men. Ain't. Shit."

"You know who *is* shit, though?" Melody asks.

"Please, God, do not say Axle," says Mona. "Mel, how many times do I have to tell you that single people truly want to jump off a cliff and die every time you gush about your fiancé?"

"I was *not* going to say Axle," Melody retorts, lowering her voice to a whisper. "Don't worry, Josie, we'll cut this. Unless, of course, something winds up happening between you two, in which case, oh my gosh. So cute. We'd have to keep it as a memory . . . but I was gonna say *Timmy*."

The three of us turn toward the window, where we can see Timmy outside, standing by the two security guards and look-ing around the street aimlessly with his hands in his pockets.

"Listen, I know you guys keep saying your hangouts aren't dates, but you seem to get along so well," Melody says. "We've known Timmy his whole life, and I've never seen him so excited to spend time with a girl. Like, how cute was he about showing you around Paris?"

"Shut up," Mona says. "No, he didn't. Josie, you beautiful slut! Are you kidding? Is that why you and Timmy were wearing matching shirts in that picture Melody sent? You were going on a date???"

"It wasn't a date," I insist, making my voice extra chipper to mask any trace of disappointment. "We're really just friends."

"Are you *sure* you're just friends?" Melody asks. "There's definitely a vibe between you two. Don't think I haven't noticed you guys flirting it up in between shoots."

Flirting?! Do Timmy and I *flirt*?! A retroactive feeling of embarrassment washes over me as I imagine Melody watching Timmy and me "flirt." It's one thing for Lou to know I sort of, maybe, have a little bit of a crush on him. But Melody and Mona are like his sisters. They can't know. It's too mortifying.

"I wouldn't say we're flirting," I insist, my face turning increasingly bright shades of red. "We're just friends! I mean, you were there when Timmy said it himself. He doesn't like me like that. Neither of our hangouts were dates. And, I mean, I am very much not over my crush on Isa—er, the boy at school." I know Melody says we can cut all of this, but saying Isaac's name in front of a camera a second time just feels too risky.

"Um, we've known Timmy since he was in diapers," says Mona. "Let me assure you he *does* like you like that. The guy texted our mom just to get your number! That has to count for something."

"It does." Melody solemnly nods. "Axle doesn't even text Mom on her birthday. Too scary."

"Timmy has known your mom forever," I tell them. "It's different."

"Well, whatever the case, I wish you two would make it work," Melody says. "Timmy is such a nice guy. He deserves someone like you. A genuinely good person."

"Melody's right. Timmy is an exception to the rule of all scumbag men. He's nice. And not in like the fake 'but I'm a nice guy' way. No, Timmy's just actually a good dude."

"Yep," Melody says. "He really is."

"Yeah," I agree, my heart getting increasingly mushy at these testimonials to what I already suspected was Timmy's top-notch character. "He's super nice. I know. But, seriously. We're just friends."

"Wait!" Mona says, totally ignoring me. "Why doesn't *Timmy* take you to prom?! That's the perfect way to make it clear you should be more than friends. Ask him as your date. It will be perfect. Let me get him in here right now. TIMM—"

Before Mona can finish his name, Melody thankfully slaps her hand across her mouth. "Shh!!!" Melody whisper-yells at her. "First of all, you're embarrassing Josie."

"No," Mona retorts, ripping her mouth away from Melody's grip. "I am *not*."

"Look at her!" Melody exclaims. "She's gone silent, and she's as red as that Lamborghini Dad bought when he was going through his midlife crisis."

I catch a glimpse of my reflection in the squiggle-shaped mirror hanging across from us. I have no idea what Ali's Lamborghini looked like, but she's right. My face is crimson.

Mona looks me up and down. "Okay, I see what you mean."

"And, besides, she *can't* go with Timmy," Melody says. "How are we supposed to say they know each other? This is all supposed to be a secret until the show airs, remember?"

"*Fine,*" Mona says as I mouth "Thank you" to Melody. "You are *such* a rule follower. But, Josie, just promise me you'll bang Timmy."

"Oh," I say. "I . . . well . . . I'm, um, I'm a virgin."

"Whatever," Mona says with a shrug. "Then make out with him. I don't care. You guys are *clearly* into each other. Why let that kind of sexual tensh go to waste?"

"Okay," Melody interrupts before the embarrassment of this conversation fully kills me. "Let's get back to shopping. Shall we, ladies?"

"Actually," I say, not able to hold it in a second longer. "Do you guys mind if I go to the bathroom real quick? I know Meesha's in the one here, but maybe there's another one? I promise I'm not trying to bail on the scene! I just . . ."

"Josie, chill out." Mona laughs. "You can obviously go to the bathroom. Actually, I have to go, too. There's one we can use down the hall in the private entrance."

Mona's security guard, Kirk, and Majid follow closely behind as Mona and I exit Vik's back door into the private hall reserved exclusively for celebrity shoppers to enter and exit the boutiques on this strip without having to worry about paparazzi. By the time we make it into the spa-worthy bathroom, I practically run into my stall and release what honestly feels like the Niagara Falls.

"Mona?" I ask as I finish scrubbing my hands with the bathroom's Le Labo soap. "I'm done, so I'm going to head back to the store. Don't want Melody stuck filming alone for too long. See you in there?"

"Yeah, sounds good," she says from behind the mahogany door guarding her stall. "I'll be there in a minute."

Now I'm walking back down the private hallway to Vik with a little extra oomph in my step, having cleared my bladder and also (hopefully) tabled any and all Timmy talk for the rest of the day. I'm just about to figure out how to respond to a random text from Grant that reads *this is gonna be LIT* (What's gonna be lit? Melody's wedding? Prom? A party at Oli Blair's? Did he have the wrong number?) when a familiar voice interrupts my thoughts, followed by a tap on the shoulder. "Well, would you look at this? Chewy?! What are you doing *here*?"

Oh my gosh. No, no, no, no, no.

Chapter 25

"Oh," I say, turning around to face my archnemesis. "H-hey, Genevieve."

Shoot. How in the world am I supposed to handle this situation? How do I explain why I'm here? We're, like, two feet away from the store, where I can see Melody peeping out of Vik's back door to see what's going on out here.

"I'm serious," Genevieve says. "What are *you* doing *here*? You know, my dad built this entryway. They are *super* strict about letting any regular people in. Wait, ew. Did you, like, stalk me here?"

Stalk her?!?!?! The nerve on this woman.

"Uh-h, n-no," I manage to stammer. "I didn't stalk you here."

"Well, are you working here as a janitor or something?" Genevieve asks. Then she adds with a laugh, "I *know* you're not shopping at Vik."

"I, um, I think Vik is closed right now," I say, not sure how else to respond to her insult.

"I know," she says, rolling her eyes. "For a *Making Mashad* episode, duh. You know, I used to date an intern on the show, so I know the ins and outs."

"Right," I say. "You might have mentioned that once or twice."

"But I'm not with him anymore, of course," she continues. "Because I'm with Isaac. You know, the one whose locker you used to stuff with those pathetic little love notes back in fourth grade?"

She bursts out laughing her stupid Disney villain laugh as I stand there trying my best to hold back the tears, knowing Melody, Timmy, and the whole crew are all well within earshot of this humiliating conversation.

Before I can remind her that she would help me stuff those "pathetic little notes" into Isaac's locker in fourth grade, she continues. "You know, sometimes when we're done . . . *you know* . . . we pull those out—he still has them—and we read them out loud and laugh and laugh and laugh. My favorite is the one where you talk about getting lost in his—what did you call them? His *perfect* hazel eyes that gaze directly into your *soul*?"

"It . . . it was a long time ago," I say, both mortified at what's happening and partially flattered that Isaac kept my letters. "I don't remember."

"Whatever," Genevieve says. "The funniest thing is that *you*, the hairy loser who can barely get out a sentence without barfing, genuinely thought you stood a chance with *my* Isaac. Do you seriously think he *likes* you just because he uses you to help him cheat in math class every once in a while? The guy thinks you're a freak, just like everyone else does."

Before she can finish annihilating every last ounce of dignity I have, we both spot Mona marching her way over to us from the bathroom. Kirk and Majid attempt to stop her, but she shakes them both loose. From across the hall, Melody tries frantically motioning for her to stop, but she loudly yells, "I DON'T GIVE A SHIT."

And all of a sudden, she's here.

"Genevieve," Mona says, staring directly at her. "Right? That's your name?"

"Y-yeah," Genevieve says, suddenly looking smaller and more pathetic than I've ever seen her. "I dated an intern on your show a few years ago? Well, we didn't really date. We got high and went to City Walk. Mickie Waller. D-do you know him?"

"Hmm, no. Doesn't ring a bell. But, anyway, I thought I'd introduce myself. I'm Mona Mashad," she says, placing an arm around me. "Josie's sister."

Genevieve's eyes widen as Mona's words sink into her brain.

"Yeah, yeah. Our dad had an affair, we have a sister. He wasn't the world's most perfect husband after all," Mona says. "Now that you're all caught up, let's get back to what's happening here. Based on how you're panting, it seems you're familiar with who I am, which means you likely know how seriously I take protecting my family. You talk to my sister like that one more time, and mark my words: I will *ruin* you."

"I-I-I'm so sorry," Genevieve says. "Mona, really . . ."

"It's not *me* you owe an apology to, you pathetic twat," Mona says, staring daggers at her. "It's my sister."

"Um," Genevieve says, turning her attention toward me. "J-Josie, I'm . . . I'm sorry."

An *apology*?! From *Genevieve*?!?!?! I quickly pinch the inside of my wrist to make sure I'm not dreaming. Nope. This is really happening. Mona actually managed to knock Genevieve off her stupid high horse. A truly impossible feat. Maybe she should run for office.

"For what, Genevieve?" Mona asks. "What are you sorry for?"

Listen, I know it's not nice. I know that, no matter how evil she is, Genevieve is still a human being at the end of the day, and I should feel bad watching her squirm like this. But watching this exchange unfold is just undeniably thrilling.

"Mona," I interrupt, making my half-hearted attempt to be the bigger person. "It's fine. Seriously. I don't even want her apology." (That's a lie. The apology was hands down the best moment of my life.)

"It's *not* fine," Mona insists. "This girl is the biggest bitch I've seen in my entire life, and I've met at least twenty-five different Bravo stars. Genevieve. *What* are you sorry for?"

"Um," she tries. "For making fun of your sister?"

"WRONG," Mona yells out, her voice echoing down the hallway. "Here, let me help you out. I'm going to have you repeat after me, okay?"

Genevieve nods enthusiastically.

"I, Genevieve," Mona starts slowly.

"I, Genevieve," Genevieve repeats.

"Am a giant bitch who takes out her insecurities on people far superior to me because I'm jealous," Mona continues.

"That's right. I'm *jealous* of Josie Lawrence because she's everything I'm not in all the best ways. She's sunshine, and I'm rain. She's good, and I'm evil. She's a Mashad, and I'm *normal.*"

Okay, that might be going too far.

"Mona," I say, blushing. "*Stop*. Please. This is too much." This time I mean it. I got my apology. We can keep it moving.

Mona looks me in the eyes, then looks back at Genevieve. "Fine," she says. "But I want you to remember it was *Josie* who stopped me from humiliating you further. Maybe consider writing her a thank-you card."

"Th-thank you, Josie," Genevieve says. "I-I'll definitely be sending you a thank-you card."

"Come on, Josie," Mona says, wrapping her arm around me and guiding me back into the store. "We've got a prom dress to pick out."

I know Mona just broke one of Mary's cardinal rules, and I know there's no way this ends well. But I would be lying if I said that in this moment I felt anything other than pure, unadulterated happiness.

Chapter 26

I thought my life turned upside down the moment I got that letter from Ali. But no. Now I realize that was just a small tilt at best. One of those minor earthquakes you sleep through. Comparatively, the aftermath of Mona's exchange with Genevieve has been like a tsunami ripping through every foundational square inch my life has been built upon.

I keep replaying that conversation I had with Timmy at the *Island Rock* concert. *He tried to warn me. He knew.* How could I have been so naïve? Obviously this was going to happen. I wasn't just signing up for a TV show. I was signing up for this. For *fame*. I peek outside my window, quickly shutting the raggedy sheets I'm using as makeshift blinds before the hundreds of paparazzi camped outside our apartment can snag a picture of me. How can anybody possibly want this? I think about the money, about Stanford, trying to remind myself of why I'm doing this. Why I *did* this in the first place. But I just . . . I can't remember. Will I even be able to go to Stanford with all this attention on me? I cringe, imagining meeting my random roommate for the first time with Majid by my side and hundreds of middle-aged men with cameras camped outside our dorm.

I don't think I fully realized what a big deal it was going to be when Mary got a tip from her PR team that the security footage from the private entrance had been leaked. I mean, I knew that footage included Mona telling Genevieve off. And yes. I expected the exchange to probably make its way to social media. And yes. I got the *hey u good?* text from Lou a few minutes after the fact. And yes. I saw the worried look in Timmy's eyes when he told me to let him know if I "need anything" after Mary called us at Vik.

But . . . I guess I never really took into account what all of that really *meant*. Like, for me, personally. How is any normal human being supposed to create a realistic expectation for this magnitude of fame? You just can't.

TMZ released the video of Mona just a few minutes after Mary got the call, and it went viral pretty much instantly. Even *Matt*, who still refers to TikTok as "TokTwik," had come across the clip of Mona confronting Genevieve within seconds of its release. I was in the middle of crafting my *hey Matt uh something happened today* text when he sent me the clip alongside a thousand question marks. Apparently three different coworkers showed it to him seconds after it went up. Not to mention the countless customers he heard murmuring about the "Mystery Mashad" at their respective tables.

"Jeez, Jos," he said, once he got back to our apartment, to find me crouched under my bedroom window, avoiding the mob of reporters outside. "I'm sorry. I should have thought through letting you do this more. Your mom . . . she was the one who was good at thinking things through. The more I try to do the right things, the more I seem to mess this whole parenting business up."

"I mean, crouching under the window to avoid paparazzi shots isn't ideal," I tried to joke. "But it's fine, really. I mean, did you actually watch the video? Mona fully told Genevieve off! It was awesome."

It really was awesome. I guess that's my one silver lining amid this nightmare. My sisters.

I just wish that being part of their family didn't come with . . . this. By the time we were leaving Vik, a literal mob of reporters and fans had formed, and they followed us all the way back to Mary's house, where she screamed at Mona for what felt like two hours straight. And then to my apartment, where dozens more reporters were somehow already waiting for me.

At first, they didn't know my name. They just called me the "Mystery Mashad."

WATCH MONA MASHAD DEFEND MYSTERY SISTER, wrote TMZ.

MONA MASHAD CALLS OUT BULLY WHO ATTACKED MYSTERY SISTER, wrote *Seventeen*.

MYSTERY MASHAD? MONA MASHAD REVEALS ALI HAD SECRET LOVE CHILD, wrote *Page Six*.

MONA MASHAD REVEALS THERE'S A FOURTH SISTER & SHE'S SUNSHINE, wrote *Elite Daily*.

MYSTERY MASHAD CAUGHT ON TAPE IN NEW VIRAL VIDEO, wrote *Us Weekly*.

By the end of the night, #MysteryMashad was trending on TikTok.

Turns out, Alicia Saraki, of all people, had come forward with my identity. Lou was the first to text me the article, along with an eye-roll emoji. Then Timmy reached out:

Let me take a wild guess . . . this person is not your best friend.

Alicia had gone on the record with TMZ, leading the reporters straight to me. "The Mystery Mashad is my best friend, Josie Lawrence," she's quoted as saying. "We've been like sisters since kindergarten. I've always known Josie was a Mashad, but she had me *sworn* to secrecy until now."

She even provided them with my yearbook picture from last year, which features me with no makeup, a faint unibrow, and a giant piece of spinach the photographer forgot to tell me I had left in my braces. That's the other thing about fame. I suddenly get why the Mashads are so image conscious. Before, this picture was just a picture in my yearbook I hardly ever had to look at. Now it's everywhere. Not only is it everywhere, but millions and millions of strangers now have the opportunity to chime in on my blemishes. It's like having an army of Genevieves down your throat at all times.

"Jos and I laughed so hard when we saw she forgot to take the spinach out of her teeth," she told *People*. "It's one of our favorite mems."

Along with the yearbook picture, she included the one

picture ever taken of us together, at the clean-air rally we orga-
nized sophomore year. The picture has since gone viral in arti-
cles with titles like MYSTERY MASHAD'S BEST FRIEND REVEALS
HER IDENTITY, MYSTERY MASHAD REVEALED TO BE BUDDING
ACTIVIST "JOSIE LAWRENCE" BY BFF, and BFF GIVES INSIDE LOOK
AT LIFE OF MYSTERY MASHAD JOSIE LAWRENCE.

That's when things got legitimately out of hand. I tried
going onto Instagram only to see I had two million new follow requests. TWO MILLION people wanted to see my
Shakespeare quotes and selfies with Lou. I had so many emails
on my Valley High account that it crashed my Safari app as
soon as I logged on. To my major surprise, like, 90 percent
of the messages were nice. Lots of people talking about how
"relatable" I felt and how nice it was to "finally see someone
normal in that family."

But the ones playing on repeat in my head aren't those. No,
they're the mean ones, like the people reminding me I'm "way
too lame" or "way too loser-ish" to really be a Mashad. Or the
creepy ones, like the people offering me thousands to blow
my nose into a Kleenex and mail it to them. And, finally, the
straight-up terrifying ones, like the messages about killing me
and my mom for "ruining the Mashad family." I guess now I
get why Mary insists on having a miniature army outside her
house.

Matt, on the other hand, the public seems to be embracing
with open arms. *Those* headlines read: MYSTERY MASHAD'S
STEPDAD IS MAJORLY HOT. FORMER COMEDY CLUB OWNER
REVEALED AS ADOPTIVE FATHER OF MASHAD LOVE CHILD. MEET
JOSIE LAWRENCE'S HOT STEPDAD. So, yes. In addition to dealing

with overnight fame, I also have to come to terms with hundreds of thousands of people all over the internet thirsting for my father. Even Mona, who Mary has declared a "total and utter disappointment" following this slipup, texted me saying, *Wait. Now that the whole world agrees, I feel like I can finally say this—Matt is a total DILF.* At that point, I just had to turn my phone off entirely and submit to lying atop my bed in the fetal position.

Fame sounds glamorous when you see it in movies and TV shows. Hey, I bet it actually *is* pretty glamorous when you live like Mary or any of my sisters. But fame is just awkward and uncomfortable when you're still living with your dad in a dingy old apartment building across the street from a strip mall. Neither of us could sleep last night because so many reporters were outside screaming my name through the paper-thin apartment walls. And Mary keeps insisting that we can't "lose control of the narrative," so Matt and I aren't allowed to answer any questions. When I was walking from the car into my apartment yesterday and they were all trying to ask me a million and one questions, Mary told me my job was just to keep my head down and ignore them.

I've seen footage of celebrities doing this all the time. But it is *awkward* in real life. Another human being is looking me in the eye, asking me simple questions like "What's your name?" and I'm supposed to just duck my head and ignore them. Then, as if the exchange isn't awkward enough in and of itself, as I keep walking away from them, they scream: "PLEASE! PLEASE! C'MON! JUST CHAT FOR A SECOND!" And I'm left feeling like a total and complete jerk.

Javier told me these people could make "millions" for getting the first comment from me, and I keep thinking about why it's such a bad thing to let them have it. Maybe *they* have a daughter they're trying to send to Stanford! Who am I to not help them out?

Now Matt's skipping work and I'm skipping school for the first time in our lives because we literally can't leave my apartment. We're trapped. The number of reporters and Mashad superfans camped outside has only grown since yesterday, and Mary has us under strict instructions not to leave until she, Javier, and the rest of her PR team lay out a plan. In the meantime, she's provided us with Majid and a new security guard, Blake, to patrol the building and "keep us safe."

FYI: Nothing makes someone feel *less* safe than telling them you need to hire a twenty-four seven security team to keep them safe. But I do have to say I like our security guards. Majid and I have gotten to know each other a bit more since Paris, and I recently learned he's actually Ali's dad's second cousin. He came here from Iran about fifteen years ago, and, according to Mary, he's an "excellent street fighter." So much so that, when he first came here, he became an MMA champion. When the car pulled up to my building and I saw the hundreds of people camped outside, Majid pulled me in for a quick side hug and whispered, "It will be okay, azizam."

Later, when we were done securing the apartment, he tearfully told me I looked just like my "dad" (still wish people would stop calling him that), then launched into a long story about how Ali helped him come to America and set him up with all the right people to launch his MMA career. I'm still getting used to hearing these stories about Ali. The ones about how wonderful he was. I know the people telling them think they're doing me a favor by speaking highly of the guy, but it's like they have all chosen to forget the glaring moral error he made in how he treated me and my mom. Like all that good other stuff he did should erase what he did to us.

The new guy, Blake, is a more stoic, more classic security guard. He's got a buzz cut and served in the army for over a decade before getting into private security. He doesn't really say much, but, when he shook Matt's hand, he did say that he will do "whatever it takes" to keep his daughter (me) safe. So I guess that was nice.

In the meantime, Matt has been throwing all his energy into cheering me up.

"C'mon, Jos," he keeps saying. "This isn't so bad! It's fun! A little father-daughter retreat."

But I don't even have enough in me right now to muster a response. So he goes into the living room and turns on a Jim Gaffigan stand-up special extra loud, obviously trying to entice me to come out. Theoretically, I should be excited about being able to spend this much quality time with him. The past twenty-four hours might be the most consecutive time we've spent together in years. And the distance has only grown since I started filming *Making Mashad* and actually have somewhere to go other than school, our apartment, and Lou's house.

So, yes. In theory, he's right. This is a special gift. Bonus time to spend together. A rare chance to reconnect after all these lost years. But hanging out with him at the current moment involves continuing this lie, which I just have no energy to do right now.

I mean, like I said to Louise, he's not an idiot. He obviously assumes I'm making money from being on the show. But he definitely doesn't know how much. And he DEFINITELY doesn't know that I'm doing it to get him out of debt. And I just don't have it in me right now to engage in any interaction that forces me to carefully avoid divulging those little details.

So I'll just quietly sulk in my room until Mary gets here. She will know exactly how to fix this.

Chapter 27

Mary finally came over last night with the plan: I would go on *The June Li Show* first thing the next morning to give my first interview as a member of the Mashad family. From there, she wanted me and Matt to pack up our things and move into one of her guesthouses where it would be "more secure" until the hype died down. Finally, with news of my existence out in the open, the producers believe a new opening has been made for more "relatable" storylines featuring me. Like, for example, Mary would like me to invite everyone over to her house for pre-prom so we could shoot it for a *Making Mashad* episode.

Personally, I was relieved. As terrifying as she is, there is something intensely comforting about having someone like Mary around. Someone who feels like she is perfectly capable of seamlessly plucking me out of even the tightest bind.

But Matt was . . . um, how do I put this gently? *Not* on board with Mary's plan.

"With all due respect, Mary, this is my daughter," he said in this serious voice I've never heard him use before. "And she's crumbling. This is too much."

I looked over at him, a little confused by this new overprotective vibe.

"Let's not be dramatic, now," Mary said, calmly scrolling through her phone. "She's fine."

"Look at her!" Matt exclaimed, pointing to where I was sitting on the couch in the same old Hanes sweats I'd had on for the past seventy-two hours. "I've never seen her so broken down."

"I'm fine," I tried to interject. "Really!"

I wasn't fine. Obviously. But Mary was there with a *plan*. How could he not see I was on my way to being fine?

"So she's being a little dramatic," Mary said, still scrolling through her phone. "She's a teenager. That's what they do."

"That may be what *your* teenagers do—or did, I don't know how old all your kids are," he said. "But not mine. I may not always get it exactly right, but I've done everything in my power to make sure that she's happy, that she feels secure."

"Right," Mary said. "We're all aware of the lengths you've gone to, Mr. Lawrence."

Matt asked what she meant by that, and Mary matter-of-factly just went, "Oh? Did Josie not tell you?" And I don't even really believe in God, but, in that moment, I shot out a little prayer: *Dear God, please, please, please, make me invisible.*

"Josie," Matt asked, turning to me, his eyes now slightly glassy. "What is she talking about?"

"It's nothing, Matt," I lied. "Seriously."

"Well, it can't be nothing," he persisted. "Because she just said, 'Did Josie not tell you.' So what did you not tell me?"

"Oh *God*," Mary said, throwing her phone into her Birkin bag. "I don't have time for this little soap opera. She knows you're in debt. We both do. That's why she agreed to come on the show. To make enough money to bail you out of debt, cover her own tuition, and buy back your comedy club." She took a look around our apartment before adding, "And maybe a new house."

You know how people look when they enter a surprise party they really, really didn't want their family to throw for them? That's how Matt looked. Just absolutely stunned in the worst way possible, his eyes looking like they might roll back into his skull because he so badly didn't want to face us.

"Josie," he finally whispered. "Is this true?"

I *wanted* to give him more of an explanation. I wanted to jump up and hug him. And tell him that I wasn't trying to deceive him. I just wanted to do something nice for him—for *both* of us. That I don't judge him for going into debt. That I'm just trying to help out, to make life easier for both of us. And I opened my mouth to say all that!!! But no words came out. All I could muster was a nod.

"I don't understand," he said. "Why would you lie?"

And this is when something shifted. I don't know what happened. Maybe I was temporarily possessed. Maybe I was stir-crazy after so much time cooped up in the apartment. Maybe it was just years of pent-up feelings bubbling to the surface. But I exploded.

"What do you *mean* you don't understand?!" I asked, tears suddenly streaming down my face. "How could you not understand?? I lied to you because I *had* to lie to you. Ever since Mom died and you gave up the club, it's felt like you're barely hanging on by a thread. And I can't afford to do anything to fray that thread any thinner. Losing Mom was devastating. Losing you after that would be . . . worse. So I put everything into being the perfect teenager for you. I get perfect grades and I don't make a fuss when you ditch me to work so many shifts that it seems like you're trying to avoid being home, and, yes, when I had an opportunity to bail you out of debt, I took it. And I don't feel sorry! I think I did the right thing. I missed you and not just the tired shell of you who comes home and passes out on the couch after a triple shift. I missed the *real* you. I want you to have your club back, to be out of debt, to sleep on a real bed. I want you to be really, truly happy again. So I agreed to go on the show. And I lied about why so your pride wouldn't get hurt. Is that so egregiously bad?"

"I'm sorry I've been such a burden to you," he said, tapping the ceiling above him before turning away from us. "Seems like you two have everything figured out here, so I'll just let you get back to it."

And, with that, he walked out. Not just out of the room, but out of the apartment. Past the reporters, past the screaming fans calling him "zaddy." Just casually strolled into his car and drove off.

"You know who's even more dramatic than teenagers?

Men," Mary said, throwing some of my clothes into a Louis Vuitton duffel bag she'd brought along with her. "He'll be fine. Let's head to my place."

✦ ✦ ✦

It's barely morning and Mary and I are sitting in the back of a black car headed to *The June Li Show*. I actually don't think I've ever seen the 101 this empty. My life in cars in Los Angeles has been decidedly marked by bumper-to-bumper traffic. And, to be honest, I usually don't mind it. I like looking into all the other cars and seeing what other people are doing, how they're choosing to pass the time. Without that familiar distraction on this car ride, all I can think about is Matt. I follow him on Find My Friends, so I have a vague idea of what he's been up to. Like last night, from my bed at Mary's, I saw he was spending the night at his friend Mario's. Now he's at California Pizza Kitchen. Probably just working. I wonder if he's being hounded by people. Or maybe they have him just doing dishes in the back to avoid the crowds.

But mostly all I keep doing is replaying in my mind everything I said. Did I take it too far? I didn't even mean everything I said. Okay, I sort of meant it. But maybe it came off too harsh. Maybe I could have softened the blow a bit. Highlighted the fact that I love him, that I appreciate everything he's done for me. But didn't I mention the fact that I appreciate everything?

He sent me one text last night:

Hey Jos, I'm sorry I stormed out. That wasn't cool. Just
need some time to think.

I've texted him thirteen times since then, and he hasn't
responded once. Well, he thumbs-upped them but that hardly
counts as a response. Doesn't he get that he's just proving my
point? *This* is why I had to lie to him all these years. He can't
handle the truth! I hold back a tear as I consider the idea that
he might never get over this. And now I feel a pang of anger.
How could he be such a baby? Doesn't he get that *I'm* the
teenager here? I'm sick of being the bigger person. Can't he
do it for once?

I swallow the anger and send him one more apology text.

"Have you heard from him?" Mary asks, looking over at
my phone as I refresh Matt's location for what must be the
fiftieth time.

"Not since last night," I admit. "He's a pretty conflict-averse
guy. I don't think I'll hear from him until he's calmed down.
I remember my mom would always say that when they got
into fights. 'He just shuts down. Mes leh eenkeh bah deevar
dahram harf meezanam.'" *It's like I'm talking to a wall.*

"The exact *opposite* of your birth father," Mary says with a
laugh. "Oh my God, that man adored conflict. Sometimes I
think he would start fights just to start them. You see where
your hotheaded sister Mona gets it from. I still can't believe
what she did. You know what the problem is? She doesn't
trust me. She doesn't understand that I know what I'm doing.
That when I say 'We need to keep this a secret until the show
airs,' I have a reason. That I've seen the numbers. We needed

to execute this perfectly to keep the show *alive*. Your presence needed to be carefully teased out on our own terms—not just carelessly blurted out in the heat of the moment."

Mary has really not let this Mona thing go, and I would be lying if I said I don't feel a little responsible. I mean, after all, she's in this much trouble for defending *me*.

"I know she broke the rules and ruined your plan," I say. "But . . . the cameras didn't fully pick up why she came out to begin with. That girl Genevieve is really *so* mean, Mary. I think it came from a good place."

"It always comes from a good place," Mary says. "She's a nice girl. But she's also a *privileged* girl. She doesn't understand that everything—this show, the fame, the money, the fans—all of it can be taken away at any given moment. She's too spoiled to realize how fickle this all is. And that's my fault. I gave her the world, and now she's left incapable of understanding how easily it can be taken out of her hands."

"I'm sure she gets it on some level," I try. "I'm sure they all do. They see how hard you work."

"The other girls I worry about less," she admits. "They're privileged as well, don't get me wrong. But they don't have that reckless streak Mona has. They follow instructions, even if they don't fully understand them. Mona doesn't. And she got that from your father. Both of them—great people. So kind. But, unfortunately, good intent is not enough to make reckless behavior right. Luckily, you don't seem to have gotten that from him. Must have taken after your mother."

"She could be reckless sometimes, too," I quietly admit. "That's how she died. She was speeding way over the limit.

She would always do that, and I would always tell her not to."

"Well, maybe *that* is why you're so cautious," Mary says. "In opposition to her."

We sit there in silence a while longer, letting the heavy words just sort of hang in the air between us.

"How well did you know her?" I ask. "In Mr. Schwartz's office that day, you said you did. But how?"

Before Mary can answer, the car comes screeching to a halt.

"I'm so sorry, ma'am," Mary's driver this morning, Vanessa, says from the front. "We got a nail in the tire. I thought we would be able to make it to Burbank without changing it, but it looks like we're going to be stuck here."

Chapter 28

The car broke down in Glendale, which is a predominantly Armenian neighborhood, but Mary knows a great Persian restaurant nearby. According to her, they have the best kaleh pacheh in America. So although her assistant has offered to get us a new car or even a helicopter, Mary has decided it's fate. We were meant to get stranded here this morning to revisit one of her favorite restaurants. Of course, it's four in the morning and the restaurant is closed, but Mary gets ahold of the owners, and, within fifteen minutes, we're seated at a booth with Mary digging into her kaleh pacheh as I teeleet my ab goosht.

"Are you sure we won't be late for June Li?" I ask nervously as I tear my sangak bread into little pieces.

"We are fine," Mary reassures. "This is why I insist on leaving two hours earlier than necessary for anything. Yes, we left in the middle of the night. But when things like this happen, we're fine. Plus, we already had your glam taken care of. You could get there fifteen minutes before showtime, and it would be fine."

"Okay, cool," I say, the knots in my stomach slowly

uncoiling. "I can't believe they have ab goosht here. It's my favorite, and I can never find it at restaurants."

"I noticed you having it at my Nowruz party," Mary says, pausing for a second to savor a bite of piping hot kaleh pacheh before adding, "I love it, too. You know, I had so many Persian people not understanding why I would serve it at a Persian New Year party. I told them it's because I love it! I wanted every delicious Persian dish imaginable, so the world could see *all* our delicious foods in that episode. Not just some sabzi polo mahi."

"Yeah, it was my first time having it since my mom died," I tell her. "She would always make it for me growing up."

"I used to make it for the girls when they were growing up, too," Mary says. "But truthfully, I was never much of a cook. Ali was the great cook between the two of us."

We sit there quietly for a bit, until I can't help but just ask her one more time.

"So, um, I know we sort of got cut off in the car, but—"

"She was my cousin," Mary answers before I can finish. "My cousin who I told you I lived with when I moved to America. My cousin was Sharzad. And her mom—my Khaleh Farrah—was your grandmother."

I drop my spoon.

"I'm sorry, what?"

"Your mother was my cousin," Mary says matter-of-factly. "One of my only living relatives. I loved her like a sister. That is, of course, until she moved into my home and slept with my husband. But you know? Even then, on some level, I still loved her. I was at her funeral, you know?"

"What?" is, again, the only word that comes out of my mouth as the room starts spinning around me, my brain feeling like a soda can you just opened after shaking it to death.

"I heard she died," Mary continues. "And I knew I couldn't be seen or anything, but I drove a small black town car with the windows completely tinted, parked far enough away that nobody would spot me, and just sobbed."

"You *sobbed*?" I ask, trying to visualize it. "At my mom's funeral?"

"I sobbed," Mary confirms. "She was my little cousin. Yes, we had a falling-out. But I didn't expect her to die. I would be lying if I said I didn't wish it upon her when we were at the height of it all, but I didn't really want that to happen. I loved her."

I stare at her, the room still spinning around us, and suddenly those vaguely familiar features start coming into focus a little more sharply. They don't look alike because they're both Iranian. They look alike because they're cousins.

"She never told me about you," I say. "Ever. She never even mentioned a cousin."

"I don't blame her," Mary says with a shrug. "I haven't exactly raved about her to my girls, either. Melody was just a toddler, but she might have some early memories from when Sharzad was living with us. And Meesha and Mona vaguely know the story. But I've never told them the whole truth. If they know, it was their big-mouthed father's doing."

"So, she was living with you guys?" I ask, still processing. "Like, in your house?"

"Yes. Your grandmother had just died, and your mother was going through this messy breakup, so I offered for her to come stay with us for a bit. She was thirty-eight, but she was still struggling with figuring out what she wanted to do with her life, who she wanted to *be*. She kept saying that. 'Marjan, who do I want to be?' So I told her to come stay with us and we'd figure it out together. You know, I helped her get that catering business going. She was always a great cook. It was an obvious career choice."

You know when you try to open a buggy new window on your browser and the entire computer just freezes? That's how my mind feels right now. Stuck. Frozen. Incapable of processing.

I stare at Mary, dumbfounded, as she continues, "So things were going great as far as I was concerned. Yes, she and Ali were close. But I just thought he was being a good husband. Taking care of my family. Spending extra time with my cousin while she was struggling. Then, of course, I found out. It was the day I found out my embryo transfer had been successful, and our surrogate was pregnant with Mona. I told Ali, and, instead of being happy, he burst into tears. He told me about your mom. Apparently, *she* was also pregnant with his child. She had just told him a few days prior. *That* is what killed me. That he told me."

"But he had to. How could he not tell you?"

"No, you're missing the point," Mary says. "*He* is just a dumb man who couldn't keep it in his pants. *She* was my cousin. My only living blood relative, aside from my children. My sense of home bottled up into a singular human being. She had betrayed me, and she didn't even have the guts to tell me. And, in doing so, just like Iran, she became another intangible home. A figment of my imagination."

The attack on my mom feels like a refresh on my mind, instantly jolting me into protective mode.

"I'm sure she was going to tell you," I insist. "Really. My mom was a good person. I'm sure she felt bad."

"I think she loved him," Mary muses. "Really. I think she truly fell in love with him. And I can't blame her for that. I know what it is to love him. He was a good man."

Not this dumb narrative again.

"Everyone keeps saying that," I tell her. "But he wasn't. Look at what he did to you! He had an affair with your cousin. He tore your family apart! And look at what he did to us. He abandoned my mom and me completely. I get that maybe he made that choice to save your marriage, but what he did to us was not okay."

"That was a complicated situation, Josie Joonam," Mary says. "And I'm not sure it was all Ali's doing. Nothing is black and white. Even your mom. Oh, I was furious. I was so hurt. So betrayed. The two people I trusted more than anyone in the world had stabbed me right in the back. It took years for me to stop feeling furious. But when I look back on it now, I realize it wasn't so simple. My marriage with Ali was not in a great place. He was lonely. Your mother was at a low point in her life, but she was *present*. I was checked out. I was a top agent at CAA then. I barely had any free time, and, after I had Meesha, doctors had warned me having a third kid was unlikely, so the few free hours I did have to spare were solely devoted to going to different fertility specialists, desperately trying to find a way to conceive Mona. Your mother made Ali feel needed. He swept in with his charisma and his charm, and he made her feel taken care of in her darkest hour. It's how I fell for him. I understand how it happened."

"So . . . you forgave her?" I wonder if my mom once wanted the answer to be yes as much as I do in this moment.

"No," Mary answers calmly. "Never. To be very clear, I don't forgive Ali, either. They betrayed me. And I will never forgive that action, for the pain they caused me during what should have been one of the most joyous moments of my life. But do I think they were both inherently bad people? No. I loved them."

"Did you ever talk to her? After the fact?"

"I tried getting in touch with her a few times," Mary says. "A couple years before she died. But she wanted nothing to do with me or Ali. I said some unforgivable things when it first happened. And, the way she saw it, he chose me over her. I'm sure that played into it. She was done with me, with us, with all of it. But I did miss her. You know, she held a special place for me, she was family in a way nobody else on the planet was, or ever will be for me."

"I feel the same way," I tell her. "Different. But the same. Nobody else will ever be able to be my family the way she was."

We sit there in silence for a few minutes, neither of us touching our hearty breakfast soups as we let her memory sink into the empty space between us.

"This is the two of us," Mary says, pulling up a picture of an old print photo on her phone of two young brunette girls hugging outside of LAX. "The day I got to LA. Khaleh Farrah took this picture of us. I was so terrified, but this little girl came running to me so excited that it forced a smile out of me. It was probably the first time I smiled since hearing about my parents. Your mother always knew how to make me smile. I deleted every trace of her from my life after what happened, but I could never bring myself to get rid of this picture."

Mary takes one more look at the picture on her phone before locking the screen and throwing it back in her bag.

"I know she's my mom, but I really am sorry, Mary Joon," I say, my defensiveness melting away. "I'm sorry you had to go through that."

"Nobody gets everything they want exactly the way they wanted it, Josie Joonam," Mary says. Then she adds with a chuckle, "Last week, the *New York Times* called me the 'living embodiment of the American dream.' And yet here I am, stuck eating kaleh pacheh on the side of the road with the love child my dead husband bore with my dead cousin."

Mary's here next to me, but it feels like she's gone. Like she's hopped in a portal and gone straight back to that time in her life.

"Is it hard for you?" I ask. "Having me around?"

She thinks about it for a moment before responding. "It's complicated. On the one hand, you're the product of their love. The same love that devastated and destroyed me. I spent so many years trying to forget whatever happened between them happened. And now here you are. Living proof of their betrayal."

Mary sighs, and I try my best to keep my eyes focused on my ab goosht. How can I look her in the eye after she pretty much just called me betrayal personified?

"But then, the fact remains that once upon a time they were the two people I loved most in the world," she continues. "I see them both inside of you, and it's like I have these little pieces of them both back. Your inability to be anything but yourself, that's her. Your openness, and the way you have approached your sisters with such depth and kindness, that's him. And here's what I wasn't expecting at all: Your ability to set everything else aside to do what's right for your family? Well, that's me."

"I remind you of . . . yourself?" I ask, not sure I see it. "Really?"

"Of course you do," Mary says. "Look at what you're doing right now. You are doing what is right for your stepfather and for yourself in the long run, even if it hurts a little bit in the moment. You know how to suck it up and get the job done. That's me," she repeats. "I will do whatever it takes to protect my family—even if my own family members don't realize it in the moment. It's funny, I was so focused on how you'd be a reminder of them, I forgot that, through her, you just might have a tiny bit of me in you, as well."

I don't *want* to cry in front of Mary, but a single tear breaks loose and makes its way down my cheek.

"Don't cry," Mary says, signaling the waiter for a check. "The car will be here any minute, and you don't want your eyes looking bloodshot on *The June Li Show*. Next thing we know, people will be saying you have a drug problem."

Chapter 29

I have never met anyone like Mary Mashad. To be honest, I have a hard time believing anyone else like her even exists in the world. Half an hour ago, we were trapped in a tiny little Iranian restaurant having what might be the most emotionally intense conversation I have ever had in my life. Now she is squeezed next to Javier on the white leather love seat in my dressing room as they both send emails, her demeanor as professional as ever.

I don't want to be staring at her, but I can't help it. How could she have possibly gone through all that? And she doesn't even seem to hate either of them. What does this say about my mom? Did I have her on too high of a pedestal? What does it say about *me* that I needed the affair to not be real? So what if she really fell in love with a married man? Wouldn't it be anti-feminist of me to be judging her so harshly for that? It clearly was a weak moment, and, if Mary can have compassion for her choice, shouldn't I also be able to?

Ali, on the other hand, I don't think I can ever understand.

Okay, he cheated on his wife. Okay, he fell for her cousin. That's all fine. I can get past that. But the fact remains he left my mom and me. Mary doesn't get it. None of these people here in his orbit do. They weren't there, watching my mom try to scrape by to make ends meet. They weren't there for all the awkward silences and pitiful looks she had to endure when people asked where my dad was. They weren't there for the Father's Days we had to sit out until Matt came around. I was there for all of that. And, no matter how good of a man he was in other realms, I don't think I can ever forgive Ali for putting my mom—for putting us *both*—through that.

Mary makes a noise and I get excited that maybe she wants to resume our conversation, but she's just clearing her throat before hopping on some sort of wildly early business call. Does this make Mary my . . . aunt? I imagine calling Mary "Khaleh Marjan" and wince. No. It's too weird. I look down at the time on my phone: 4:45. Still way too early to talk to Lou.

Ugh. I need to distract myself. I cannot sit here tossing this new information around in my mind any longer or I'm going to burst. I open Snapchat on my phone and scroll past the drunken stories of Lou, Isaac, Grant, and the rest of the popular kids out after the basketball game last night and notice Genevieve is notably absent. According to Lou, she hasn't been at school since the video came out, either. Should I be feeling more guilty? I did really enjoy watching Mona put her in her place that day. But I didn't think it would get *this* out of hand. I just wanted her to say sorry. Not to make her live in hiding.

My pang of guilt is interrupted when my Snapchat feed automatically progresses to Timmy's story. First of all, I forgot he added me as a friend on his super secret private Snapchat account when we went to the concert. Second, the reason I forgot was because he never seems to post any stories or anything. But here it is. A new story from Timmy. And it's a selfie of him and a pretty girl with icy lavender hair and flawless skin that looks like it could never possibly be plagued with a zit. *Who is that?* I mean, why do I even care? We're just friends. Timmy is allowed to have really pretty girlfriends who he posts Snapchat stories with. Maybe they're dating! Maybe that's why he didn't want either of our hangouts to be a date. And maybe he really was just going to tell me I had a booger by the Eiffel Tower that night. But, again, why do I care? None of my business.

My phone vibrates with a text and I'm thrilled to have a distraction, immediately tapping out of Snapchat to find a text from Matt:

Good luck Jos. Love you.

Okay, I think. *Maybe the damage here isn't quite as bad as I thought.* I quickly heart the text and write him a *love you* back.

"Delivery!" a PA on the show exclaims, knocking twice before entering with a giant bouquet of pale pink hydrangeas. "Josie, this is for you."

"Thanks," I say, taking the giant bouquet from her and placing it on the coffee table in the center of my dressing room. "These are gorgeous. Do you know who they're from?"

"There's a note," she tells me, pointing to the small envelope pinned onto the vase. "And, just so you know, you're on in thirty. Break a leg!"

"Thank you, Beth," Mary says, somehow knowing the name of the PA without even looking up from her phone. "We're looking forward to it."

Maybe it's recency bias after having seen his story, but a small part of me hopes the bouquet is from Timmy. Like, I know we're just friends. But sometimes friends get friends supportive bouquets of flowers, right?!?

Apparently wrong. The card is from my sisters: *You've got this!!! Love you, Jos. XO Meesh, Mo, & Mel.* I highly doubt Meesha signed that herself, but I'll take it.

"Okay," Mary says, putting her phone down. "It's time to do a quick refresh on strategy. Javier, are you ready?"

"One second," Javier says, finishing typing something before he finally stuffs his phone in the pocket of what I can only assume are his designer jeans. "All right. Yes. Well, I think we nailed the look. Right, Mary?"

"Yes," Mary agrees, looking me up and down. "It's very girl next door."

"But taken up a notch," Javier adds. "Like, the girl you *wished* lived next door."

I'm glad they're happy with the final product, considering how much went into curating this look for me. Last night, Mary and Javier had a meeting with six different stylists and what Mary referred to as their "entire glam council" to decide what I would look like for this appearance. "This is your introduction to the world," Mary kept telling me. "No detail can be taken lightly."

They were so set on my look that Mary had me wake up at three in the morning to get my hair and makeup done by Becky and Alfie because she didn't trust the beauticians on staff at *The June Li Show* to fully "nail the Mashad element of the aesthetic." Even now, Mary insists Becky and Alfie have to come in to do my touch-ups before I go on. "Nobody else gets it like they do," she keeps saying. "Hair and makeup is an *art*. You cannot just introduce new artists with new visions to come tamper with the masterpiece at the final hour." As prickly as they have been toward me since our first encounter, I've noticed myself sharing Mary's sense of trust in Becky and Alfie. They do know what they're doing. And, at this point, I just feel like I have too many things to worry about to add an out-of-place hair or bags under my eyes to the list. I'm not hoping for the otherworldly looks my half siblings go for. I just want to look *unremarkable*. To leave people with nothing to say in that department. And I trust Becky and Alfie can get me there.

As for the clothes, the team of stylists decided to have me in some loose-fitting ripped light-wash Re/Done jeans, a pair of sparkly silver Golden Goose sneakers, and a fitted white Vince T-shirt. Normally I'd insist on wearing my own clothes, but to be totally honest, I'm scared. I have absolutely no idea what I'm about to get myself into. And if there's one thing about Mary, she knows how to play this game. So I'm just going to do exactly what she says and hope for the best.

"Your strength," Mary is now saying, "is that people relate to you. You're one of *them*, who also happens to be one of *us*. We need to play that up."

"Remember, you're the *awkward* sister, which is a blessing, in a way," Javier adds. "You can't go wrong. Even if you freeze, that's great. People will feel sorry for you. I mean, ideally you won't freeze. Just do that awkward blabber thing you do, and it should all go great. You're just so *normal*, you know? People go nuts for normal."

I'm not sure how many normal teens are out there wearing thousand-dollar sneakers, but Javier doesn't seem like the kind of guy who's open to feedback and Mary is in no mood to be challenged when it comes to this appearance. "This is *very* important, Josie Joonam," Mary keeps saying. "You need to go up there and just be totally honest and relatable. The people will love you, which, in turn, will get us ratings. If you just listen to us, this could be the most viewed season of the show yet."

Mary and Javier pause to discuss whether or not they would be better off having me in a gray T-shirt to contrast with the white couch as I feel a buzz on my phone. A text from Timmy. I immediately burst out laughing when I see it's just a selfie of himself doing a funny face. Then another text:

Since I can't be there to do it in person.

"Look!" Javier exclaims, pointing to me. "Josie is smiling. She loves the gray. Right, Josie? Tell Mary you love the gray."

"Oh," I say, putting my phone down on the vanity table.

"Sorry. Um, I was just looking at a text. I'm fine with whatever."

"See?" Mary says, turning to Javier. "Josie doesn't care, which is why I think we should go with black. It will be a starker contrast."

"Black is too mature," Javier insists. "We want her to seem young. Bright. Soft."

"That is a good point," Mary says, nodding intensely.

I peep back down at my phone, Timmy's funny face instantly taking the edge off the stressful vibe in here. I start to write back *Thanks. Wish you were here*, then delete it. Too clingy. Then I try again. *Thanks! What are you up to?* Nope. Too nosy. Also, it's not even the crack of dawn yet. There isn't much he could possibly be up to. Okay, wait. I have it:

Thanks! Here's to hoping this goes better than filming the dinner party scene.

My heart skips a beat when I see he immediately gives my text a "haha" and responds:

We already established that was as bad as it could possibly get! Only up from there. You're gonna crush it.

I smile down at my phone for just long enough that it may be creepy before I remember the lavender-haired girl. I check Timmy's location on Snap Maps and see that he's at his parents' place down the street from Mary's in Beverly Palms. I wonder if she's there with him. Did she spend the night? When he took that selfie to send me, did she ask what he was doing? And if she did, what did he say? Does she know I exist? I mean, even if we're not, like, romantically into each other, we're pretty good friends at this point. I hope he would *mention* me. But, to be fair, he never mentioned her to me. So *are* we even that good of friends?

"Knock, knock." June Li redirects my train of thought as she bursts into my dressing room. "Mind if I interrupt?!"

I'm not a huge celebrity person, but something about seeing June Li in the flesh makes me want to squeal like a tween at a Harry Styles concert. She's just so . . . she's JUNE FREAKING LI. The entire country wakes up to her every single morning. She's as American as apple pie and white picket fences. I'm too busy gawking at her to muster any response, but luckily Mary seems to be fine taking the wheel.

"JUNE." Mary rushes over to her friend with her arms wide open. "My June Joon!!! Get over here, you!"

"MARE BEAR," June squeals as she rushes into Mary's arms. "How the heck are ya?"

"You know," Mary says. "I'm better now that I see you."

Javier interjects. "June. Help settle this for Mary and me: Should we have Josie in a black T-shirt or gray?"

June looks me up and down, then, without acknowledging me at all, shifts her attention back to Javier. "Gray," she responds resolutely. "Absolutely gray."

"I knew it!" Javier exclaims, before stepping outside—presumably to somehow source me a gray T-shirt. With him gone, it's just me in this tiny room alone with arguably the two most powerful women in Hollywood.

"So, tell me," June says, turning her attention back to Mary. "Did you know? About her?"

"Yes." Mary nods. "I did. We were hoping to release it all on our show. You know, on our terms. But, we figured, since the news is out, who better to handle it than you? Basically family."

"Of course," June agrees, taking Mary's hands in hers. "Well, I've got this all under control. Don't worry. She's going to be America's favorite little bastard by the time this interview is over."

I gulp hard at the word *bastard*. It sounds weird in reference to me. But it sounds even weirder coming out of June Li's mouth. Her whole thing is spreading the love. As in, her show's slogan is quite literally *Spread the love with me*. Something about calling a teenager whose presence you haven't even fully acknowledged yet a bastard doesn't feel like spreading the love to me.

"All right," she says. "I'm out of here. Love you, Mare."

"Love you, Junie Joon!!!" Mary shouts back as she takes a seat back on the leather couch. As soon as June closes the door, Mary turns her attention to me. "Isn't she just the best?"

"Uh, yeah," I lie. "You guys seem close."

"We are," Mary says, her voice lowering a few octaves before adding, "but you have to remember this is all business. What June is trying to get is the best story, which, as of now, is you being Ali's love child."

"Right," I say, a pit starting to take shape in my stomach. "I sort of got that vibe."

"Your main job here really is to divert," she says. "Tease

something else that might pop up this season. Make people want to watch. The novelty of this Ali affair business is going to wear off. We need to give viewers a taste of something more."

"But what?" I ask. "What else am I supposed to give them?"

"Don't worry about that," Mary says. "I've taken care of everything. All you have to do is get out there and answer her questions honestly."

Chapter 30

I'm standing just off the stage of *The June Li Show*, staring at the scuffed-up black floor because one of the producers told me June "hates" eye contact before we're live. I wonder if the producer would have said that with Mary standing next to me. Probably not.

Honestly, I'm not mad about the no eye contact thing. It's kind of meditative staring at the floor here. No need to look at the cameras, the stage, the audience full of excited middle-aged women. No need to look at June as they touch up her makeup where she's sitting onstage. All I have to focus on is this floor. As my heart picks up speed, I try to think of my mom. She would have been totally unfazed by all of this. Nothing intimidated her. Her birthday voicemail starts playing like a song in my head, my muscles slowly relaxing each time my brain repeats it like a mantra. *Hi, Josie Joonam, you're asleep just one room over from me, but it's midnight and you're officially eleven! Happy birthday, azizam. I love you so much and can't wait to see you in the morning.* See? This is why I don't listen to it on my phone. Because forcing myself to keep it memorized means I can carry it with me wherever I go.

"She's the hashtag MysteryMashad we've all been buzzing about for the past forty-eight hours," I hear June announce before I can repeat the voicemail a sixth time. "JOSIE LAWRENCE, EVERYBODY."

"Aaaand *go*," the producer whisper-yells behind me as she shoves me onto the stage.

The cameras don't faze me as much as they did that first night of filming *Making Mashad*. But something about being onstage makes me want to puke. It's like the time Lou made me sign up for *Into the Woods* with her in eighth grade. Only worse because, instead of a crowd full of parents, this time I'm facing a crowd full of strangers. And instead of playing the role of Tree #3, I have to play *myself*. But not really myself. The version of myself Mary and Javier have created, the one who wears three hundred–dollar jeans and "relates" to the general public.

I can do this. All Mary told me to do was be honest. Just be honest. I don't even need to overthink anything. I don't have to pick and choose my words carefully. And I don't even have to look June in her ice-cold brown eyes.

The spotlight is directly on me as I cautiously make my way over to the couch across from June where I'm expected to take my seat. To be clear, there's literally a giant light following me as I walk. It's boiling hot, but kind of soothing in its own way. Like a giant warm hug following me wherever I go. I try to focus on how the warm light feels on my skin and not on the fact that this is all being streamed live to millions of people.

"Welcome, Josie," June says with the same warmth she had in greeting Mary earlier. "We are *so* happy to have you on here!"

"Thanks, June," I say, trying my best to look at the camera, and only the camera. "I-I'm really excited to be here. I'm a huge fan."

"Now, for those of you who haven't heard," June says, turning her attention to the crowd as she reads off a teleprompter. "Josie Lawrence is the eighteen-year-old love child of Ali Mashad and a woman by the name of Sharzad Lawrence. Josie's identity was revealed just two days ago when her half sister Mona Mashad was filmed defending her against a high school bully. Check it out."

A screen drops down behind us and the video of Mona telling off Genevieve plays for the entire crowd.

"So, Josie," June says as the video ends. "Tell us about this day. What was going on?"

I catch a glimpse of the crowd staring at me intently, hungry for whatever's about to come out of my mouth, and my stomach drops like I've just entered the upside-down part of a roller coaster ride (as if I ever go on roller coasters, LOL). I try to shift my eyes back over to the cameras and think of the selfie Timmy sent me. My lips slowly curve upward as I picture the image of him with his chin tucked into his neck and his eyelids flipped upward.

"Well, um, we were actually filming an episode of the show," I finally say, imagining Timmy standing behind the camera operator encouraging me to keep going. "I've got my prom coming up soon, and we thought it would be fun to film an

293

episode with my sisters helping me pick a prom dress. So we were at Vik, and I had to go to the bathroom, and, on my way back, I ran into a . . . um, a friend . . . from school."

"That girl did *not* look like a friend to me," June says with a laugh. "At least, Mona didn't think so. What was she saying to you that got your sister so mad?"

Just be honest. Just be honest. Mary's words play over and over like a song I can't get out of my head.

"Yeah, well, actually, I've had a crush on this guy forever, and she's dating that guy," I say. "So she was just sort of making fun of me. Saying I could never be with him because I'm a hairy freak and that they laugh at the love letters I used to write him in fourth grade."

"Well, that is just *awful*," June says, shaking her head in disapproval. "I see why Mona felt the need to intervene."

"Yeah," I say. "She didn't have to do that, obviously. But I appreciated it."

"That's what sisters are for," June says with a smile. "Speaking of . . . how long have you known your sisters?"

"It's, well . . . it's only been a few weeks," I say. "I actually just found out who my birth dad was recently."

"Wow! Only a few weeks!" June exclaims. "And now you're on the show, with your sister fighting tooth and nail to defend you. Must be a big change of pace."

"It's huge," I say. "Really different from my normal."

"What *was* your normal, Josie?" June asks, her eyes narrowing. "Tell us about yourself. Who *is* Josie Lawrence?"

"Um, well, there's not much to say, really," I admit. "I'm a senior in high school. I'm going to Stanford in the fall to study pre-med. My mom always wanted me to do that. She passed away in a car crash a few years ago, so it feels extra special that I can finally make that dream come true for both of us."

"I am sorry to hear about your mother," June says. "Do you know how she crossed paths with Ali?"

I freeze. Mary wanted me to be honest. But would she want me to be honest about *this*? I make eye contact with her where she's standing just off the stage, and she nods for me to keep going.

I take a deep breath and spit it out. "She was, um, she was actually Mary's cousin."

The crowd gasps.

"Her cousin?" June asks, appalled. "So you are saying Mary Mashad's cousin had an affair with Ali Mashad?"

"I mean, I think it was more complicated than that," I say, suddenly wanting to protect my mom. "Well, yes. I guess, to answer your question, they *technically* had an affair. But Mary's marriage was in a hard place. And my mom was also in a hard place. It was all complicated. My mom was a great person. Until my stepdad, Matt, came and adopted me, she was a single mom. It was just the two of us for the first few years, and she never made me feel like I was missing something. And even once Matt was there, she always put everything she had into making sure I felt loved and taken care of."

"Well, everyone," June says, squinting as she turns to face the camera. "Let's all remember my message. Spread the love. Josie's mother may have had an affair with her own cousin, who just so happens to be my best friend and America's favorite mother, Mary Mashad. But the woman was also a wonderful single mother, and it sounds like she raised a wonderful daughter. *Every* family is complicated. And I suppose that's why we keep watching the Mashads. They openly share their complications with us, and each new development makes us feel a bit more normal."

I stare at her, confused. Where was this loving energy in the dressing room?

"So, Josie, I have to say. *You* seem so normal." June turns back toward me, a slightly condescending smile breaking across her face. "Has it been difficult fitting in with your megastar sisters, considering you come from such vastly different backgrounds? And, well, considering the circumstances of your birth?"

"No," I say, still trying my best to be honest. "It actually hasn't. They've been so nice and welcoming. Mary, too. They all have. I feel really lucky."

"Wow," June says, scooting herself closer. "Now, I have to ask . . . what about Meesha?"

Oh gosh.

"Wh-what about her?" I ask, already nervous about where this could possibly be going.

"Well, I did notice one thing in that video. She's not there! I mean, the video obviously features Mona," June says. "And Melody can be seen trying to stop her in the background—classic Melody, so kind and cautious. But Meesha seems to be missing. Sources are saying she wasn't even spotted at the store when the confrontation took place. Did she not snag an invite to the prom dress shopping trip?"

Okay, easy. I can answer this without lying.

"No! She did," I say. "She was there. She just was in the bathroom when that happened."

"In the bathroom? With you and Mona?"

"No! Actually, she was in the bathroom at Vik. That's why Mona and I went to use the bathroom in the hallway."

"And she was still in the bathroom when you got back? And for that entire feisty interaction?"

"Um, yeah," I say. "She was."

"C'mon, girl," June Li says with a knowing look. "Every diehard *Making Mashad* fan knows those girls lock themselves in the bathroom when they're over filming! What happened? Spill the tea."

"She, um, I think she got in a bit of a tiff with Melody and Mona and needed some space," I say. "It'll be on the show!"

I hope that plug makes Mary proud.

"A tiff? Juicy!" June exclaims, scooching closer. "What was it over?"

I pause for a minute before responding, thinking through exactly how I'm going to answer this.

"Mona was just . . . frustrated with her," I finally say. "I don't really have an opinion on the situation, but she thought Meesha was kind of in a bad mood, so she said something, and Meesha left."

"Why would Meesha be in a bad mood?" June pries. "Was something going on?"

"Uh, I'm not sure," I say. "Like I said, I don't really have an opinion. I didn't pick up on her acting any differently than usual that day. But, you know, I don't know her as well."

"Do you think it's you?" June asks. "Does being around you put her in a bad mood?"

"Um, well, like I said, I really don't know her super well," I say, beads of sweat forming on my forehead. "So I wouldn't really know her bad mood from her good mood."

"Right," June says. "But do you think something happened between the two of you, specifically, that might have her on edge?"

"Uh," I say, trying my best to picture Timmy's face but instead seeing Pete's chiseled back. "N-no. Not that I can think of."

"What about her relationship?" June asks. "There were rumors she and Bunny barely spoke at Coachella. Anything going on there?"

I look over at Mary, who just shrugs before mouthing, "BE HONEST." I can't be honest about this. This is a secret. But I guess Mary doesn't know this secret. So is it *really* a lie if Mary doesn't know I'm lying? I doubt she wants me to out her daughter's cheating scandal to the nation on live television.

"Hmm," I say, trying to buy time before I have to answer. "Um, I'm not sure. I've only known everyone for a few weeks, so I'm not super familiar with their love lives."

"Really?" June asks. "That's hard to believe, with you roaming around Mary's house for filming. I'm sure you've seen something or other going on."

What in the world is this? Why will she not drop it?

"No," I lie. "It's pretty boring stuff, really. I guess I did see Meesha with Bunny once at Mary's Persian New Year party. But they were super cute."

"Huh," June says. "What about Pete Sanderson? Have you met him at all? Those two seem so close. I wonder how Bunny feels about that."

Oh my gosh. She knows. Which means Mary knows. That's why she kept insisting that I *be honest*. She set this whole thing up. She *does* want me to out her daughter, to pump even more drama into the news cycle before the new season even airs. To give the show another twist. But I can't.

"Just over FaceTime once," I say, which isn't technically a lie. "He was nice. And I don't know Bunny well at all, so I can't really speak to her feelings on anything."

I see Mary out of the corner of my eye, instructing me to "STOP BEING BORING AND GIVE HER WHAT SHE WANTS."

"Interesting," June says. "So you haven't seen anything . . . fishy? Anything to indicate Meesha and Bunny might be on the rocks?"

"Nope," I say, avoiding all eye contact with Mary. "Nothing."

"Hmm," she says, visibly disappointed. "All right then, folks. There you have it! America's newest reality royal, Josie Lawrence. Next up, Poison Puppet here to discuss his latest album."

Chapter 31

"You had ONE job," Mary yells at me as she stands above my bed in her guesthouse. "*Be honest*. And you couldn't do that. This is my fault. Why do I even try? Between you and my daughters, when will I learn? The only person I can depend on to get anything done around here is myself."

"How could you put me in that position?" I ask through tears. "I thought one of *your* brand tenets was family first! What about throwing Meesha under the bus would have been family first?"

"I thought you got it," Mary says, shaking her head. "Were you not listening at the restaurant? Sharing this tidbit—'throwing Meesha under the bus,' as you so eloquently put it—*is* putting family first. In this family, we do what we have to for the numbers. *That* is how we put family first."

"But you're the number one show in the world," I try to remind her. "Couldn't the numbers have waited just this once?"

"Don't you *dare* try to give me pointers on how to do my

job," she says so sharply that the words slice right through me. "You know how this show has stayed number one for all these years? Me. I let my husband die on camera for numbers. We streamed the love of my life's funeral live on Yay! for numbers. We mourned his death on camera. Then that got old, and we needed something new. That's when Mona started dating Max. And for years I let the world watch my baby girl's first love unfold. He was a toxic jerk, but America loved him, and the storyline was a nice, lighthearted numbers boost after all the grief and death. Then they broke up—he dumped her for that model, the one he's engaged to. That was *really* great for numbers. When the hype of that died down, Meesha came out. And the world got to watch an Iranian family deal with the revelation that their daughter and sister is gay. Another fantastic numbers boost. Then things mellowed out again, so I invited you, my dead husband's love child with my beloved cousin, on for yet another boost—"

"So that's all I'm here for?" I say, surprised by how much her words sting. "A numbers boost?"

"That was the plan before your sister went and screwed it all up by getting caught on that security camera," she says. "But, even then, I still had hope! Maybe you somehow inherited Ali's unwavering ability to pull through for me at the last hour. Maybe you could go on *The June Li Show* and just tell the damn truth like I asked you to. But no. You couldn't even do that."

How could I have ever trusted this woman? She doesn't even have her own children's best interests at heart. Let alone mine.

"How long did you know I knew about Meesha?"

"Since the day it happened," she says. "Obviously. There are security cameras on every inch of this compound. I review each one before bed every night. I saw. I knew. And I knew the footage couldn't go on the show without Meesha's consent, so I was waiting for our moment to use it. THIS WAS IT. And you blew it."

"So you were using me," I say. "And you wanted to use your daughter?"

"Aren't you going to Stanford? How do you *still* not understand this?" she asks, as if I truly don't possess a single brain cell. "Capitalizing on these storylines is how I *protect* my family. The designer clothes, the nice homes, the fancy cars, the only life my children have ever known. All of it goes away if we don't mine what we have. I thought you, of all people, would get it."

"What do you mean?" I ask, offended. "Why would I get your cold-hearted logic?"

"Because I *thought* we were similar," Mary says, more gently this time. "I thought you knew what it was to do what you have to do to take care of your family."

"I *do*," I insist. "And you're right. That's why I agreed to come on the show. For money. But money is not why I've stayed on the show. I've stayed because . . . I love my sisters. I didn't expect to. But I do. And I would never do anything to stab them in the back, even if it loses me money."

"Well, that is very sweet of you," Mary says sarcastically. "But nobody loves your sisters more than I do. They are my *daughters*. And I will do whatever it takes to protect them—to keep this dynasty going. If that means seizing an opportune moment to air some dirty laundry that they aren't quite ready to share, I expect you to trust my judgment on that."

"Did our car even really break down this morning?"

Mary scoffs. "Are you accusing me of *faking* a flat tire to sit in a restaurant and eat kaleh pacheh with you?"

I don't even flinch. "Yes."

"No, I did not fake the flat tire," Mary says. "Our car broke down, and I was hungry."

"But everything you told me about my mom. That conversation conveniently happened right before the appearance, and then June asked me all those questions about her and Ali."

"Josie, I do not stage conversations off camera," Mary says with a sigh. "If you remember correctly, *you* were the one who asked me about her. Did I capitalize on the timing and give June's producers a heads-up after the fact? Of course. That's just good business sense. And thank God I had it. If I didn't, the whole segment would have been you yammering on about your mundane school life and dodging June's questions about Meesha."

"So you exploited our heartfelt moment," I say. "*Immediately* after it happened." Right after I say it, I wonder if she'll exploit this conversation, too. Who am I kidding? Of course she will.

"Will you stop being so naïve?" she says with an eye roll. "Please. It's disconcerting. That storyline—the things you said about your mother being a kind single mother despite what happened with Ali. That made *you* look good. It made *you* play well. You came off as simultaneously interesting and sympathetic. And, for millions of Americans who come from broken homes, it made you all the more relatable. You are a likable person. Your story is endearing. I was helping you play that up."

"It doesn't feel that way."

"How you feel about my methods is not my concern," Mary says. "They work. I have kept this empire afloat for well over a decade. *This* is how I do it. This is how I take care of my family, which—like it or not—you are now a part of."

And with that, she gets up and strides right out of the guesthouse.

Chapter 32

Lou is the only person I want to talk to right now. She did send me a text after the show ended:

Watched with Grant this morning. Yikes. Did she know about Meesha?? Will have to debrief at school tom.

But tonight, she's going to a celebration dinner for Grant's acceptance to Villanova with his family, so she's too busy to listen to me cry about Mary exploiting me.

I can't even talk to Matt. It's not like we were ever really the tell-each-other-everything kind of stepfather and daughter. But the familiarity of silently watching one of our favorite Netflix stand-up specials sounds wildly comforting to me right now. Based on Find My Friends, he's back at the apartment. Probably watching some old *Curb Your Enthusiasm* episodes. I was hoping the nice text he sent me before the show meant he's ready to talk again, but nope. He's back to ignoring me. I tried calling him twice this evening and even sent him another *I'm sorry* text, but nothing. Radio silence. A small part of me wonders if I've ruined our relationship forever, but I can't even let myself go there.

So I'm just sitting here, replaying everything Mary said in my head on a loop, little snippets of our conversation popping out at me like a series of movie teasers. On the one hand, I feel completely taken advantage of. Like I was a pawn in her game. But, on the other hand, I'm starting to realize that may be how Mary shows love. Does Mary *love* me? She did call me part of her family.

Before I can consider the possibility further, I hear a knock on the door. "Who is it?" I ask.

"Me," Meesha says as she lets herself into my guesthouse. "Mind if I join you?"

My stomach immediately drops at the sight of her, weeks of her icy attitude toward me creating an almost Pavlovian fear response to her sheer presence.

"Oh," I say, jolting upright on my bed. "Sure."

"Cool," she says, taking a seat next to me. "I brought popcorn. Do you like popcorn?"

"Um, yeah," I say. "I do."

"Great," she says, pulling the bag of popcorn out of her canvas tote bag. "Let's share. This bag has everything—kettle corn, cheddar, caramel, just plain buttered. I like to take a big handful and have them all at once."

Cheddar and kettle corn sound weird together, in my opinion, but I don't want to be rude, especially not to Meesha. This might be the first time she's ever said more than four words to me. So I tentatively grab a small handful out of her bag and cautiously give it a chew.

"Wow," I say. "This is *so* good."

"Right?!" she asks, more enthusiastic than I've ever heard her. "Cheddar and caramel. You'd never expect the combo to be good, but it's out of this world."

"Yeah," I say grabbing another handful and shoving it in my mouth. "Wow. This is nuts."

"Back when I was modeling, popcorn was the only thing we could snack on," she tells me. "Just plain popcorn. Almost no calories. I ate so much plain popcorn that I couldn't eat it again for a year after I retired."

"What would you get at the movies?" I ask.

"Bon Bons," she says. "Or Twizzlers. Anything fattening. I was so *over* dieting and everything having to do with it. I still am."

"But you started eating popcorn again," I say. "That's nice."

"Well, only if it's doused in butter and sugar and cheese," she says. "This popcorn is *not* model popcorn, let me tell you."

I let out a polite laugh, and we sit there quietly eating our popcorn, only speaking when one of us squeaks out an awkward "Oh, sorry" when our hands touch in the bag.

"So, um, are you going to Mona's party tomorrow?" Meesha asks. "She is fully freaking out about the guest list. Her ex and his fiancée are coming."

"It's crazy that her ex has a fiancée. I know he was older than her, but only by a little, right? Mona is practically my age. We're so young. I'm not trying to be judgmental, but who has a *fiancée* around our age?"

"You almost have to calculate celebrity ages in dog years," Meesha responds. "Max and Mona both grew up so fast. I think what's heartbreaking for Mona is just seeing that, until now, they were doing all of their growing up together."

"Why would she invite him and his fiancée to her party in the first place?"

"She wanted to be the bigger person," Meesha says. "Well, let me rephrase that. She wanted to *look* like the bigger person. She wasn't exactly expecting them to actually respond yes."

"Maybe they won't show up," I say. "Allergies are really bad this season! Maybe one of them will have awful allergies and want to skip it."

"I'm sure that's what Mona's hoping for," Meesha says with a laugh. "But anyway, you should definitely come."

"I don't know," I say with a shrug. "She's texted me about it a few times. But it seems intense for a school night. Plus, tomorrow is going to be my first day back at school since . . . everything. It all just feels like a lot to throw into one day. I just hope she won't be mad if I don't go."

"She will," Meesha says matter-of-factly. "But, luckily for you, Mona's rage lasts about an hour tops. She'll be over it by the end of the night. And . . . I'd be happy to cover for you if you need some backup."

"Thanks," I say with a smile. "You really don't have to do that."

We sit there, quietly eating more popcorn for a few more minutes, until Meesha finally blurts out, "Pete is my best friend. Sorry, that was an awkward way to bring it up. I know

Javier dubbed you the Awkward One. But I'm a real contender, too. I have a hard time just . . . opening up."

I watch her icy exterior slowly start to thaw as she scrunches up her cute little button nose to avoid tearing up. Is Meesha . . . *embarrassed*?

"Meesha, you really don't owe me an explanation," I say, sensing her almost palpable discomfort. "Really. It's your life! I'm not judging."

"No," she insists. "I want you to know this. Pete has been my best friend since birth. Honestly, until I got into fashion, he was my only friend. I was so shy. The only reason I got invited to any parties in high school was Pete."

"I get that," I say. "Sort of like my friendship with Louise."

"Yeah," she agrees. "Exactly. Like, my real true ride-or-die best friend. Anyway, the point is I've always loved him. But I didn't love him *romantically* until recently. That moment you saw in the bathroom—that was only, like, the second time we . . . uh, you know."

"I know," I confirm, blushing like a fifth grader in sex ed. "No need to dive into details."

"I always liked girls," she says. "Even as a kid. While my sisters were crushing on Jacob Elordi, I was crushing on Zendaya. I would try to make it work with guys. I'd do everything in my power to like them back when they pursued me. I'd go on dates and stuff. But every time they touched me, I felt repulsed."

"That's okay," I say. "You just weren't into it."

"It's easier to say that now. But, growing up, it was

embarrassing," she says. "My sisters were obsessed with boys. So was every girl on every TV show. I thought I was a freak."

"I can't imagine what that would have been like," I say. "I'm so sorry."

"It wasn't great," she says with a laugh. "My sexuality became my big secret, even from Mona and Melody. Pete's actually the only one I ever told. I remember we were twelve, and we were—I know I'm about to sound like a total douchebag—but we were on a yacht with our families sailing the Greek isles. Pete and I were sitting on the deck, and he was talking about this girl he had a crush on in our grade, Annie Love. He was going on about how hot she is and how cool she is and how funny she is, and I got it. Like, I fully got what he was saying because I felt all those things about Annie, too. So I told him."

"How'd he take it?" I ask. "Was he fine with it?"

"Yeah," she says. "He couldn't have been cooler. Just gave me a fist bump and said 'I guess we'll see who can get with Annie first.'"

"Who got with Annie first?!" I ask. "Now I'm invested."

"He did, of course," she says with a laugh. "I was the shyest person in the world, and this was my deepest, darkest secret. My—uh, our—dad was more chill, but I was terrified of my mom's reaction. She may seem all modern and cool on TV, but she's old-school Iranian. I was so scared of how she'd react. Not just her, though. Everyone. I didn't want anyone to know."

"So, what changed your mind?" I ask.

"Bunny," she says without missing a beat. "Bunny changed

everything for me. I'd just quit modeling and finally sort of felt like I was coming into my own. Mona and Melody were always so sure of themselves. They knew who they were, they were comfortable in their skin. I always wanted to crawl out of mine. But then, one night in New York, Bunny was the guest performer when I was hosting *SNL*. And it was just—I'm seriously sorry for the cheese overload here—but there is no other way to describe it than fireworks. Absolute fireworks."

I cannot believe I forgot Meesha hosted *Saturday Night* freaking *Live*.

"I am going to need so much more detail on you hosting *SNL*. I am, like, a superfan," I gush. "But first, finish telling me about Bunny."

"Oh, hosting was *terrifying*," she says with a laugh. "But meeting Bunny made it all worthwhile. I was far from being publicly out yet. I'd only ever kissed a few girls here and there at parties. But Bunny just knew. She could sense it in me. We went clubbing together that night in New York, and she invited me back to her room at the Soho House. I knew she was gay, but I still wasn't sure if she was *into* me into me, or just being nice. Like, a friendly sleepover. I was so naïve. I truly couldn't believe someone as amazing as her would be into me."

"But she was."

"Yep," she says. "She was. So we wound up hooking up that night, and we both extended our stays in New York and just had this amazing month together, straight out of a rom-com. We'd walk the West Side Highway, get drunk with our friends at Zero Bond, row boats in Central Park, lay out by the pool at Dumbo House and just *talk*. We talked about everything. About our childhoods, about our fears, our dreams, everything. It was like a thirty-day-long conversation interrupted only by amazing sex."

"That sounds . . . great," I say. "I mean, what an amazing experience."

"It really was," she says. "It just felt like this whirlwind of love. Real, deep love. Not just the surface-level stuff. The feeling of knowing the person you're most in awe of on the planet chose *you* to be with. And not just the facade of you, either. The real you. The you with the insecurities and the bitchy tendencies and the failures. She saw *that* version of me and was still down. It felt like a fairy tale."

"I mean, I can't say I relate," I say with a laugh. "The only guy who's ever told me he loves me is my dad. But this sounds pretty aspirational."

"Well, don't get too excited," she says. "You know how the story ends, remember?"

"Right," I say, my heart involuntarily sinking a bit. "Pete."

"Yes," she says. "Pete. So things really started strong with Bunny that month. We were in love. Like, we were saying it. 'I love you.' And it was weird for me, not sharing this amazing thing in my life with my family when we're so close. Ironically, *Pete* was the only one I did feel comfortable introducing her to at first. He loved her. Said she was a perfect fit for me. That he'd never seen me so happy."

"That's so nice," I say. "It sounds like he's such a good friend."

"He really is—er, was—is? I honestly don't know what

to call him anymore," she says. "But, anyway, Bunny really wanted me to come out. To share who I really am with the world. And I was kind of ready to, as well. I loved her so much. I was sick of living a lie. So first I told my family."

"How'd they take it?" I ask.

"Well, my—sorry, I keep doing that . . . *our*—dad was already gone at that point. But everyone else was honestly way less dramatic than I had expected. I did it on the show, so my mom was happy because of the ratings jump," she says with a laugh. "And Mona and Melody said they already knew. They were just waiting for me to tell them. It was kind of ideal. And, I mean, of course it helped that they loved Bunny. Everyone loves Bunny."

"She seems really cool," I say. "You know, based on Instagram and stuff."

"She is," Meesha agrees. "She's the coolest. And I'm still so grateful to her for giving me the courage to do that, to come out. And, at the time, that really was my truth. I'd only ever liked women. Why would I not assume that made me a lesbian? And I was so scared to share it with everyone, so scared of what they might say. Terrified. Like, playing out hypothetical scenarios of it kept me up for at least five hundred nights. But when it really happened, everyone was so amazing. Not just my mom and my sisters. *Everyone.* Even still, I get letters from fans from all over the world, thanking me for coming out."

"That's so nice," I say. "I'm sure you gave so many people the courage to do the same."

"Yeah," she says, tearing up. "Not just that, but my mom's

acceptance gave so many Middle Eastern parents who watch the show the push they needed to embrace *their* LGBTQ+ kids. It all just became bigger than me. I became a symbol. Our whole family did. So then . . ."

"When you fell for Pete," I say, filling in the blank.

"Yeah," she says. "It complicates things."

"I can imagine," I say. I suddenly get it. Her issues with me were never about *me*. It was more that by catching her and Pete in the act, I became a physical reminder of her deepest, darkest secret. And she just couldn't face that.

"I don't know where it came from," she says, barely audible. "It all happened so fast. Pete and I were hanging out at his place, playing video games like we've done a million times before. Bunny was out of town. I was tired and didn't feel like driving all the way home, so Pete offered to let me sleep there—another thing that's happened a million times before. But something was . . . different that night. I don't know how else to describe it. There was a sexual tension that just had never existed before—not only between the two of us, but between me and *any* dude."

"So was that the first time you hooked up?" I ask.

"Not that night," she says. "I slept in the guest room that night and the next morning I had to wake up early for a meeting, so I popped into his room to say bye. And he offered to walk me to my car—a first in the million times I'd slept over. We were both walking super slowly, almost purposely. Like we wanted the walk to not end. He was going away to the Bay Area the next day for basketball, so I figured that was partially it. But also, that same weird tension was there. So, when we finally got to the car, he kissed me. And . . . I liked it. It was those same fireworks all over again, but with a dude. With *Pete*."

"But you were still with Bunny," I say. "And you'd just come out. That must have made it all so confusing."

"Yeah, it's like coming out all over again," she says. "But worse. I don't even know what I identify as. Pansexual? That feels the most right. But honestly, I don't know. Other than Pete, I've exclusively been into women. I have no idea what that makes me. And I'm terrified of speaking too soon. Of incorrectly defining myself all over again."

"Well, maybe you don't have to define yourself at all," I suggest. "Who cares? You're allowed to love whoever you want to love."

"The thing is, if I don't define myself, the media will. I know what people already say about our family. That we'll do anything to make headlines. What if people think I just came out for ratings? To get a few more Instagram followers? 'Meesha Mashad lies about being a lesbian in most pitiful Mashad PR stunt yet.' I can already see the headline. Oh God. And the people I helped come out. What happens to them? Or the parents I convinced being born gay is a real thing? I can already picture the dinner table conversations: 'Meesha Mashad was a lesbian, sweetie. And now she's not! I bet you can turn straight, too.'"

"Well, you didn't *turn straight*," I remind her. "That's silly."

"I *know* it's silly. Pete is the only guy I've ever had even an inkling of a feeling for," she says. "But what you and I know doesn't matter. It's all how people perceive it. My whole life is defined by how people perceive my choices, and it's fucking exhausting. Oh, and let's not forget to add in the fact that the Sandersons are our *best* family friends. Mona was right, on the phone with you guys. One of us dating a Sanderson is basically incest."

"Well, at least it's not *technically* incest," I say, trying my best to uncover a silver lining here. "That would be bad."

"Yeah, I guess we have that going for us," she says with a laugh. "Not *technically* incest."

"So . . . what are you gonna do?" I ask. "Your mom knows."

"Ya *think*?" she says with a laugh. "That interview had Mary Mashad written all over it."

We both sit there quietly for another minute, picking at the last bits of popcorn left in the giant bag.

"Thank you, by the way," Meesha says. "For today. I know I haven't exactly given you any reason to be loyal to me."

"Of course," I say. "That wasn't my business to tell. Loyalty or no loyalty."

"I'm sure my mom gave you an earful for that," she says. "She does *not* like when things don't go according to her plan. I wouldn't be surprised if Mona is out of the will for good after spilling the beans about you."

"Yeah," I say. "She wasn't really . . . pleased."

"If it makes you feel any better, I can safely promise you she's been just as mad at her own daughters at one point or another," she says. "So take it as a sign that you're really family."

"I don't know," I say. "She did call me family at the end of our conversation. But she also admitted she only wanted me on the show as a plot twist. So I'm not really sure where that leaves us."

"Hey, what you did for me today," she says. "That was some real sister shit. That's family. Don't pay too much attention to what my mom says when she's mad. She loses it and says dumb things. She once threatened to legally emancipate me for getting a C on a report card."

"Whoa," I say with a laugh. "That's intense."

"*She* is intense," Meesha says. "And she's the MOST intense about the show. She's so weird about it. It's not like any of us actually need it financially at this point, despite what I'm sure she tried to tell you. It's just—I don't know how much she told you about her upbringing. . . ."

"She told me," I confirm. "I can't believe she went through all of that."

"Yeah," Meesha says. "It's dark. She really did lose everyone she loved. Then, when she lost our dad, she was terrified of losing us. So now she has it in her head that if she loses our show, we're going to stop spending time together as a family. And she'll do whatever it takes to keep this dumb show going, because in her head, it's the only way to keep us around."

"That must be so stressful," I say, imagining being convinced my family's love was contingent upon a reality television show continuing to air. "Poor Mary."

"I wouldn't go feeling too sorry for her," Meesha says. "The woman needs serious professional help. But all of her craziness—even the mean rants—do come from a good place. Codependent. But good."

"Huh," I say. "I guess that makes it sort of sting less."

"Good," she says. "Glad I could help."

The two of us sit there quietly, no more popcorn left to pick at, until Meesha finally breaks the silence. "I'm going to come clean about everything soon—I am," she promises. "Bunny doesn't deserve to be cheated on. And my fans don't deserve to be lied to. Plus, Pete and I deserve a real shot to see where this goes. I just . . . need some more time to process everything."

"That's fine," I say. "Do whatever you need to do. Your secret's safe with me."

Meesha gets up and starts walking toward the door, but pauses before she makes her way out. She stares at me for a moment too long, opening and shutting her mouth.

"Is everything okay?" I ask. "Did you forget something?"

"There's just . . . There's one more thing I have to tell you."

Chapter 33

"Wait, so how did Meesha even get these emails?" Lou asks in the car on the way to school. Brent, Mary's driver, is giving us a ride. "Weren't they in Ali's inbox?"

It's my first time back at school, and Mary insisted I go with security and her driver in this bulletproof car. I asked him to pick Lou up on the way so we have some time to privately discuss. Well, as "private" as a discussion can be with Brent driving and Blake and Majid seated behind us.

"I guess she was helping him with something on his computer when he was sick, and she just accidentally stumbled upon this thread," I tell her. "And she kept going back and forth on whether or not she should show me, but she decided she had to at least tell me they exist."

I think back to last night, when Meesha tentatively showed me the emails on her phone. At first, I couldn't even bring myself to physically touch the phone. It felt like she was dangling a chunk of lava in front of me. I knew it would burn me if I touched it. And I guess, on some level, I was right.

"This is wild, Jos," Lou says, her eyes still glued to the phone. "It literally says there are four thousand six hundred emails in this thread."

"I know," I say, rubbing my eyelids against my sandpapery dry eyeballs. "It took me hours to muster up the courage to open the thread after Meesha forwarded it to me, but, once I did, I couldn't stop reading. I was up all night."

"So he *did* want to meet you?" Lou asks, her eyes wide as she skims over the thousands of emails Ali sent my mom throughout my life. "For years?!"

"Yes," I say, still in total and complete shock. "He emailed her practically every single day begging to meet me, and she refused. Even when he got cancer! He *told* her he was sick, and she still refused."

"Well, she probably didn't think he would actually die," Lou says, setting the phone down on her lap and facing me directly. "Nobody did. He was so energetic and fit. It was hard to imagine he would ever die."

"Well, whatever the case, she was set on me not having anything to do with him until I turned eighteen. No matter how much he begged to see me earlier."

"But I don't understand," Lou says, her brow furrowed. "Ali Mashad was the most powerful man in the world. Couldn't he just sue her and make her let him see you?"

"He didn't want to," I say, remembering the impossibly kind tone he used toward her in every single one of his emails. "He wanted to be amicable with her, to not create any drama for me."

"So what was her reasoning for not letting him?" Lou asks,

her attention back on the emails. "She *had* to have given him something."

"I don't know," I say. "She was honestly pretty short. For the thousands of emails he sent, she probably sent forty back over the years. He would send these long essays begging to meet me and, every now and then, she would just respond saying 'We had an agreement. You can meet her if she chooses to meet you at eighteen.'"

"Maybe she was being loyal to Mary," Lou suggests. "After all, Mary *was* her cousin. Maybe she felt guilty and thought having you guys back might upset Mary even more than she already had. You were a kid then, so you being in his life would have meant her being in his life, and her being in his life might have been hurtful to Mary. Or maybe she felt so guilty about what happened that she just wanted a blank slate. To not see either of them anymore."

I want to believe that story. I desperately do. But part of me just . . . doesn't. Honestly? I don't know what to believe anymore. It feels like my life is a soccer ball someone kicked off the ground and sent spinning wildly into the sky.

"Mary did mention that my mom wanted nothing to do with them," I remember. "But I don't know. First, I find out about what she did to Mary. Now this? She let me believe he didn't love me, when he very clearly did. Did I even know her? Or is my memory of her just a total figment of my imagination?"

Before I know it, I'm crying, and Lou's dropped the phone to wrap both her arms around me.

"Of course you knew her," Lou says, rubbing my back. "There were just some parts you . . . didn't know."

"I listened to the voicemail," I tell her, my voice quiet as I soak her shoulder with a few more tears. "When I was done reading all the emails. I listened to it."

"Like, out loud?!" Lou asks. "Not just in your head?"

"Out loud," I say. "I just needed to prove that I knew her. That there was *some* part of my memory of her that wasn't a total lie."

"And?"

"She doesn't call me azizam," I say, my cute girly cry transitioning into a more snot-filled ugly sob. "She calls me joon eh man."

"Josie," Lou says. "That is so minor. It's one tiny word."

"But it's not minor!" I exclaim through tears. "I have repeated that voicemail in my head so many times with her saying 'azizam.' I've been so smug. That the iPhone transcription was so dumb—"

"Well, she did not call you Boob Man," Lou interrupts. "Let's not discount that."

"But she didn't call me azizam, either," I insist. "I completely forgot she ever called me joon eh man. Did she ever even call me azizam? Did I fully make that up?"

"She *did* call you azizam," Lou says. "I was there."

"But not in the voicemail," I remind her. "And I thought I had that voicemail memorized. That voicemail was my only proof that I still knew her. Now I don't even have that."

"Ladies," Brent says before Lou can respond. "We're going to be there in a minute."

I pull out a tissue from the box of Kleenex in the back of the car and start wiping my tears.

"What are you doing tonight?" Lou asks. "You're not filming or anything, are you?"

"No," I say. "It's Mona's birthday party, but I think I'm going to skip it and just have a night at home. Well, at Mary's home. I'm still staying there. She thinks it's safer, and things are so awkward between Matt and me right now that I don't mind."

"Oh. I was going to suggest a school-night sleepover to finish discussing, but . . ."

"Yes!" I exclaim before she can finish. "Just come to Mary's. You've already signed an NDA, and we're not filming. It will be fine."

"Great," Lou confirms. "Okay, you ready for school?"

"I'm not sure."

Up until now, fame has been something happening to me from a distance. Something I hear outside my bedroom walls, see outside the car window, or read about online. But now I'm in the back of this fancy car on the way to school, and suddenly this myth-like story I've been hearing about myself for the past three days is about to become reality.

"You'll be fine," Lou reassures me, sensing my compounding nerves. "Seriously."

But I don't know. The crowd outside the school is so massive that Principal Schwartz already had to send a school-wide email this morning instructing all students to come in through the school's back entrance behind the football field. The main entrance to the school is so congested with fans and reporters that the entire block had to be shut down. Even from a couple blocks away, as the background to my sobs, I can hear people screaming: "JOSIE!" "WHERE'S JOSIE?" "WE WANNA MEET JOSIE!" I guess, on the bright side, Mary was right. Something about the interview did seem to make me likable.

"Okay," Brent announces. "We're here."

"Could we just have one more minute to catch up, please, Brent?" I ask as he puts the car into park. "I don't know if I'm ready to go in."

"Jos," Lou says, grabbing my hand. "You're never going to be ready. Come on. I'm here with you. It will be fine."

We're parked in the underground lot under the football field, so, luckily, there aren't any reporters or fans here. But I do see Isaac in the distance with Grant. Genevieve is nearby as well, but she isn't hanging all over Isaac like she normally is. Interesting.

I take a few deep breaths and instinctively hear my mom's voice in my head, telling me to *cheelax*.

"Wait," I say, stopping Lou before she opens the car door. "Did my mom really say 'cheelax'?"

"*Yes,*" Lou confirms. "Every time you were freaking out. And, if she was here, she would say it to you right now. Josie, you didn't know everything about her. But you *knew* her. Now come on."

By the time I set one foot out of the car, pretty much every student in the parking lot has made their way over to us. Every student except Genevieve, that is. She's cowering alone by her BMW. She looks terrible, honestly. Like she hasn't slept in days. Her usually perfectly blown-out hair is totally unkempt, and a little greasy. And I can't really tell from here, but I think she might be wearing pajamas.

If the tables were turned, and *I* had completely given up on life as a result of something *Genevieve*'s sister had said to me, she would love it. She'd probably print out a life-size poster of me looking all defeated and sad and hang it in her bedroom for her and Isaac to laugh at when they're done making love. Then she'd record them laughing and make me watch it, just as further torture. But I kind of want to give her a hug.

"Stop looking at her with those puppy dog eyes," Lou whispers. "She is the *devil*, remember?"

"Right," I say, diverting my attention to the mob of people in front of us. "Right."

"Josie!" Alicia Saraki exclaims, cutting between me and Lou. "I'm so happy you're back, girl! Did you finish brainstorming ideas for promoting the clothing drive? I have *tons* I've got to run by you."

"Hmm, I wonder how you managed to find the time to come up with ideas," Lou chimes in. "I would think lying to any half-baked reporter who will listen is pretty time consuming, is it not?"

"*Louise*," I say, nudging her. "Be *nice*."

"Josie, come ON," Lou exclaims. "The girl is the most blatant social climber who's ever lived. You don't *have* to be nice to everyone."

"Sorry, Alicia," I say. "But do you mind if we catch up later at the meeting?"

"Sure!" she practically squeals. "See you there! Same seats?"

"You know it," I say with feigned excitement. "See you there."

"I don't know how you do it," Lou says, shaking her head

as we make our way through the crowd of familiar faces suddenly acknowledging my existence. "It took all the might in me not to punch her in the face."

"What's the point of being mean?" I ask. "If anything, that takes *more* energy, at least as far as I'm concerned." My attention flashes back to where Genevieve is still standing, looking the most pitiful I've ever seen her, camped outside her car away from the crowd.

"Maybe I should just say something to her," I tell Lou, nodding toward Genevieve. "Really quickly. I mean, I know what it's like to be the ostracized loser. I don't want anyone to feel like that. Not even my literal worst enemy."

"Josie, oh my God," Lou says. "*No.* Now is not the time to be a hero."

But before I can make my way over to Genevieve, a deep voice screams "JOSIE!" Then someone swoops me up from behind and throws me into the air. "Blake!" I scream as I shoot upward toward the gray concrete ceiling. "Majid! HELP!!!!"

What happened next was a total and complete blur. I only remember it in flashes. Lou shouting, "No! It's just Grant!" as Blake tackles Grant to the floor. Grant's muffled voice barely able to utter the words "Just . . . wanted . . . to . . . welcome . . . you . . . back" from underneath Blake's three-hundred-pound body. Me falling safely into Majid's arms, each of which is the size of one of me. The entire parking lot staring at me even more than they were before.

"I'm so sorry, Grant," I keep saying. "I'm so, so, *so* sorry."

"I'm sorry, too, man," Blake chimes in. "You seem like a good kid. But, you know, this is my job."

"You've got to be more careful, dude," instructs Majid. "You can't just go tackling famous people up from behind. You do shit like that, and we've got to take you down. That's just the way it goes."

"Got it." Grant winces. "Thanks for the tip."

We're all waiting around the bench outside of the nurse's office, which I honestly didn't even know existed until now. Really would have loved to know about it the thousands of times I thought I was dying on this campus. But Grant can barely talk and is holding on to his chest like his heart might fall out of it at any given moment, so I think it's safe to say he needs the nurse more than I ever did. Lou keeps kissing him on the top of his head and saying she's so happy he's safe, as if her own heart would fall out if his did.

Speaking of love, Isaac is here, too. Let's face it, I never do *great* around Isaac outside of math class. When I don't have derivatives and limits to distract me, the intensity of my attraction to him wraps around my body like a king cobra and squeezes all the sense and personality out of me.

And this time I also have to reconcile with the fact that I pretty much declared my love for him on live television yesterday morning. I was so focused on being honest and following Mary's orders at that point that I didn't even take my own life into account. And now I've got to look him in those perfect, gorgeous honey-and-grass eyes and accept the fact that he saw me say what I said, alongside the rest of the world. But, then again, maybe he didn't. *The June Li Show* really does focus on a more middle-aged female crowd. He is *not* their target audience.

"Mr. Miller," the nurse shouts from his office. "We'll see you now."

Isaac, Lou, and I get up to follow Grant into the room, but the nurse throws an arm out. "This isn't a pep rally, people," he says, using one of his big hairy arms to push the rest of us back into the hallway. "I'll *just* be seeing Mr. Miller. The rest of you can get to class."

"Mr. Laputo," Lou interrupts. "Can I *please* come in with him? I'm so worried. Please."

"Yeah, can she please?" Grant winces. "I know I'll feel more comfortable if I have my Lou Bear by my side."

"Fine," Mr. Laputo says, rolling his eyes. "You two come in, the rest of you stay out."

"I'll wait right out here!" I yell. "Love you! Er, that was obviously to Lou, Grant! I love *Lou*. Not . . . you. Not that I have hard feelings! I *like* you! You, uh . . ."

"Pretty sure they can't hear you anymore," Isaac says with a laugh, nodding toward the shut door. "No point in trying to say anything."

"Right," I say. "Nice call."

Then we just sit there silently on opposite sides of the bench, guarded by Blake and Majid on either side of us. I consider starting a conversation but can't think of anything not math related. My brain briefly flashes to Timmy. Even when we have silent moments, it's never this awkward. But maybe that's exactly what makes Timmy a friend and Isaac a crush. Maybe Timmy and that lavender-haired girl have plenty of awkward silences when they hang out. Maybe that's what it's supposed to be like when you hang out with someone you're romantically into. Maybe when there's an intense physical attraction between two people, it cancels out the indescribable X factor that makes two people feel completely and totally comfortable with each other.

I grab my phone to distract myself, and my eyes flash over to the icon for my Gmail app. I'm tempted to do another deep dive into my mom's emails with Ali. It was late. Maybe there was an email I missed! One where he was a total jerk. Or where she told him he's welcome to see me but scheduling just didn't work out.

"You good?" Isaac asks, prompting me to put my phone down as he scoots closer to me on the bench. "You seem a little . . . out of it."

"Oh, uh, yeah," I say. "Sorry. I just, I've had a lot going on lately. My brain's kind of everywhere."

"I can imagine," he says. "I saw you on *The June Li Show*." Oh no. No. No. No. No.

"Um, really?" I ask, my stomach plummeting downward as it waits for him to rip me a new one for embarrassing him in front of the world. "That was all such a blur. I barely, um, even remember what I said."

"You did good," he replies. "Was cool seeing you on there. You didn't seem to be nervous at all. Do you ever get nervous? You're so fearless."

I laugh but stop quickly when I realize he's being serious. Fearless? The guy doesn't know me at all. You know who does know me? Timmy. Ugh, why does Timmy keep popping into my head like some sort of relentless reminder to update my computer software?! There are more pressing things happening right now. Isaac, the biggest dreamboat of all time, is sitting right here in front of me, giving me compliments. Who cares if they're totally unwarranted and unfounded compliments? They're still compliments! And he's still gorgeous!

"Oh! Well, I'm glad," I say. "You know, uh, glad you liked it. Not just, like, glad in general." *Real smooth, Lawrence.*

"Actually, um, Josie," he says. "I did have one question for you."

Here goes my stomach again.

"The guy you mentioned," he continues. "It was me, right?"

"Y-yeah," I say, my voice shaking like it's aboard the *Titanic* just moments before hitting that iceberg. "Um, it was."

"Cool," he says, a huge, gorgeous smile flashing across his face. "That's what I thought."

Ugh, that's what he thought? Is that a good thing or a bad thing?

I've gotta change the subject. This is too much.

"You watch *The June Li Show* regularly?" I ask. "I didn't really think anyone at school watched that kind of stuff. Any other daytime talk shows you're into? I've been trying to think of one to get into myself. Seems like a nice way to start the day."

"Well, I don't really normally watch," he says, the cutest smirk to have ever been smirked by any human boy creeping across his face. "But my mom does. She might have some recs for you. She watches them all, every morning. And June's her favorite. She was so excited when you were on; she's always loved you."

"Carol!" I exclaim. "Yeah, I love her, too. That's why I asked about her at, you know . . . Oliver Blair's party. But I know you don't remember that. I don't mean that in, like, a passive-aggressive way! Ugh, I know that sounded passive-aggressive. I get that you were drunk that night. No big deal!"

Out of the corner of my eye, I can see Blake texting Majid. I wonder if they're side texting about what an awkward freak I'm being right now.

"No," Isaac says. "That *was* a big deal. I shouldn't have done you like that. I was just super faded, you know."

"Yeah," I say. "Totally get it. Seriously. It's all in the past. No big."

"Cool," he says. "I know I've said it before, but I really do love that about you. You're so chill."

I'm dead. That's it. Who cares about Timmy and his stupid lavender-haired secret maybe girlfriend? Isaac Taylor has now basically professed his love for me *twice*. There is no way this is happening and I'm also alive. I've died and gone to heaven. That's the only logical explanation.

We sit there for a few seconds longer, an army of butterflies ready to burst out of my chest.

"My mom actually said the funniest thing while we were watching you on TV," Isaac says. "She asked why you and I never got together."

"Oh," I say, forcing a laugh. "I mean, technically we *did* get together. You know, for that one day."

"Right," he says. "In fourth grade. Great day."

"Really?" I ask. "You think so? Because Genevieve . . ."

"Forget Genevieve," he says, shaking his head. "That girl is wack. I don't know why I've been wasting my time with her for all these years."

"I mean, well, I'm sure you loved her . . . ?" I say, not sure why I'm feeling this small sense of protection over the sanctity of his relationship with the literal devil. "Like, on some level, you must have, right? To be together for that long?"

"Whatever. I'm not trying to talk about her," he says, turning his body around to face mine. "I was actually trying to talk about *us*."

At this point his PERFECT, GORGEOUS, SPOTLESS hazel eyes are staring directly into my brown ones.

"Uh—us?" I ask. "You want to talk about *us*?"

"Yeah," he says, taking my clammy hands in his giant ones. "*Us*. You know, Josie, the truth is I've had a crush on you forever, too. I guess I was always just nervous you were out of my league."

"Really?" I ask. "Because I've always just assumed *you* were out of *my* league."

"Well, I'm not," he says, a perfect smirk flashing across his face again. "So what do you say we go to the prom together? You and me? The way it always *should* have been."

"Um, I'd say YES," I practically scream. "And, uh . . . since we're inviting each other to things . . . actually, before I say anything more, can you sign this NDA?" I rifle through my backpack and pull one out.

It isn't until Isaac has signed the NDA and agreed to come to the wedding with me that Lou and Grant finally make their way out of the nurse's office.

"Guess what, you guys!" I exclaim. "Isaac and I are going to prom together!"

"And," Isaac adds, before lowering his voice, "Josie invited me to join you for the wedding."

Lou groans and gives me her best *Are you kidding me* look, but her negative vibes are drowned out by Grant's over-the-top excitement.

"Dude!!!!" he exclaims, his voice suddenly back to normal. "This is sick! Best friends dating best friends!!! Before you know it, the two of you will be visiting Lou and me in Philly next year."

Lou kicks him in the shin, but it's too late.

"What?" I ask. "What do you mean in Philly?"

"I was going to tell you," Lou insists. "Tonight! At the sleepover."

"You still hadn't told her?" Grant asks. "It's been weeks!"

"Babe, I love you, but nothing you are saying is helping right now," Lou hisses at him, before turning her attention to me. "Josie, I'm not going to Santa Clara. I'm sorry. It's just . . . it's not what I want."

The world feels temporarily frozen as all the memories of Lou avoiding my questions and reminders about Santa Clara start seamlessly fitting together like puzzle pieces.

"But it was part of our plan," I say, my voice flat. "It was always our plan."

"It wasn't always our plan!" Lou exclaims, before lowering her voice back down to normal. "Sorry. I know you're having a difficult day. I'm not trying to yell. But you have to understand. It was never *our* plan. It was always *your* plan that you steamrolled me into. I want to do something different! To see what's outside of California."

"So you're going to Villanova?" I ask, resisting the urge to throw up right here on the floor. "When did you get in? Did you even apply there?"

"I'm not going to Villanova," Lou says. "I'm taking the year off. I'm going to spend the first semester renting a place near Villanova, hanging with Grant, then who knows? Maybe I'll check somewhere else out. Maybe I'll come stay with you at Stanford!"

I stand there, stunned, my brain desperately trying to make sense of her words but coming up blank.

"Come on," Lou says, her eyes watering. "Josie, please say something."

"It doesn't seem like there's much for me to say. You seem to have this all figured out," I say, holding back tears of my own. "I'm, um, going to get to class."

I turn around and head toward English, ignoring all of Lou's shouts to come back as I walk away.

Before I enter the classroom, my phone buzzes with another text from Mona:

Josie! I know you're planning on bailing tonight.
Meesha's already making excuses for you. Just come!
It will be fun.

I think about it for a second. Yes, a party is typically my idea of hell. But how much worse can this dumb party be than my current hellscape of a reality?

I'll be there!

Chapter 34

"Uh . . . Josie?" Meesha asks as we pose for a series of sisters-only "pre-prom" pictures outside Melody's clifftop Malibu mansion. "You okay? You've barely spoken since you got here."

"Yeah," Mona agrees, signaling for the photographer to pause. "You're kind of freaking me out."

"You know you can tell us anything," Melody says, her Bambi eyes wide with concern. "Really."

I stare back at the three of them blankly. How did I get here? How are the only people who I can seemingly trust in the world three virtual strangers I met a few weeks ago?

I mean, can I even trust them? Look at what Mary did to me when I thought I could trust her. Look at what my own *mom* did to me. Not to mention my own best friend!

I press my lips into a tight smile and force a shrug. "I'm fine."

It's just not worth getting into it.

"She's reminding me of you," Mona says to Meesha, a look of visible disgust on her face. "I'm, like, disturbed."

"You don't have to get into it," Meesha reassures me, ignoring Mona. "Let's just have fun tonight."

"Yes," Melody says. "Just know we're here whenever you *do* want to talk."

"Mm-hmm."

Mona signals for the photographer to resume, and my mind almost leaves my body entirely as I pose for what feels like thousands of photos with my sisters, then with Mona's army of A-list young Hollywood friends. It's almost like my brain short-circuited. It's no longer functioning. I feel like a robot, dressed in this ridiculous early 2000s–inspired designer "prom" gown Mona's stylist selected for me, mindlessly going through the motions.

"Josie Joonam," Mary says, tapping me on the shoulder as the photos wrap up. "Can I get a word with you?"

"Now's not a good time," I say, the words falling out of my mouth without an ounce of thought. "Sorry."

I don't even feel like me anymore. I feel like a Sim being operated by someone else entirely.

"Well, you are clearly upset," Mary says. "Azizam, I know I might have been a bit too harsh yesterday. But we are family. We need to sort this out."

"Mary, this honestly has nothing to do with you," I say, no energy for niceties. "We're good. Really."

"Fine," Mary says curtly, straightening up her suit. "Then we're good."

I look over at her, preemptively annoyed as I wait for her to press the issue further. But she doesn't.

"Josie!" Melody calls out from the other side of the sprawling yard as her mom turns away. "Come here!"

Without saying another word to Mary, I make my way over to where my sisters are now standing by the nonalcoholic bar Melody has set up by her infinity pool. The bar is stocked with fresh-squeezed organic juices and mocktails, and all the beverages are being served in red Solo cups to look "more high school."

"Look what Melody got me," Mona says, pulling a flask out from her diamond-encrusted bag. "How cute?"

I stare at the chrome flask, MONA written across the front in bright pink rhinestones.

"I got them for all of us," Melody says, handing me one with my name written across it. "There's a 'speakeasy' bar in the bathroom where everyone else can get their alcohol. But I thought these would be fun for just us to have. Totally feels like something people would have at a real prom, right?"

I look around the elaborate party filled with hundreds of impossibly good-looking people wearing expensive early 2000s prom outfits as they take unnecessarily grainy selfies using the pink digital cameras everyone was handed in their goody bags. Melody has transformed her home gym into a "real" school gym, complete with bleachers and a dance floor, and hired some famous deejay to curate the music. Like she said, her downstairs bathroom has been turned into a "speakeasy" where all the guests can have access to all the alcohol and drugs their hearts desire off camera. Nothing about this feels like a real prom.

"Yep," I say, taking my flask from her. "Thanks."

"I know you don't drink, so I filled yours with Pellegrino," she reassures me. "But I figured it would be fun for us all to match, you know?"

"Come on," Mona says, wrapping an arm around me. "Let's all cheers before Max and Chya get here. I am still *way* too sober to see those two."

"Wait!" Meesha interjects. "Pete and Timmy just walked in. Let's have them cheers with us."

For the first time all night, my heart slightly perks up. But then I look over and see Timmy trailing behind Pete, the lavender-haired girl by his side. Of course, she's even prettier in person.

"You guys!" Meesha yells over to them. "Come take a happy birthday shot with us!"

I gulp. I cannot do this. Not tonight. How in the world am I supposed to chitchat with Timmy and his hot girlfriend when I feel like *this*?

"Actually," I whisper to Mona, "could I have a sip of yours?"

"Um, fuck yes," Mona says, excitedly handing me the flask. "Love this fun vibe out of you."

"You sure, Josie?" Melody asks, her sweet face scrunched up in concern. "I don't want you feeling pressured or anything."

I think about all of the studies I've read about the effects of alcohol on the developing teen brain. The hours I spent panicking over the Vibe Tea. But I can't seem to muster up the strength to care about any of that anymore. I mean, if there ever was a human who needed "liquid courage," wouldn't it be me, right now?

"I'm sure," I say, grabbing the flask from Mona and taking a giant swig. For a second I think I might puke, but I keep my mouth pressed tight, forcing the disgusting liquid down my throat. Why do people like this stuff? It's chilled so it's freezing cold, but it somehow still manages to burn every inch of my throat as it makes its way into my stomach.

"Hey," Pete says, scooching into our circle next to Meesha. "Timmy's being a loser. He won't drink with us."

"It's cool," Meesha says, clasping his hand in hers. "Come on, let's take a birthday shot for Mona. You can have a swig from my flask."

I've been so caught up in my own head that I practically forgot Meesha dumped Bunny and told her family about Pete this morning.

"I'm still not over this," Mona says, her eyes glued to their clasped hands. "Like, it works. But wow."

"I think you guys are *adorable* together," Melody says. "My new favorite couple."

"Okay, enough dillydallying," Mona says. "How is Josie the only one who's already had a drink?"

We each take a giant swig in honor of Mona, then Pete and Meesha go off to be with the lavender-haired girl and Timmy, and Melody goes into the gym to handle an issue with the deejay.

"Shit," Mona suddenly says, grabbing my arm, her palm uncharacteristically clammy. "Shit. Shit. Shit."

"What?" I ask, a comforting buzz starting to settle in. "What is it?"

"Don't be obvious about it," Mona instructs as she whispers in my ear. "But they just walked in. They're talking to my mom."

I try my best to slyly look over to where Max, who is so famous that even *I* recognize his face, is standing with his arm wrapped around Chya as they chitchat with Mary. Chya is dressed in what looks like an exact replica of Kate Hudson's dress in *How to Lose a Guy in 10 Days*, her blond hair pulled back into a low bun that accentuates her bright blue eyes, and he's got on a crisp tux with yellow accents to match her dress.

"Oh no," I say. "I was really hoping they wouldn't show."

"Same," she says, refusing to look in their direction. "*Fuck*. I wonder what they're talking to Mom about. Can you believe him? What kind of psychotic sociopath comes to his ex's birthday party with his new fiancée? It was *obviously* not a real invite."

"It is weird," I concede. "I don't get it at all."

"He just wants to get in my head," Mona says. "I know him. Even though he doesn't have me anymore, he still wants to *have* me. Like, he wants that control. Ugh. *Fuck* him."

We watch as Chya and Max leave their conversation with Mary to greet some other friends by the pool, both giggling as he slides a corsage onto her wrist and she fastens a boutonniere onto his lapel. As much as I hate to say it, they look happy together.

"So," Mona says to me, an eyebrow raised. "What do you say you and I get absolutely sloshed?"

+ ✦ +

The rest of the night is a mortifying blur, starting with me marching up to Max and Chya to defend Mona. Well, I thought I was defending Mona. What I really did was give an incoherent speech about why Mona is the best for about ten minutes straight until Max had to ask who I was and why I was talking to him and his fiancée for so long, which just prompted Mona and me to start laughing in his face, and (I really hope I'm making this up, but) I also vaguely remember Mona screaming "BOOM, BITCH" as I gave him a wet willy?

And believe it or not, that wasn't even the most mortifying portion of my evening. At some point (time is very loose here), Melody and Meesha pulled me aside and told me they wanted me to join them for a choreographed dance they had been planning to surprise Mona with set to 50 Cent's "In da Club." Apparently, that was her favorite song with Ali. I knew none of the moves but somehow decided I would be fine, and—shocker—I was not fine. I spent the whole routine tripping and tumbling all over the stage. When the video montage of Ali and Mona dancing to the song on her birthdays over the years dropped down on the projector behind us, I also added ugly tears into the whole messy, drunken mix.

And that's when I saw Timmy and the lavender-haired girl. They were standing there, front row center. This was probably all in my drunk head, but it felt like Timmy was staring at me, which prompted me to stare back at him, which ultimately resulted in me completely losing my balance and falling off the stage into his arms. And not in, like, a romantic way. In an extremely embarrassing, slightly physically painful way.

The end of the night is the fuzziest. All I have are brief flashes of me being in the passenger seat of Timmy's old Toyota Camry, him occasionally pulling over the car to hold my hair back while I puked on the side of the Pacific Coast Highway.

This is all to say: Why does *anybody* like drinking?

Chapter 35

I wake up the next morning with a splitting headache and the overwhelming urge to puke, which is shocking considering how much I already puked last night. Ugh. What is wrong with me? On the worst night of my life, I somehow managed to do the one thing that would make me feel even worse.

I stare up at the white popcorn ceiling, briefly unclear on where I am. Then my surroundings start to familiarize. *That's right. I asked Timmy to bring me home.*

I look over at my nightstand, where a bottle of Advil is sitting next to a glass of water and a note: *Text me when you're up, you party animal! — Timmy.* Despite feeling like my insides are revolting against me, I smile.

Thanks for everything last night, I start typing to him. Ugh, no. Not funny enough. I delete and start typing again: *I'm alive!* Nope. Too casual. I wish Lou were here to help me. I hover my finger over her name in my Favorites, but can't bring myself to press call. I'm still too hurt.

"Jos." Matt interrupts my texting with a knock on the door. "Mind if I join you?"

"Sure," I say, my headache immediately a little better after hearing his voice. "Come on in."

He walks in quietly, taking a seat at the foot of my bed.

"That Timmy is a good kid," he says, nodding over at the nightstand. "I was working a late shift last night. When I got home, he was sitting next to you with a finger by your nose making sure you didn't die."

"Was I that bad?" I ask, horrified. "Like, almost *dead*?"

"I think he was being a little overly cautious," Matt says. "But you definitely looked like you had yourself a good night."

"It wasn't even good," I admit. "I just spent the night embarrassing myself, and now I feel horrible."

"Well, that Advil might help," Matt says. "Start there."

I follow his instructions, downing a couple pills with the water. And then we just sit there quietly for a minute, Matt looking aimlessly around the room before asking, "So why aren't you at Mary's?"

"I asked Timmy to bring me here."

"Why?"

"Because this is ridiculous!" I accidentally shout, prompting a sharp wave of pain to shoot across my brain. I pause to chug more water before quietly adding, "I miss you. You're my dad. I know I lied, and I'm sorry if I hurt you with what I said the other day in front of Mary. But I need you right now more than ever."

"Jos, you know I'm always here," he says. "You're my

favorite girl. I'm never not going to be here. No matter what you say."

"But, Matt, how am I supposed to know that when you ignore me the one time that I'm ever fully honest with you?" I ask, realizing my makeup from last night must still be on as a fresh stream of tears forces my fake eyelashes off my eyelids and down onto my cheeks. "I've sent you hundreds of texts, and you've just gone dark! How is that being there?"

Matt sits quietly for a minute, nodding slowly as he processes my words.

"I get that," he agrees. "I handled this all wrong. I'm the adult here. You're the kid. I shouldn't be the one throwing tantrums and ignoring you. You *definitely* shouldn't have to be the one apologizing to me."

"Do you want to make up?" I ask, instinctively biting the inside of my cheeks as I wait for him to answer.

"Of course I do," he says, scooching up toward where I'm sitting as he wraps me in a hug and gives me a kiss on the top of my head. "Jos, you were right," he says as he lets me go, his voice quivering. "Not just right now. But you were right on Monday night, too. I *have* been in constant pain since your mom died—pain that I've probably been trying to ignore by avoiding spending time at home. I wanted to be the perfect dad, to swoop in and make everything okay for you. You had already been through so much. But the fact of the matter is you were the one who wound up making everything okay for me, and, whether it was conscious or not, I think a part of me had grown used to that dynamic. On some level, I think I knew all of that. But hearing you say it all that day, it made it so real, and I just . . . I hate myself for letting you exist in that position."

"It wasn't all bad," I tell him. "Remember when I was in *Into the Woods* with Lou and you stayed up all night sewing my costume? Or when I organized the Shakespeare reading and you were the only one who showed up? Or when I won the Albright Award at school, and you started a one-man 'JOSIE' chant in the crowd? Just look at where you're sleeping! Every single night you kill your back on that couch, just so I can get a good night's sleep."

"I told you!" Matt exclaims with a small smile as he loudly cracks his back. "The couch is *good* for my back."

I laugh, but eventually the two of us are sitting silently again, both seemingly unsure of what to say next.

"I should have told you," he says, quietly. "About the money. I knew I should. I just . . . could never quite bring myself to do it. I already felt like such a failure, and keeping that one promise we made to you seemed like the only remaining way to redeem myself. To keep your mom's legacy alive. Then I lost the club, and it started to become increasingly clear that I couldn't even do that. It was devastating. I felt like I was letting you *and* your mom down. Like I was a failure. I couldn't deliver on the most important promise she asked me to keep."

"Nobody is perfect," I reassure him. "Really. I know that."

"Your mother was pretty damn close," he says, a wistful smile making its way across his face. "She was unlike anyone I had ever met. She somehow made every single person in her orbit feel like the luckiest person in the world, just for having been loved by her."

I think about everything I have learned about her over the course of the past few days, not sure if I want to ruin his perfect image of the woman he still loves so deeply. But then I remember I love her that deeply, too. And maybe this has been my problem all along. Maybe I was too hung up on needing her to be perfect in order to warrant my love and adoration. Maybe Matt is, too.

"Did you know that she purposely kept Ali from me?" I ask. "Meesha showed me all these emails. He sent her hundreds of emails begging to meet me, even from his deathbed. And she refused."

"What?" Matt asks, his eyes wide. "She *what*?"

"She kept him from me," I say. "*And* she was Mary's cousin. Did you know that? She had an affair with Ali when she was staying with them for a bit."

"A coworker mentioned that part to me after your *June Li* appearance," he says solemnly. "I had no idea. But you know, to be fair, she didn't know every detail about my exes, either. What was in the past was in the past. That's how we always operated."

"The Mary thing I can wrap my head around," I say. "I mean, it was a shock when Mary first told me. I get that relationships can be complicated. It's just . . . the keeping us apart. On purpose. Until it was too late."

I watch as Matt tries to process this all in real time. "Sharzad was always going by instinct," he finally says. "Remember? She would always do what her gut told her. If that was her decision, even if you or I can't make sense of it, I'm sure she had a feeling it was the right one."

I still don't think it excuses her actions, but something about Matt highlighting a facet of her personality that feels so intensely familiar makes me feel . . . I don't know . . . validated? Yes. That's it. Validated. It's a reminder that I didn't just make up my entire memory of her. The hot bowls of ab goosht when I was feeling down. The nights staying up belly laughing at old sitcoms. The impassioned pep talks reminding me that I'm great *exactly* as I am. The too-tight hugs and the too-wet kisses. All of that was real. The woman I loved was real. She just also happened to be the same woman who kept me from my birth father.

I nod in agreement. "It's not like I needed him as a dad, anyway," I add. "I had you."

"You *have* me," Matt corrects, pulling me in for another hug. "How are you doing with all this information?"

"I don't know," I answer honestly. "I guess I'm just coming to terms with the idea that maybe I didn't know absolutely everything about her like I thought I did."

"Well, that makes two of us," Matt says with a slow nod. "But the version of Mom we knew? That was real, Jos. That woman loved you—loved us both—with every fiber of her being. I can promise you that."

"Does this change how you think of her?" I ask. "Knowing she had an affair with her cousin's husband and kept all those emails from us?"

"I would be lying if I said I wasn't shocked," Matt says. "But, for me, it always goes back to the love the three of us had. And nothing can ever take that away from *either* of us."

Matt gets up to grab a box of tissues as our eyes well up with tears at our shared memories of her and of our life together.

"Jos, I have to ask," he says, once we've both wiped our tears. "Are you happy? Because if what your mom really wanted was for you to choose whether or not you wanted a relationship with the Mashads, you were robbed of that. . . . *I* robbed you of that by leaving you in such a vulnerable position."

"Honestly? In a weird way, you not being able to afford college was one of the best gifts you could have ever given me," I tell him. "I would have never done the show if it wasn't for that. And it's led me to all of these new people who have turned my life upside down in the best way. Don't get me wrong. The past few days have been hell, and fame is absolutely something that's going to take some getting used to for me. But I'm suddenly part of this close-knit bonus family. I never expected to even have anything to talk about with these people, let alone *love* them, but . . . I do."

"I'm happy for you," he says. "Even if I showed it terribly. I really am. Your mom always wanted a big family with lots of kids. Now you sort of have that."

"Would you maybe . . . want to spend more time with them?" I ask, my teeth once again clenching down on the flesh of my inner cheek. "Then maybe they don't just have to be *my* bonus family. Maybe they can be yours, too."

"Sure," he says with a smile. "I would love that."

"How about this weekend?" I ask, perking up at his positive response. "The wedding. Melody mentioned I could invite you a while ago. Why don't you come?"

"You know what?" Matt asks, clapping his hands together. "If you're there, I'm there."

Chapter 36

"Are you sure about this guy?" Matt whispers to me after Mona snaps another picture of Isaac and me at Mary's private airport hangar. "I don't know if I get the best feeling."

Lou gives me a *Told you so* look from where she's standing next to Matt, and I shoot back with my own look that I hope says, *ISAAC is not the one who actively lied to me for months.* Ever since the other day at school, this is pretty much how we've been communicating. Loaded looks and the occasional passive-aggressive comment.

"I agree, Mr. L," Mona says, seamlessly inserting herself into our private conversation. "He absolutely has tool energy. But you have to admit the guy is hot."

The four of us stand there, awkwardly taking in Isaac's perfectly chiseled jawline as he snaps a selfie alongside Grant in front of Mary's massive plane.

"His face *is* very symmetrical," Lou concedes. Then she quickly adds, "Still hate him, though."

Even though I've been focused on icing her out, I could tell

Lou was nervous on our car ride here. But as soon as she met my sisters, it was like she had known them her whole life. Well, to be fair, she has watched them on TV for so many years she practically *has* known them her whole life. But the feeling seems mutual. Mona, Meesha, Melody, and even Mary all seem to be totally at ease with Lou. Mary even offered to represent her! "You have a look, Louise Joonam," she told her. "Like a young Megan Fox. And, if your outfit today is any indication, impeccable taste. You belong in the fashion industry. I don't typically take on clients outside of my family, but you're basically family. Let me help you." I know the compliment meant a lot to Lou. She may not have looped me in on the decision-making process like she normally does but I can imagine how many hours she put into the seemingly effortlessly thrown together baggy jeans, ribbed white tank, and chunky belt she's currently wearing with a pair of trendy-looking sneakers. And even though I am still *so* mad at her, I have to admit I was a smidge happy for her in the moment.

But then, to my total and utter confusion, Lou just responded to Mary by saying she's "still figuring things out right now." What is there to figure out? Mary just offered you up your wildest dreams on a silver platter!

"Boys," Mary says, marching over to Grant and Isaac from where she was standing chatting with the pilot from our flight to Paris, who she managed to snag after all. "Remember. You are not to share those photos *anywhere*. Unless you want to owe me millions."

"We're chilling," Isaac says, taking another selfie. "I won't post these."

351

"You have my word, ma'am," Grant says, reaching out his hand to shake Mary's. "These photos are not going anywhere. I promise. I read that NDA front to back. I'm class president over at our high school, so I'm always reading documents like that."

Seriously? Lou is dating *this* kiss-butt, and I'm the one getting eye rolls?

"Very well," Mary says, ignoring his hand entirely. "So we're clear."

She leaves the two boys awkwardly standing, casually strolling past them over toward the futuristic bar she has set up in the very back of the large hangar.

"*Oof,*" Mona says, covering her mouth with her hand. "That was cold, even for Mom."

"Oh, Louise, I'm sorry," Melody says, instinctively making her way over to us upon noticing Lou's reddening face. "We'll have our mom apologize to your boyfriend. She can be harsh sometimes."

"No, no, it's fine. I should probably go hang with him anyway. Grant, babe," Lou says, rushing over to him. "Let's walk a few laps around here before we have to actually board. It will be good for your blood flow."

"You take such good care of me, baby," Grant says, giving her a too-wet kiss on the lips. "I'm the luckiest guy in the world."

I stare at them quizzically as she grabs his hand and leads him for a walk around the massive airplane. Is she literally walking her boyfriend like a dog?! According to the nurse, Grant just had the wind knocked out of him that day. No broken bones or anything. But Lou's still been doting on him like he's a soldier who lost a limb in war.

"Matt Joon," Mary says, coming to where we're standing. "You must come join Farida and me for a celebratory drink. We are so happy you came here. Weddings are all about family, and ours would not be complete without you here with us."

"Thanks, Mary Joon. I'll join," Matt says, before looking down at his watch. "But isn't it a bit early for drinks?"

"Oh, nonsense," she says, waving her hand nonchalantly. "We're on vacation!"

I resist the urge to vomit at the mere mention of alcohol.

"So, um, I actually got you something," Isaac says, making his way over to where I'm standing once his selfie session has come to an end. "You know, as a thank-you for having me?"

"YES," Mona yells before I can even answer. "Gifts are perfect. Great photo op."

We both look at her, confused.

"What?" she asks with a shrug. "If you guys are maybe going to be official one day, you're going to want lots of content for social."

"Well, I don't know if we'll ever be *official*," I say, beads of sweat multiplying all over my face. "This is our first date, and it's not even really a date. Well, I mean, I guess, Isaac, you're technically here as my date—"

"If it's okay with you," Isaac says, cutting me off. "I'd love if this was a date. Like, a real one."

"Oh!" I exclaim. "Then, um, great. Sure!"

So it's a date. A real one. Not a Timmy *friend* date. A real date with my real crush. I look over at Lou, hoping she heard every word, but she just rolls her eyes and continues walking laps around the garage-like room with Grant following her like a little puppy dog.

"So anyway," Isaac says with that freaking gorgeous smirk. "I hope you like these, Josie. I chose them myself, especially for you."

"Oh," I say, pulling away before he can hand me the bouquet full of peonies. "They're peonies!"

"Yeah," he says. "Uh, is there a problem with that?"

"No," I say, keeping my body as far away from him as humanly possible. "They're so pretty. So, so pretty. And oh man, they smell amazing. But, um . . ."

"SHE'S ALLERGIC TO PEONIES," Lou screams from where she's clearly been eavesdropping across the hangar. "IDIOT."

So she's barely spoken to me in almost forty-eight hours, but she suddenly has the vocal strength to *scream* at Isaac? The nerve.

"Oh," he says. "I'm so sorry."

"No! Don't worry about it," I say. "How would you have known that?"

"HE COULD HAVE ASKED," Lou yells again.

"Dang," Meesha says with a laugh as she hangs up her call with Pete and walks over to us. "I see why this chick is your best friend. Hilarious."

I turn my attention to Isaac, who looks sort of like he did in Algebra II three years ago when Mr. Mohler asked him what a single-term algebraic equation was called and he didn't know the answer, even though Mr. Mohler had *just* told the class they were monomials.

"Seriously," I reassure him. "It's fine! I don't need flowers."

"Cool," he says, visibly relaxing. "That's my chill girl."

So now I'm *his* girl?! His?! I mean, I'm not his property and I'm obviously going to have to take him through why that phrase is so problematic at a later date. But, like, I know he meant it in an extremely romantic, cute, non-patriarchal way.

"You know why I chose peonies?" he asks, quickly flashing Mona's iPhone camera a glance. "They're beautiful, just like *you*."

"Awww," Melody says. "He seriously reminds me *so* much of my Axy. So cute!!!"

He takes one more long look at Mona's camera as he grazes my cheek with one giant hand and whispers, just loudly enough for everyone to hear, "But no peony in the world could be as beautiful as you."

I hear Lou snort out a laugh from across the room. What is her *deal*? Like, yes, that was kind of corny. And, yes, it was probably slightly disingenuous, because I know for a fact that peonies are Genevieve's favorite flower so that's more likely why he originally chose them. But can't she just let me have this moment? My lifelong crush is (kind of) professing his love for me!!! This is the stuff dreams are made of!

At least Mona gets it. "Okay, so that was cringey," she's saying. "Very cringey. BUT would make for a cute photo op, so Isaac, do you mind grazing Josie's cheek like that again real quick?"

"I could graze Josie's cheek for the rest of my life," he says, looking directly into Mona's camera.

"Thanks, Isaac," I say, as he rubs my cheek up and down like it's a llama at a petting zoo. "Really sweet of you."

I expected a touch from Isaac, the literal love of my life, to drum up some sort of jolt of excitement within me. But, instead, it sort of just makes me want to . . . vomit? And not in the anxious way I normally want to vomit. Or in the hungover way I wanted to vomit after Mona's party. More in a disgusted way, like when we had to dissect a pig brain in biology class freshman year.

I try my best to keep my facial expression nonchalant as I perk up at the sight of a text from Timmy lighting up on my phone screen. The truth is we have been texting nonstop since Matt and I made up. And the more I text him, the more I want to keep texting him. But also, I'm here with Isaac. Isaac, my lifelong crush! Isaac with the sharply chiseled jawline and perfectly chiseled face! Isaac, who literally just told me he wants this to be a date! (Yes, he's also Isaac whose touch repulses me, but we're choosing to forget about that.)

Timmy has made it abundantly clear we're just friends. Not only has he literally said verbatim that the two times we hung out were not dates, but he obviously has a girlfriend. A really pretty girlfriend with cool lavender hair. I mean, he did ditch her at Mona's party to take me home. Well, at least from what I can remember. But still. She's in his Snapchat stories and was his date to Mona's party. They obviously have *something*.

So it's not like I'm doing anything *wrong* by texting him while I'm on my date with Isaac. But I am aware that maybe

I'm possibly spending a bit too much of my Isaac time thinking about Timmy and how much I wish he was here with us right now. And it's not just here. It's everywhere. I know I haven't known him for long, but I've concluded that every experience is at least slightly better if Timmy is involved. For me, at least.

"You guys!!!" Meesha calls out, slightly out of breath as she rushes across the gigantic room to open the entrance door. "Pete is here! We can go!"

"Holy shit," Isaac whispers to me as Pete enters the building. "Pete *Sanderson*? He's here?!"

Chapter 37

This place is so out-of-control fabulous that it makes the past several weeks in Mashad World feel like a stay at a road-side Best Western. When we arrived, we were introduced to our personal butlers, who escorted us each to our private bungalows.

And now, Isaac and I are sitting next to each other on the front deck of the Sandersons' yacht while everyone else hangs inside. Normally I would be morally opposed to something like this, but Mr. Sanderson reassured me that their yacht was built entirely with recycled materials and the engine is electric. So I really have no choice here but to enjoy.

"So, do you like comedy?" I ask, realizing this might be the first time we've fully been alone together maybe ever. "I'm really big into stand-up." It's a shot in the dark, but I've already exhausted every math-related topic we could possibly discuss and need some fresh material.

"Um, yeah," he says. "Sure."

Bingo.

"Cool!" I exclaim. "There's this new woman I've been following, Destiny Williams. She is *hilarious*. Have you seen her at all? She just released the best Netflix special."

"Oh, uh, yeah," Isaac says. "I think I watched that. She seems cool."

"Yay!" I say, hoping Lou can hear the connections being made from where I know she's still eavesdropping inside. "I knew we had so much in common."

"Yep," he says. "Totally."

"Her bits are so funny. Like, the whole story about peeing in the Ralph's parking lot," I say between fits of laughter. "Sorry. Oh, man. That one always gets me. It's so me."

"What?" Isaac asks, looking at me like I just recited a poem in Mandarin. "I don't get it."

"Oh," I say, my laughter immediately subsiding. "From her special. The story she tells? About peeing in the Ralph's parking lot?"

"Ah," Isaac says. "I must have missed that one."

Well, now I know he never saw the special, because she literally opens with this story. But! Isn't there something to be said about the fact that he cares enough to lie to me? My heart swells at the idea of *the* Isaac Taylor telling a white lie to impress me.

"It's easy to miss," I lie, desperate to change the subject and keep the ball rolling. "So, um, who's your favorite comedian?"

"Uh . . . Mac Josephs?"

"Oh, like the guy who started that sports betting company?" I ask. "Is he a comedian?"

"His shit is *hilarious*," Isaac says. "He does this awesome thing where he rates sports teams based on how hot their cheerleaders are. You'd love it."

"Well, that sounds kind of sexist," I say, unable to help myself. "But I'm sure there's more nuance in the videos. Can you show me a clip?"

"I would," he says. "But I don't have my phone, remember?"

"Oh, right," I say, remembering all our phones were confiscated by security upon arrival. "Duh."

"Yeah," he says. "Bummer . . . So, um, you like sports?"

"Not really—"

"Josie, can I talk to you for a minute?" Lou interrupts, her voice the least hostile it's been toward me since Wednesday. "Please?"

"Um, sure," I say, not wanting to make a scene in front of the literal love of my life. "Isaac, are you gonna be good here alone?"

"Yeah, for sure," he says, getting up from his seat. "I think Grant's in the bathroom, but I'll just go chill with your dad and Pete Sanderson's little brother over there."

I watch as Isaac makes his way over to where Matt and Timmy are gabbing by the bar area inside and say a little silent prayer that their interaction with Isaac goes more smoothly than mine just did.

"Yes, Louise?" I ask Lou, doing my best exasperated sigh as I place a dramatic hand on my hip. "What did you want to talk about?"

She pauses briefly to adjust the gold belly chain sitting between her black bikini top and her half-buttoned jean shorts.

"I just wanted to check in," she finally says. "On how things are going between you and Isaac."

"They're great," I respond, a smidge too quickly. "We just had the *most* soulful conversation."

"Interesting," she says. "Because it looked like you were both going to die of boredom."

Okay, rude! Maybe our conversation wasn't *riveting*, but it was beautiful in its own unexpected-start-to-a-rom-com sort of way. Lou just doesn't get it.

"Well, Louise, looks can be deceiving," I say. "Speaking of deceiving, you know what was *really* deceiving? You lying to me about Santa Clara." I smile, proud of my zinger.

Lou dramatically rolls her eyes.

"Can we just take a time-out on our fight for *one* second to have a real conversation?" she asks. "Josie, you clearly don't have anything in common with him."

"So what?" I ask. "Did you ever consider the possibility that I *like* how different we are? It keeps things interesting! Maybe I'll learn something from him. Really, it's honestly beautiful."

"You know what? Fine," she says, storming away. "Enjoy your fairy tale."

"I *will*," I fire back, stomping over to where Isaac is now standing with Matt and Timmy.

"So, Isaac," Matt is trying when I make my way over to them. "Tell me about yourself! Are you a big comedy nerd like Josie here?"

Oh no. Not this again.

"Yeah," Isaac says as he cracks open what must be his fourth

Bud Light since we hopped aboard ten minutes ago. "I was just telling her I love Mac Josephs."

"The guy who owns that fratty sports company?" Timmy asks, just as confused as I was when he told me Mac Josephs is his favorite stand-up comedian. "Is he a . . . comedian?"

"Oh my God, bro," Isaac says. "Yes. The guy is hilarious. Plus, you should see the chicks he gets with. All tens."

"Wow." Timmy nods. "Totally. Seems like a cool guy."

"His TikToks are gold," Isaac continues. "I wish I had my phone. I'd totally show you guys."

"On the plane back!" I suggest, feeling secondhand embarrassment over how excited he is about this misogynistic guy who I know for a fact is not even a comedian. "We'll watch then."

"Yo!" Grant calls over to us from where he is now hanging out on the front deck of the yacht with Lou, Pete, and Meesha. "We're gonna shotgun some beers! You guys down?"

"Come on, Jos," Isaac says, reaching for my hand. "Let's do it. I'll grab you a beer."

I tentatively put my hand in his, surprised to feel that same pang of nausea I felt when we touched at the airport hangar.

"Oh, um, my dad is here, so I wouldn't want to—"

"Don't let me stop you, Jos," Matt says, motioning for me to go join them. "I don't even think drinking at your age is illegal here."

"It's not," Pete says, walking over to the bar near us to grab another beer. "International waters, baby."

"So, you coming, Jos?" Isaac asks, his hand gently tugging on mine.

"I, uh . . ."

"SHE DOESN'T DRINK, YOU IDIOT," Lou screams from across the boat. Gosh, her hearing is good.

"I *do* drink," I say. "Actually, I got pretty wasted the other night at Mona's birthday. Timmy was there! Right, Timmy?"

I look to him, hoping for backup.

"Yep," Timmy warily confirms. "She was definitely wasted."

"A little too wasted, if you ask me," Matt adds. "Timmy had to carry her home!"

My heart melts a bit as I watch Timmy flash Matt a sheepish smile. *He has a girlfriend*, I remind myself. *You're with Isaac.*

"She literally fell off the stage during our dance performance!" Meesha yells out from where she's standing with Lou. "It was wild." Ooh, nice touch, Meesha. Really sealing in my party girl image.

I catch a glimpse of Lou staring at me quizzically and immediately know she's feeling exactly how I felt at school the other day. Like everyone else suddenly knows your best friend better than you do. I feel equal parts guilty and triumphant.

"But, um, yeah," I say, pushing past the guilt as I pull my hand out of Isaac's. "I think I need a breather after all that raging. You go ahead. I'll hang back here."

"You sure you don't mind if I go with them?" Isaac asks, like a nervous fourth grader asking his mom for permission to see an R-rated movie. "It seems like they're having so much fun. . . ."

"Go for it!" I exclaim, loud enough so Louise can hear. "This is what I love about us. We don't have to do everything together. Super healthy. No codependency to see here, amiright?"

"Uh, yeah, totally," Isaac says, before turning to Timmy. "Sorry, bro. I forget your name. Pete's brother . . . you want in on a little shotgun action?"

"Uh, I'm good, man. I'm not much of a drinker," Timmy says, looking over at me. "I'll hang back here with Josie."

See? I remind myself. *This* is why I can't be with Timmy. Well, aside from the whole girlfriend thing. We're too similar! I need to be with Isaac. The yang to my yin.

"I'm trying to rush Lambda at USC," Isaac says completely seriously as he makes his way over to Grant. "So, you know, it's a grind, but I gotta practice my drinking."

"Right." Timmy nods. "Well, good luck with that!"

"Yeah!" I echo. "I hope you win!"

Okay, so I now know that nobody "wins" shotgunning. Apparently, it's not a game. It's more just people finding a messier, more complicated way to chug a beer? I don't get it, honestly. But Isaac and Grant got *way* too into it. By the time we had to get to the rehearsal dinner, they were toast.

"So, where are your dates?" Timmy asks me and Lou as we take our seats next to him at the dinner. "Too many shotguns?"

"Actually, yes," Lou replies with an eye roll. "They're such amateurs. They completely passed out."

"I honestly thought they were dead," I say, my heart rate

spiking as I consider the idea that they still might be. "Matt had to stay in the bungalow with them to make sure they don't choke on their puke."

"Let's be clear," Lou adds, smoothing out a wrinkle in her floral-printed linen dress. "Matt is with them because you *made* him stay in the room with them, after you made us flip both of them over to their sides."

"Um, you're welcome for saving your boyfriend's *life*," I retort. "People choke on their puke and die all the time!"

"You think Isaac's frat bros are gonna be flipping him over at Lambda?"

"I would hope so!" I exclaim. "Isn't that what *brothers* are for?"

"Not those kinds of brothers," Timmy says with a laugh, clearly trying to release some of the tension between me and Lou. "But, hey, I'm happy you guys were able to make it. How awesome is this place?"

This venue is one of the most magnificent—I know that's a dramatic word, but I don't know how else to describe it—things I've ever seen. There's a giant infinity pool taking up most of the space, sort of like the one at Mary's, but this one overlooks the ocean below us. Our table is a huge U-shaped hunk of marble that wraps around the pool, and it's draped with thousands and thousands of the most beautiful tropical flowers I've ever seen. Oh, and we happen to be here *right* at sunset, so we see the almost neon-orange sun making its way down below the cotton candy–pink sky. Melody and Axle are seated at the center of the table. To Axle's right is his side of the party, starting with his groomsmen. To Melody's left is her side of the party, starting with Mary, then her bridesmaids, ending with me. Next to me is Lou, then Timmy, then Pete.

The rest of the fifty-person table is lined with famous people. Truthfully, aside from the ones Lou took a break from being mad at me to point out, I don't know who any of them are. But if there's one thing from all this I've gathered about famous people, it's that they just look shinier than regular people. You can spot them from a mile away, even if you don't keep up with that stuff at all, just because they *sparkle*. It's to the point where I wonder if there's a special body glitter that's afforded to you once you hit a certain amount of Instagram followers.

After Melody thanks everyone for being here and Axle leads everyone in a guided meditation "designed to mimic the effects of rolling on molly" (obvi I did not participate), the speeches start.

"Melody Joonam," Mary begins. "I am so happy to be here today celebrating your love. Ever since you came into the world twenty-two years ago, everything in my life has been better. All of it. The highs, the lows. Everything is better because I get to go through life knowing you are my kid. I know your father felt the same way, too. Some nights we would truly fall asleep talking about how we got so lucky with you. I mean, the kindest, warmest, most genuinely loving person in the world came out of *me*. Can you believe it?"

Mary pauses for a moment, a satisfied grin making its way across her face as the crowd laughs at her self-deprecating joke.

"And now my kind, warm, loving baby is marrying her

soulmate," Mary continues, her attention on Axle. "And, Axle, just know Ali would have loved you and welcomed you with open arms. I know my marriage was far from perfect. But, from college to the day he died, Ali and I were together for thirty-five years. And I did pick up a few things on what makes a relationship last over the years."

It might be in my head, but I swear Mary's focus is on me now. I shift uncomfortably in my seat, trying to avoid eye contact. We still haven't really spoken since I blew her off at Mona's, and, while it's not quite as bad as my vibe with Lou, things have definitely been a bit . . . weird between us.

"Every time you open your heart up to someone, whether it be a sibling, a parent, a friend, or a spouse, you take a risk," she says, her attention still seemingly on me. "That's just the truth. You're placing your raw, beating heart in their hands and hoping they handle it with care. The problem here is, of course, as far as I know, no human being has truly achieved perfection. My Melody might be the closest we've come, and even she still constantly forgets to turn the lights off when she leaves a room."

She pauses a bit for another laugh before continuing. "This is all to say, every single one of us is fallible. We are all inevitably going to hurt and be hurt by the ones we love. Even when we are trying our absolute best. Even when the love we share is *spotlessly* pure. We do things that hurt each other."

Okay, her eyes are now directly on me, and I'm tearing up. I know this isn't just a speech for Axle and Melody anymore.

"So that beating heart is going to get a bit scuffed," she concludes, facing Melody and Axle again. "My advice to you?

Trust in the love. Let it fill the spaces between you and soften the inevitable blows. Because, at the end of the day, no human is ever going to love you perfectly. All you can really hope is that they care enough to try their best."

After giving her hugs to Melody and Axle, Mary makes her way over to where I'm seated—now fully sobbing. It's like her speech somehow hit the release button on all this resentment I've been holding. Not just toward her, but toward Ali. And, most recently, toward my mom. Now it's all pouring out of me in tear form.

I practically pounce on her, wrapping my arms around her freakishly strong body and continuing my sobs into her shoulder.

"Thank you," I whisper in her ear.

"Of course, azizam," she whispers back, giving me a kiss on top of my head. "Now stop crying so much. You're going to ruin your glam."

Chapter 38

I've really only ever been to one wedding, and it was when Matt's sister Linda married her second husband, Josh, in Minnesota. The actual ceremony was at her church, and the reception was at the community center down the street. There were about ten plastic tables covered in polyester tablecloths with foldout chairs, a barbecue buffet with surprisingly really good mac and cheese, and a small dance floor in the middle of the room that was being deejayed by Linda's son, my thirty-year-old stepcousin Ricky.

The fact that the term "wedding" can be used to describe both that ceremony and this one makes me think it might be time for the English language to do a little update. Unlike Aunt Linda's no-frills Minnesota church wedding, Melody's wedding was in the middle of the freaking ocean. Like, they legitimately set up a glass aisle and altar in the middle of the ocean. It was also *shockingly* secure, which is something I'll have to ask Melody about later. The thing barely shook, even with almost a dozen people on it! And it was just floating in the middle of the ocean! Still makes no sense to me.

Instead of seats, all the guests got to watch the nuptials from little bamboo gondolas that their butlers sailed them out on. People on Melody's side, including Isaac, Grant, and Lou, were docked to the left of the aisle, and people on Axle's side were docked to the right. Once all the guests were seated, the wedding party made its way toward the altar, which was really a traditional Persian sofreh aghd, in two larger gondolas, one with Axle and his groomsmen and one with Melody and her bridesmaids.

Axle was the first to get off his boat and make his way down the aisle, alongside his mom, and then it was my turn. I walked down with Axle's brother Hunter, who smells nothing like patchouli and works in finance in New York. I can't believe they're related. Axle has three brothers, so it worked out nicely. His other two brothers escorted Meesha and Mona. Then, finally, Mary walked Melody down the aisle alongside a hologram (!!!) of their—*our*—dad. It was all very emotional, there wasn't a dry eye in the room—uh, ocean. Like, I even think I spotted Isaac tearing up in his gondola with Grant and Lou. Either that or his cheek was sweaty.

Mansour, an old friend of Mary's, performed a nice, relatively quick ceremony, which was perfectly catered to Melody and Axle. There were traditional Persian elements, like an explanation of the sofreh aghd, a display of different elements meant to bring them luck as they enter their marriage, and a few readings of Rumi poems.

Right after Mansour instructed them both to lick honey off of each other's fingers, the Persian equivalent of *You may now kiss the bride*, Melody and Axle just dove right off the altar into the ocean. That's where they finally kissed for the first time as husband and wife—in the middle of the ocean, fully dressed in their wedding-day attire. And the crowd freaking loved it.

All the guests were laughing and crying and clapping as the two made out, Lou and Grant style. After about five minutes, though, they were *still* making out, and it was honestly starting to get a little weird having all fifty of us watch and cheer on what was starting to look more like foreplay.

"I *knew* they would be in such a rush to bone," Mona kept whispering to me and Meesha as we stood on the altar. "Nobody should wait twenty-two years to have sex. It's unnatural."

✦ ✦ ✦

Mona described the wedding reception as being like "Scorpios in Mykonos but more lit," and I'm not really sure what that means, but I'd venture to guess it's glamorous person speak for *This is the most out-of-control, wild party ever.*

There's a huge dance floor set up on the shore, and we've already had performances from half the Grammy-winning guests.

"Man, am I glad to see you," Timmy says as I get to the bar to grab a coconut water. "Everyone here is *wasted.*"

I take a look around the party and realize he's right. In addition to an open bar with every drink imaginable readily available, there are multiple waiters roaming around with trays filled with fruity cocktails for people to try. And it looks like the vast majority of the guests have taken full advantage.

Matt is currently fully engaged in what appears to be a dance-off with multiplatinum singing legend Aaliyah Thomas. Farida has been twerking on her new boyfriend, a young male model named Yoan, for the past hour. Javier and Mona have been taking body shots off of Majid's perfectly chiseled abs. I'm pretty sure I saw June Li moon a yacht passing by earlier. And Meesha and Pete have been rolling around in the sand making out for the past twenty minutes, which is extra awkward considering both of their parents are here. But honestly, I don't think they seem to care, because I just saw Mary busting into the splits with a margarita balanced atop her head as Mr. and Mrs. Sanderson chanted, "MVP! MVP! MVP!"

"Yeah," I agree with Timmy, my eyes making their way to a person who I'm pretty sure is a member of the royal family doing the funky chicken onstage as some trendy deejay named Boxhead does his set. "I don't think I've ever seen anything like this."

"Agreed," Timmy says. "So, where's your date?"

"Oh, he's taking shots with Grant and Lou," I explain. "He was super hungover, but Grant says he's going to have to learn to push past the hangovers if he's going to be in Lambda *and* be on the basketball team."

"Right."

We stand quietly for a bit, and I consider asking Timmy where *his* date is—I would be lying if I said I hadn't noticed the lavender-haired girl sitting next to him at the ceremony—but decide against it. He still hasn't even told me about her. I can't be creepy.

"Oh!" I exclaim, my eyes shifting over to the corner of the bar where Lou, Grant, and Isaac are clinking their shot glasses. "There they are. Come on, let's go hang out with them."

"Lou, baby, come on," I can hear Grant saying as Timmy follows me to where they're all standing, backs facing toward us. "You have to admit. She is a *little* off."

"Not just a little," Isaac says with a laugh. "The chick just started quoting some comedian out of the blue and expected me to know what she was talking about. I always knew she was a freak, but I didn't realize she was, like, *off*."

Timmy and I both stop in our tracks.

"Excuse me?" Lou practically yells at Isaac. "You're talking shit about my best friend *to* me while you're only here as *her* date to this wedding?!? Are you good?"

I want to jump in. To give Lou a hug and tell her they're not worth it. That we should forget about Isaac and forget about our stupid fight. But I can't. It's like every feeling I've ever had for the last eighteen years—all the mortification, the grief, the loneliness—is melting out of my body like superglue, pinning my feet to the sand beneath them. Forcing me to keep listening.

"Relax, babe," Grant says. "You didn't really expect him to want to be with Josie . . . ?"

I look down, hyperfocusing on a seashell next to my left pinkie toe in order to avoid the look of pity I know Timmy has in his eyes right now.

"Then why would you ask her to prom?" Lou asks. "If you just think she's some freak? Why come to her SISTER'S WEDDING??"

"Um," Isaac says. "Isn't it obvious?"

"Well, I would ASSUME that it's because she's one of the most incredible people to have ever walked this Earth and is an abundantly better person than Genevieve is or ever will be," Lou says. "But please. Enlighten me on your take."

"It's because she's a Mashad, Lou," Grant cuts in. "Obviously. My boy had to shoot his shot! Being able to say you took a Mashad to prom is worth maaajor clout when you get to college. That story alone is going to give him a fast pass into Lambda."

"Uh," Timmy whispers as tears start to dampen my eyeballs, "should we go?"

"No," I whisper back, my voice coming out a little shakier than I'd like it to. "I think I need to hear this." Clearly, I had ignored who Isaac really is for years. Maybe this is the only way to get over him. To stand here frozen, watching as he exposes his own true colors.

"All right," Timmy says, another one of those crazy shocks shooting up my spine as he places a hand on the small of my back. "But, for the record, these guys are jerks."

I make eye contact with him for the first time since we got stuck here and am pleased to see there's not one trace of pity in his eyes. Just his standard chicken soup smile.

"So," Lou is now saying to Grant, "let me get this straight. You *agree* with him using my best friend for popularity?"

"Come on, Louise," Grant pleads. "She's not *really* your best friend, is she?"

"OF COURSE SHE IS," Lou screams. "SHE'S BEEN MY BEST FRIEND SINCE I WAS FOUR."

"But," Grant interjects, "you're so hot and cool. And she's so—"

"I would seriously consider how you choose to finish that sentence," Lou says, her voice so ice cold that she could pass as Meesha. "Very. Seriously."

"Dude, Louise, stop being such a bitch," Isaac says. "It's cool she's your friend. But just admit it's, like, charity. I get it. It's just like when I have to be partners with her in math class."

Grant snorts. "Dude, you're partners with her in math class? That's hilarious."

"Hey," Timmy whispers, delicately wiping a stray hair away from my face so he can look me directly in the eye. "I'm assuming you already realize this because you've apparently seen Isaac try to do math, which I'm sure was a hilarious experience in and of itself . . . but you know these guys are idiots, right? They make Axle look like a Nobel laureate."

I look back at Timmy, his crooked smile softening the impact of Grant's and Isaac's blows. I notice there's an intensity in his gaze, like he desperately needs me to not just hear his words—but believe them. And I do. If I am being fully honest, I always knew Isaac wasn't the brightest bulb. But until now I think I almost found some safety in his subpar intellect. As bad as it sounds, deep down I didn't think he could be the bad person Lou insisted he was because I didn't think he was smart enough to be that calculated. Now I know it's possible to be simultaneously evil and stupid.

"You are both genuinely horrible human beings," Lou tells Isaac and Grant. "You deserve each other."

"Babe," Grant says. "Chill! We're just joking around. So Josie is a bit of a freak. Whatever!"

"Oh my God," Lou says. "What am I even doing here? We're done."

"LOUISE!" Grant calls out. "WAIT! COME ON. I'M CLASS PRESIDENT! YOU CAN'T LEAVE ME."

But it's too late. She's already walked away from them and is now standing, frozen, facing me and Timmy.

"Uh, I should probably let you two chat," Timmy says, giving my hand a squeeze before leaving us for where his parents are standing at the other end of the bar.

Lou and I stand there for a second, just staring at each other, not sure where to begin.

"H-hi," I finally say, trying my best to rapidly blink the tears out of my eyes.

"Hi. So, uh, did you hear all of that?" Lou asks, fidgeting with her fingers the way she does when her mom yells at her.

"Yep," I say, letting a few tears finally make their way out of my eyes. "I did."

"Like, *all* of it?" Lou asks, now also tearing up.

"Uh, yeah," I say. "Pretty sure."

"Oh God, Jos," she says, wrapping me in a bear hug. "I'm so sorry. I'm so, so sorry. I hate them. I hate them both."

"You really didn't have to do that," I say through sniffles.

"Grant is probably gonna be prom king. You should be there with him next week."

"I would rather be chained down to a table while a team of tiny elves slowly sawed off my limbs one by one with their tiny saws than be caught dead with him ever again."

I pause my crying to let out a laugh. Lou has always been able to come up with the world's most bizarre hypotheticals.

"But seriously," she continues. "How could I ever be with someone who doesn't love you?"

"But I don't want you guys breaking up over me," I insist. "I mean, he's not necessarily wrong. I *am* a freak. And you can't just go dumping every guy who thinks that. You'd be left with, like, two guys to date. Matt and Timmy. One is a middle-aged widower, and I'm pretty sure the other has a girl-friend. It's not a great pool."

"We're not breaking up over you," she says. "We're break-ing up over him being a legitimately bad person who has no respect for me and my loved ones."

"Yeah, I guess he's not the world's nicest guy."

"No," she retorts with a laugh. "He's not. We were super attracted to each other, and it was fun while it lasted, but I think this is for the best. He was taking over my life."

I look back at her, surprised. I just sort of assumed I only felt like Grant was taking over her life because I was being a jealous best friend. I never thought *she* felt that way, too.

"Isn't that normal, though?" I ask. "Like, for the beginning of a relationship?"

"To a certain extent, I guess," she says. "But I feel like I was starting to lose a piece of myself with him. He was always trying to make me be part of *his* world but made zero effort to be part of mine."

"I guess I was sort of guilty of trying to mold you into someone I wanted you to be, too," I admit. "Lou, I'm sorry. Really. You deserve to do whatever you want to do with your life."

"I'm sorry, too," she says. "I shouldn't have lied to you."

"But I get why you did," I say. "I never even really gave you a window to tell the truth! I was so set on our—er, *my*—plan. I literally filled out your Santa Clara application for you. That should have been my first sign maybe college wasn't for you."

"Maybe," Lou says with a laugh. "And who knows? Maybe it will be eventually. I just . . . need a minute to explore other options."

"So what are you going to do now that you and Grant are done?" I ask. "You know, you could always make your first stop Stanford . . . *not* that I'm trying to force you into anything."

"I don't know," Lou muses. "Do you think Mary was serious about helping me out with getting into fashion? She brought it up again when I talked to her after the ceremony. She said she thinks I could start as a model and eventually have my own line the way Meesha does. But I don't know. Maybe she was just drunk."

"Drunk or not, I don't think Mary ever jokes about anything," I say. "Especially not when it comes to business. Do you think you're going to take her up on it?"

"I mean, it would literally be a dream come true," she says. "But do you think I could *model*?"

I take a long look at her. It's funny. When you have known someone so deeply for so long you become almost immune to their physical appearance. But Lou is undeniably stunning. Her simple black lace-trimmed slip dress sits perfectly on her body, and her green eyes are so bright against her dark glossy waves that they shine like two little stars sprinkled across her face.

A very real part of me wants to warn her about the cutthroat nature of the modeling industry and remind her that a business degree could really help her with more complex negotiations, but I tell that part of me to shut up. This is her life. And I need to let her live it.

"You definitely should," I say instead. "I'm sure Meesha could give you pointers, too."

"I should probably think on it," Lou says. "It almost sounds too good to be true."

"Hey, if you're not going to go to college near me, the next best thing is to have you be famous with me."

"You wouldn't feel like I was sort of interfering with your new family?"

I let out a laugh at the thought.

"Are you kidding? Absolutely not. You were my family first. This just feels like my families are blending. It's a dream come true."

We stand there quietly for a bit, watching the party unfold in front of us.

"Is that . . ." I begin to ask.

"Mona licking five-time Grammy Award winner Marco's face? Yes."

"And that . . . ?"

"Pop singing legend Aaliyah Thomas grinding on Matt? Also yes."

We both laugh.

"So, we're really good?" Lou asks. "You actually forgive me?"

"I'm for real over it," I promise. "And you're for real okay with the breakup? Lou, seriously. If you want to be with him, I'm fine with it. I just want you to be happy."

"Trust me," she says. "I'm *happy* to be done with Grant. Isaac can be his prom date. Also, OMG, I hate to say I told you so about Isaac, but . . . COME ON. Please, just let me have this moment."

"Ugh," I groan. "Fine. You were right."

"I was RIGHT," she says, jumping for joy. "So we can be done with him? Like, for good?"

"Yeah, I think it's going to be tough to get past him pretty much admitting to using me to both pass math and get into a frat."

"Thank GOD." She sighs dramatically. "You deserve so much better. Like, sooo much better. Like, Isaac is below ground, and what you deserve is in outer space."

"Trust me," I say. "I know. And, honestly, it wasn't just that he's a user. He's also just kind of . . . boring. Like, we truly *do* have nothing in common. I kept trying to convince myself that we had an *opposites attract*–type thing going for us, but if I'm being honest, it was like pulling teeth trying to talk to him this weekend. Even in math class, we talk. But it's not like our conversations are exactly *riveting*."

I let out a big exhale. I've spent so many years trying to convince myself that there was something inexplicably special shared between Isaac and me that it feels liberating to admit that we just don't vibe.

"Well, I guess we're both single now," Lou says, wrapping her arm around me. "Hey, now that you're this huge partier, what do you say we take some shots?"

"That was a one-time rock-bottom decision and just left me convinced that I will literally never ever drink again," I explain. "But I'll come with you."

"Fine," Lou says, making her way over to where my sisters are taking shots on the dance floor. "But you have to promise to show me video footage of you falling off that stage."

"Deal."

Before we can reach my sisters on the dance floor, the party is interrupted by an extremely loud helicopter landing on the helipad above the nearby clubhouse.

"What is happening?" I ask Lou, squinting up at the blurry scene. "Do you think another celebrity just got here?"

"Oh my *God*," Lou says, her eyes fixed on the same scene. "It's Isaac and Grant."

Oh my gosh. She's *right*. Slowly but surely my eyes are able to make out exactly what's going on as Mary's security team escorts a wasted Isaac and Grant onto the helicopter, their luggage in tow. I look around the reception. The music has stopped, and everybody is watching as Grant way-too-loudly tries to remind Mary's security team that he's class president.

"Josie Joonam, it's all taken care of," Mary says, walking over toward Lou and me with Mona, Melody, Axle, and Matt following closely behind. "Your rude little friends are going to be transported to the nearest public airport, from where I've booked them both coach seats back to the Valley. *And* I used a landline to call both of their mothers and inform them of their sons' behavior."

"You are *so* extreme, Mom," Mona says with a chuckle. "It usually annoys me but, TBH, I am loving it right now."

"I have to say, I am, too," Matt says, sending a waft of his Irish Spring soap scent up my nostrils as he wraps an arm around me. "I probably should have said this earlier, but thank you, Mary. For everything you've done for Josie."

Mary smiles, and I'm surprised by the way my shoulders ease up in response to their little exchange. I had no idea how much the tension between them was causing *me* tension.

"I just did what had to be done," Mary says matter-of-factly. "Josie Joon, you speak Farsi. Those boys were textbook pedar sags."

"Huh?" Lou asks. "What's a pedar sag?"

"It's kind of like how Americans say *son of a bitch*," Mary explains. "But, instead, it means *Your father is a dog*. Get it? Basically, they're jerks."

"Got it." Lou nods as the helicopter flies away. "I'm all in. They're both pedar sags."

"Did you all hear the whole thing?" I ask, my cheeks flushing with embarrassment.

"Josephine," Axle says, clasping both of my hands in his. "Do not waste time with frivolous worries of what others think."

"Um, my full name isn't Josephine. It's just Josie . . . but thanks?"

"Oh, Axy," Melody says, giving him a kiss. "Now that we're family, you're going to have to learn *all* my sisters' names."

"Yeah, everyone knows," Mona tells me, completely ignoring the interaction with Axle. "One of the bartenders overheard, and word got around pretty quickly after that."

"When I was told, I knew they were no longer welcome here. I will not tolerate any pedar sag treating you or any of my girls that way," Mary says, giving me an extremely unexpected kiss on the top of my head. "Now go enjoy the rest of your sister's big day."

I watch, stunned, as Mary strolls over to where Mr. and Mrs. Sanderson are hanging by the bar. She has a unique—and, frankly, super dramatic—way of showing it, but I guess Mary really does care about me.

"Who wants shots?" Meesha says, Timmy and Pete trailing behind her as she makes her way over with a tray of pink shooters. "Jos, I bet you could use one right about now."

"Yes!" Lou exclaims. "Come on. It's no fair that they all got to see drunk Josie and I didn't."

"Lou, I promised I'll send you video footage!" I exclaim. "But I'm never drinking again."

"How about a virgin shooter?" Timmy asks, handing me a fruity-looking concoction to match his own. "I got two in case you'd want one."

"I'd love one," I say, shooting him an appreciative smile as we clink our glasses together. "Thanks."

We hold each other's gaze for about one second longer than is socially acceptable, until I notice everyone else staring at us.

"Actually, um, Timmy," Meesha interjects. "I almost forgot—your mom mentioned she lost her diamond earrings out by the docks."

"What?" Timmy asks, his eyes wide. "Those were her thirtieth wedding anniversary gift from my dad. She loves them."

"I know," Melody says, her lips curving downward into a pout. "She was super upset."

"Would you mind finding them?" Pete asks. "You're the only sober one here."

"He's right." Mona nods. "The rest of us would be looking until sunrise."

"Jos, you should go with him," Lou suggests. "You know, since you're sober, too."

"Yeah, I'd love to," I say, a little more excited than I should be at the idea of some alone time with Timmy.

I scan the crowd for the lavender-haired girl and notice she's over by Mary and the Sandersons. Ugh. So she's in with his family. They must be serious.

"You sure?" Timmy asks me. "You really don't have to."

"No, really," I insist. "I want to help." It's true. He might be in a relationship, but Timmy is still one of my favorite people on Earth to do literally anything with.

When we make our way over to where the docks are, we immediately spot a little picnic blanket set up by the shore, covered in rose petals and candles.

"What is this?" I ask, making my way over to the blanket. "Are Axle and Melody supposed to come here later?"

Timmy reaches down and grabs a small card resting at the center of the blanket and quietly reads it.

"Well," he says. "My mom didn't actually lose her earrings."

"What?" I ask. "What's going on?"

"I have no idea," Timmy says, passing me the card. "But I think . . . this is for us?"

I read the card: *To J & T, The earrings are fine. This is for you. Enjoy. XO.*

My face immediately turns bright red. Was my crush on Timmy really *that* obvious? Oh gosh. And now he's literally being trapped on a romantic date with me against his will? While his girlfriend is here, no less! This is a total and complete disaster.

"Timmy, we really don't have to do this," I say, moving to make my way back toward the reception. "We can go back to the party. I'm sorry. I know you're with that girl. This is so not okay."

"What?" Timmy asks, his face scrunched in confusion. "What girl?"

Is he really going to force me to spell this out for him? Haven't I endured enough humiliation tonight?

"The pretty one," I shyly reply. "With the lavender hair."

"Wait, *Emma*?" Timmy asks with a laugh. "You thought Emma was my girlfriend?"

I notice he hasn't moved an inch. He's still standing calmly by the picnic blanket.

"If Emma is the girl with the lavender hair, then yes," I admit, making my way back over toward him. "How could I not? She was in your Snapchat story, then you brought her to Mona's party, and now she's at the wedding!"

"Josie," Timmy says. "Emma is my cousin. She's visiting from Michigan, so I've been showing her around."

I feel like an absolute idiot, but I'm so relieved that it doesn't matter.

"Oh," I say. "Well, good." *Shoot.* The word slipped out before I could think any better of it.

"Good?" Timmy asks, an eyebrow raised. "So it's *good* that I don't have a girlfriend. Interesting."

I rack my brain for explanations that are not *It's good because I wish I was your girlfriend* but come up short. Who cares at this point? Enough people know I have a crush on him that they literally set us up on a staged date during a wedding. I'm in this deep. I might as well go for it.

"Fine, I'm just gonna go ahead and say it," I say, shoving the words out of my mouth as quickly as I possibly can. "But before I say what I'm going to say, you have to promise that things won't be weird between us if you don't feel the same. Okay?"

"Promise," he says solemnly, the smallest sliver of a smile on his face.

"Well, all right, here it goes," I say, instinctually tapping Matt's go-to "I Won't Back Down" on my thigh. "I like you. A lot. But seriously. It's totally fine if you don't feel the same way. I just . . . figured if I don't say it now, I probably never will."

I stare up at him, the pink sky slowly turning to navy above us.

"Josie," he says, his eyes beaming down at me as the small sliver of a smile grows wider. "I like you, too. A lot. Isn't it obvious?"

"Not really!" I insist. "The two times I thought we were maybe on dates, you insisted they weren't dates. Then there was the whole cousin girlfriend conundrum. You are a confusing man."

Timmy laughs. "You were the one who pulled away when I tried to kiss you after the concert, remember? I only said they weren't dates after that because I assumed you weren't interested, and I didn't want to make it weird."

"Yeah," I admit, wincing at the memory. "Well, now that we're being honest here, I'll tell you the truth. I pulled away because I've never kissed anyone before, and I freaked out."

I stare up at him, waiting for him to laugh or look embarrassed for me. But he just smiles and shrugs.

"That makes sense," he says, sending a small spark up my spine as he gently takes my hand in his. "Well, how about we try again?"

"I would really like that."

Timmy gently wraps his arms around my waist and inches his face toward mine, his familiar scent of dryer sheets and sandalwood intensifying as he closes the space between us. Man, I *really* want to kiss him. Like, it's wild how strongly I'm craving this experience I've never even had before. My brain scrambles, trying to remember all the YouTube kissing tutorials Lou and I watched in middle school. Shoot. What if I suck at this? What if I'm a bad kisser? Honestly, it would be really on brand for me to be bad at this. . . .

But the minute Timmy's lips meet mine, something shifts. My mind goes blank. There's no more thinking. There's just feeling.

At first, it's just one little peck, then it's a bunch of little pecks, which feel so good that I instinctively push myself closer into Timmy. He pulls me in even farther, now squeezing me tightly as our little pecks turn into one long, continuous peck, ending with him slipping his tongue into my mouth. I always thought the whole rubbing tongues part of kissing sounded gross, but I instantly get the hype. His tongue is all minty fresh, and feeling it groove alongside my own shoots *full-on* fireworks up my spine. Multicolor explosions!!! Like, forget the stupid little sparks I was feeling before. This is those on steroids. And not the kind of mild topical steroids my dermatologist makes me take when I get really bad eczema. No, more like the illegal kind of steroids that professional athletes inject themselves with to enhance their performance. The kind that make you feel invincible.

Timmy's arms stay wrapped around me, but he pauses our kissing for a second, a shy smile spreading across his face as his chocolate-brown eyes gaze down directly at mine.

"Why'd you stop?" I ask. "Shoot. Was I a bad kisser? Ugh, I *knew* I would be a bad kisser."

"No!" he exclaims with a laugh, blushing a bit. Then he softly adds, "You were a *very* good kisser. Best kiss of my life, hands down. It's just . . . I'm so happy. I wanted to pause for a second to take it all in."

I look up at the dark navy sky, littered with bright white stars whose reflections shimmer on the surface of the ocean in front of us.

"Want to jump in?" I ask Timmy, the words flowing out of my mouth before I can really think them through.

"*You* want to jump into the ocean?" Timmy asks. "You're not afraid?"

I pause for a second, frankly shocked by how totally and completely calm I feel in this moment.

"I'm . . . honestly not."

"Well, in that case," Timmy says, flashing me a giant smile. "Last one in has to sneak Axle a nonorganic beverage!"

His hand breaks away from mine as he books it into the ocean, still fully dressed in his beige linen suit. I dive into the salty warm water after him, laughing uncontrollably as my long flowy gown gains what feels like ten pounds of water weight.

"WAIT FOR US," I hear in the distance, looking over to see Lou, Mona, Meesha, Pete, and Melody running toward us.

"What are you guys even doing here?" Timmy asks, laughing as his brother and Meesha dive into the ocean after him.

"Oh, please," Mona says, casually stomping her stiletto-clad feet into the water. "You think we were going to set this entire thing up and *not* spy on you from the bushes the whole time?"

"How did you guys even plan all of this?" I ask, looking back over at the insanely romantic picnic.

"It was nothing," Meesha says. "When things didn't work out with Isaac, we knew it was time to make something happen for you two. So we got the staff on it. They had it ready in, like, ten minutes."

"I honestly had no clue what was going on," Lou says. "Mona just whispered the plan to me when you guys were being all cute with those nonalcoholic shots."

"But, Melody, during your own wedding?" I ask. "This night is supposed to be about you."

"Are you kidding? This is the cutest thing I've ever seen!" Melody squeals, her beautiful white gown now completely soaked for the second time this evening. "Two human beings I love, getting together on my wedding day?! What could be better?"

"You seriously did *not* have to come over here in the middle of your own reception," I say, my heart warming at the fact that she did so anyway. "Where's Axle?"

"Mom's off briefing him on some sort of PR crisis," Melody says with a shrug. "But as soon as they told me you two were kissing, I had to come. My little sister's first kiss!"

"*Our* little sister's first kiss," Meesha corrects, pulling me in for a side hug as she wades over from where she was standing near Pete.

Before I know it, Melody, Lou, and Mona have all pounced on the hug and the five of us have toppled over out onto the sand.

"ARE YOU GUYS OKAY?" Timmy calls out from where he's still standing in the ocean with Pete.

"YEP!" I call back between giddy bouts of laughter. And even though I'm getting squished down here, I mean it.

I look back up at the starry night sky, my lungs feeling like they might collapse under the weight of my four favorite women on Earth. This might be the best night of my life. And not just because I had my first kiss, and it was perfect. Or because I made up with Lou. Or because Melody got married. Or because I finally saw Isaac for who he really is. Or because my dad is here having the most fun I've seen him have since my mom died. Or because I'm at this impossibly fancy island with these impossibly fancy people.

Because of *this*. Because of these people who make me feel so loved for exactly who I am. Because I did something terrifying. And it landed me here.

Epilogue

"So, Josie Joon," Farida instructs. "Give the viewers some backstory on what's going on tonight."

"Well, it's prom." I speak into Zadie's camera as Becky applies some sort of clear goo on my eyebrows. "And Mary suggested Lou and I get our glam and do pre-prom pictures here at her place."

"This definitely beats getting our makeup done at the mall," Lou adds from the seat next to me. "Alfie, you are a genius. I didn't even know my hair could look this good."

"Oh, honey, this is nothing," Alfie says. "Give me some time to throw a gloss and some highlights in, and you'll be a whole new woman."

"Who are you girls going with?" Farida asks. "To the prom."

"I'm going solo," Lou proudly declares. "I was supposed to go with my boyfriend Grant, but he turned out to be a spineless twerp, so I dumped him last weekend."

"You're not going solo," I correct Lou, then turn my attention back to to the camera Zadie is still pointing at me. "*I am* her date, and Timmy is already fully aware that he is coming as *our* third wheel."

"Josie, Timmy is your boyfriend," she reminds me. "It's okay that he's your date."

My lips curve upward at the sound of the word *boyfriend*. I mean, I know it's lame and antifeminist to be freaking out over having a boyfriend. It's not like I did anything noteworthy to achieve this. But c'mon. This still feels major. I can't believe *I*, Josie Lawrence, have a boyfriend. And not just any boyfriend. *Timmy*. The best boyfriend.

"Knock knock," Mary says, letting herself into the glam room. "Josie Joonam, it's time for pictures. And, Louise, while I have you here, what are you doing tomorrow? I have an opening from eleven to one if you would like to come for a strategy session regarding your potential modeling career."

I shoot her an excited look. I knew Mary wasn't just bringing up the modeling stuff for no reason. And modeling actually feels like a really good fit for Lou.

"I would love that," Lou says, her cheeks adopting a pinkish hue. "If you're up for it. Seriously, Mary. No pressure or anything if you're busy or don't want to."

"I would not offer if I did not want to, azizam," Mary says matter-of-factly. "You have a great look, and I think *both* of us could make some good money off it. I've already told Meesha to block some time off, as well. She can mentor you."

"That would literally be a dream come true," Lou gushes, Becky rushing to reapply her eyeliner as her eyes water a bit. "Thank you."

"Becky, Alfie, you two should probably be here also, if you're available," Mary instructs. "We'll get her glammed up and take a few headshots while we're at it."

"I'll be here," Becky says as she dusts a bit of gold eye shadow on my eyelid.

"I'll be here, too," Alfie says. "Lou, babe, what do you think of a cut? A lob would look gorge on you."

"I'm up for whatever," Lou says with a shrug. "You guys know better than I do."

"So it's settled," Mary says. "I'll see you tomorrow morning. Now you girls hurry up and get outside."

When we finally enter the backyard, Timmy is already waiting with everyone else by the infinity pool, fully dressed in his tux. Not to be, like, a pervy girlfriend, but he looks so hot I might have to shove him in the pool to cool him off a bit. I always thought Timmy was cute. But something shifted after we kissed. Now I find him to be smoking hot. It's like those fireworks I felt whenever we'd touch burst all over me every single time that I see him.

"Wow," Timmy says, his squinty eyes widening as he sees me entering Mary's backyard. "You look—"

"Hot," Mona cuts in, finishing the sentence for him. "Man, they *always* pull through at Vik. That dress looks so good on you it should be illegal."

"Thanks," I say, looking down at my simple but perfectly formfitting long black gown. "I really do love it."

"Oh, Jos," Matt says, his eyes welling up as he looks me up and down. "You look beautiful. I wish your mom could have been here to see this."

"Me too," I say, my eyes also watering a bit before I turn toward Timmy. "She would have loved you."

"She really would have," Lou chimes in. "Anyone who treats Josie as well as you do would be top of her list."

"What's not to love?" Pete asks, giving his brother a hug. "This guy is the best."

"Okay, this is a sweet moment, but you guys have to pause so I can FaceTime Melody in. I promised her I would as soon as you came out, Josie," Meesha says, pulling out her iPhone. "She has such FOMO."

"Isn't she on her honeymoon?" Lou asks. "In, like, Italy?"

"Yeah," Mona says. "The girl's FOMO truly knows no bounds."

"Oh my GOSH," Melody squeals as soon as she answers from the master bedroom of their private Italian palazzo. "Axy, wake up. You have to see Josie and Lou. And Timmy!"

"Ah," Axle says, a smile slowly forming across his face as his groggy eyes take each of us in, one by one. "How beautiful. The gift of love did not stop at our wedding, you see? It simply continues to give and give and give. Look at what it has blossomed into."

"Are you saying your love somehow sparked Josie's prom?" Mona asks. "You know it was scheduled for, like, months, right? Before she even knew you?"

"What I'm speaking of is the *love*," Axle maintains. "The love that is only brought about by more love."

"What Axle is trying to say," Melody says, grabbing the phone from him, "is that we are so happy for you guys! And we wish we could be there."

"We wish you were here, too," I tell her. "But having an entire Italian palazzo to yourself probably beats taking a few pictures of me before prom."

"Speaking of which," Mona cuts in as she pulls out her phone camera. "Let's get one of the three of you all close together."

"Oh, this is great," Matt gushes, pulling out his own phone to snag a picture of us posing in front of Mary's infinity pool. "And, um, Timmy, I hope you don't mind, but could I get one of just Lou and Josie? I promised Lou's mom I would send her a few shots since she can't be here tonight."

Lou pulls me in tight, and the two of us take a different version of the same best friend picture we've taken ahead of every school dance we've ever been to.

"You're right, Mom," Meesha says, peering over Matt's shoulder. "Lou definitely translates great on camera. She could go really far. I see her doing something trendy. Maybe a Loewe campaign?"

"I told you," Mary says. "She has *it*."

"You guys think so?" Lou asks, blushing as she looks down at her gold-studded gown. "Really? Loewe is, like, one of my all-time favorite brands. Not that I can ever afford to shop there. But I'm always stalking their stuff on Instagram. I would freak if I could do *anything* with them."

"You definitely could," Meesha confirms. "You're so natural in front of the camera. I think headshots tomorrow will be a breeze."

"This is *so* exciting," I whisper to her. "What if you actually become, like, a supermodel?"

"Stop," Lou says with a laugh. "That's, like, too crazy to even dream about."

"Crazier things have happened," I tell her. "Look where we are right now."

"Fair," she says. "Very fair."

"Uh, Josie, when you're done, I got something for you," Timmy says, pulling a corsage out of his pocket. "I hope you like roses. The only other option was peonies and I remember Lou saying you were allergic to those. Right?"

"See?" Lou says as he slips the corsage onto my wrist. "*This* is the sort of commitment you deserve. A guy who knows which flowers aren't going to make you break out into hives."

"Wait!" Mona exclaims, grabbing my phone out of my bag as she rushes back over to us. "Take it off and put it on again so I can get pictures of the whole thing."

We laugh as I let Timmy slip the corsage onto my wrist for a second time, hundreds of little shocks shooting up my spine as his hand grazes mine.

"Uh, Josie," Mona says as she pauses her photography. "You just got, like, a psychotically long 'I'm sorry' text from Isaac. . . . Oh, and now there's a follow-up of him asking for help in calc. He says he's gonna fail and have his offer rescinded from USC if you don't help him?"

Everyone stops, silence washing over us, save for the "You have *got* to be kidding me" I hear Lou mutter under her breath.

I look over at Timmy, unsure how to properly navigate the whole text-from-an-old-crush-in-front-of-the-new-boyfriend situation.

"I don't care if you want to help him," Timmy says with an unbothered shrug. "Seriously." His voice is completely genuine.

I feel my heart melting a bit as I stand on my tiptoes to give him a kiss. I know it's too soon to be using the *L* word, but I know deep in my bones that I love him. Part of me felt like it would never happen, but with Timmy I really did manage to find a love like Matt and my mom's. One where I feel totally loved, too, and trusted and seen for who I really am.

I guess what I didn't consider was how finding the love I always knew I deserved would change me. The way it would seep deep into my psyche and make me feel brave in a way I never thought was possible before.

At any other point in my life, I would have helped Isaac in a heartbeat. Not just because I had a colossal crush on him, but because I would have been terrified of what would happen if I *didn't* help him. What if he hates me? What if it's awkward in class next week? What if I have to find a new math partner this late in the semester and my entire routine gets completely thrown off? But I'm not scared anymore.

"You good?" Timmy asks, interrupting my introspection with a quick kiss on top of my head.

I smile up at him. "Yeah," I say, taking the phone from Mona and blocking Isaac before throwing it into my clutch. "I'm not gonna reply. He can figure it out on his own."

"Well," Timmy says, flaring his nostrils and pulling his chin inward to make what might be his funniest face yet. "I'll be here no matter what you decide."

I let out a laugh. I mean, come on. How could I be scared of anything when the scariest thing I ever did landed me here?

"Um, did you just completely ignore a string of desperate texts from Isaac Taylor without even reading them?" Lou asks, her jaw practically on the floor as she grabs my hand in excitement. "Who are you, and what have you done with my best friend?!"

"I don't know," I say, smiling as I give her hand a squeeze back. "I guess I've changed."

45 Years Earlier . . .

"Ladies and gentleman, Pan Am welcomes you to Los Angeles," the captain announces as the plane hits the tarmac at LAX. "The local time is eleven thirty a.m., and the weather is currently seventy degrees Fahrenheit. We hope you enjoyed your journey here from Paris."

Marjan pulls the compact mirror out of the Celine box shoulder bag her mom got her last year for her birthday and stares at her reflection. *I look awful*, she thinks. *Haggard. Old.* In twenty-four hours, she swears she's aged thirty years. This would be a difficult realization for anybody, but it's especially difficult for Marjan, who has been told her whole life that she's beautiful. Not just beautiful in a regular prettiest-girl-in-your-class sort of way, either. *Showstoppingly* beautiful. People would literally stop in their tracks just to stare at her. Now they still stop in their tracks. But it's more to ask what's wrong. Why she's crying so much. Why the collar of her brand-new DVF wrap dress is covered in snot. She breaks down again, heaving loud sobs as she files off the airplane. *Get it together,* she tells herself. *You can't be a baby anymore. You're on your own now.* She takes the compact out again, wiping away her tears, and puts her bravest face on as she steps off the plane.

Marjan hasn't seen Khaleh Farrah and Sharzad since before they left Iran for America three years ago. Sharzad was only ten then. Marjan has no idea what she looks like now. She isn't even completely sure that they'll be there waiting for her. She was hardly focusing when they made these plans, still feeling like she was trapped in some sort of never-ending nightmare.

But as soon as she gets off the plane, they're there.

"Ghorboonet behram man," Khaleh Farrah says, running over to her and smushing Marjan's face into her ample chest as she squeezes her in a tight hug. "Fadat sham." She smothers her in kisses, and, for a split second, Marjan feels like she's in her own mom's arms again. But then she remembers her own mom is gone, and she starts sobbing all over again.

Sharzad watches as her beautiful, chic older cousin breaks down in her mom's arms. She knows it's been a few years since they've seen each other, but Marjan has always been her idol. Even with giant dark circles rimming her eyes and snot crusting her cheeks, she's stunning. It's not just that, though. It's everything about her. The way she carries herself. Like even if she weren't stunning, she could trick you into thinking she was. Sharzad gets a bit of a confidence boost just knowing they share some DNA.

"Marjan Joonam," Farrah says, still holding Marjan tightly as she shifts her attention toward Sharzad. "You remember Sharzad, right?"

"Of course," Marjan says, wiping her tears away. "Sharzad. Hi. You look so grown up."

Sharzad blushes, honored her cool older cousin even remembers her.

"Thanks," she sheepishly says. "I'm . . . I'm so sorry."

Marjan bursts into tears again, and this time Sharzad joins in on the hug.

"They're gone," Marjan keeps saying through sobs. "They're all gone. And I'm stuck here alone."

"But, Marjan," Sharzad gently interrupts. "You're not alone. I promise. As long as I'm here, you'll never be alone."

Marjan looks down at her little cousin, who doesn't look quite so little anymore, and gives her a small smile. For the first time since she got that awful phone call from Khanoom Hashemi, she feels just a little bit better.

Acknowledgments

Mom, I will try to keep this brief considering I wrote an entire chapter about you in my last book, but, at the end of the day, you inspire so much of who I am and what I do. Like I said in the dedication, I hope this book is a celebration of strong women. Frankly, I hope most of what I write is a celebration of strong women. And that's all thanks to you. My muse! I am always confused when anyone describes women as weak because the strongest human I know is and has always been my mom. Behem posht daadi.

Dad, this book wouldn't exist if it weren't for you. I wish every girl were lucky enough to have a dad like you—one who really listens to everything they have to say, who shows up without fail whenever they need him, who makes them belly-laugh at his outrageous stories, and who encourages them to be exactly who they are. I imagined Ali Mashad being to the Mashad girls what you are to me. The best dad. You set me free to explore what I loved as a kid and encouraged me to continue doing so as an adult. This book is a direct result of that. Thank you.

Brian, not many straight men would joyfully sit through hundreds of sessions of their wives reading out loud a book largely targeted toward teen girls. Thank you for listening so intently, for crying, for laughing out loud, and for brainstorming ideas with me whenever I hit a wall. For being my number one fan. I love you and I'm so lucky.

For the women in my family who had a hand in raising me alongside my parents—Mommy Eshi, Masham, Aunty Farnoosh, Aunty Moj Joon (who I can't mention without also mentioning her counterpart, my Uncle Farr), Aunty Bahi, Aunty Fereshteh, Allaleh, and Avisheh. Thank you for loving me so wholeheartedly and for infusing little bits of yourselves into who I am today. When writing Mary's storyline, it only made sense that she would go to her aunty's house when her life in Iran fell apart. My aunties have always felt like my soft places to land. And I hoped Josie could find that same sense of love and belonging with the Mashads.

Nilou and Fari, the sisters in the book are inspired by you both. Not their personalities necessarily but the way they show up for each other. Nilou, you read more versions of this book than anyone not making money off it should have to read. There is nobody whose opinion I trust more, who knows me better, who more accurately calls me out. I wanted the Mashad sisters to feel close, like *real* close, the way we are. To be for each other what we are for each other. At the end of the day, through thick and thin, I know I always have you and you always have me. Fari, you were and continue to be the quintessential cool older sister. Even as a dweeby middle schooler I felt a disproportionate sense of confidence just knowing I shared some DNA with you. Thank you for loving me so unconditionally, for choosing to spend hours on the phone with your kid sister when you were a full-grown adult living in another continent. I wanted the sisters in the book to embrace Josie, because you always embraced me—to me, that's what sisters do.

My mother-in-law, Raissa, thank you for letting me spend countless hours curled up on your couch working on this book. And thank you for raising Brian.

My best friends! Morgan, Shannon, Annie, and Cori, you were my high school sweethearts. My best friends growing up. And four of my best friends to this day. Meg and Nora, when I got to college I was lucky enough to find two more lifelong best friends in the two of you. A lot changed about this book over my years writing it, but the one thing that never shifted was Josie's relationship with Lou—I wanted that to feel like her main love story. Little bits of each of our friendships went into inspiring their dynamic. Because of my friendships with each of you, I know exactly what it feels like to have a human being feel like your own personal living, breathing life raft during some of life's worst moments. Morgan, I also have to note you literally edited chapter 2 for me on the plane to your bachelorette. And, Annie, you're the reason I had Josie actually go on her date with Timmy.

Zareen and Bahar, thank you for so beautifully bringing this book to life. The cover and the interior of this book came out more beautifully than I could have ever imagined. I so appreciate your vision for and your devotion to this project.

Karen, Sylvia, and every other copy editor and proofreader who took their time to give notes on different iterations of my manuscript, thank you for the detailed reads of this text. I am many things, but detail-oriented is not one of them. Thank you for making sure this copy was as tight and consistent as it could possibly be.

To everyone else at Hyperion and Penguin Random House who had a hand in transforming this project from something I wrote on my mom's couch over the pandemic into a real book that will be out in the world with real readers—thank you, thank you, thank you. You brought my imaginary friends to life.

My teens! Oliver, Blair, Alina—you guys read this book before anyone else did. Even before my agent! Nothing about it would exist if it weren't for you. Thank you for helping this out-of-touch loser get in touch with the youths.

Kevin and Alexia, the best thing *Elite Daily* gave me was you guys. I am so lucky to call you my friends and to have you as people whose opinion I endlessly trust. Thank you both for the reassurances, for the vent sessions, and the never-ending editorial feedback.

My editor, Rebecca, I don't know where to begin! You were the best editor I could have ever asked for. Thank you for believing in me and—most importantly—in this story. You were able to infuse *so much* heart into this book. You took a fun little book and turned it into the heartfelt story that I knew I wanted to really tell. Thank you for seeing that. I feel so grateful to have gotten to work with you and hope I'm lucky enough to get to do a hundred more books with you.

My agent, Amy, you signed me on as a nonfiction client and continued to believe in me and work with me when I came to you with this crazy idea. Thank you. I feel so lucky to always have someone as professional, devoted, and truly phenomenal at their job as you in my corner.

Finally, thank you to my inspirations: Meg Cabot, Lisi Harrison, and Cecily von Ziegesar—my holy trinity of YA authors. And, of course, the Kardashians. The original Mashads.